I0612817

This is a work of fiction. Unless otherwise indicated, all the names, characters, businesses, places, events and incidents in this book are either the product of the author's imagination or used in a fictitious manner. Any resemblance to actual persons, living or dead, or actual events is purely coincidental.

Copyright © 2024 by Alan Howard Butterworth

All rights reserved.

No part of this book may be reproduced in any form or by any electronic or mechanical means, including information storage and retrieval systems, without written permission from the author, except for the use of brief quotations in a book review.

THE TRICK

ALAN HOWARD BUTTERWORTH

"They don't like it up 'em"

Sun Tzu, *The Art of War*

1

WWJD

May 13th 2001
8 days before the General Election

As I wait to be called forward, I can feel a vein in my eye starting to pulsate. I wonder if this is visible to anyone else. More specifically, if it will be visible to the check-in attendant. I can also feel sweat running down my forehead; that can't be good. The woman looks friendliest. I hope she calls me forward before the man in front of me. He has one of those meticulously crafted beards with really sharp lines that makes him look like an evil cartoon. Jimmy told me not to look like I'm trying to pick my own agent though, just like I'm bored and maybe in a hurry. I'm not bored though, I'm frantic. My trick requires constant concentration.

Have you ever seen Kabaddi? It's an Indian sport and it's usually played on the beach, I think. It used to be on TV really early in the mornings. I'm not a good sleeper. Good at falling asleep, not good at staying asleep. And this was before I figured out my trick.

Anyway, Kabaddi: It's in teams and they take turns. When the raider from one team is in the opponent's side, he has to hold his breath the whole time. There is no timer. He can stay in their side as long as he wants, but if he takes a breath, he's out. It gets pretty intense because the frantic thirst for oxygen sets in pretty fast in the middle of an athletic contact sport. The way that they can tell if the person has taken a breath is if he stops talking. He has to constantly repeat the words "Kabaddi kabaddi kabaddi" again and again with no gap, no chance to take a breath. If there is even the tiniest gap between the words, he is out. The words flow into each other, and it's impossible to breathe as you are saying them. Try it, I'll wait.

So, that's how it is with me and making things smaller. I don't have to say words or anything, but I need to have it at the forefront of my mind, the object, really small, like a visualisation. And if, for even a fraction of a second, I visualise something else or my mind wanders, before there is even time to realise what has happened, it's like a gap between one "kabaddi" and the next. Even if you didn't take a breath, if there's a gap, you're out. If I lose the thought for even a moment, then there it is, full size.

I used to practice on my bed at school. I wasn't on my bed. I mean I used to shrink the bed for as long as I could before it came clattering back to size. This was the last thing they wanted us to be doing at school towards the end, but it was kind of fun. I guess it gave me a kind of ownership of it, of my trick, and the more I practiced, the better I got. I guess not all tricks are like that though. Some seem to arrive fully formed.

There was a kid in my class, Deitre, her eyes would glow yellow if you smiled at her. We all thought that was literally it, almost not a trick at all, not a miracle either but about as manageable as tricks come. Then this obnoxious boy Remmy had smiled at her, and she had started to cry. We got it out of

Deitre eventually that when her eyes changed she could see peoples' memories, sometimes their darkest secrets, and Remmy had drowned his young brother in a paddling pool when his parents were making daiquiris. Deitre had kept it quiet because she thought people wouldn't want to be friends with her if they knew what she could do. And she was right because, not long after that, she was found with her neck snapped. She'd been thrown from a high window. I say thrown, they said it was a suicide, but she had a blindfold tied around her eyes and I don't think you'd do that to yourself. Maybe Remmy did it, but more likely a teacher or something. Word gets around, and a lot of people had smiled at her just to see her eyes change.

Constant concentration, visualisation, no lapses, no breaks, no sleep. Kabaddi kabaddi kabaddi.

The guy with the cartoon beard calls me over, and it occurs to me that the person I had taken all my smuggling advice from was a convicted drug smuggler.

Four heavily armed guards are standing close by. I don't want to look like I'm checking them out too much as both Jimmy and basic common sense tell me that's a bad idea, but some of their weaponry is pretty ominous looking. They have regular machine guns for sure. I don't know what kind exactly, but they look like they would get the job done. That isn't what is drawing my eye though. One of the guns looks more like a harpoon. There is a metal rod with a spiked arrowhead attached with a long cable to the guys backpack. I guess he has a huge battery in there, or maybe some sort of liquid. There are very few tricks that would enable a person to survive a hail of bullets from a machine gun, but the arms industry sure has taken up the challenge with gusto.

Jimmy's logic was that, as there would be no sense in smuggling drugs out of Natbag, security should be relatively light.

There would be no profit in it, drugs that is. Most party drugs are pretty expensive in Israel, so there would be no sense smuggling them out. What Jimmy had omitted to take into account is that this airport was no stranger to international terrorism and would be searching passengers about as thoroughly as human decency would allow, perhaps more so if they were suspicious.

"This trip was for business or for pleasure?"

"No."

I'm worried that if I concentrate too hard on the conversation that I'll forget my trick and explode all over the airport.

"No?"

"Sorry, I mean 'yes'."

"What was the purpose of your trip?"

We'd prepared a cover story that I hoped I wouldn't have to use. I'd practiced reciting phrases as naturally as possible while keeping Jimmy shrunk to the size of a dachshund. Tess was throwing these proper curve-ball questions at me, and I didn't lose it once. We'd all agreed that I'd definitely be fine and there was nothing to worry about. It was only occurring to me now that of course that's what they were going to say. They where trying to convince me to smuggle the stupid thing.

Any experienced drug mule will tell you that the safest way to get a package through customs undetected is internally. This was certainly the technique that Jimmy had used for an apparently huge number of successful drug runs through some of the world's most secure airports. Jimmy swallowed his packages of course, but I didn't want to do that. The problem with swallowing something is that you are pretty much at the mercy of your digestive system if you need to extract it in a hurry. And the human digestive system can be a fickle mistress.

I step through what I assume is a metal detector and wait for a moment to see if anyone starts shouting at me, or shooting at me. Someone behind me coughs, and when I looked back at them, they give me a "hurry-along-now" wave of the hands, which I guess means I'm through. Yay!

I try not to look too obviously pleased, which is easy enough. There is, after all, no good reason to be pleased. I wasn't even on the flight yet, and then there would be five and a half hours in the air. There was a lot that could go wrong yet.

The TVs by the departure gate are showing *Darwin*. I think it's live, at least I haven't seen this one before, and it seems too boring to have made it to a highlights show. A really tall man is holding what looks like a metal rod with a loop around the end. I think it's one of those games where you have to pass the loop all the way from one end to the other along a long twisty piece of wire without letting them touch. Except that this is *Darwin*, so if they touch, rather than something innocuous happening like a buzzer going off, it looks like a huge electric current will pass back through the long rod and into the tall man. The camera keeps cutting to the base of the wire to show that it is sparking with high-voltage current. I'm not sure if it is genuine or just a bit of theatrics from the producers. They are clearly trying to inject some drama into the situation because, despite the high stakes, what we are watching is actually quite tedious. The wire loop is pretty high up, so I suppose a normal height contestant would have the added difficulty of holding their arms above their head. This can get tiring pretty fast and would no doubt encourage them to try and get through the obstacle rapidly. This guy is easily eight foot tall though, so he's able to rest his arms on his knees and take a break. I'm not sure if being that tall is the whole extent of his trick or he can do something else with it.

There's a couple sitting across from me. I think they must be watching the same thing because the girl makes a "boo-hoo" sad face. The screen shows a close-up of the man; he isn't resting, he stopped because he is crying. I've seen this happen before on *Darwin*, and it's not good news. If he has any sense, he'll give up for this show and just try to find a safe spot to wait it out. Once people get emotional, they have a tendency to take unreasonable risks, the kind of unreasonable risks that *Darwin* relies on.

A mountain climber was recently in all the papers because it turned out he had a trick. He had got a new record a while back for some sort of mountaineering feat, the fastest or the highest something. Anyway, the bigger story was that it turned out that he maybe had a trick. He didn't need as much oxygen as a regular person to maintain his mental faculties. He argued, very reasonably I thought, that it wasn't really a trick, more of an aberration, and that climbing mountains, even with a surfeit of oxygen, is still a pretty challenging endeavour.

My point is that before the *scandal* he'd said something interesting, "You learn nothing about a good climber from the mountains he has climbed. You want to find a really good climber? You should pay attention to the peaks they have turned back from. You find someone who's got so close he could almost touch it, but for whatever reason, he just felt this wasn't his day and turned back. That's a true climber."

I think the climber had ended up on *Darwin* as well. I can't remember if he survived or not, but his point stands. The tall guy should give it up and live to fight another day.

He doesn't, of course. He shakes his head and gives himself a couple of shouts of encouragement before standing up and almost immediately electrocuting himself. It was a particularly bendy bit of wire in front of him, and he had tried to take it way too quickly. The whole floor is metal, and you can see sparks shooting up his legs. The lights in the stadium dim. I'm pretty sure that's just for effect. They must be on a different circuit, but they dim all the lights whenever there is an electrocution, like it's taking up the power for the whole building. Before his body even stops twitching, the phrase "Death by Misadventure" appears on screen and the broadcasters cut to a different contestant.

The guy opposite makes an "I told you so" gesture to his girlfriend. I've got to be careful, this is exactly the kind of thing that will explode me all over the airport. I was too busy thinking about what he could have meant with the gesture. Maybe he agreed with me on the mountain climber theory, or maybe he just thought tall people never do well on *Darwin*. A lot of people think this, as there have been a number of memorable decapitations, but I'm not sure it's true. There are more than enough regular obstacles where being above average height conveys a significant advantage to balance out the increased decapitation risks.

Monstrous as it may be, it would be hard to argue that *Darwin* does not make for compelling viewing. Exactly the kind of thing that would totally grab my concentration for the moment it would take for the package to revert to full size. The package was about two metres on the longer side before I shrank it. Best not to think about it.

My passport is fake, or at least, it's not my passport. Until three days ago, I'd never even been on a plane. I was once enrolled in a special school, which means my name is on a register of differently-abled people. Even if I was allowed a passport, there would be no way they'd allow me to fly on a commercial jet with my trick.

I'm not too worried as the woman at boarding waves the passport under some sort of special light though. It had been good enough to get me onto the plane from London. I figure Jimmy, or maybe even Felix, have some sort of inside man at the passport office. It had only taken a few days to get the documents, which I'm pretty sure isn't normal for these kinds of things. But then she looks right at me and says, "Wait, there is an issue."

She talks to her colleague. They are all looking at my documents, and I can't help but imagine the myriad of different ways this could go wrong. I try to make the facial expression of a regular traveler confronted with an unexpected delay, something that totally isn't their fault. I'm concentrating so hard on my facial expression that I miss the first few sentences from the boarding person talking at me. Her face looks devastated, like she's telling me I have a new form of cancer that's going to persist into the afterlife. When I realise it's actually good news, the wave of relaxation that washes over me is so intense I nearly explode.

Apparently, they can't get me a seat in first class. I had forgotten that my seat had even been first class. This had all been part of Jimmy's plan. He insisted that first class was essential.

As I was traveling with the package internally, it was going to take a pretty invasive search for anyone to find it. Airport staff aren't entirely bashful about putting on some rubber gloves and having a good look around inside a passenger, but there are a few things we could do to discourage it. Firstly, I had intended to arrive 45 minutes before my flight. This had been intensely stressful and had significantly contributed to my eye-twitching nerves as I arrived. You see, if you miss a flight because the airport staff has detained you without a "justifiable reason for suspicion", they have to pay the airline a penalty. If you arrive with only about 45 minutes to go before your flight, then you are in exactly the sweet spot where they are going to let you check in for the flight, but a full body cavity search, or even an X-ray, would likely cause you to miss the boarding time. I trusted Jimmy on this because he sounds like he knows what he's talking about, and I'd never even flown before, let alone been a mule.

The problem was that you can't just show up at the airport with plenty of time to spare and then check in 45 minutes before your flight. Hanging around in front of airports waiting to check in 45 minutes before a flight is just the kind of "justifiable reason for suspicion" that would exempt the airport from any financial penalty and practically guarantee you a thorough internal inspection. So I'd had to book a cab from two miles away, which I hoped would pull up outside of the airport at just the right time. It had got stuck in traffic because Jerusalem is currently a phenomenally popular holiday destination. The whole city is rammed with Billy Winn devotees.

Anyway, I made it to the airport with only about 25 minutes to go before the flight. Cut it this fine and you run the serious risk that they won't let you check in at all. This is where flying first class can be a big help. They are far less likely to inconvenience people that are routinely dropping five times the standard ticket price or however much it is. The price on the ticket was in shekels, and I'm not sure how much they're worth, but it seemed like a lot of them.

It turns out that it's the huge number of shekels I had paid for my ticket that is filling the people at the boarding desk with so much concern. Apparently, a passenger on board the plane is unwell, and the stewards have generously upgraded them to a first-class seat, my first-class seat.

I magnanimously assure them that it is totally fine. I'm so relieved that I'm not about to be arrested for travelling with false documents or for trafficking huge shrunken contraband that they could have told me I was going to have to make the journey strapped to one of the wings and I'd still have been thrilled.

A flight attendant apologetically shows me to my seat like they're a naughty child presenting a demanding parent with a terrible report card. She assures me that I will still be receiving a first-class meal and that she'll be right over with some champagne the moment the plane takes off. Champagne seems like a terrible idea. If there's one thing almost guaranteed to cause a fatal break in my concentration, it's alcohol. Bubbly alcohol seems even more perilous. I assure her that I will be absolutely fine and take my seat. Then I realise I am in huge trouble.

I begin to suspect that whoever had been allocated this seat isn't sick at all. I bet they are just one of those frequent flyers that knows all the right things to say to get an upgrade. They had no doubt sat down and immediately realised what I have just realised, that the little kid sat behind was going to be intermittently kicking the back of their seat for the entire five-and-a-half-hour flight. Well, the joke's on them. When I explode, there's a healthy chance I'll take the whole plane down with me, first class and all.

When I eventually did cause the plane to crash, it actually turned out to be fairly survivable. I'm sure this is very little consolation to the people that didn't survive, but I thought it was worth noting. My biggest fear had been that I'd blow a hole in the fuselage somewhere over the ocean. One where people maybe get sucked out as the plane gradually disintegrates. My whole concept of flying was derived from movies. I'd assumed that planes crashed a lot more in movies than they did in real life, but that doesn't help ease my mind much. Jackson once told me that almost all plane crashes are survivable, but he has bouncy bones so that doesn't really count.

But let's backtrack a bit to when I was trying desperately not to cause a plane crash. The kid is continuously kicking the back of my seat, and I'm already pretty worried that I won't to be able to take this for five hours. Every time the seat moves, I have this little rush of frustration and anger. This is the kind of thing that would cause me to lose concentration on the package for the split second it would take for it to suddenly expand back to full size. This happens with a pretty intense force. If I'm in control, I can gently ease things back to size, but if it happens because I've forgotten about it for a moment, they just kind of explode. I would probably know nothing about this, as if it explodes, I'll explode.

There is an almighty thump on the back of my chair, like the kid has been frustrated by my lack of reaction to the last few jolts and has really decided to make a point. I turn around and take a deep breath before saying anything. It doesn't help that he has the kind of haircut that could only have been administered as some sort of punishment. Maybe that's where all his rage came from.

"Hi, I'm not sure if you've noticed, but these chairs are... chairs. What I mean is that when you kick the back of my chair like that, I can feel it. I'd really appreciate it if you could just keep your legs on the floor. Would that be OK? It's just, I'm trying to concentrate on something really important."

I think that's what I said. It felt polite. Maybe it wasn't that polite.

The package exploded just as we were approaching Luton Airport.

On reflection, I have to admit that the crash was largely my fault. We'd just come out from some clouds, and suddenly I could see the ground with grass fields and buildings that didn't even look that little, and I thought for a moment that maybe Jackson was right, that at least if we crashed now, I'd probably be OK. We didn't seem very high up at all, a few more metres and I could basically jump from here. This was entirely wrong of course. We were still hundreds of metres from the ground, higher than the tallest buildings in the city, and I've never thought I'd be all right jumping from one of them. But I think it was that tiny moment of relaxation that caused me to let go of the thought, and I heard a loud cracking sound of what was most likely a large immovable box suddenly appearing inside the aeroplane.

The good news, from my perspective at least, is that it wasn't inside me when it happened. The bad news is that it seems to have torn a huge gash in the tail of the aircraft.

I'm reticent to admit that the kicky kid with the ridiculous haircut saved my life, but he was definitely a contributing factor. I'd gone to the bathroom to get a break from him about 45 minutes before the crash. I started thinking about the tall guy on *Darwin* pushing on through his tears only to stupidly electrocute himself, and then about the advice from the mountain climber. Am I the mountain climber just moments from the summit who realises he's not feeling it, or am I the tall guy crying my heart out? I should turn around and go back to base camp, live to climb another day. I had extracted the package and stowed it in the paper towel bin in the bathroom. I'd figured that if I made it until landing without letting go, I could always come back and get it. No one is likely to stop me if I just make a dash for the bathroom as soon as we touch down. And if the worst were to happen, at least I wouldn't immediately explode.

I barely registered this at the time, but what apparently happened was that a large section of the fuselage just in front of the tail ripped off. This big chunk of metal then smashed into the tail of the plane and tore a big chunk of that away as well. What I did notice at the time was that the giant box had burst through the bathroom door. I'd looked to see if anyone else had noticed it and saw an air steward, the kind one who had been super apologetic about the seating mix up, staring right at it. In a moment, she was gone. We were low enough that there wasn't any explosive decompression, but we were still going at hundreds of miles an hour. Perhaps it was a gust of wind or perhaps it was the lurching of the whole plane to the right as the tail came away, but seemingly in a fraction of a second, she'd gone from standing dumbfounded in the aisle to being outside the aeroplane altogether. I wonder if she had managed to figure out what had just happened. I'll never know I suppose, as I'm assuming that, for her at least, this was not a survivable landing.

An aeroplane without a tail doesn't do a lot that a rock wouldn't do in terms of aerodynamics. We are only a few hundred metres from the ground though, so maybe a closer analogy would be an aluminium tube full of sausages being tossed down a staircase. It's not going to be pretty, but maybe one or two of them might be salvageable for your... barbecue, I guess? I don't know why you would be throwing sausages around.

I should probably point out that my trick is limited to making things smaller briefly. In other respects, I am as vulnerable as any other human/tube-sausage.

I hear a shout of "brace, brace" over the intercom. It's loud enough to hear over the thunderous sound of the air battering against the gaping hole in the cabin, so I guess they must have a special volume level that clicks in at crash time. Loud enough to wake any passenger who might otherwise sleep through the whole thing.

"Heads down, stay down."

I realise that I'm already pretty much in the brace position. Then I worry that maybe I got into the brace position *before* the explosion.

I must have blacked out for a moment; at least, I don't remember the landing itself, but I remember feeling people pushing past me to get to the door, which seemed pretty rude.

They could have given me a nudge or a shake or something. I did cause the crash I suppose, but they didn't know that. At least, they didn't know that yet.

I look back and see with horror that the box is no longer on board. It must have finally fallen out the gash in the side of the plane when we touched down. After a crash like this, they collect up every single frayed bolt and child's Barbie and lay them all out in a giant warehouse to inspect them. I've seen it on TV. It seems pretty unlikely that they won't figure out what caused the crash eventually, unless I can somehow retrieve the package and shrink it again. Also, and even more pressingly, the cabin seems to be filling with smoke.

I try to stand up and I can't. A huge blast of pain shoots up my leg. Christ, if I can't even walk, I'm just going to choke to death on the smoke in a matter of moments. And then I realise I still have my seatbelt on. I get the belt off and start crawling towards the exit over the wing. I think the one at the back of the plane might be closer, but everyone seems to be going for the wing one, and I can see a shaft of daylight that can only be coming through an open door. And then there is a firefighter dragging me towards the light. If firefighters are here, I must have been unconscious for longer than I thought. Surely there couldn't have been time to scramble a fire engine. There wouldn't have been any warning, after all. It was a perfectly normal landing for the most part.

Suddenly I'm shooting down one of those inflatable slides. I'm outside and I take a deep breath of clean air and begin to think more clearly. I'm ushered over to a horde of walking-wounded. You'll be pleased to hear that the kicking kid made it out seemingly unscathed by the experience. I'm sure I hear him asking his parents if they'll still get to the next flight on time. This kid is relentless. He's already basically brought down one airliner this morning, and he can hardly wait to get on to the next one. He raises an interesting point though. I have no idea what the process is going to be from this point on. Presumably, they can't just bus us to the terminal and push us down the *nothing to declare* line. One of the passengers is still on fire. As a firefighter douses her in foam, I see the box in the distance. It must have fallen clear of the plane halfway down the runway. It can't be long before someone notices it. There is a large group of passengers that I suppose are the least wounded, some are hugging and there is a lot of praying. It was a flight from Israel, after all.

I've not tried doing my trick at anything like this distance. I'm not sure it will even work. I've shrunk objects on the opposite side of a room before, but even that felt harder. To shrink something, I have to imagine it in a three-dimensional space, and then it is almost like I squeeze it together with invisible arms. It's harder to imagine it as a three-dimensional object when it is further away. This is why tricks are so difficult and the special schools could have been incredibly useful. They didn't turn out to be useful at all. They were mediocre at best, and then boring and pointless, and then largely fatal.

It seems that almost every trick functions differently and that my way of doing mine could be totally different to some other trickster's way of doing something similar. I've not heard of anyone else that can shrink things, but there was a kid at school that could vibrate stuff at pretty significant distances. Maybe he could have told me how he did that and I might have been able to apply it to mine. We'll never know; he's presumably long dead.

Anyway, this doesn't seem like a time to try something new, and even if I did shrink it, I'd have to go pick it up at some point. I can't chance leaving it out here on the runway at any size. If I just start running towards it, though, I'm almost certain someone will stop me. Or someone will shout at me, and everyone will wonder what I'm running for and see the large box halfway down the runway.

And then I see a woman away from the main group. She is shouting at the sky in a language I'm not familiar with and going around and around in a figure of eight pattern. The thing that strikes me is that no one seems to be paying her any particular attention. Maybe that's the answer. As long as I don't look like I'm particularly motivated to go in any specific direction, perhaps people will just ignore me. There is a still-smouldering passenger jet to occupy everyone's attention, after all. It shouldn't be that difficult to slink away.

I stare upwards and hobble around in a couple of tight circles. I'm basically mimicking the crazy woman, but I can't bring myself to shout. I have no idea what I would even say. After a couple of loops I start trying to put some distance between myself and the plane. I don't head straight for the package though. I want to give myself some room to seemingly aimlessly meander back towards it. In no time at all I'm most of the way there and turning towards it. I'm congratulating myself on how brilliantly this is going when I hear a paramedic ask if I'm OK. It occurs to me that there is no good answer to this. If I say "I'm fine", they're going to want me to come back and stand with the other passengers. If I say "no", then they are going to want to check me over. For want of a better plan, I shout, "I've lost my glasses."

"Stay where you are."

"I just need to find my glasses, they must be back here somewhere."

I'm not going to be able to outrun them. I hate having to think fast. Whenever I panic, I just tend to instinctively shrink whatever is in front of me. It's like my whole *fight, flight, freeze* response has been replaced with *shrink*. Once, an unusually aggressive ticket inspector on a train had shouted at me, and I'd panicked and shrunk him to the size of an ice-cream cone. As a kid, this was embarrassing, these days it would be deadly. Fortunately this time, what I'm looking at is the crate, and I successfully shrink it. I must still be at least fifty metres away, a new personal best by a long margin. Now I just need to get the thing.

"I see them, I see my glasses."

I just start to run straight for it. I'm assuming that after intensely traumatic events like a plane crash that generally rational people sometimes do some fairly crazy things, so hopefully running as fast as I can at an imaginary pair of glasses won't strike them as too strange. I glance back and see that two of them are coming at me now. Whether they think I am somehow complicit in the crash or just a disorientated victim in need of assistance, they have definitely decided I need to be stopped.

I just keep running as fast as I can, but the pain in my leg is intensifying. And then one of the paramedics, in what has to be a break from his emergency medicine training, rugby tackles me to the ground. So close, I must be so close.

"You're OK now." Which is an odd thing to say to someone you've just smashed to the ground.

He helps me back to my feet and wraps me in one of those space blankets. Oh Christ, I see it.

"My glasses."

I bend down and palm the now tiny box.

"I'm sure they can get you a new pair."

I guess I'm going to have to get a pair of glasses. It would seem pretty strange at this point if I told him I didn't need them.

"Are you OK to walk?"

This is going to be bad. In the distance, I can see that as well as the emergency services, other first responders have begun to arrive. There are police vans filled with officers setting out a perimeter around the wreck. Far worse though, I see two black vans with large white crosses on the sides. What if someone saw? What if they search me?

We had run through a whole bunch of possible scenarios for things going wrong, but nothing like this had occurred to any of us. I had to think quickly. What would Jimmy do?

Against my better judgement, and any sense of taste or decency, I casually put the shrunken box into my mouth. As the paramedics guide me to an ambulance, I swallow.

2

THE OLDEST TRICK IN THE BOOK

It's very unlikely that Felix Trent was the first person to ever have a trick. He does, however, have the dubious distinction of being the first person to use his trick as a form of defence in both the British and American legal system. Extra points for it not even being for the same crime.

There is, of course, a huge amount of debate about who the first person to have a trick actually was, and almost all of it is utterly pointless, like those people who still meticulously research the Jack the Ripper case so they can argue about it with a bunch of other mass murder fans, as if it would make any difference to anyone now. Incidentally, I can tell you that Steve the Ripper, who murdered four sex workers in Derby in 1998, did have a trick, albeit not a very good one. He was apparently part Bobbett.

It's pointless to argue whether or not Rasputin or Houdini had a trick or were just exceptionally hardy/talented/practised. It seems hugely unlikely to me, but either way, the point is that it's pretty clear that a small percentage of the world's population can do a trick of some sort. There are few accurate figures because, for reasons that are hopefully becoming clear, it's not something people tend to be forthright about, not anymore. The reason I want to tell you about Felix Trent is that his case leads somewhat directly to where I am now... or at least where I was until I inadvertently destroyed an aeroplane.

Felix is a mind-reader. This is not that uncommon. I mentioned the unfortunate Deitre, and I've met at least a couple of others that I know of. I am very much not a mind-reader (I once asked a date if they always had a sad face or if they were just having a particularly bad time, and they said it was the latter, but I reckon it was also a fair bit of the former), but my understanding is that, like most tricks, it's different for each person. It's not like they can all read every thought that every person has at any moment. For Deitre, it was darkness and regret, whereas I believe Felix tends more towards desires.

He won his first poker tournament at the age of only 18, the youngest age he could legally gamble in the UK. I've got to assume that he'd been aware of the trick before that exact point, but he'd just not been able to use it for gambling yet. It wasn't until a few years later, though, in 1991, when at age 21, he traveled to Las Vegas and won the World Series of Poker, that the world started to take note.

I'm no poker expert, so correct me if I'm wrong. Actually don't, no one cares anymore as no one will ever play poker for serious money ever again. There is a fairly solid foundation on which all high-level poker is based, what to do when you have such and such a hand and something something is on the table, etc., that will give you statistically the best chance of winning. Let's call that *perfect play.* If you play according to those principals against anyone other than a very skilled player, you would generally make a profit, as most deviations from *perfect play* will decrease your chance of winning. In professional poker, however, it is deviations from *perfect play,* based on hard-won experience and intuition, that make a champion.

There was a staggering amount of statistical analysis performed of Felix's play after he won the World Series. There needn't have been, as even a cursory glance could have told anyone competent that Felix wasn't so much deviating from *perfect play* as seemingly entirely unaware of it. More damningly, the unlikely folds, brazen calls and gutsy all-in plays were successful at a rate that many experts testified was statistically impossible without him having some knowledge of the other person's cards.

His first court case was in a civil court in Nevada, a case brought by the Poker World Series organisers and, as they were often referred to, presumably against their wishes, a "consortium of losers". It was a long and technical trial, so I won't bore you with the details. I'm sure you're eager to hear how I'm doing after that plane crash. Essentially, their case was this: "We have no evidence that he cheated other than that it is statistically impossible that he didn't."

That doesn't sound enough to me, but Nevada is a state that lives by statistics and dies by statistics, and Felix was informed by his very experienced defence counsel that if he couldn't come up with a plausible explanation for his unlikely winnings, he was about to be killed by statistics.

And so, Felix explained his trick.

Firstly he made it very clear, in the hope that this would be the technicality that saved him, he had no specific knowledge of what cards his opponents had in their hands. Felix's preferred game, and that of the World Series of Poker, is Texas Hold 'Em, where a player's hand is made up of a combination of their cards and the gradually revealed community cards on the table.

What Felix could know, with varying degrees of certainty, was what his opponent was hoping the next community card would be. If they hit their card, he'd fold, and if they missed, he'd keep betting. This was the full extent of his system, if it could even be called that. He explained this to a courtroom packed full of statisticians and professional gamblers. Felix became the butt of many a worldwide joke in the style of "Card Cheat Puts Up Defence You Won't Believe!"

The defence team then tried one last approach. Felix proposed a card game in the courtroom, he would play the "consortium of losers". He would need the money they were playing for to be real, as his trick works best where strong emotions are involved, so he put up a million dollars from his winnings as his stake. The consortium would each also need to put up a million dollars. If they agreed, he stated that not only would he beat them, but he'd explain how he did it as they played. No one from the consortium seemed keen to go along with this until Felix explained his final condition: He would not look at his own cards even once.

The judge seemed thrilled to now be the host of a world-wide televised poker showdown with genuine legal merit. The players were pretty much compelled to stump up the cash and give it a go, lest they forever be known as "the consortium of losers too scared to play a man who doesn't even know his own cards".

And so began the first of what would eventually become a tiresome procession of people demonstrating their tricks on television. Felix's trial became a front-page phenomenon as people, for the first time, undeniably witnessed a human ability previously thought impossible.

For the first few rounds, Felix would wait until right before the showdown to explain his choices.

"Tommy was waiting on a 10 on the flop, so I've got to assume it's the straight he was after, and this big bet on the river has got to be a bluff, so I'll call."

Felix got lucky with a pocket-pair that hand.

As his confidence grew, he would talk through every hand,

telling the players exactly what they were hoping for on every single card drawn.

As Felix's chip lead grew, and player after player in the consortium dropped out, the last player made a startling realisation. Knowing what his own cards were had become a disadvantage. If he knew what his cards were, then Felix was going to know what his cards were. He would have a better chance of winning if he played the same way as Felix and just threw in his bet sight unseen.

"And now I don't know anything apart from that he wants to punch me in the face real bad," said Felix.

"I can't deny that, Your Honour."

The plaintiffs were in a tricky position legally as it was now clear that Felix had not cheated in any conventional sense. Poker is a game of skill, and Felix had used his skills to win — they just happened to be skills that no one had ever anticipated anyone having. In a gesture of goodwill, Felix returned the money to the members of the consortium that they had lost in the demonstration game. It was agreed that he could keep his World Series winnings on the condition that he never play cards in a Nevada casino again.

———

You really want to use cold water for bloodstains. If you use hot water, it tends to fix the stain in place so it can never be removed. I don't understand the science of this exactly, but I know it to be true because I once tried to clean up a creeper murder scene with warm water, and the cost of the carpet I apparently ruined is still being deducted from my already meagre paycheque. Creeper murders tend to be bloody. To be clear, it wasn't the creeper that had been murdered, sadly. They were the murderer. Because they can't bring weapons with them, they are usually limited to whatever is lying around the victim's house. This often means the victim will have been bludgeoned or stabbed to death, either of which is fairly bloody.

"Cold water for blood, idiot head!" my boss Mr Gustav would shout at me on a pretty much daily basis, like he was ordering a drink incredibly rudely, which is, I imagine, exactly how he would order a drink. Mr Gustav is the kind of boss that you only work for if you have no other choice. The kind of person who could say they run "a small business that specialises in cleaning up violent crime scenes", and it would be a surprise to absolutely no one.

Creeper murders are less frequent these days. And to be clear again, I mean murders *by* creepers. Murders *of* creepers are likely on the rise significantly, but I haven't had to clean up one of those yet. The kind of crime scenes I get tasked with tend to belong to fairly affluent members of society, albeit of the newly deceased variety.

Tom Barnett would certainly fall into that category, or rather, both of those categories. His London townhouse was spectacular. It was spread over four floors, each with these grandiose high ceilings. They were connected with a huge spiral staircase. I mention this only because it was key to Tom's current situation.

Tom had tied a piece of nylon rope around a couple of bannisters on the fourth floor and tied the other end off around his neck. This is the kind of ostentatious death by hanging that only the truly wealthy can afford. My old roommate hung themselves on a bathroom doorknob. I didn't even know that was possible. They weren't very tall, I suppose, and they had small arms and three thumbs on each hand. I don't know why I mention that. I sometimes wonder if they tried in vain to loosen the knot on their way out.

Anyway, there would be no time for second thoughts with what Tom had set up. The spectacularly high ceilings of his city pad had allowed him a lot of leeway as to rope length, and he had given himself about 12 feet, which those in the know will tell you is a real neck-snapper. Those *really* in the know will tell you, that for someone of Tom's quite considerable weight, it's a real head-snapper-clean-off.

Tom had gained some weight recently, maybe that's why I didn't recognise him at first. This wasn't from his severed head, I'm happy to say. The police have a special team that clears all that away before Mr Gustav gets a call. There were, however, a huge number of photos of him dotted around the house, so I guess he was one of those people. But it was only when I saw a picture of him standing outside the high court, in a clipping from a major newspaper, that the whole furore came flooding back.

For a while, his face had been everywhere.

Thankfully, the vast majority of passengers from the plane are essentially unharmed, which is pretty miraculous when you consider that half the tail fell off the thing. There are a number of people listed as *critically injured,* and one air hostess is currently listed as *missing*. That's not exactly surprising as I'm pretty sure I saw her fly out the back of the plane. Weirdly though, the whole "I could basically jump from here" logic that got me into this mess seems to have been not that far from true.

By the time I am helped into the back of an ambulance by the guy that had tackled me to the ground, a large bus has already taken about half the passengers back to the terminal. They figure I should go straight to the hospital, not because of any obvious external injuries, but I think because of my slightly manic run to supposedly find a lost pair of glasses. They ask me a lot of questions, but I don't think they're suspicious yet. I think they're just tying to figure out if I've sustained some sort of brain injury.

"Where were you flying from?"

"From Israel."

"What day of the week is it?"

"Thursday."

"And who is the President?"

"Of America?"

"Yes."

"Billy Winn."

I try not to put any specific inflection on the words but it's tricky. Billy Winn tends to insight strong opinions, so it's slightly strange not to have one, but I don't want to arouse suspicion.

"Follow this light."

He shines a light into my eyes, and I try my best to do as he says.

In the hospital, I am trying to figure out if I'm being detained. This may sound strange, but I don't want to just come out and ask someone, just in case I'm not but I somehow make them think it's not a bad idea. It's not like they've handcuffed me to a bed or anything, but I haven't been left alone for a single moment.

From the ambulance, I'm pushed along in a wheelchair to a few different places while some doctors have short chats. There are images from the plane crash on TV already, and the paramedic cheerily introduces me as "one of the survivors."

Eventually I get sat in a room with a woman with a huge newspaper. I don't think she's one of the survivors. I don't mean she's dead, I just don't think she's one of the plane crash survivors. I guess she survived something else. I ask her what.

I'm not particularly interested really. I just ask because it seems like the sort of thing a normal person would do, a person that isn't afraid of being revealed any moment as a smuggler that blew up an aeroplane. It's pretty bizarre though. Well, you be the judge.

A seagull had flown into her mouth, and she'd accidentally bitten its head off. She'd just been eating a baguette, and she says she chomped down on it as a reflex. She says her mouth "filled with warm blood and the seagull was still flapping." She says she came into the hospital to see if she needed "a rabies jab or tinnitus or something." She didn't know if seagulls had any specific diseases, but it had tasted dirty. Mostly, she had decided to go to the hospital because it just didn't seem right to go on with her day as if nothing had happened. I think I get where she's coming from. You can't just bite the head off a seagull and take a swig of Pepsi and carry on with your day, even if it was an accident. Which I am almost certain it was... And then for a moment I think of Tess.

"What are you in for?"

"Plane crash."

I try to be casual, not make a big deal of it. Judging by her reaction, I may have been a little too casual. Her mouth is hanging open like she's looking for another bird.

"The one on the TV?"

"I wasn't injured or anything."

She folds down her newspaper and turns the TV back on.

"It's all they've been talking about all morning. What was it like? What happened? Are you OK?"

"I'm fine, it was just a rough landing."

"The TV said it was probably terrorists. Most likely Islamists, like at the old power station."

"Really?"

"Because it was coming from Israel and they're always after the Jews."

"They said that on TV?"

"Were there a lot of Islamists on the plane?"

I begin to think that the seagull might have been the smartest thing to come out of this woman's mouth in some time.

She's not wrong though. The guy on the TV is taking some pretty bold license with the surely very limited information he has. He says the network is "so far, unable to confirm the involvement of either Islamic terrorists or militant tricksters" in the plane crash. Crikey, when he finds out it was a collaboration between the two, this guy's going to lose his mind.

"Your brother is here to see you."

I look across to the seagull-eater, assuming that the nurse is talking to her, but she just carries on reading the paper.

"Are you talking to me?"

"Regular visiting hours are after 2 pm, but he says it's important."

As I don't have a brother, I continue to expect a response from my roommate. She sees me looking.

"You going to see him or what?"

"Oh, I thought they were talking to you."

"I don't see why, my brother is dead."

"Oh, it's just I wasn't expecting…"

"He was killed by a lion."

This is all pretty strange as, even if I did have a brother, I can't fathom how he would know where I am. I can't even focus on this, though, because my mind is so distracted trying to reason how this woman had a brother that had been killed by a lion.

"How?"

"Got him by the neck, I presume. That's how they usually do it, anyway."

"In England?"

"Everywhere," she says indignantly, like I should know better.

And then there is this guy right next to me all of a sudden.

"What do you think caused it?"

I lurch instinctively away from him out of pure shock at suddenly having someone in my personal space.

He adopts a kind of squat pose, with his arms outstretched in front of him like he's anticipating a wrestle.

"The crash, what do you think caused it?"

I can only assume that this is the person that had introduced himself as my brother. The fact that this was apparently somewhat believable did little for my self-confidence.

"Who are you?"

"I just thought you might want to get your side of the story out there, your version of events."

I get a horrible sinking feeling.

The man's eyes dart to the left and the right of me, and he slowly backs away in his weirdly crouched position.

Kabaddi, kabaddi, kabaddi.

"What's in the box?"

He's getting a camera out now. Is it because he knows I'm about to explode?

No, I'm not, I just need to keep concentrating. It seems painfully clear that a bunch of fairly startling things are about to happen, and the key thing is that I not be surprised by any of it. Surprise is the worst possible thing for my trick. It causes the mind to wander in all sorts of dangerous directions. It was a few hours ago that I swallowed the package. I have no idea where it could be by now. Anyway, there's no way I can get it out now, so I'm just going to have to ride this out.

"Our readers want to know, what's in the box? Where is the box? You make it invisible? Is that what you do?"

I heard the sound of smashing glass behind me. *Nothing*

surprising about that, I think, just a normal everyday sound. And then I'm shot in the face with a kind of translucent green goo. This isn't actually that surprising, I suppose, at least not explosively apparently.

The police have a fairly standard arsenal of supposedly non-lethal weaponry for dealing with potential tricksters. The goo is probably the most often used of the lot. I've never been goo-ed before, but I have spoken to tricksters and non-tricksters alike that have, and no one has described it as a particularly horrific experience. It's a strange sensation to be sure, like an unexpected porridge to the face. The point of the goo is largely to hold the suspected trickster in place while they fetch a better weapon. In my case, it works excellently. The fact that I now can't really see anything definitely discourages me from attempting a sprint for an exit. And then there is what feels like a second goo blast to my feet. If it didn't make a running escape impossible, it would definitely make it prohibitively slow. At the risk of sounding like a fawning critic, I can definitely see why it's a popular weapon. It would incapacitate some of the most talented tricksters I can think of. It glows brightly in the dark as well, apparently, which is effective against tricksters with camouflage abilities.

And then there is a shout from the other side, and suddenly I'm hit with something else. These people are evidently taking no chances. I try to shout "I'm not resisting" but my mouth is full of goo. I realise what I've been hit with. It's a net thing. I've heard of these but never seen them. Picture a small fishing net and then... change absolutely nothing about it. That's what it is, a really small fishing net. Some politician surely received a significant backhander to get these commissioned because I can't imagine anyone legitimately thinking it would be a good idea as a weapon against a trickster, or anyone else for that matter, apart from perhaps a fish with very poor eyesight, in a small pond. I figure they must give them to trainee officers as a hazing thing or maybe a punishment for showing up late for work.

And then I hear an ominous buzzing sound and quickly fall to my knees.

"Got it!" shouts the idiot with the fishing net.

The buzzing sound most likely comes from some form of taser. Tasers and other electrical weapons are the second big staple of anti-trickster weaponry, the other being goo. Sadly, nets can't be considered a staple. It would make life a lot easier. It's not that we're specifically vulnerable to electricity, it's that we're about as vulnerable as everyone else. Oh, apart from *me* right now, that is. If I get shocked with a taser, I'm almost certainly going to lose concentration on my trick and explode.

That's why I fell to my knees, for the record, not because of Poseidon, God of tiny fishing nets. And it's lucky that I do because the guy with the taser fires that very second. Even luckier, it misses me and hits the journalist who definitely isn't my brother.

I lie down on my gooey face and know that this terrible day is surely about to get a lot worse.

3

COLD WATER FOR BLOOD

The second trickster to come to mass public attention was probably Billy Winn. I say "probably" because he may even have been first, and "trickster" because he'd hate it. Billy Winn is not a fan of tricks but more on that later, no doubt.

Annoyingly, Billy Winn has arguably the most genuinely useful trick anyone has yet seen.

Billy is from Tennessee, which if anything, probably delayed the amount of time it took for people to take note of his trick quite considerably. It's testament to how many preachers, evangelists and sons of God himself there are in the United States' Bible Belt, a lot of them pretty adept at faking miracles, that Billy had been performing genuine, honest to God, physical miracles on a weekly basis for years before anyone of consequence started to take notice.

I'm sure you've seen the kind of thing. Billy was traveling from town to town, so sometimes it would be in a church but more often a public hall or even a large tent. Everyone would have a whoop and a holler and a pray, and then Billy would read some choice passages from the Bible. There would be a bit of a sing-song, and Billy would bless some people. It wasn't a particularly unusual at this kind of gathering for a preacher to ask for anyone suffering from any physical ailments to come down to the front of the room for their own blessing. In the early days, before word got about and people were being ambulanced in from the ICU, these would tend to be the kind of ailments that the generally elderly Christian audience were susceptible to. Trouble with eyesight, a lot of diabetes, occasional heart problems, maybe a cancer here or there.

Billy would touch the person on the head, or sometimes the arm, or wherever the injury was, close his eyes and nod, and that would basically be that. Later he would add a "praise Jesus" or a "God, I am your weapon of choice, make me your magic man today" (one of those may not be accurate). And the person would say that they feel better or they can see better or "I'm cured, praise Jesus." But the problem from Billy's perspective was that people had been saying that kind of thing for years whenever any preacher popped by to lay hands on them. It must have been infuriating.

The first case to gain any kind of mainstream attention at all was that of Mary Denton. Mary had apparently only come along to the service to accompany her elderly mother. She considered herself a Christian, but she wasn't the kind to regularly attend a church service. She had only come down to the front as her mother had been keen to get a blessing for her own arthritic legs.

After Mary's mother shouted a particularly joyous "praise Jesus" and exclaimed in relief that all of the pain in her legs was gone, she threw her walking stick to the floor. Mary instinctively grabbed it and warned her mother to be careful. Billy sensed her scepticism and asked what he could do for her.

"I'm fine, thank you."

"Nothing at all?"

Like I said, Mary was a Christian, but she wasn't the talking in tongues kind, the "hallelujah" kind, the bumper-sticker kind.

"Lupus, I have lupus."

And she did. I can't remember the exact kind, but it was a definitively diagnosed incurable form of lupus that she had been living with for the last twenty years. And Billy touched her head, gave her a wink and, without even a "praise be", he was on his way, and Mary "didn't have lupus no more."

As they left the service, Mary was still keeping a close eye on her mother, who continued to insist she was fine to walk without her stick all the way back to the car. It wasn't until the following weekend, though, when Mary met her mother for lunch and noticed that she was still walking without a cane, that she really took note.

"I'm cured. That Billy Winn is a miracle worker."

Mary was less credulous than her mother and asked if there had been any changes to her arthritis medication recently.

"The only change is that I don't need to take those pills no more. The Lord cured me."

"You stopped taking your medication? Did you ask the doctor about this?"

"Your lupus is gone too."

And, the thing is, that of course it was. Mary hadn't had an ache all week.

"Of course not."

"I can see it in your face."

There used to be a slight redness around Mary's nose, some days worse than others, but not consistent enough that she had noticed when it entirely vanished.

She looked at herself in the hallway mirror.

"Well I'll be."

Tom Barnett's body had come to rest on a large white sofa in the entrance hall of his spectacular London flat. I say "come to rest", but I'm sure if I'd been here at the time, I probably would have described it more dramatically. His body had come cleanly away from his head as a result of the long drop and it's large girth, and then it had fallen a further couple of floors. The bit that was most relevant to me, though, was that it had eventually landed on an off-white-coloured sofa. It was currently a really-off-white-coloured sofa because basically a whole body's worth of blood had been soaking into it for the best part of a day.

I was no stranger to cleaning up some pretty unpleasant situations. In fact, that was basically the only work we got. Credit to Mr Gustav, he had found himself a bit of a niche. Employment law surrounding people with tricks is a little complex, and a lot ridiculous, and I'm sure I'll have to break it down for you at some point, but for the time being, suffice it to say, I was lucky to have any kind of job at all.

There is a cardinal rule to getting by as a trickster: Do not, under any circumstances, use your trick. I was incredibly aware of this, to the point that I would routinely wish that I didn't have a trick at all. It's not like it had ever done me any good, anyway. To be able to live a normal life with normal friends and a normal job seemed like a much better deal than what I currently had going on.

And I'd been being good recently. I hadn't used my trick at all since Monday. I'd promised myself I wouldn't after the cyclist incident.

I had been walking home from work and I was exhausted. Someone had exploded in a chemist, and it had taken all day to clean up the scene. I had spent most of that time individually wiping down cosmetics so they could be sold, presumably without telling the customers that some poor person had exploded all over them.

Anyway, the shop owner had gifted me a sandwich, albeit one that even they had agreed was not salvageable for sale, and I was about to take a big bite out of the thing on my way home when this cyclist had pulled out of the road and onto the pavement. They were heading straight for me. I was off balance, tired, and mostly thinking about the sandwich, and my instincts kicked in. Suddenly the cyclist was gone.

They weren't really gone, of course. I'd shrunk them and their bike to about the size of a budget lemon, and they were currently veering at high speed around people's feet on the crowded pavement, before screeching to a halt at the edge of the curb. The drop, to them, must have looked like a sheer cliff edge.

I'm sure I don't need to tell you by now that if anyone knew it was me that had done this, the results would not be good. I half walked and half jogged, trying not to draw attention to myself whilst desperately concentrating to keep the cyclist shrunk. I was a couple of blocks away before I felt them blast back to full size.

I got away with it, I think. At least I didn't hear anything more about it. The register of tricksters, though, had a record of what we could do. I was the only person at my school who could shrink things like I do. It was not impossible I was the only person anywhere who could. Some tricks were like that. If the cyclist realised what had happened and made a fuss, there may still be hell to pay.

Anyway, I had promised myself that I was done. No more shrinking anything, ever. It just wasn't worth it. From here on out I was going to live my life like a normal person, a normal person but with less rights and a terrible job. The worst of both worlds, that was the life for me.

So it was strange that as I stood staring at the blood-drenched sofa, I just knew I was going to shrink the thing. If I shrunk it, I figured I could just chuck the whole thing in the washer and dryer and I'd be done in a couple of hours.

When I'd first started at the special school, it had been one of my jobs, doing the laundry. The headmaster had been recruited from a posh boarding school, and he had looked to recreate a lot of the same rules and principals in the special school. New kids at his old school had a rota of chores they had to do, things like sweeping floors and cleaning toilets. I guess these were designed to teach the kids that they weren't above menial work. On reflection, this seems a little strange, as everyone I've met since that went to a boarding school seems to have very much not learned that lesson.

Anyway, at the special school a lot of us had abilities that meant we could do chores that were genuinely useful. Like one young kid was really fast and would run around delivering everyone's post to their rooms before breakfast. Not the most inventive use of that skill but I think he liked it. Which was a shame because things didn't work out well for him in the end. For me, it was helping with the laundry.

A big lad called Jeffy would go around the whole house collecting up everybody's sheets in a big sack. That wasn't his trick. He was just pretty strong in a traditional way, strong enough to drag a huge bag of sheets about. His trick was that his sweat was a kind of protective gel. It was toxic and oozed out if he was nervous. That wouldn't have helped much with the laundry though.

I'd shrink down the big bag of sheets to a fraction of its size, and we'd chuck the whole thing in a regular domestic washer/dryer. Apparently, before I'd come along, they'd had to send everything off to a commercial laundry.

But Jeffy was either an idiot or a sociopath. He'd gaffer taped up his classmate, Ben, and put them in with the sheets.

You wouldn't have known it from how he dragged them in, certainly I didn't. Ben was pretty small already, I guess, and Jeffy was properly strong.

Ben had been in the washer/dryer with the sheets for at least 10 minutes before it occurred to me that something was wrong. I'd been sat in front of the machine in my usual spot. It didn't take a huge amount of focus, but I did have to make sure that nothing broke my concentration.

"How hot is it?" said Jeffy, as casually as he could.

"It's a hot one, that's for sure." It was a warm day, and I wasn't really listening to Jeffy.

"The machine. How hot is..." He looked at the dial, "90 degrees".

"I don't know what to tell ya, Jeffy, it's 90 degrees."

"I mean, would it burn you?"

I put my hand on the machine. "No, it's... that's the temperature inside the machine. It wouldn't burn you unless..."

I saw the fascinated look on Jeffy's face and hit stop on the machine. The infuriating thing wouldn't let us open the door without running the rinse cycle first. I shouted at Jeffy until he near yanked the door clean off with the bizarre strength he had.

I don't think Ben had been badly burned. The machines took a fair while to get up to temperature, and he had probably drowned in the first couple of minutes.

That was the last time I used my trick to do the laundry, until today. I was optimistic that this time would go better. It was an optimism that turned out to be very much misplaced.

Firstly, there was a cat staring at me.

I supposed it was Tom Barnett's cat, it certainly seemed at home. When people died, the authorities would normally take their pets to a shelter or to a relative or something. I supposed maybe it was an outdoor cat. Maybe it had been away for a few days and only just came back to find this. Poor guy must've been devastated. Then I reminded myself it was just a cat. There was something very human about the expression on its face though, an intense curiosity to it.

It reminded me of this article I'd read that said animals didn't really have facial expressions, it was all in our minds. And this had made me think of Jackson for the first time in a while. So much so that I was distracted when I was moving the sofa out of the washing machine and into the dryer. There were already some sheets in there. I didn't take them out, as I thought they might stop the sofa from getting too bashed about, and it's not like I needed the space.

I'd noticed that the sheets had slight remnants of a blood-stain on them. If I had been a bit smarter or thought about it a bit harder, I could have saved any number of lives right then and there. But I wasn't, and I didn't. All I thought was "cold water for blood, idiot head."

The following week, Mary was more conscious of the fact that there was no swelling in her knee joints, none of the occasional aches she would usually suffer. But she was also conscious of not wanting to seem like a sucker. She didn't mention Billy Winn to anyone just yet, but she was curious enough to book herself in for a doctor's appointment.

Mary worked as a reporter for the *Kansas City Star*, and like any decent reporter who thinks they might be onto a big story, she started by putting in some research. There was nothing published yet about Billy Winn in any major news source, which was either really encouraging, as she was about to break a huge story, or not... because it was ridiculous. It was obviously ridiculous. Her usual beat was politics, but if there was even a fraction of truth in this, then it could be a career-making story, and stranger things have happened after all, just look at that British mind-reading poker cheat.

The following week, after a barrage of blood tests, urine tests, X-rays, and repeat blood tests, it was confirmed to Mary that she did not have lupus. Her doctor explained that the only possible explanation for this, and he was reticent to admit it as he had made the diagnosis himself, was that she had never in fact had lupus in the first place. The type of lupus she had been diagnosed with was incurable, but she no longer had any form of lupus, ergo the initial diagnoses was incorrect.

Mary was beginning to suspect otherwise, however. Her mother had just completed a six-mile fun run.

As Mary continued to correspond with a few of the people that Billy had cured, she began to form a theory as to how he could be performing these incredible miracles without attracting more attention. Of the people she had spoken to, and there were at least a dozen she believed to be genuine by now, not one had returned to a Billy Winn service. They genuinely thought that they'd had an interaction with God, and as one charmingly put it, "He fixed my lungs, he fixed my heart, I didn't want to push my luck."

But Mary did want to push her luck. She was very aware that if she presented her editor with what amounted to a bunch of people from her mum's church who said a man named Billy had touched them and God had cured their angina/vertigo/deep-vein thrombosis, she'd soon be out of a job. She confided in a friend, a freelance videographer, and they set up an experiment.

They had debated finding patients with non life-threatening conditions to reduce the risk of deeply traumatising these poor people when Billy was inevitably exposed as a fraud, but then they decided to throw caution to the wind and found three stage-four cancer patients willing to give it a shot.

They taped interviews with two oncologists testifying to the status of the cancer and its untreatable nature.

"Doctor, is their any hope at all for Victor long-term?"

"Nothing short of a miracle."

Cut to: The Reverend Billy Winn.

Mary was well aware that a TV special about an evangelical preacher wasn't the sort of thing that would win her a Pulitzer, but she also felt that extraordinary claims required extraordinary evidence. There was going to be an article, there were going to be interviews and there was going to be hard science, but she also wanted to have video footage of the Reverend Billy Winn performing his miracles.

She assumed that he would not be averse to publicity. He was, after all, an evangelical preacher, and they were not generally a publicity shy type. But she was worried that he would play to the camera if he knew he was being filmed. It would give the whole thing the cheesy infomercial feel she was trying so hard to avoid. Footage from a hidden camera, on the other hand, had just the right feel; grainy, covert, hard-won, with the added advantage that she could grab quick interviews with the congregation. As they took their seats in the hall, the lady beside her said that this was her first time at a Billy Winn event but she'd "heard he was the real deal." She'd travelled one hundred and sixty miles, so he had "just as well better be able to sort my lumbago."

Billy started out with some well-worn Bible content. There was an occasional "praise Jesus" and the odd whoop and holler, but nothing exceptional, until Billy cracked in to Mark 1:40, in which Jesus cures a leper. People were getting pretty pumped up now. A man stood weeping in the aisle.

"You can make me clean!"

That's what the leper had said to Jesus in the story. It wasn't a subtle point that either of them were making. And before long, more people were pushing down towards the front of the hall. Mary nudged her cancer patients.

"We had better get down there."

There was an urgency in this meeting that had not been there in the last one. There was nothing tokenistic or perfunctory about the movement to the front of the room. These people were here to get cured.

I won't tell you the exact amount I got paid for cleaning up an entire crime-scene, it's embarrassing. But put it this way, getting the bus home would significantly impact the day's earnings.

Those earnings had already taken a hit from a visit to the cheapest supermarket in town. I bought tinned food, bread and water. It turned out I bought too much. Looking back on it, I wonder if this was my subconscious messing with me. Is that possible? Maybe I'm reading too much into it and it was just a good deal on a multipack. Maybe I'd just wanted the security of having enough food to last a good long while.

Recently, work had been good though. From a financial perspective anyway, really good. I think the apt phrase here is *be careful what you wish for*. What I wished for was violent crime scenes. Scenes so grim that Mr Gustav's was the only company willing to take the job on for a reasonable rate. The government was cutting costs all over, and so I'm sure they didn't ask too many questions. Mr Gustav could keep his prices low because he wasn't going to do any of the work himself. I was, or some poor schmuck like me.

As well as the suicide and the person exploding in a supermarket, I'd had three other jobs so far this week. It was a personal record in terms of income. Again, not so much that I wanted to splurge on something as fancy as a bus ride, but may have been a factor in my buying too many tins of beans to comfortably carry home.

A yellow person had been hit by a train, a dentist had been shot to death, and there had been four people electrocuted in a paddling pool at a barbecue. That one had been particularly nasty. This had all been since the start of the week, and it was only Thursday.

I was pretty sure this sudden spike in violent deaths could be largely attributed to the Church's new anonymous reporting system. I saw Verity Pool on TV talking about it. (I didn't have a TV, but there had been one on at the dentist's office). She said that the "grip of fear that these abominations had over the country was so extreme" that people were reluctant to even report the ones they were aware of, lest they be discovered. But no more. The Church of Divine Justice's new reporting system was so secure that "not even the Church themselves would know the source of the information." What's more, they were "committed to thoroughly investigating every single tip." This new system had only been in place for a week or so, but I think I had already seen the results. The CDJ has historically had a bit of a *shoot 'em all and let the Good Lord sort 'em out* approach to problem solving, and this was just the latest example.

The dentist, for example, had been reported as having laser eyes, like Superman in the old comics. Someone had phoned up the service and said that he had used them to drill a hole in their molar before he filled it. Overall, they said they were happy with his dentistry, but they thought they should report him as he was definitely using his trick as part of his job, which is a violation of the Winters Act. The Church sent an X-Force team to investigate.

The investigating team had understandably been heavily armed, as they were potentially about to be confronted with someone who could fire lasers out of his eyes. One thing led to another, and I had an incredibly bloody crime scene to clean up. In case you're interested, the *one thing* was the dentist opening his door and saying "how can I help you" but with a "dark glint in his eye", and *the other* was him being shot seventy-five times in the head and chest with armour-piercing rounds. I wasn't convinced he even had a trick. Judging by the reading material in his office, it looked like he was actually quite an avid fan of the CDJ, so he would have had to have been in some pretty radical denial. Certainly not the kind of person I imagined casually showing his trick to a total stranger just to remove a molar. Also, I'd never heard of anyone being able to fire lasers or anything like that. It seemed a little implausible even to me, and I can shrink things.

The paddling pool lady had been a similar story. The team that had come to investigate her had been under the impression that she was going to be able to turn invisible at will. This, at least, is fairly achievable for some tricksters. Unfortunately, they had decided that the best way to counteract this would be to pre-emptively electrocute her with a taser. This was a brand new taser that the officer had never used before though. He'd set it to the highest setting because, on the older model, that's where you'd want it to be to properly incapacitate someone. However, this new model apparently had a setting designed specifically to take out tricksters with thick skin or a specific resistance to electric shocks, so the max setting was more than fatal to the woman having a barbecue. The taser was still firing at full blast when she fell backwards into the paddling pool, and it was strong enough to electrocute the three children that had been taking a dip.

No one explained to me why the person in the supermarket had exploded, but I think we can safely assume that it wasn't from natural causes.

So, where were we... I had a few tins of beans and a loaf of bread and some huge water bottles. I was really looking forward to getting home and having a shower and cooking the beans, something that I could do simultaneously, such was the size of my accommodation. There were rules prohibiting tricksters from occupying most types of property which, I think unintentionally, didn't yet include houseboats. Boats were consequentially hard to come by, but fortunately I had seen the previous owner being hit by an SUV at about 70 mph, and I quickly moved in before someone else could grab it. There wasn't any drinking-water plumbed in on the boat though, hence the huge bottles I was currently struggling with.

I'd only gone a couple of blocks when I'd decided that this walk was going to be exhausting with my heavy shopping. I stepped into a phone box and, with only a quick glance behind me, I'd shrunk the shopping bags and stuck them in the front pocket of the hoody I was wearing. They would have fit comfortably in a trouser pocket but I didn't want to squash the bread.

It seemed so natural, I barely even thought about it. I used to do stuff like this all the time. Why would you carry anything big and heavy ever if you had the option to just shrink it? This was certainly Jackson's opinion, anyway. He's probably the only person I've ever met who likes being shrunk. Sometimes he would take a nap in my hoody pocket like a baby kangaroo.

So yeah, it wasn't like this was new to me, but it was frustrating that after swearing myself to abstinence only recently, I had so casually used my trick twice in one day.

I could swear that pigeon was staring at me. This definitely seemed like the sort of thought that a paranoid person would have, but it felt like a number of animals had been looking at me strangely recently.

It was acting super weird, hovering at my eye level about three feet away from me and just staring right at me, like it was a humming bird and I was... nectar? I'm not so sure what humming birds are into.

And this was the second one, the first had been the cat, and the third was a fox. I was jogging along the canal, getting close to home, when I first spotted it. If you're not from London, I should point out that it wasn't unusual to spot a wild fox or two, especially in the evening. They say that foxes are probably more scared of you than you are of them, but I wasn't sure that was true here as I think this one was armed. I'm almost certain that he had a handgun strapped to his side. More unusual still was that he was being ridden by what looked like a miniature monkey jockey. The miniature monkey, which turned out to be a gibbon called Tony, was the fourth.

I picked up my pace. Whatever this was, it couldn't be good news. I wasn't sure I could outrun a fox in normal circum-stances, but the weapon and mini-monkey had to be weighing him down some. Even so, it was taking a lot of effort to gain ground on them. Tony was holding on with one hand to the fox's neck and apparently waving at me with the other. It didn't look like waving though, more like the convulsions of some sort of rabid test subject. Perhaps he escaped from a lab or something. Regardless, I ran as fast as I could, right past the burned out barge I lived on. I just kept on going until I couldn't run any further and I had to stop and catch my breath. I jumped into a hedge and just sat on the ground for a moment, panting as quietly as I could.

I pulled my hood over my face and tried to look as casual as possible as I made my way back along the path to my home. I stopped every few metres and had a look in every direction. Surely I'd see them. They weren't exactly inconspicuous.

Pumas, on the other hand, are notoriously stealthy. I was in the river before I even saw it, just a fragmented glance of a huge black cat that had definitely just pushed me into the river, slinking back into the night.

I grabbed for the shore. I am a mediocre swimmer, and the shock of the cold water wasn't helping. I flailed at the concrete bank, but it was just too high. I'm going to drown, I thought, I'm going to drown and the bread is ruined.

I threw my hand as high as I could and, to my relief, I felt a strong grip as Tess pulled me up.

Billy had luck and timing on his side, and as he placed his hand on the forehead of one of the cancer soon-to-be-survivors that Mary had brought along, either because he was just seeing the recording equipment for the first time or he recognised Mary from their previous encounter, he looked straight into the camera, and a calm smile grew across his face. The sun came out from behind a cloud and shone bright through the window, with the window frame superimposing a cross onto his chest. And in that moment, Christianity had it's new poster child, God help us all.

The oncologists were baffled as they confirmed that, in each individual case, the patients did indeed appear to be cancer-free. Their first instinct was to question the original diagnosis. Mary had been right to go big though. Not only were these cases where the patients almost inarguably definitely had cancer, but she had four separate cases all with similar results. No doctor was going to come right out and say the word *miracle*, but when the segment first aired, on the same day that Mary's *Kansas City Star* piece was published, it was clear that that was what a lot of people were thinking.

A number of commentators of a Christian persuasion had not been shy about denouncing Felix as a devil. After all, denouncing people as the devil was a relatively popular pastime, and here was a flamboyant British guy using apparently inhuman abilities to win card games in Sin City. He was a soft target. But even better, only a few months later, they had a long-haired golden boy literally curing cancer with his bare hands. Surely no one was going to call this the devil's work, so praise be, it must be the Lord.

Before long, numerous camcorder videos of Billy's miraculous powers were being distributed at church functions all over the nation, with names like Cancer Cures 3 and Broken Back Beauties.

4

A JUMPER THAT HATES YOU

Tess was only eleven years old when the special schools closed. It was in the second week of her first term. This was pretty terrible timing on her part as it meant she was on the register for differently-abled people without having even had some useful lessons out of it. If it had been even a month or so earlier, she surely would have chosen to keep her trick secret.

As you probably guessed, Tess is able to control animals. Pretty much any animal as I understand it, and I've seen a few. She can only do one at a time though, and not humans. Oh, and she needs to be pretty nearby. She doesn't *become* the animal or anything, but she has to be pretty close, like with a remote control car or something. It doesn't sound incredibly impressive as these things go, but it's a surprisingly versatile trick.

After fleeing from her school, she had waited until evening and then strolled around the residential streets of a salubrious part of town accompanied by a pigeon. Whenever she spotted a nice-looking house with few or no lights on, she would have the pigeon fly up and have a closer look. It wouldn't take long for her to find one with an open window, and she'd fly in and have a quick look around. As it happened, the first house she tried was in fact occupied by an elderly gent. He had chosen to have an early night and had turned off most of the lights. Needless to say, he was quite startled to see a pigeon peering around his bathroom door as he performed his ablutions. She left the pigeon there for the man to deal with and moved on down the road. I'm not saying that every time you've found a bird in your house there's been some trickster having a nosey. I'm just saying that there's a non-zero chance that that's what happened.

Anyway, eventually she found a house that was not only empty but had a window open on the ground floor that she could get to. So she spent her first night on the streets in a warm double-bed with a pigeon standing guard at the door. For comparison, I spent mine on a literal park bench.

Oh, if Tess falls asleep while she's controlling a pigeon or whatever, it falls asleep too. So it wasn't so much standing guard as sleeping outside her room. She says most animals are lighter sleepers than her though, so it makes for a pretty good early warning system.

By my current standards, she'd basically already solved life, but she wasn't satisfied. See, it had taken her nearly two hours to find a suitable place and, unless she stuck with the same house every night, this was going to be a big drain on her time. Finding somewhere permanent seemed like a bad idea though. Eventually someone was going to notice a young girl coming into or going out of a house where a young girl didn't live. It was key that she keep moving, so she had to be able to find new places to rest up easily.

She had passed a lot of houses that she had guessed probably were empty, but she hadn't been able to get in to be sure. There had even been a house that was perfect, but it had only had an upstairs window open and she couldn't get up there... she began to forge a plan.

The next day she'd hopped on a train to London, this was easy enough to do as the gates to the platform aren't usually manned and it's easy enough to slip in behind someone. Tess is small and she has an innocent face that belies her cunning nature.

Her biggest fear was being confronted by a ticket inspector on the train. She had no money to pay for a ticket, and one thing could lead to another until authorities were called and databases were searched and a lot of things that could potentially end with some sort of horrific death, all for the sake of a £20 train ride. And so she'd brought a pigeon with her.

She'd found a bored-looking one and walked it along about twenty feet behind her. When the train pulled up, she had the bird hop on one carriage down and tucked it in behind a jacket on an overhead baggage shelf. She hoped that if a ticket inspector did confront her, that a pigeon wandering in or pecking at him, or defecating on him, or some combination of those things would be enough of a distraction for her to be able to get off at the next station.

As it happened, no one ever asked for a ticket, and the pigeon got a free ride to London for no good reason whatsoever. She had started to feel bad about the one she left in the old man's house though — maybe he wasn't the kind of person to gently usher a bird towards an opened window, maybe he'd shot it or thrown things at it. So this time she made sure to walk the pigeon to a park so it could, like her, begin it's baffling new life in the big city.

<u>May 9th 2001</u>
12 days before the General Election

I can only imagine a fair bit of time had passed from me being pulled from the river because when I woke up, my clothes were dry and it felt like I'd been asleep for ages. But also, I had no idea where I was. There was something covering my eyes. I thought it was maybe one of those sleep masks that people use on aeroplanes. I wasn't sure if I'd been blindfolded by the kidnappers or if they'd just wanted to make sure I got a good nap.

I was lying on an old squidgy sofa, the kind a grandparent might let their dog sleep on.

I sat up and Tony pushed a plate of chocolate-covered digestive biscuits towards me.

"Thank you." I took a biscuit and pushed them back towards him as he seemed to be eyeing them keenly.

"Where am I?"

He didn't say anything, just kept his eyes intensely focused on the digestives. I wasn't sure if I expected a reply, what with him being a gibbon and all.

The room had no windows, and the walls looked to be made of thick old bricks. There was carpet on the floor but it wasn't fitted, just a rug that had been placed onto the bare earth.

"Who are you?"

"Tony. You know he can't talk, right? He's a monkey."

Tess' voice came from behind me.

"I think he wants a biscuit."

"Biscuits make him fat."

Tony jumped forward and grabbed a digestive. He broke a small piece off the corner. With pleading, angry eyes, he put the rest of it back on the plate and pushed the plate away.

"Your bread got soaked in the river, sorry. The tins are OK though. They all went back to full size when you fell in. Is that how it works?"

"How what works?"

"Your trick." She flipped back the hood of her oversized raincoat, and I was surprised by how young she was.

"You lost your concentration when you fell in, right? It's like with me, I bet. It depends on the animal, but if I take my concentration off of Tony for even a moment..."

Tony jumped from Tess' shoulder and onto the table. He had a whole fistful of biscuits only centimetres from his face when he froze in motion. He seemingly willingly put them back on the table, but his eyes were telling a whole different story.

"I..."

"Or is it like a time thing? I don't think it's a time thing. That sofa, you had that in the washing machine for the deep-clean cycle, that's over four hours. So it can't be a time thing."

"What sofa?"

"Let's not do the 'trickster, me? I'm just a humble...' whatever you are, cleaner, I guess? Like a really disgusting cleaner?"

"The cat, you were the cat."

"The cat," she repeated, feeding Tony a tiny piece of digestive. She flipped the big hood back over her head. "Let's get to work."

Tess had spent her first morning in London shoplifting, and so far she had a good torch, a large rucksack and a selection of assorted tools from a hardware store. Also an ice lolly. She had no compunctions about stealing and was well practiced at it. I suspect that her generally angelic demeanour is an affectation she developed purely to help facilitate her robbing, rather than there being any kind of internal conflict. I suspect she's not conflicted. She's a happy, smiley thief.

She spent her afternoon trying out animals at the zoo. While there was an obvious benefit to pigeons and the like in that they were so ubiquitous that they didn't draw any unnecessary attention and it was generally no trouble to find one, her instinct was that something closer to human was going to be more useful for breaking and entering. That's not to say she didn't consider simply having a grizzly bear or a baby hippo just batter down some poor unsuspecting homeowner's door.

A chimp would have been the obvious choice, but when she'd tried one out, she found a strange sensation. She could control it, but it was almost like the will of the chimp was fighting back against her, trying to regain control of its limbs by doing the exact opposite of what she wanted it to do. It was like wearing a jumper that hates you. When she exited the chimp, it seemed to have a little fit, jumping on the spot and flailing its arms. Perhaps it was too close to human. She had tried to control humans before, but even with children, it was like there was this huge wall of angry consciousness fighting her back, the total opposite of a penguin. Penguins were her favourite so far, like slipping into a bath of ice cream. They were joyously fun to control, all waddle and hop and slip and slide, like cycling downhill with stabilisers on. Even better, when she exited a penguin, it didn't seem to be in any desperate hurry to regain control, and more often that not, it just continued to waddle along in whatever direction she had been pointing it.

She didn't think a penguin would be a particularly useful partner in crime though. As well as being slow and cumbersome out of water, they had very limited dexterity and were sure to attract attention in town.

She'd asked a zookeeper if they had anything else in stock similar to the chimps. They explained that "there really wasn't anything similar to a chimp" before showing her something that totally was similar to a chimp, but much better: a gibbon. These furry little apes ticked all the boxes. She took a blond one for a test drive, swinging it between branches of trees in its enclosure before running up and down on the ground to see how fast she could get it to go. With the handling and pace of the chimp in a smaller and more agile package, she knew she was onto a winner. Also, there seemed to be a lot less mental fight than with the chimps. It wasn't as easy to slip in and out of its mind as it was with the penguin, but it wasn't far off. And they came in all different colours. Thinking that a grey one would be ideal for night work, she picked the one with the friendliest face and christened him Tony.

Just when she was thinking how easy this had all been, she remembered the difficult part was yet to come. She had to get Tony out of the zoo.

There was a small crowd of people congregating around Penguin Beach for the penguins' feeding time, and Tess figured this might afford her an opportunity. Security was lax around the penguins it seemed, especially around feeding time when they would basically just follow a bucket of fish round. Tess stood with the crowd until a gate was left unguarded, then she jumped into the mind of the penguin nearest to it and waddled him as fast as she could towards the exit. Once he was on his way, she swapped into the mind of another and sent it in the same direction. The penguins would basically just keep shuffling along wherever she pointed them, so mind-hopping from one flightless bird to the next, she had soon amassed a small troupe of a dozen or so waddling little black-and-white minions. They were soon out of Penguin Beach and on their way to the gibbon enclosure.

The specific kind of chaos provided by a dozen penguins was exactly the kind of thing that Tess was after; it was a light-hearted panic. Not the kind of fear-fuelled mayhem that might have resulted from a big cat being on the loose (another half-considered plan), but enough that every park employee in the area was fully focused on the penguins as Tony began to saw casually through his wire enclosure with a small hacksaw.

Tess wanted to be careful not to damage Tony on his first night, so she decided to stick to first-floor windows. Still, this gave her a lot more flexibility than before. People are much less fastidious about closing upstairs windows, presumably because they don't anticipate a small gibbon shimmying up the drainpipe and letting himself in. Once inside, Tony removed the small torch that had been gaffer taped to his back and turned it on to have a look around. Aware that this was not an ideal solution, Tess made a note to pick up some sort of head torch when she could. Did they come in children's sizes? Seemed unlikely, but she'd have to figure something out. Seemed unfair to keep gaffer taping things to him.

Still, she liked the effect of the torch. It was safer than just turning the lights on. Firstly, light switches were hard to find in a stranger's house, and secondly, Tony was only about two feet tall, so he often couldn't reach. But most importantly of all, if she had missed someone on the pigeon fly-by and the owner of the house turned out to be home, she hoped to spot them with the torch rather than turning on a light to present them with the startling sight of the gibbon that had just broken into their house.

After a thorough search, Tony headed downstairs to the front door and opened the lock from the inside to let Tess in, like the tiny simian butler she now realised she had always wanted.

Tony led the way down a dank corridor. He scrambled and swung from the pipes running along the walls and ceiling. A wise choice on his part, if it was his choice, as the floor was occasionally covered in broken glass and nondescript liquids.

"What is this place?"

"It's temporary."

"Really?"

A lanky guy with big hands waved at us. Or maybe he was just waving at Tony because the gibbon swung down onto his shoulder and scratched the back of his head, and the lanky guy seemed OK with this.

"Because it looks kind of old."

"He in?" said Tess.

The lanky guy gave a single nod.

"What? News?"

He gave kind of a shrug.

"Tell me!"

Tony smacked him on the back of the head.

Lanky gave a more emphatic shrug and pushed open the heavy door he was stood outside.

Tess stepped inside. I looked to see if I should follow but there seemed to just be another door in front of her.

"Come on, I won't bite."

I stepped in next to her. What else was I going to do?

Tony jumped onto Tess' shoulder, and Lanky shut the thick door behind us.

"This is cosy."

A screen flickered on in the top corner of the tiny room. There were two cameras next to it. At first the camera showed the two of us. I thought I looked a bit unwell. Maybe it was the camera, maybe it was that I hadn't eaten in the best part of a day. Stupid puma, ruining my bread.

"Where are my beans?"

"It's a precaution, against anything really fast, both doors can't open at once."

Tess pulled back her hood and waved to the camera.

The image changed to what I presumed was a thermal map because we were now two orange blobs and a small red blob. I guess Tony was hot.

"Or anything invisible."

"And the chap outside, what's his deal, he mute?"

"Chris? Not at all, the opposite if anything."

I wasn't sure what the opposite of mute was. "He didn't seem very chatty."

"If he spoke at all, they'd hear him a few blocks away. This close it would probably rupture an eardrum."

"OK, he's my new karaoke duet partner."

"What's karaoke?"

A green light went on above the second door, and there was the sound of a heavy lock clunking open.

Jimmy looked really angry. He also looked like he had way too much skin, or a tiny face, or maybe both.

He had his back to us but waved us in over his shoulder. He kept his eyes on the screens. One of them showed the thermal image from the room we had just been in, another showed Terrence Bobbett giving a speech from atop a ridiculously decorated tour bus. It said "Freedom Healthy for Coventry South" on the side, and someone had, presumably hastily, painted "and the UK" underneath. The others screens seemed to be feeds from security cameras. I assumed they were all in the building as I was pretty sure one was in the room I had just woken up in. There were a couple of children sat on the sofa now. I was half wondering how long they'd been waiting for me to leave to take my sofa, and half trying to listen in to Jimmy's phone call. I guess I was hoping he might explain why he was so angry, or if not, then maybe why he had so much skin.

"...at this point, I think we might need to figure if it would be worth just calling it lost and just putting all our efforts into a contingency plan."

During the long pause as we waited for a response, he handed Tess and I each a thick slice of cheddar cheese from a pretty substantial Tupperware box that seemed to be filled entirely with different kinds of cheese. It was an unorthodox greeting, but I was glad of it.

I later found out that the delay was caused by the phone call being relayed in a fairly convoluted manner for security purposes. Jimmy would phone a payphone in a big bank of phones and have an accomplice answer. They would then place a call to whoever Jimmy wanted to speak to, usually Felix, on the phone next to them. They would have to relay each part of the conversation to both parties. This was time consuming, impractical and, as it turned out, far from perfectly secure.

"Well, you were always the optimist."

After he hung up the phone, he did in fact explain why he was so angry. The Prime Minister had been in touch with Felix to tell him that they had had some private polling done and the results were absolutely disastrous. According to their figures, the government was about to be voted out in a historically unprecedented landslide.

Generally, I would have had little interest in this. The Prime Minister reminded me of an economy-brand version of my old school headmaster, so it didn't seem like a terrible thing if he was voted out of office. Also, this administration's rules regarding people with tricks had contributed to making my day-to-day existence pretty awful most of the time. However, for reasons I'm sure I'll elaborate on, the opposition party getting into power would be considerably worse, potentially fatally worse.

So I guess what I'm saying is that politically, most tricksters are effectively in a frying pan thinking, "You know what? This actually isn't that bad. It's almost a pleasant temperature. That fire on the other hand, looks devilish hot."

And it turned out that polling suggested the general public were about to vote for the fire by a margin of seven to three. The leader of the opposition was, incidentally, a chap called Virgil Barnett, who just happened to be the father of Tom

Barnett, whose blood I had recently been washing out of a sofa. Small world.

Apologies if this is a lot to take in all at once. I'll leave it there with the Barnetts for the time being. I'm sure I'll get back to them later because they play an annoyingly large role in this tale.

"But that can't include Bobbetts, right? A Bobbett's not going to do an opinion poll," said Tess.

"Smart, that's exactly what Felix said."

"And..."

"And it's not enough, not by a long shot, even if they were evenly distributed about the country, which they aren't."

And then he looked at me, seemingly for the first time. Although surely he'd noticed that there were two people and a monkey in the airlock room, or that security measure was utterly pointless.

"Can I help you?" he said, in that assertive manner the majority of Americans seem to value. Maybe I'd been staring.

"Why have you got so much skin?"

"Who is this?" he asked Tess, like I was invisible again.

"The answer to all our problems."

I was sure no one looked more unconvinced than me after Tess' proclamation, and Jimmy looked pretty unconvinced.

5

INSIDE EVERY FAT MAN

Jimmy had taken a long time to realise that he had a trick. This isn't uncommon. Sometimes there is very little to separate someone who has a trick with someone who is just in maybe the 99th percentile of what a regular person can do. Also, this was in the pretty early days of people with tricks starting to gain attention, and it wasn't yet clear how prevalent the phenomenon was.

Jimmy can eat a lot. He apparently ate a cow, like, a whole cow. He grew up on a ranch, and it wasn't unusual for there to be an entire butchered carcass in his family's freezer. One of his brothers (he has three of them) had, as older brothers often do, dared him that he couldn't, and so he did. It took him the best part of a day, but apparently that was mostly taken up with cooking the thing.

His parents were understandably furious. This was the family's meat supply for the next few months. His father threatened to whip him with his belt, something he reserved for only the most serious of disobediences. His brother, the same one who had made the dare that started the whole thing and was perhaps feeling partially responsible, brokered a peace. If

Jimmy could pay back the cost of a new cow, the whole incident would be forgiven. He even had an idea of how Jimmy, a
sixteen year old with few other tangible skills, might be able to
raise the $500 required. The county fair was taking place in just
a few weeks, and it featured a burger eating contest with a
substantial prize for first place. Surely if he could eat a whole
cow by himself, he would stand a good chance of winning the
thing? He would, and he did. And then his life took an unusual
turn.

Opinion is apparently pretty divided amongst professional
drug smugglers regarding the best way to take drugs onto a
flight. Some favour hidden compartments in checked luggage.
The advantage being that you can carry fairly large quantities
in one go. The downside is that airports, especially in popular
trafficking locations, are getting better and better at finding
drugs in luggage, so there is a significant chance that the mule
will be stopped and the entire shipment lost.

For this reason, many traffickers favour swallowing the
drugs. Not themselves, of course, one thing that all drug traffickers are agreed on is that it is best to have someone else do
the actual smuggling for you. It's a lot harder to search a person
than it is a bag. You can't just skewer them with a pointy stick
and see if cocaine comes out. Well you can, but most customs
officers choose not to, and so there is a much lower chance of
losing the whole shipment. The downside is that you are much
more limited in the amount that you can get through in one
trip. Airfares aren't cheap, and mules are usually paid the same
for a small load as a big load, so this leads to comparatively
small profit margins.

It was this situation that an inventive drug importer was
trying to improve when he decided to visit the Iowa State Fair
and got himself a front-row seat for the annual burger eating
tournament. He watched Jimmy romp home to first place
with seemingly very little effort at all, and immediately

realised he may have found a solution to the age-old problem.

A particularly talented eater might offer a *best of both worlds* solution, the capacity of a suitcase with the security of a human. Provided, of course, the young lad was as talented at swallowing condoms filled with cocaine as he was burgers.

It turned out he was.

Jimmy made over thirty trips before he was caught.

The cat was clearly eyeing up Jimmy's lunch.

I'd shrunk the cat to about the size of a large grape so, to him, the cheese board must have seemed as big as a modestly sized house.

"Are there any side effects?" Jimmy seemed genuinely interested now.

"I get kind of tired if I do it a lot."

"For the cat."

"I don't think so."

I relaxed and let the cat snap back to full size. It seemed to take it in stride. In fact, it nearly managed to grab a mouthful of cheese before Jimmy grabbed ahold of it. He held it aloft and stared into its face.

"Seems fine."

"What are you looking for?" said Tess.

"I'm not sure, it doesn't look angry or anything."

"How can you tell if a cat is angry?"

"Trust me, I can tell."

Tess wouldn't let me demonstrate on Tony. She seemed to have enough confidence in my abilities to proclaim me "the answer to all their problems" but not quite enough to risk harming her monkey puppet.

Tess' trick allows her to "sense and guide" (her words) an

animal in a pretty wide area though. It had taken under a minute for her to have a cat scratching at the front door to be let in and shrunk.

"Could you shrink me?" said Jimmy.

Jimmy was probably about six foot. It was difficult to tell how much he weighed, but because of the extra skin, he was substantial. I couldn't remember the size of the thing I was shrinking ever being an issue though. I mean, I'd shrunk a sofa earlier and Jimmy wasn't bigger than that.

"Sure you want me to?"

And, to his credit, he didn't hesitate.

"Yup."

Most people didn't like the idea of being shrunk.

Little Jimmy looked briefly confused and then nodded appreciatively as he stared back up at us.

"So, that's it? You guys want me to shrink something?"

"Of course."

"A person?"

"Kind of," said Tess.

"What does that mean? What's 'kind of' a person?"

"I don't think I can tell you."

"Well I'm not going to do it if I don't know what it is, obviously."

I looked back to Tiny Jimmy but he was gone.

"Uh-oh."

"What?"

"Where'd he go?"

It turned out that the cat had got him.

The cat hadn't done too much damage (full disclosure, Jimmy tells it different). He'd picked Jimmy up and shaken him about a fair bit though. I suppose this was why people didn't like being shrunk.

"Was it angry?" said Tess.

"Of course I'm angry," said a still slightly disorientated Jimmy, happy to be back at his impressive full size.

"No the... never mind."

"I'm sorry about that." I don't know why I was apologising, these people had basically kidnapped me. "I don't usually shrink people, not... I should have kept an eye on you."

Tess looked closely at Jimmy, examining him the same way he had examined the cat.

"What?"

"You seem fine."

"I'm having a drink."

Jimmy headed towards the cabinet in the corner of the room, but Tony was faster. I could just about make out the glint of liquor bottles inside before the little gibbon slammed and locked the door.

"Seriously?"

"If we're going to do this, we should start planning right away. And we are doing this, right?"

There was a moment before Jimmy resolved himself to a "Sure, let's give it a shot."

"No."

Tess looked at me like I'd just turned down an ice cream.

"You don't even know what it is yet."

"Exactly. You want me to shrink something, something super-secret, I'm guessing a person? Or an animal maybe? And somehow you think this is something that can change the result of the General Election."

"It definitely will," said Tess enthusiastically.

"It probably won't," said Jimmy, taking a seat and a bite of cheese.

"How could it? How could shrinking someone change the way people vote? Unless you want me to shrink Virgil Barnett. Even then I don't think it would make a difference. His

supporters are nuts, religious nuts most of them. They'd probably just call it a miracle and vote for their new miniature
supreme leader."

"Exactly," said Tess, somewhat too happily to be properly
cryptic.

"And you do know it's temporary, right? If I'm killed or incapacitated, and I'd almost certainly be both of those things if I
went anywhere near someone like Barnett, I'm pretty sure
they'd go straight back to normal. If I stop concentrating for a
fraction of a second, I lose it."

"What's the longest you've ever done? The longest you've
kept something shrunk."

"I don't know."

I did know.

"Hours, like ten hours maybe."

It was sixteen.

"Yes!" said Tess, as Tony did a little dance I was not
convinced he was enjoying.

Jimmy mulled it over. "Doesn't leave a lot of room for
error."

It took three months for the prison guards to realise that Jimmy
had eaten his cellmate. Drug smuggling is a federal crime, and
Jimmy had accordingly been sent to a maximum security
federal institution while he awaited sentencing. There was
little doubt that he was going to be pleading guilty to all
charges, but lawyers were haggling over the details.

Jimmy was trying to keep to himself in prison. He knew he
was going to have to do some time, but he was hoping that as a
first-time offender, he might get off with a light sentence. The
problem was that his case had been all over the news, so
everyone knew who he was. There was a photo of him stood

next to the big pile of cocaine that had been inside him that the customs people had taken. It was a ridiculously huge pile of narcotics next to a rather sad-looking fat person and accordingly made it into just about every newspaper in the world.

Apparently, being well known isn't always a bad thing in prison, unless it's for something against children or whatever, but a bit of a criminal profile can actually be an asset. For Jimmy, though, it was different. Firstly, Billy Winn's then fledgling religious movement had a pretty big following in the US prison system, so Jimmy already had a target on his back as a suspected trickster. One of the bigger gangs had apparently already put it about that they wanted him dead, just out of principal. He figured he could maybe last a few weeks, or at most a couple of months, before eventually someone got to him, unless he did something about it.

On the upside, Jimmy's ability to eat large objects had a far greater market value in a prison than it generally did on the outside. Getting contraband inside had never been an insurmountable obstacle in any prison system, and this was no exception. Weapons, cigarettes and narcotics were predictably the most popular items. Every step of the process had a cost though, and searches were frequent, so concealing these items on a day-to-day basis could be just as important a skill as getting them in, in the first place. This just happened to be something that Jimmy was almost uniquely qualified to do.

He realised he had no choice but to pick a side, so he approached the biggest gang in the prison, the only one he figured had the muscle to protect him. In exchange for their protection, he could swallow anything they wanted to keep hidden from random searches. US prisons, as yet, had no special facilities for people with tricks, so Jimmy was treated just like any other prisoner. Initially, they had wanted to X-ray him on a daily basis. The authorities made the argument that he could well be concealing deadly weapons, and they were absolutely right. Jimmy could swallow an AK-47 if you served it with gravy. However, Jimmy's lawyers successfully argued that this kind of consistent X-raying would put him at a significant risk of cancer over time, and a judge agreed. He ruled that Jimmy was to be X-rayed no more than any other inmate, which meant basically never.

So that was what he could offer the gangs. He could basically be their bank for contraband. The gang's leader had some sway with the guards, and he had Jimmy moved to a cell with one of their most trusted lieutenants, a sociopath by the name of Manny Charles. Gang members would bring whatever they needed hidden to Manny, and Manny would bank it in Jimmy for a small fee. They started cautiously at first, but before long, Jimmy was chock-full of enough drugs and weapons to make him a target for a whole new reason.

As loyal as Manny was to the gang, it didn't take long for him to realise that he was sharing his cell with a large percentage of the gang's wealth, and that the only thing that stood between him and it, was Jimmy's stomach. This would be a challenging crime to get away with, but prisons aren't usually full of people that are strong long-term planners.

Jimmy had started to have nightmares. He later realised that this was caused by Manny whispering to an accomplice in an adjacent cell late at night, making plans on how best to kill Jimmy and get all the goodies out from inside him. Fortunately for Jimmy, the paranoid state the nightmares had left him in meant he was barely sleeping at all, and so he happened to be lying awake when Manny made his move.

Manny had cut strips off his bed sheets and plaited them together into a strong, thin rope. Thinking Jimmy was asleep, he quietly passed the rope over his neck and began to pull it taut. Jimmy was frozen stiff, like a rabbit in headlights, as he saw his inevitable death racing towards him. The cord was getting tighter, cutting off the oxygen to his brain, and all he could think about was how ridiculous the whole thing was and what an idiot Manny was. Surely for Manny, the best-case scenario was that he was going to be found in his cell with his dead cellmate and a whole pile of contraband. Unless he had an inside man. Maybe someone from another gang or a guard was going to come by in the night to grab all the goods. Christ, they were going to gut him.

He was about to lose consciousness when his leg kicked. His body was starting to do what he asked it again, and all he was asking was for it to flail madly. From where he was in the top bunk, all he could think to do was to kick against the wall. On the second big kick, he managed to topple the whole bed over. He got lucky, and Manny's arm got trapped between the bed and the sink that it had just clattered into, enough of a knock that, for a moment, he let go of the cord around Jimmy's neck.

Jimmy stood facing Manny. He wasn't out of the woods yet, but surely with all the noise someone would come to investigate. Manny must have paid off whichever guards were on duty. He didn't even seem worried. And then, Jimmy felt an ominously familiar sensation, the sickly taste of adrenaline. He began to vomit. At first, just his large dinner, then the most recent deposits, a few tightly wrapped blocks of black tar heroin, and then two screwdrivers; he remembered them from a couple of days ago. He wouldn't normally accept stabbing weapons, unloaded guns were OK, provided any hard edges were taped up, but he wasn't going to swallow a knife. Jimmy's digestive system was clearly very different to most people's, but he was pretty sure that wouldn't feel good.

However, the guy with the screwdrivers had been smart. He had deliberately smuggled them out of the workshop as a pair and then sharpened each one to a vicious spike. The clever bit was that he'd hollowed out a hole in each of the handles so that the point of the other one would fit in. When they slotted together as a pair, with a little bit of tape around them to keep everything in place, they looked perfectly edible, an innocuous little block that now lay in a pile of vomit on the floor between Manny and Jimmy.

As luck would have it, Manny was as shocked by the sudden huge vomiting as Jimmy had been. There was a moment's hesitation as they both remembered the guy with the two sharpened screwdrivers. They reached at about the same time but Jimmy was just a little faster, or a little more willing to shove his hand into a pile of vomit. He was frantically trying to get the tape off the things. As Manny desperately lunged toward him, the two screwdrivers came apart in his hand and he thrust both sharpened ends up towards Manny's face. The first one caught him under the jaw, and he slammed the second, as hard as he could, into the side of Manny's head.

And then he sat down for a moment in the middle of his cell next to a corpse and some heroin and wondered quite how his life had ended up like this. Still, no guards had taken an interest. They must have assumed it was all the noise of Manny cutting him open. They wouldn't want to come near in case they were caught on camera somewhere close by. There were security cameras out in the communal areas, so the guards would have timed a coffee break or something to coincide with the hit. When the tapes were reviewed, they might look incompetent, negligent maybe, but not criminal. Nothing that would get you even a reprimand with a strong union on your side. He knew this because it happened all the time. What he didn't know was how much time he would have before someone realised that his murder hadn't gone according to plan.

He rinsed the heroin in the sink and ate that first. He didn't know if there was anything to be done about his dead cellmate though. It seemed the best he could hope for was going to be pleading self-defence. Manny presumably had a violent past, so it might be enough for reasonable doubt. And then, like a python eyeing up a wounded gazelle, he started to consider it. Manny wasn't a particularly big guy.

By the way, I think this is how a lot of tricks work. You just have a small sense that you might be capable of something extraordinary, there is a little innate nudge that tells you to give it a shot.

He lay down on the floor and opened his mouth as wide as he could. I've mentioned that Jimmy has a bizarrely tiny face, right? Anyway, he started to wrap his jaws around the top of Manny's head, and before he knew it, the whole thing was in his mouth. By that point it seemed as easy to carry on as it would have been to back out, so he just kept on going. Within around twenty minutes, the whole bottom of his face had opened up to about the size of a fat toddler, and he had got down as far as the bottom of Manny's torso. It took around forty-five minutes to eat the whole thing, by which point he could barely keep his eyes open. He just about summoned the strength to push the bed back up against the wall and went to sleep.

The next morning, Jimmy was woken by an irate guard hammering the railings outside his cell. He'd slept straight through the morning wake-up siren. He'd never done this before. It wasn't easy to do as they blasted a fire alarm type sound out of speakers all around the block. Then again, he'd never eaten a person before. He was happy to discover that there wasn't even much of a bulge in his belly anymore. Flashbacks from the horrific events of the night before jumped into his mind, and he could picture his stomach as he went to bed looking like he was pregnant with a fully grown man. People say that "inside every fat man, there's a thin man trying to get out." Fortunately in this instance, it looked like the thin man had already been at least partially digested.

The guards were shouting, in fact, it was really starting to kick off, but Jimmy was still so tired that he didn't say anything to spoil it. See, all the ruckus was directed at the missing prisoner. Manny had also not been outside the cell for roll call of course. When the guards had arrived at the cell to find one prisoner missing and the other unconscious, they had assumed that Manny had somehow escaped from his cell sometime in the night, presumably after knocking Jimmy out. This was spectacularly good news as far as Jimmy was concerned. He had fallen asleep wondering what the punishment for cannibalism might be.

A guard was tapping at window bars with a baton. The moment the guards noticed Jimmy was conscious, he started shouting in his face, "Where is Manny Charles? How did he escape? How long has he been gone?"

Jimmy wondered if this guy had been in on Manny's murderous plans. At least one of the night guards must have been. Maybe this guy had also been paid off. He would have been the one to find Jimmy's corpse, after all. Maybe he had been paid enough to make sure it got filed away as a suicide with no questions asked. If he had been expecting a big payday, that he now realised wouldn't be coming, it would explain the genuine anger he seemed to be experiencing over Manny's disappearance. Jimmy decided to play dumb.

"He's gone? What time is it? My head hurts like crazy. I don't remember anything. I think he must have smashed me over the head with something maybe."

This line seemed to go down pretty well, and a medic was summoned to take a look at him. And then Jimmy had the terrifying thought that if they were too thorough over his injuries, they may X-ray him. An image of the entire human skeleton inside his skeleton flashed into his head, and he started to act a lot less concussed. He'd be fine, he said, once he had had his breakfast.

And that was basically it. He would have got away with it if it wasn't for the fact that Jimmy is not the type of person to eat just one of anything. About three months later he ate another cellmate. I wouldn't go so far as to say that he was probably just hungry, but the second one sounds a lot less like self-defence. However it happened, Jimmy ended up with another dead bunk mate and decided that it would be easiest for everyone involved if he ate them. This time, though, a guard decided to do a walk-through of the floor and had shone a torch into the cell to see what must have been a fairly startling sight — Jimmy, waist-deep into consuming an entire human being head-first. Not least because, and I know I've mentioned this before, Jimmy has a really tiny face.

By that point, the investigation into how Manny had escaped his cell unseen by the cameras had gone in any number of exciting directions. People speculated that he could have the same trick as an invisible serial killer that had recently escaped a super-max prison in Texas. Perhaps he had just been biding his time, waiting for an opportunity. Prisoners talked of a tunnel that the guards didn't find. For the right price, they had all the info. So it was a little bit of a disappointment when it eventually turned out that obviously Jimmy had just eaten him.

It also turns out that, in fact, there was neither a federal nor a state law forbidding cannibalism, provided the livestock had been reared in accordance with FDA regulations. Another fun fact is that the cells in which his victims had been housed were considered just about fit for purpose for live cattle, although too small for an organic certification. Jimmy had bigger concerns though, as he was more than likely to face the federal death penalty for murder in furtherance of drug trafficking. The prison hospital had taken the precaution of pumping Jimmy's stomach in a search for further victims. They didn't find any, but they did find an astonishing quantity of narcotics as well as assorted weaponry and other miscellaneous contraband. By this point Billy Winn was calling people with tricks "abominations unto the Lord", and he seemed to be unstoppably popular.

So, when a British doctor showed up and told Jimmy that he was being transferred to a new facility, a facility outside of the legal jurisdiction of the United States, for a moment he thought it might just be a lucky escape.

"I'm not doing it," I said. Obviously. Until very recently I had thought that this was about the only possible reaction a person could have when someone suggested you smuggle something internally. But also obviously, I did it, didn't I? I've already told you I did. But I guess I didn't want you to think I was the sort of person who would just go shoving any shrunken thing anywhere I was told without asking questions.

"Why?" This was one of the key questions.

"Because," said Jimmy, taking it very much as a given that the package would have to be smuggled somewhere inside me (this was, after all, his area of expertise).

"We only have a very narrow time window. If you can only keep it shrunk for 10 hours and you've swallowed it, even if you've made it through customs this end, there's no guarantee we'll be able to get it back out of you before it bursts back to full size." Wise words, as it turned out.

"If I'm going to do this…"

Tess made a prematurely celebratory clenched fist.

"Big 'if'. I'm going to need to know what's in the package."

"Why?"

"Tell me," I don't think I was being unreasonable.

"Go on." Said Tess.

"But what if we tell you and then you don't want to do it?"

"You're not making it sound any better."

"It's highly confidential," said Jimmy, stepping closer.

"No one believes it anyway," said Tess.

"Are you Christian?"

"God no," I blurted out. In all honesty, it wasn't something I thought about that much before the Church of Divine Justice started doing their thing. I'd been to the occasional Christmas service, I suppose. I'd never really been bothered by whatever people chose to worship in the privacy of their own home, but these days Christianity was so entwined with our persecution that it seemed a borderline ridiculous question to ask someone with a trick.

"Why?" I felt like I was asking this a lot.

Jimmy stood silently for a moment. Either he was contemplating whether it really was a good idea to let me in on this secret, or he was pausing for dramatic effect.

"It's Jesus."

"What is?"

"The package we need you to smuggle. It's Jesus."

"No it isn't."

"I told you so," said Tess.

"Seriously, it's the remains of the body of Jesus Christ."

I was no expert on these things, and this certainly wasn't something that they covered at the Christmas services.

"This is something that exists?"

"Yes."

"Where?"

"The Israeli government have it. We have a contact within their security services who is going to hand it over."

"Why haven't I heard about this?"

"It's a secret," said Tess, unhelpfully.

"Up until now, it's been one of the most closely guarded secrets in the world. Only a few people at the very top level of the government there knew about it."

"Uh-huh. If it's heroin or something, just tell me it's heroin. I'll smuggle the stupid drugs for you." This was ridiculous.

"Think about it."

"You think about it." These people were idiots.

"What good would it have done to tell anyone about it? I don't have all the details, but my understanding is that there were a few candidates of human remains from the right era that may have been Jesus. These have all been preserved. Relatively recently, scientists have been able to use DNA testing to ascertain with a pretty good degree of certainty which body was his."

"Jesus' body."

"Yes."

"Why haven't I heard about it? What was the point in all that testing if they weren't going to tell anyone?"

"Why would they? It's not like that whole area isn't contentious enough already. If they start proclaiming that they've got Jesus' body, in the current climate it's liable to kick off a holy war!"

"It's definitely not just drugs."

"It's not like it would do them any good. It's just a body. It's not like it does anything," said Jimmy.

And then suddenly I saw it, the whole plan these morons had come up with, almost in its insane totality.

"Until now."

"Exactly," said Tess with a devilish grin.

"It really is Jesus?" I was pretty sure I sounded sarcastic.

"We think so," said Jimmy.

"And you want me to shrink him and... smuggle him, internally, through customs."

"For maybe eight hours," said Tess. "That's about how long the flight is plus customs."

"It's the best way," said Jimmy.

I just want to point out, lest you think that I'm even more gullible than I clearly am, that I wasn't totally convinced that this package was anything to do with Jesus. This seemed like the kind of thing that someone could only believe if it was literally their only hope, a position that both Jimmy and Tess had seemingly taken. Going along with it for now, though, seemed like the best way not to anger a girl with a puma that did her bidding and a man who had eaten at least two people.

"And that's it," I said. "I just need to get it back to the airport. I'm not taking him to Hull."

"Why not? It's not much further. It would be easier if he was smaller."

"No." I had to draw the line somewhere, and I thought I was already being pretty generous.

"Firstly, this is possibly the stupidest plan I've ever heard, and that's saying something. Secondly, you'll never be able to get in there. It's totally locked down now. No one is allowed in or out. The security will be insane."

"We will," said Tess, somewhat defensively. "There's an exception."

"For what?" I said, genuinely forgetting.

Tess glanced at the TV showing Terrence Bobbett. He was throwing some sort of fruit at a bemused-looking crowd.

"OK, now this is definitely the stupidest plan I've ever heard."

Once we were agreed that I was indeed going to be participating in their historically terrible plan, it was decided that I should be introduced to the rest of the organisation (I don't think "organisation" is the right word, but it will have to do until I find a better one). Because we only had a limited amount of time, though, Jimmy decided that this should form part of my training.

Jimmy insisted I get as much practice in as possible before the flight. This entailed getting an object to act as a stand-in for the box containing the Jesus remains. Tess insisted that not only should I shrink the object, I should transport it "as I would on the real flight." Because Jimmy was a pragmatist, he suggested the object be small enough that should it return to full size it would, at least, be non-lethal.

"But enough to give you something to think about," said Tess, a little too happily, as Tony fetched a large banana.

This was by far the most tricksters I'd met since school. You wouldn't know it by reading the news, but people with tricks are actually kind of rare. The highest estimate I've seen only has it at around five percent of the population, and that number includes Bobbetts. Whether or not Bobbetts should be included in trickster statistics was actually a pretty contentious subject. You can make up your own mind about it when I invariably have to explain something of the workings of the Bobbett community, but for now let's keep the madness to a workable minimum.

Chris, the quiet/loud guy, introduced me to his girlfriend Phoebe. He did this in sign language so as not to burst everyone's eardrums, which Phoebe then translated for me, as I didn't tell her that I could sign. So, slightly surreally, she said, "This is my girlfriend, Phoebe."

"I'm pleased to meet you," I said. I wasn't sure if she had a trick. I know that's what you're thinking, what can this one do? It's rude to ask, and besides, I was mostly concentrated on the banana.

There was also a guy who I think was called Barry but was rather generously nicknamed *Spider-man*. This gave him a superhero caché that I wasn't sure his trick warranted. As far as I could tell, the only spider-like thing about him was that he had a small extra set of arms coming out below his normal arms. Even if we forgave the maths of it, he was hardly going to be swinging between buildings anytime soon. When I met him, he was cooking an omelette while shuffling a deck of cards. I suppose it was a very slight time saver.

Jimmy thought it would be good for me to sit in for a few rounds of cards, an extra distraction to see if it would break my concentration.

The game was Texas Hold 'Em, a form of poker I'd actually played a bit of at school. It had been popular back then, I think largely because of Felix being a hero to a lot of young tricksters.

It turned out no one had any money, so we played for literal peanuts. This added the extra complication that if Tess was distracted or annoyed, Tony would tend to dive into the centre of the table and devour the pot. At which point, the first person to catch him and wrestle the uneaten nuts back off him would be entitled to them, house rule.

Spider-man was not a good poker player. He was colour blind and often confused the suits. He did, however, let me have some omelette. Chris was a good player, in that he was definitely tricky to read. I think maybe just not being able to talk at all was basically an advantage in poker. He generally seemed to rely on sign language for people who understood it, and basically pointed at stuff for people who couldn't. Both were pretty effective, although it turned out a whole bunch of signs that I thought I knew might have just been stuff Jackson made up.

If Chris wanted to get your attention and you weren't looking at him, he would hum as quietly as he could. The first couple of times he did this, I thought it was the sound of a not-too-distant train.

The players to really watch out for were Jimmy and Tess. I think Jimmy had played a fair bit of poker with Felix in their time incarcerated together. If it was a serious game, I've little doubt he would have cleaned up, but I think maybe his mind was on other things, or perhaps he just didn't really want the peanuts. Anyway, I was winning. The only other person with a good stack of nuts left was Tess, and she had just gone all-in.

There was an ace-high straight available from the flop, and with the strength of Tess' bet, that was evidently what she wanted me to think she had. I wasn't buying it though. Not because of anything in her play specifically, or even in her demeanour, but because Tony looked intensely worried. He was hopping from foot to foot with wide eyes and gritted teeth. I guessed that some of Tess' emotions must've rubbed off on him, she controlled him that much. That or it was some sort of intense double-bluff, which seemed like a lot of effort to go to for some nuts. So I called.

I was pretty sure she had been bluffing because Tony immediately started scooping up tiny fistfuls of my nuts. I made a leap for him, but he was fast. Spider-man had a go at grabbing him as well. If he couldn't manage it with four hands, I was thinking, what chance did I have?

"Every damn time!" reprimanded Jimmy.

I stopped chasing and just started laughing. The whole thing was ridiculous. And then Chris started laughing. He was clearly trying to hold it in, but it still sounded like a thunder-storm shouting.

The others covered their ears and then their faces, no one wanted to catch Chris's eye and make him laugh any more.

Implausible as it sounded, given the nature of the situation, I was suddenly filled with an overwhelming feeling of warmth, of belonging. For the first time in a long time, I felt... normal? This was immediately, and rapidly, replaced with an over-whelming feeling of a large banana.

6

JESUS SAVES

Aplane-spotter had been recording the landing. Well not exactly, they had been recording another plane taxiing to another runway as apparently it was more interesting. And then part of the tail of our aircraft had blown off and suddenly we became more interesting. The camera whips across just in time to see the plane's first shuddering contact with the runway. It's pretty spectacular. I didn't even know that plane-spotting was a thing, but they've got to be pleased with this. Maybe they aren't though. Given that this person presumably films planes successfully landing all the time and is happy enough with the results, maybe this is their worst recording ever. Thinking it might be important, they had sent the video to the police. Thinking it might be valuable, they had also sold it to a tabloid newspaper.

Spectacular as we all agree it is, the crash landing bit is not the part of the tape that Detective Brewer is interested in. There's another detective there as well, but no one tells me his name. Also his main job seems to be running the video machine, a job he doesn't seem to be particularly adept at.

The evacuation of the passengers from the plane is on tape, and it seems we are going to have to sit through the whole thing. Brewer says, "Is this you?" as a few blurry people clutter down the slide onto the tarmac, and I'm genuinely not sure.

"Rewind and freeze," says Brewer, radically overestimating his colleague's competence with the tape machine. The screen goes black for a bit, and then we are watching some footage from earlier in the day, or maybe a different day. By the time it gets back to the crash again, it's decided we should just watch the whole thing through without trying to pause or rewind anything. This is fine by me, I'm not in any hurry. On one hand, there is a decent possibility that I will explode at any minute, on the other, I can't foresee things getting any better in the future. I am, after all, currently in the custody of the regular police. It will surely only be a matter of time before I'm handed over to specialists in dealing with the differently-abled, and it's been a long time since that has been seen in any form of positive light.

About twenty minutes later, we finally arrive at the bit of the video they are interested in.

Seemingly bored of filming the surviving passengers, the plane-spotter returns to filming his actual passion, the plane. He zooms in real close to the hole in the fuselage and, muttering to himself, commentates on the footage.

"It's like there was a bomb blast right here, and then you can see where the tail has been damaged here. It's a wonder they were able to get it down safely at all. Let's see if..."

He pans away down the runway to see if he can spot any of the tail of the aircraft. This guy's camera has an impressively powerful zoom lens.

"What's that, is that luggage?"

The package, apparently containing the earthly remains of the son of God, is blurry and grainy from this distance.

"You see that?" says Brewer.

And then it's not there anymore.

"No."

"Wind that back."

We both look at Detective video-playback, this could be his toughest case yet.

And then there is me, running stupidly. I don't think I've ever seen myself running before. It turns out I kick my legs up really high. It looks ridiculous. Was that just something I was putting on? I don't think so. Why hasn't anyone ever told me that I run like a deranged person?

"That's you right there, is it not?"

"I hope not."

"Why were you running?"

"I can't remember, everything happened so fast."

The video shoots back to life. Remarkably, it's in about the right place. There is undeniably a big box of some sort sitting on the runway and then, moments later, it is gone. I've never really seen myself shrink something before either. I mean, I've seen it, but I've never really seen it in detail because I'm concentrating on doing it. It looks more like it disappears than shrinks, it's that fast. Definitely less embarrassing than my running.

"What happened there?"

The duo of inept-cop and incompetent-cop look at me like they've just cracked the case wide open.

"I don't know what you mean. The crash?"

"You know exactly what I mean," says Inept. "There was a case there, a trunk or something, and then it disappeared just when you got close to it."

"What case?"

On the screen, the paramedic is checking my vitals.

"What kind of freak are you?" says Incompetent. "I don't think that case disappeared, I think you shrank it. I think you smuggled it onto the plane and something went wrong with your powers or whatever and it came back to full size and crashed the plane. Then I think you shrank it, and then I think you picked it up off the runway."

On the screen, I'm holding my hand up to my mouth, like I am masking a cough.

"And then I think you ate it."

I guess he's not that incompetent, I should probably find out his actual name.

———

In the early days, there had actually been a fair amount of legitimate scientific research into tricks. Initially, they were assumed to be some sort of genetic mutation. The implications of this would presumably be that they would be inheritable. Immediately, people were predicting that in only a few generations, the vast majority of human beings would have superhuman abilities. This was the prevailing theory for a number of years. It's probably not true.

Humans are really slow at breeding. Before you get all defensive and start waving your eight adorable children at me, I mean in comparison to something like fruit flies.

When it comes to genetic research, fruit flies get the job done fast. They breed like crazy, have short life spans, a fully sequenced genome, and they share a large portion of their DNA with humans. If you want to see how a genetic trait moves down through generations and you don't have a lot of time, fruit flies would likely be your go-to subject. The problem is that a trick is not something that will necessarily manifest itself physically. Take my trick for example. How are we supposed to know if a fruit fly has the ability to shrink things? Hey, maybe they all do but they lack the mental capacity to act on it. Admittedly unlikely, but you see the issue.

Scientists followed a promising lead when a relatively

common trick was believed to have been found in fruit flies. This is not a good trick and is often sighted by the more religiously inclined as an example of the whole thing being the Devil's work. Some people can extend an arm, sometimes both, to around two to three times it's normal length. That's not bad in itself. Not world-changing, sure, but it might be handy if you needed to get something down off of a high shelf or something. And that's how it would usually happen. The person would be trying to grab something just out of reach, and the trick would kick in, and suddenly their arms would be twice as long, but therein lies the rub.

This trick seems to only effect the muscles and the skin. Their bones are seemingly no different to a regular person's. If a regular person's hands were yanked so hard that they were suddenly ten feet away from them, it wouldn't be a pretty sight, right? It isn't. Most of the internal carnage is hidden from view, as the skin does stretch out, but the bones usually dislocate at the elbow or break at the humerus. When the arm's muscles pull back to their regular length, the skin has lost all elasticity and the person is left with one (if they are lucky) or two stretched out sacks of bones where their arms were just a moment before. As I said, it's not a good trick. People with this trick tend to be referred to somewhat unfortunately as *arm-floppers*. There are also occasional *leg-floppers* and apparently even *neck-floppers*, although thankfully that is very rare as it is almost universally fatal.

I don't know what arms are called on a fruit fly. Could it be legs? But one of the more promising pieces of early research involved tracking fruit flies that had one or two elongated front legs through the generations. Biologists believed that these flies' elongated legs might genetically correspond to the aforementioned terrible stretchy arms trick. In the end they didn't. It turned out that some fruit flies just have gammy legs.

So essentially the only way to study how tricks work at this point is in humans, which is incredibly slow. Not only are we slow to reproduce, but often a trick won't manifest itself until adolescence or even later. There are some examples of tricksters with children who also have a trick, sometimes the same trick, but there are countless more examples of people with a trick whose children are totally normal. But as studying even three generations of humans would take maybe fifty years, it is understandable that we so far know very little about how tricks work genetically.

Apparently his real name is Detective Inspector Timothy Timpani, which is rather charming, I suppose. Although it doesn't seem to suit his gruff exterior. Maybe that's why he joined the police. He wanted a job title with some heft to it to balance out his slightly twee name. But I digress. It seems unlikely that I will survive the day.

It is only a matter of time before the package returns to full size. This is either going to happen with it still inside my digestive system, which will be immediately fatal, or with it outside my digestive system, which will probably be only slightly less immediately fatal.

They decide to stop interrogating me, as I'm apparently not being cooperative enough. I'm returned to an Intense Observation Cell, where I'm definitely being observed, and it is very much intense.

I'm trying to avoid using the lavatory facilities provided, for reasons that are about to become obvious. Firstly, they aren't so much lavatory facilities as something you might use to pack a lunch in. Secondly, as soon as I finish making use of the sandwich box, a man dressed as a scientist comes running in with a camera and starts photographing it. I say "dressed as a scientist" because I can't believe he actually has any medical qualification. What he does have is a pair of tweezers, a macro lens, and a total lack of shame. I think maybe they just gave him a lab coat to help him feel slightly better about his job as the excrement inspector.

Anyway, he doesn't find the package, and he definitely would have if it was there, so it is almost certainly still working its way through me. Which means it is very important I don't get distracted for even a moment. Not helping with this at all, is a small robin tapping rhythmically on the window.

The cell doesn't have real windows, windows you can open. I'm assuming it was purpose-built for suspected smugglers. But there are a couple of sizeable square holes near the ceiling letting light in. They are sealed off with that strong glass with wire running through them.

Tap, tap, tap goes the robin. Which I should have realised at the time is a little strange. More the kind of thing that happens on Christmas cards than in jail cells. I don't, for a couple of reasons. Firstly, I'm trying hard not to think about anything other than the package, and secondly, it sounds like something is kicking off in the hallway.

I think I hear gunshots.

It's difficult to tell because the cell is really well insulated, I guess to prevent whoever is being observed from disposing of any evidence. They have made it basically a fully sealed room. But I hear what sound like four or five loud bangs and then a muffled sound of people shouting. I push my face up to the tiny window in the cell door to get a better look, just in time for some more gunshots. I know they are definitely gunshots this time because I see who is being shot. He is running directly past my cell when he takes at least five rounds in the back.

Unsurprisingly, this knocks him to the floor. Somewhat more surprisingly, he gets right back up.

He has a bag taped over his head, and I don't think he can

see where he is going at all. He is tearing at the bag when one of the guards tackles him to the ground.

"Keep the hood on him, for God's sake," says another.

"What's wrong with it?" says the guard, pulling the hood down as far as he can and wrapping tape around him.

"If he sees light, he'll run."

It kind of looks like he's about to make another run for it anyway, before they shoot him in the head.

———

It's usually pretty easy to tell the difference between regular police and the X-Force. Firstly, the latter are going to have much better kit. While the police have slowly been acquiring new gear to help in combatting specific tricksters, they are far more budget-constrained than the Church of Divine Justice's volunteer army.

The four balaclava'd troops that lead me from my cell have got more specialised weaponry between them than probably the entire police force of Greater London. They each have a large rifle-type weapon thrown back over their shoulders. No two are the same, each is of a slightly different size and shape, but more obviously the barrel of each is painted a different bold colour. I'm guessing this is so they can quickly pick out the right weapon for a specific job and also easily see what kind of heat their buddies are packing.

Given that I don't have any sort of defensive trick, I'm assuming that any one of the weapons will be spectacularly fatal. They'll probably turn me into something like the chunky red mist I recently cleaned off the ready-meals in the supermarket. These aren't even their primary weapons mind, two have what look like electric harpoons slung over their fronts. I can just about see a spiked end protruding from the barrel, and there is a humming sound coming from one of them. I guess he decided to charge the thing up in case I make a run for it.

And I am, right? I am, at some point, going to have to make a run for it. The prospect seems like suicide, but what am I going to do, just go quietly along to FIDA? In the best case scenario, I'll almost certainly never be released.

I can't even shrink anything. I'm only able to shrink one thing at a time, so I'll have to get the package out of my digestive system first. What will I even shrink though, these four guys? I guess it will be a start. Maybe if I shrink them, I can just stamp on them. It will be horrific once they came back to full size but probably quite effective.

Apart maybe from the guy to my front left. He appears to have some sort of reinforced exoskeleton. I suppose I can call it body armour, but that really doesn't do it justice. This is either metal or perhaps carbon fibre, and it covers his legs as well as his torso. I honestly think that even shrunk I might have trouble crushing him with a boot. I don't know what he's done to deserve it that the others haven't. He might just be independently wealthy. My understanding is that X-Force are more than welcome to buy their own kit if they can. Maybe this isn't even his main job, just a hobby. He definitely looks like he's enjoying himself.

"Prisoner is secure, release the gate on 3, 2..."

Also he has "Jesus Saves" written in bold letters on his gun. This is potentially accurate, as I suppose it is mostly due to Jesus' shrunken corpse working its way through my lower intestine that I didn't have a good go at squishing him right then.

There is a loud buzzer sound before the rear doors of the police station open up. Just one vehicle in the car park, a large armoured van with no markings whatsoever on the side.

"Keep moving," says one of the troops behind me.

I stop walking. This seems like my very last chance to make

a break for it and there is just no way. I would be lucky to make it even two paces. They wouldn't even have to use their guns. My hands are cuffed behind my back, and I think if they even give me a shove, I'll just fall on my face.

There are two birds circling overhead. I give a skyward half-shrug in case one of them is Tess. Neither of them seem to have any advice.

7

THE OTHER PASSENGER

The interior of the van is sparse. There is a bench on each side facing the centre and seatbelts for the passengers. I'm assuming this is to comply with some unavoidable regulation or other, as I'm not convinced that the safety of the passengers is these people's primary concern.

A guard removes the handcuffs from behind my back.

"In you get, left side."

I'm still looking up at the circling birds.

"We haven't got all day."

Once I'm sat down, he re-handcuffs me, this time locking the cuffs around a chain attached to the bottom of the van.

"What, have you got dinner plans?"

"No," says the guard as the pair of them take seats on the bench opposite me. He's staring.

"I just meant because you seem to be in a big hurry, I wasn't asking you out."

The other guard closes the van doors behind us, and they thunk into place.

"Rear door secured," he says into his radio.

"Roger," his radio buzzes back. It is the driver. I can literally hear the driver's voice through the wire mesh between us and the front of the van, louder than I can hear the radio.

"We are ready to depart," he says, again into his radio.

"Please repeat," says the driver.

I lean as close as I can get to the front and say, "He says we are ready to depart."

But the driver seems to be occupied with something else.

We sit there in silence for at least a minute before the two guards' radios squawk back to life.

"OK, we need you to stand down, guys, we need the room for another passenger."

"Say again."

The driver just leans back and talks through the wire mesh like a normal person.

"We've got another one for FIDA."

"Shouldn't they just send another team?" and then whispers, "I thought this was the number one priority?"

It's stupid, but I do feel a little good about being called the "number one priority," even if it is only quietly.

"No," says the driver, now also whispering, "the orders are that they go in the same van."

"We could stay back here as well."

"That's not the order." This is the driver's angriest whisper yet.

I say, "You guys want me to step outside while you hash this out?"

Apparently they don't. What they do want me to do is sit inside the freezing cold van with the doors wide open for what seems like an age while they anxiously await this mystery prisoner.

His identity remains a mystery somewhat, even after they sit him opposite me, as there is a thick black bag tied over his head.

They handcuff him to the same chain as me and he says

nothing. I doubt he can see anything at all through the bag. Fortunately, there isn't room for all of the X-Force along with the extra passenger. Huge exoskeleton man and a quiet one stay behind, so I have just the two guys in the front and my surprisingly-still-alive fellow prisoner for company.

"Hi," I say, not wanting to be rude.

Nothing.

The back doors are shut and finally we are on our way.

"Package one is secure, package two is secure, and we are en route to you, ETA approx three hours," says the heavily armed trooper in the front passenger side. They had stacked all four of their larger weapons, his and the driver's, vertically in the footwell. This looks like an accident waiting to happen, if you ask me. Most of the new trickster-specific weapons are barely more than prototypes. It wouldn't be a huge surprise if one went off unprovoked. He gives us a thorough once-over through the grate and then turns back to the road.

The hooded guy waves at me.

"You were outside my cell."

He nods.

"They shot you."

He nods enthusiastically.

There are a few things you should probably know about Jackson. Firstly, he gets shot a lot. Beaten, stabbed, punched, thrown off buildings, thrown in front of a train once, I think he's been pushed down stairs several times. Someone slammed his head in a car door one time, I think. You get the picture. Or maybe you don't. Jackson has a trick. He describes it as "bouncy bones", a phrase he borrowed from his mother. She had been trying to explain to his father how their young toddler had survived a fall from a second-story window, and that was about the best she could come up with. "He just bounced and kept right on going." In fact, he crawled back up to the second floor for another go. And therein lies one of the many problems with Jackson.

Jackson nods down to his hands. He is signing, or at least his version of sign language.

"We're going to escape."

Fun fact, the sign language for "escape" is the same as for "elope", but given the situation, I'm pretty sure it's the former.

I've been so slow. "You did this deliberately. You got arrested to come get me."

He nods but with a shrug, like it's the most normal thing in the world.

This is unbelievable. I don't want to get into it with you now, but this is a lot to unpack. There are a myriad of reasons that I wouldn't have expected Jackson to come to my rescue like this. If I start thinking about them now though, I'm almost certainly going to explode Jesus all over the van.

On the upside, perhaps if Jackson has essentially put himself into this situation, then maybe he has already figured a way out of it.

"How?" I whisper.

He gestures lightly towards the mesh separating us from the guards.

"Uh-huh."

I check that the guards aren't looking at us, still not sure how much Jackson can see through the bag.

And then he signs something I am very familiar with, and I realise we are in trouble.

"Shrink me."

My heart sinks.

"Can't."

He shrugs. "Why?"

"Because," I lean as close as I can. "I've already shrunk something else."

"Backs to the benches."

The passenger side guard is pointing a handgun at us through the grill.

"Sorry, I fell asleep, I think."

"No talking, you two."

Jackson waits not long enough before signing "un-shrink it." This is one that I'm pretty sure is a sign of his own invention.

I point to my stomach, as a rough guess at the current package location.

"What is it?"

This is going to be tricky to explain with partially visible sign language, so I opt for simply "nothing good."

———

Baby Jenny was born at a weight of 7.1 lb on Christmas Day 1992 to the huge surprise of the medical community as a whole, her family in general, and most specifically her mother, Poppy, who until a few ill-judged decisions around six weeks earlier, had been a virgin. The almost-virgin Poppy reluctantly informed both the doctors and her incredulous parents that she had only had intercourse with one person, and with that person only once. The father could only be her high school gym instructor, a man in his mid 30s by the name of Terrence Bobbett.

At first, no one believed Poppy. Let me clarify, they very much believed that she'd had sex with her gym teacher. Terrence Bobbett looks like, and is, exactly the kind of teacher you would expect to be taking advantage of his students. He briefly denied the accusations, claiming that he could not possibly be the father of the child. He was represented by a lawyer from his teacher's union who, somewhat half-heartedly, requested a paternity test. The test duly confirmed that he was the father of baby Jenny, and he was dismissed from his position at the school. This was only the start of a huge number of problems for Terrence though. As Poppy had only turned sixteen around three months before giving birth to baby Jenny, it didn't take a super-detective to realise that this placed the likely date of conception very much on the statutory-rape side of the law.

Class act that he is, Terrence insisted under caution that he had been "one hundred percent certain that Poppy was over the age of consent" when their liaison had taken place

"I checked her ID and everything, always do!"

See, class act.

Terrence continued to protest his innocence and had been due to be laughed out of court and presumably into some significant jail time sometime the following year. He would surely have been convicted were it not for two things: Firstly, a mind-reader had a TV show now and a guy who can cure cancer was beginning to make headlines, so apparently magic people seemed to be a thing now. Secondly, five-month-old baby Jenny was now nearly four feet tall. Doctors estimated that, physically at least, she was developing at somewhere between ten and fourteen times the rate of a regular person. Mentally, it was harder to tell, she definitely wasn't as developed intellectually as you would expect from, say, the six year old that she resembled. She couldn't form complete sentences and was spectacularly un-coordinated. She would run at things screaming, arms flailing, sometimes biting and clawing at anything she could get her hands on. She routinely fell down the stairs and had so far jumped from the garage roof twice. These incidents had caused her any number of broken bones, but these, too, seemed to develop at an accelerated rate and had healed rapidly. She could break a leg at lunchtime, and be wildly running towards an open window by tea.

So, little Jenny was a curiosity for sure, and certainly something for the medical community to take note of, but there were so many other startling medical firsts going on at the same time that she was pretty much left to her own devices to be raised by her mother and grandparents. Her father had other things on his mind. Either as a natural consequence of his lifestyle or as an ill-conceived attempt to prove his innocence on the statutory rape charge, Terrence had impregnated a further four women since Christmas, three of whom had already given birth to children that were developing at a similar rate to baby Jenny. Whatever it was that was causing these children to develop so quickly, it's likely origin was inside Terrence Bobbett.

Bobbetts (as all decedents of Terrence Bobbett are somewhat derisively known) are not easy to care for. I mean that both physically, as they are wildly energetic, accident prone, exceptionally loud and have voracious appetites, and emotionally, as they are generally needy, angry, lustful creatures. I'm not sure if the second part has anything to do with Terrence Bobbett's trick or is simply a more conventional result of having him as a father.

Fortunately, there was a solution for any woman who had the misfortune to bring a little Bobbett into the world. Their father was more than happy to take over parenting responsibilities for the child, provided they relinquished full custody to him in perpetuity. He set up a charitable foundation that, somewhat surprisingly, initially received significant public support and began, for want of a better phrase, hoarding Bobbetts. A number of people did point out that maybe he wouldn't need "a charitable foundation with large grounds and extensive sporting facilities" if maybe he just kept his pants on a little more thoroughly, but that wasn't something that bothered Terrence. He seemed to have found his calling in life. Oh, and the Crown Prosecution Service had dropped the rape charges, so he had that going for him too.

On the whole, the horrified new mothers were happy to hand over their bouncing baby Bobbetts to the Terrence Bobbett Institute for Accelerated Development (or T-BAIT as it is inaccurately abbreviated), with the exception of Poppy, who had decided to raise little baby Jenny herself. Little baby Jenny, incidentally, was now nearly four years old and resembled a dinner lady approaching retirement.

Publicly available documents show that in the first two years, T-BAIT adopted over thirty children, but even if you factor in that Terrence appeared to be both promiscuous and phenomenally virile, and that there may have been a great number of adoptions without documentation, it is virtually impossible to explain how he amassed quite so many Bobbetts with just himself as the father. By the time the Winters Act passed into law, by conservative estimates there were in excess of half a million Bobbetts in the UK.

The rather unnerving but somewhat unavoidable explanation was that not all Bobbetts were Terrence's children. They were his grandchildren and possibly even great-grandchildren. There's no easy way of saying this, but the Bobbetts had almost certainly been breeding with each other. This is disturbing given that intellectually and emotionally they would almost certainly have still been essentially children. Also, even if physically they are adults, they are also obviously at least half-siblings. I should have warned you in advance that Bobbetts are disgusting, you probably could have skipped this bit.

I won't say this was the biggest question people were asking, as there are just so many valid questions that should be asked about the Bobbetts, but people began to ask "Why? What is this guy's purpose in amassing hundreds of thousands of these things in a vast estate in Coventry?"

There were a lot more people asking the more obvious

questions like "How has this been allowed to happen? How is this legal? Why do people choose to sleep with this weird dude?" But let's get back to the first one because I have a theory. I think he wanted to teach them gym. As well as being his former job, teaching gym is a genuine passion in Terrence's life, and I think he saw an opportunity to do it really well.

A more cynical perspective is that the original goal of all of the physical conditioning at T-BAIT was what turned out to be the first and only legally sanctioned use of the Bobbetts. Terrence had pitched his ever growing family to the government as "an army of perfect super-soldiers." They were exceptionally physically fit, could heal from almost any injury in a matter of days, they had relentless energy, and they would follow orders unquestioningly. Who knows, perhaps through the eyes of a loving father, that is exactly how they appeared.

The reality was rather different. When they were starting to reach around their optimum condition for military service, with a physical age of around twenty to thirty, they still had approximately the intellectual age of a preschooler. They were well drilled preschoolers for sure. They had constant boot-camp type training to enforce discipline.

However, numerous live-fire exercises apparently ended in tragedy. Unfortunately, it was difficult to envision a military application for such a large *unarmed* force, so Terrence persevered with the weapons training. Eventually, apparently he did put together a number of units of fighting men and women that could be trusted to fire their weapons where he told them, rather than at each other. The downside was that physically these units had an approximate age comparable to conventional eighty-year-olds, with all of the health issues you would expect from a squad of actual octogenarians.

They still had some advantages. They could recover from injuries faster than a regular person, certainly a regular old person. But their injuries were frequent and extensive. Essentially, Terrence just couldn't find the sweet spot where the physical development of a person being so rapidly accelerated, in comparison to mental development, conveyed any kind of advantage. Certainly a seven-year-old's mind in an eighty-year-old's body wasn't it.

The military contracts were cancelled, if you believe Terrence, or were never agreed to in the first place, if you believe the government. I'm going to go with Terrence on this one. He is a pretty deplorable person, but I just don't see why he would lie about this. Also, why else would he have constructed an army of heavily armed pensioners?

It's worth pointing out that I hadn't slept in around forty hours, and even that hadn't been for long. I'd known I wasn't going to be able to sleep on the plane, so I'd tried to grab a power nap in Israel, but it had been difficult because I was in a hotel room that was unfamiliar and it was impossible to relax. Weird how that happens. Also, I was expecting a phone call from someone who inexplicably had access to the preserved human remains of Christ, so there was that too.

So it's probably just pure exhaustion that is causing me to feel like I am drifting to sleep. This certainly isn't a relaxing situation either, given that I'm in the back of a fortified van with heavily armed guards, on the way to one of the scariest places on Earth.

The van brakes hard and I lurch forward. Thankfully, it is enough of a jolt to bring me back to full consciousness. It possibly saved my life. I think I do the wide-eyed looking around *I'm totally awake* thing that really sleepy people do, and I look at Jackson to see if he's realised how close I'd just come to exploding. It's hard to tell with the bag on. That said, it is often hard to tell what Jackson is thinking.

"Do you know where we are?"

A shrug.

"Just keep driving," says the heavily armed passenger.

I try to figure out why we stopped.

"I don't want to hit them." Said the driver.

"Don't stop for any reason, that's the order."

"What if it doesn't move?"

"Of course they'll move."

"They can kick you to death, I've seen it. They fly up on the bonnet and they panic and they kick you."

I lean forward to chance a look at the obstruction. It is two large deer, standing stock still in the middle of what seems to be a narrow country road. This makes a bit more sense of the conversation. For some reason I pictured an elderly couple.

"Just drive into them slowly, they won't go up on the bonnet."

"What about the antlers?"

"It's an armoured car."

"Backs to the wall, you two..." says the driver. "Oh, you have to be kidding me."

A third deer, bigger than the others, and than pretty much any creature I have ever seen, steps into the road and stares directly at the van.

There are honking sounds from behind us. I guess we're causing quite the obstruction. This must be such a narrow country road that there is no room to pass our huge van at all. I've got to assume this means we are very near our final destination. The FIDA building is in a underdeveloped region of Wales and famously inaccessible.

"Fine, I'll sort it," says the passenger, stepping down from the van.

"What's the hold up?" says a voice from behind. At least that's what I think they say, the Welsh accent is so strong that it basically confirms my suspicions of our current location.

"Never you mind," he says to the car behind while he selects a weapon from the footwell.

Jackson taps at my foot.

"Shrink me," he signs emphatically.

The passenger has stepped out in front of the van and levels his rifle at the biggest deer.

"Can't," I say, trying my best to convey my frustration to Jackson. He is right though, if ever there was an escape opportunity, this is it. And likely our very last chance.

"Buckle up!" says the guy pointing the huge gun at the deer, before pulling the trigger.

The gun barely makes a sound. It is maybe more like you would expect from a blowpipe or a bow, just a whisper and then a thud.

The huge deer barely reacts, and then it is immediately totally ablaze. Every single part of it is engulfed in flames. I think that maybe it will jump around, but it just kind of crumples to the ground, still staring straight at us. I feel sick.

"You see that?" he says, far too pleased with himself.

This seems like a stupid question, it isn't the sort of thing you'd miss.

But then again, he might have, because it turns out that around the time the deer started combusting, a huge badger had apparently jumped up into the van. Half the driver's face is torn off. He is desperately trying to get away but he had, as advised, buckled up.

I feel the bile touch the back of my throat. I'm not a huge fan of these guys, but this is brutal.

I'm going to blame the fact that I'm still desperately trying to keep my concentration on keeping the package shrunk and because I am very, very tired that it takes me so long to realise that trying not to be sick is the exact opposite of what I should be doing. I push my left hand down to the floor, so even with the cuffs on I can get my right hand up to my face and push my fingers to the back of my throat.

It's not like I have to be subtle about it. The driver is being eaten by a badger.

On that topic, it seems that he figures his best way out of this is just to stamp his foot as hard as he can onto the accelerator. That, or he doesn't really think about anything at all, because he's being eaten by a badger. Either way, the result is the same. The van shoots forward and into, then over, the chap that had shot the deer.

I like to think that the other two deer managed to hop out of the way. I don't think we hit them anyway. We do, however, hit a sturdy tree at a pretty decent pace. I think the handcuffs are the only things that stop me from smashing hard into the front of the van. The badger is not so lucky, and the impact throws him through the driver's side window, albeit with half the driver's face still firmly locked between his jaws.

Jackson seems fine. Of course he is fine. He has also been thrown forward in the impact.

"What happened?" he signs, to no one in particular.

"We cr—uh—ed."

I have my fingers down my throat.

The driver is somehow still alive and understandably seems to be in a lot of pain. I see, to my horror, that he is reaching across the car to the stash of presumably devastating weaponry in the passenger-side footwell.

"Why?" signs Jackson.

I wretch.

"Badger attack."

I'm not sure if he is nodding or desperately trying to get the hood off his face.

The driver has a gun now, although he no longer really has a face, and he just has the one eye left.

I am sick on the floor.

I can see the driver pressing the gun up against the parti-tioning grill as I desperately search in the vomit for Christ.

The driver's gun is painted bold red. I have no idea what that means, but suddenly I worry it might be something so powerful it can harm even Jackson, given that it is now pointed straight at him.

Before I even realise what happens, I hear a high-pitched scream as, suddenly, we are sharing the back of the van with a six foot coffin.

"Freeze!" shouts the driver as he shoots Jackson in the back of the head.

This knocks him off his feet and onto Jesus, but fortunately he seems unharmed.

"What happened?" he signs, to no one in particular.

"Stay still," I shout as I shrink him.

I pick him up and push him through the partition and into the driver compartment, before snapping him straight back to full size.

The driver's scream is lower this time as there is suddenly a big blind trickster on him.

"That's it, Jackson, you got him."

I still don't think Jackson can see anything at all, that doesn't stop him wailing with his fists into the guy's already mangled face.

"Freeze!" says the other guard, as he shoots Jackson in the face.

He's done well to survive being run over, and somehow he made it back round to the passenger side door. The gun only makes the same dull thud sound as before, but this time I know what is coming.

"Three o'clock, three metres," I shout to Jackson.

And then he is engulfed in flames.

Unlike the deer, Jackson doesn't take calmly to being incinerated. He turns to his right and pounces straight at the guy. He wraps his arms around him and just holds on.

Jackson, I should point out, is entirely impervious to fire. I once saw him run into a burning building to rescue a kebab he'd been saving. The guard is not so blessed and appears to be melting in Jackson's arms.

The driver is also on fire, and I worry it might spread. I'm still handcuffed in place.

"Little help?"

Jackson is rolling on the grass.

"Tony, you star! Look and see if that guard has keys on him, watch out for the fire."

The tiny monkey starts rifling through the driver's pockets. I really hope the other guy doesn't have them. He is basically just a pile of ashes at this point.

Tony pushes a set of keys back through the grate before wisely jumping out of the window.

I step out of the van to see that Jackson has finally managed to extinguish the fire. The fire has totally incinerated the bag so he can finally see again. It has also incinerated the rest of his clothes.

"Great to see you," he signs.

"You too."

"What does he look so happy about?" says Tess.

So, that's the other thing you should probably know about Jackson.

Jackson had grown up thinking he was indestructible, until one day it turned out that he wasn't. He broke his spine at the c4 vertebrae and was permanently paralysed. However, presumably as a result of his bouncy-bones trick, Jackson's nervous system seemed to work quite differently from other peoples'. Jackson was left paralysed from the *neck up*.

He retained full movement of the rest of his body, but his face remains frozen in place. No matter how hard he tries, and sometimes it looks like he is really trying, he cannot move any muscles in his face. This is doubly frustrating because he also can no longer talk.

I should try to describe his expression, I'll only need to do it once. I think it might be a factor in why he gets beaten up so often. He looks happy, deliriously happy, a thrilled child-like open mouth joy-smile, wide-eyed and excited. He looks like that all the time. At least to most people he does. And it turns out that people don't always take kindly to super-happy looking people. At least not when they can't explain why they are so happy. Try holding your mouth open as wide as you can, then try and spell out the alphabet without moving your tongue. That's what it sounds like when Jackson tries to explain his facial expression to strangers.

Some people just try to ignore him, some people are sympathetic. These two groups are both minorities though. Most people get mad at him. People start fights with him. Because of his bouncy bones, these fights tend to go on for a long time.

I once read an article proposing a theory, a theory that I totally disagreed with at the time. They said that dogs don't have different facial expressions. They just have the same basic dog face, and it's the person looking at them that infuses them with the emotion. But the article speculated that the emotion itself is solely in the eye of the beholder. I thought it was nonsense. Dogs obviously have all kinds of expressions. Now I'm not so sure though. Given that I know with a pretty high degree of certainty that Jackson cannot change his facial expression and I find it's impossible to look at him without embodying his face with whatever emotion the situation requires.

After the cancellation of the military contract, Terrence Bobbett was left in a tricky situation, both legally and morally. Legally, he now had more dependents than any other parent in history, as he had demanded full guardianship of every child he brought into the T-BAIT program. Furthermore, a bill had recently passed in parliament that capped all government subsidies for children at a maximum of thirty per household. Given that the second largest household in the country had only eight children, it would be difficult to argue that this bill was not aimed specifically at Terrence Bobbett.

Morally, most people would agree that Terrence also had an obligation to provide a safe environment and, if possible, some sort of meaningful existence for his offspring. While they now varied in age as much as any population can vary in age, in fact there were now scores of Bobbetts dying of age-related illnesses on a daily basis, they were all mentally no more developed than children. Terrence didn't see it like this though, or perhaps he was just taking revenge on the government for the new legislation and the cancelled contracts. Either way, he decided to inflict his progeny on the nation at large.

Unmarked vans were witnessed dropping off as many as fifty free-range Bobbetts outside town centres all over the country. As acts of war go, this perhaps doesn't sound hugely distressing, but I honestly can't imagine any other event that has been more immediately destructive to a society.

Imagine a hungry, confused, angry child with the hormones of a teenager, in the body of a fifty-year-old former heavy weight boxer who'd let himself go. Now imagine a hundred variations of that, some older, some younger, some at their physical peak, some on their last legs, but all with the mind of a child raised with little more than PE lessons and military drills.

Now take those hundred bewildered, half-starved, horny creatures and imagine them all wandering around your local shopping centre, picking up clothes, food, anything shiny, with no concept of how society as a whole functions and a deep distrust of anyone who doesn't resemble them. Now picture that multiplied by a thousand and know that you are not even close to the number of Bobbetts that had been unleashed on the UK's towns and cities. There were even reports of smaller drops in rural areas, where as few as ten Bobbetts could render a small village uninhabitable in a matter of hours.

Of all the fear-mongering speculation in the early days of tricks, this was curiously one outcome that was never hypothesised.

"But why?" you might ask, and you might be alone in that as the question that most people were asking was "How can we immediately kill all of the Bobbetts?" But I'm going to take a moment to address the "why", as I don't think Terrence Bobbett is a particularly smart guy, but I have to give him his dues for this one.

The free-range Bobbetts had been gradually accumulating cash for reasons that weren't initially clear. They never attempted to pay for anything, they would generally just stroll aimlessly into any store that hadn't been swift enough to bar its doors and pick things up, put on clothes they wanted, hold on tight to anything that took their fancy and discard anything that didn't. As far as anyone knew, they had no real understanding of the concept of money, having all been raised in seclusion at T-BAIT.

However, cash definitely seemed to appeal to them. Younger Bobbetts would grab wallets or handbags from people and feverishly search out bank notes, some older slower Bobbetts would walk behind counters and pull cash from the till. Retail establishments and restaurants were immediately realising how ill prepared they were for a thief that wasn't concerned with whether or not they were caught. And of course Bobbetts were not, they had no fear of arrest or seemingly any sense of right and wrong in a traditional sense.

But it seemed that they wanted money, and it soon became clear why. The first video I saw of this was of an older Bobbett, biologically maybe in his fifties, approaching a cashpoint with handfuls of cash. It was an ATM with a deposit facility, and other Bobbetts were carefully placing the, I assume ill-gotten, paper money into the envelopes provided by the bank and handing them to him. I don't think they could have had any comprehension of the purpose of the envelopes. This must have been something that they had been trained to do. The fact that it was always Bobbetts physically at least middle-aged implies that it may have taken many years of training. Anyway, this Bobbett put in his bank card and proceeded to make a deposit of many thousands of pounds in cash. When the transaction completed, the machine ejected a receipt and all Hell let loose. The Bobbetts were frantically celebrating, holding the receipt aloft, cheering and jumping up and down. It then became disturbingly pornographic. I don't know how else to describe the incestuous orgy that kicked off in that Uckfield branch of Lloyds TSB.

The only conclusion that makes any sense is that they had somehow been conditioned to respond in this way to successful cash deposits. This was not a one-off occurrence, just the first one I saw on a news report. Before long it was impossible to visit almost any bank branch in the country without witnessing at least a minor Bobbett gang-bang first-hand.

It turns out that Terrence had been opening a lot of bank accounts, or rather, his Bobbetts had. Every legally registered Bobbett, i.e. ones with birth certificates and government ID (this was only a small fraction of the total number of Bobbetts but still tens of thousands at the minimum), had opened a basic checking account, the kind you would set up for a newborn child to start a college fund or something, with every bank in Britain over the last year or so. As soon as a deposit was made into an account, it would be transferred overseas to a numbered bank account controlled by an anonymous shell corporation registered in Delaware. From a law enforcement perspective, it would never be seen again. We've gotta give Terrence some credit for that, right? Not bad for a gym teacher.

The initial police response had been woefully inadequate. In order to arrest a Bobbett, first you have to witness them committing a crime. This, in itself, is not a challenge, as they shoplift habitually and often commit public indecency on a grand scale, but they are hugely wary of police. The moment an officer of the law approaches a Bobbett, it will flee into the nearest crowd if it can. And unfortunately that is, more often than not, a crowd of Bobbetts. As they are all related and tend to look quite similar, it can be easy to lose track of the specific one you are after. Also, and I would assume this goes back to more of Terrence's ingenious conditioning, they routinely swap clothing (if they happen to be wearing any) upon meeting, as a form of greeting.

On top of this, the laws at the time in the UK stipulated that no person under the age of ten could be arrested or charged with a crime. This unfortunately excluded almost all Bobbetts from any form of criminal prosecution, as even the oldest-looking ones were still technically aged in the single digits. That is, if there is any legal record of their existence at all.

This was soon irrelevant though, as the far bigger problem turned out to be where to put them. Every cell in every police station was chock full of Bobbetts from day one, without making any significant dent in their numbers. This wasn't helped by the fact that many career criminals and oppor-tunistic looters had realised that the police were currently overwhelmed and unlikely to respond to any criminal complaint for a while.

The government took the seemingly inevitable step of calling in the military. Large troop transporters rolled into major cities with soldiers detaining anyone suspected of being a Bobbett. Whether or not they had been seen committing any kind of crime, they would then be restrained with cable ties and loaded into trucks. Stadiums and sports halls were requisitioned to become processing centres.

This was a wildly unpopular solution. Despite the havoc they caused, it was hard not to have some sympathy for the Bobbetts. They were, after all, essentially just overenthusiastic children, which made the military response seem all the more draconian. The army had been engaged admirably rapidly but with only vague rules of engagement. Bobbetts were gunned down in the street for seemingly no greater crime than running from their pursuers. As if this wasn't enough, any number of regular citizens had been rounded up as suspected Bobbetts. These were often elderly people or people with learning difficulties who just happened to be in the wrong place at the wrong time.

Upon being handcuffed, a Bobbett will often intentionally break its wrist or dislocate its shoulder to get free, in the knowledge that it will heal within a day or two. They are usually physically strong, energetic and fearless. If you want to have any chance of successfully detaining one, even one physically far past its prime, you need to be decisive and forceful. The army had learned this quickly, however these same tactics, when applied to an elderly person who turns out not in fact to be a Bobbett, were always harmful and often fatal.

8

A MIND-BENDING PREDATORY GAY

I nitially at least, being sued by the World Championship of Poker seemed to be about the best thing that could have happened to Felix Trent. Apart from the one obvious downside, that he was unlikely to ever be able to play poker for large amounts of money again, everything seemed to be looking up. The court case had brought him a level of global fame that could surely be monetised to some degree.

For a while, he featured on just about every talk show you could imagine. Felix is both charming and erudite and would make an excellent guest on a panel discussion, even without his trick, but it was his mind-reading abilities that would make his appearances so popular.

His very first post-trial interview had been on a late night US show where he had had a nice enough chat and demonstrated a little card play, making thousand-dollar bets with the host. The guest after Felix was a big movie star; it was one of those shows where they keep all the guests out the whole time so they can chip-in occasionally. The actor had just finished an impassioned plea for everyone to go and see his latest movie, which he rather foolishly finished with, "I really think it's the best thing I've ever done."

"Is that true, Felix?"

"No."

After both the audience and the slightly flustered actor finished laughing, Felix warmly explained that while he was certainly very proud of the movie, he believed that his two children were actually his proudest achievements.

There were "aaah's" and cheers and back slaps all round, and it was clear that Felix had a golden future in television ahead. Come to think of it, I doubt that this career-making moment even required Felix to use his trick. It didn't take a mind-reader to know the actor wasn't all that impressed with the current movie. Felix could have seen it on the plane on the way over. Anyway, it was a lovely moment.

Felix's first TV vehicle was a show where couples could win prizes by lying to their partner... or was it by not lying to their partner? It was called *Two of a Kind*, and it was mediocre at best. However, both the show and Felix became incredibly popular almost immediately. Later he had his own weekly talk show with assorted not-quite-celebrity guests. That one was apparently challenging to make as legitimate stars were reticent to be interviewed live by a man with genuine mind-reading abilities.

For me though, the most compelling viewing would be when he was asked to comment on current affairs, especially the thought processes of politicians. Unfortunately for Felix, this probably didn't do him any favours when the trouble started. A little known (at the time) politician by the name of Virgil Barnett had made some fairly racist statements the day before and had been backtracking a bit, explaining how he thought "multiculturalism is a great British virtue", etc., and he only wanted all of Britain to be as strong as something or other, and Felix, clearly angry, chose to weigh in.

"I'll tell you right now," he said. "The only thing that man wants with any real conviction is to be Prime Minister. He couldn't give a toss about the country as far as I can tell."

Again, Felix wasn't exactly having to overly strain his mind-reading powers to come to that conclusion, but the fact that he genuinely did have an ability to sense what people wanted presumably gave the comments a significance they wouldn't have otherwise had.

Almost immediately, I hear footsteps beside me.

I'd left Jesus in the back of the van and just started walking.

"Where are you going?" shouts Tess.

"Home, I guess." I haven't thought that far ahead.

"You can't just go home, your face is all over the news."

The pitter-patter of feet beside me becomes more urgent, and then the little monkey creature is scampering up me.

"They're sure to find you, and they'll either interrogate you until you tell them what we're doing or they'll just send you straight back to FIDA."

Tony tugs on my ear until I turn round.

"Then I guess I'll find a new home." She is right though, this is terrible. I'd spent my last money in the world on a bottle of water in the airport, and I'm now more unemployable than ever. Where am I even going to sleep?

"Aaaaaaa," says Jackson, buttoning up the slightly burned pair of trousers he presumably just pulled off of the faceless van driver. He looks pretty pleased with himself, Jackson, not the van driver. Jackson always looks pleased, the van driver not so much.

"You coming with me, Jackson?" I don't even know that I

want him to, as if I'm not going to draw enough attention already, but it seems rude not to ask after all the trouble he'd gone to, to rescue me.

He shrugs, but I think it is kind of a yes. He is wrapping a tourniquet around his arm to give himself an injection. This is understandable, he had been very on fire only moments ago.

"What's that?" he signs, pointing at the Jesus box.

"It's not important."

"It's very important," says Tess, seeing her opportunity. "The whole future of the country, the world even, could rest on it."

"Steady on," I say.

"Why? What is it?" he signs.

She tells him. He looks excited, but he always looks excited.

The long and the short of it is that I begrudgingly agreed to help, again. Tess had been following us all the way from London on a fairly dated-looking scooter. It's a wonder she had made it this far, especially with a small monkey on her shoulders. There was no way she'd be able to get the package anywhere on her own though. I'd come this far, it would be a shame to make it all for nothing. Also, in my brief tantrum I'd realised I literally didn't have anywhere else to go. I do have conditions though. While I will shrink the package, from this point onward it is going to remain entirely exterior to my body. Secondly, I will only take it as far as Jimmy in London. Some other idiot will have to take it from there. I certainly want nothing to do with Terrence Bobbett. Fortunately, Tess has few other options, and we are agreed. Oh, also Jackson, he seems game enough.

So, we (mostly I) decide that the scooter is not an option for the long trip. Even if I shrink everyone as well as the package, there is almost no way I'd be able to keep my concentration up the whole journey. We need something bigger.

We can't be too picky. Presumably, someone must be expecting us to arrive at FIDA any moment, so it can't be long before they send someone to look for us. On the other hand, this is a very quiet country road, only a couple of cars have been past in the last 20 minutes. The first was a tractor (too slow) and the second was a mini (too small).

"Oh, oh, perfect! Go, Jackson."

It is a horse box, basically like a camper van for horses if you're not familiar with these things (I wasn't), and it is going at about 50 mph, which I suppose is pretty fast for something with a horse in it.

Jackson only just manages to step out in front of it before it shoots past us, so there is almost no time to brake. He gets hit pretty full-on by the front bumper and then gets rolled over by two sets of tires. He manages to grab onto the tow bar though and is dragged along behind.

The vehicle stops… eventually. For a moment I'm worried they are just going to accelerate away and get out of there as quickly as possible. That happened sometimes, I guess understandably. The injuries Jackson sustains in these impacts look so obviously fatal that the driver has to wonder for a moment if there is really any point in trying to help. Might as well just get out of the area as fast as you can and inspect the damage later. Fortunately, this driver is not so pragmatic. She gets out and stands by her door, seemingly wary of going any further.

"Are you OK?" she says, somewhat optimistically.

Jackson, being Jackson, is fine. In fact, he is currently unlocking the back doors of the horse box. In a real stroke of luck, there is a horse passenger onboard, which makes an ideal distraction. Tess has it scamper straight into the adjacent woods, and the driver doesn't miss a beat in running after it. However much concern she had for Jackson, she is definitely focused on the horse now.

We agree that Tess should drive. If we are pulled over for some reason, at least we might have a chance. My face is currently on every news report in the country and Jackson's face is undeniably distinctive, but there is a chance they may not be aware of Tess. She looks far too young to be driving a horse box about, but I'm sure she can find some distracting wildlife or something.

I jog up the ramp into the box, and Jackson closes it behind us.

"Thank you, Jackson."

I pop Jesus on the floor and let him back to full size.

"For everything. You didn't have to."

There's a slight shrug, his face is hard to read.

"How have you been?"

It had become clear that Felix was not unique, rather he was just the first example of a new human phenomenon. Shortly after Billy Winn was recorded making medical history in Middle America, a girl from Senegal recorded a new 1500 m world record at just under 30 seconds. The World Athletics Organisation, in a move that was prescient of how most institutions would handle the phenomenon going forward, essentially decided to pretend it had never happened and simply banned the girl from all future athletic events.

There were also a lot of people claiming they could levitate for some reason, but most early videos turned out to have been faked. The first legitimate levitator was probably a guy called Sergey Petrov from Bosnia, although I would argue that it wasn't a particularly useful skill. He could definitely levitate to a foot or so above the ground, but once he was there he was basically stuck, as there was no way to propel himself in a direction. He could either take a run at it before hovering along like a frictionless skateboarder, or he could poke himself along with a kind of mini gondola pole. He was also able to levitate over water, poking himself along on canals with a more conventionally sized gondola pole.

So Felix was not the draw that he had been in the early days. Simple mind-reading was not enough to pull in large audiences, but charming as he was, he had bumbled along on daytime panel shows for a good while, presumably making a decent living, until the first accusations appeared. A tabloid newspaper published a photo of Felix kissing Tom Barnett, the twenty-three year old son of conservative politician, Virgil Barnett, outside of a popular London night club. There was nothing scandalous about this on the face of it, and the paper didn't make any overt judgement with the headline "Young Barnett Getting Frisky With Felix."

The subtext was clear though. Virgil Barnett was was very much towards the family-values, no sex please we're British, end of the political spectrum. He had, in fact, recently spearheaded a number of education policy changes that would prohibit any discussion of homosexuality in state schools. The tabloid had known this would be embarrassing to him. The owner of the paper had bought the photographs and positioned them prominently in several publications as petty revenge for the MP's small role in blocking an acquisition of another paper he was attempting to make. Such is the day-to-day life of business and politics. Odds are it would soon have been forgotten without consequence had it not been for the ill-advised overreaction of the young Tom Barnett.

Tom had not been entirely upfront about his sexuality with either his father or, as it turned out, his fiancé. What really should have been a matter for maybe a frank and honest discussion amongst family over a cup of tea instead became a matter for the courts, parliament, and eventually the military, as they dealt with the global ramifications of the second trial of Felix Trent.

I sleep. Oh boy do I sleep. This is the first time in almost two days that I haven't had to concentrate on my trick, and the moment I shut my eyes I'm out like a light.

Jackson shakes me awake. He looks worried.

"What's wrong?"

"It's all over the radio," says Tess.

"What's all over the radio?" Wait, we've stopped? I worry for a moment that Tony might be driving.

"We are, even him." She points to Jackson. "They called him an 'indestructible robot-man with a broken face.' I've not seen a TV, but they might even have pictures by now. We need to change car or something?"

"But this is perfect."

"But it's a horse box, they're not exactly common. If they already know about the escape, they've got to have figured out that we stole this."

"Fair point." I have just woken up, but on reflection this does seem pretty obvious. "So where are we now?"

"If I'm right, we should be a short walk from Chippenham."

"Is that good?"

"If you don't enjoy long walks."

"Why Chippenham?"

"There's a direct train to Paddington, and from Paddington we can get straight into the old Post Office Railways."

"I have so many questions."

"Can you ask them while we walk?"

Apparently, while I had been sleeping, Tess had had altogether too much time for thinking, and when Tess gets to thinking, ridiculous plans seem to come thick and fast. This one, at least, has a kind of twisted logic to it.

She assumes that there are likely to be roadblocks popping up all over the country, so we will probably be discovered if we continue in pretty much any road vehicle. My face is being broadcast everywhere, and I'm not able to shrink myself. Any interaction with the police, or worse with the X-Force, is at best going to result in a brutal firefight.

Public transport, with the fewest possible changes, seems like the best option. If I shrink Tess, Jackson and Jesus, and pop them safely in my jacket pocket, and then I can get onto the train without being seen and find an out of the way spot where no one is going to see my face, we might all be able to get back to the capital.

It all sounds relatively straight-forward the way Tess explains it, but then so had the aeroplane plan and look how that turned out.

The good news is that the station is, as promised, not too long of a walk. Which is nice given that I'm the one doing all the walking. I'd popped the shrunken Tess on one shoulder so she could shout up to my left ear, and I'd put Jackson on the right because that's where he wanted to be. Jesus went in my pocket.

"Don't go in yet," shouts Tess.

"Why?" I whisper back, as inconspicuously as I can. We are halfway up the station approach.

"There's police by the entrance to the platform. They're checking everyone."

Some pigeons in the station made it easy enough for Tess to get a preview of what was coming up.

"Towards the left of the station, there's a payphone, go in there."

"Who am I calling?"

I step into the phone box and try to keep my hood covering my face without looking like I'm trying to keep my hood covering my face.

"We need a distraction."

"I don't have any money."

Jackson jumps off of my shoulder and climbs onto the top of the phone.

"It's a free number, dial 0800 6637325."

"What are we doing?" Jackson signs.

I shrug and dial the number. It seems familiar, but I can't figure why. An automated message picks up.

"You've reached the Church of Divine Justice Ability Awareness line, please hold and one of our operators will be with you as soon as humanly possible. Have a blessed day." And then there is a muffled recording of a choir singing something bombastic.

It all clicks in a moment.

"It was you."

"What?" says Tess, like butter won't melt.

"You had that dentist killed."

"That guy was an idiot."

"And the lady in the paddling pool?"

"Massive bigot. You would have hated her."

"But the kids?"

"That was a shame. If they didn't have such ridiculous weapons."

The music clicks out.

"And the guy in the supermarket?"

"What guy?"

"He exploded."

"Nope. Hope it wasn't an actual trickster."

"Church of Divine Justice, how may we be of assistance today?"

"Tell them that you've just seen someone with a trick, and they were working, but just be like 'I'm certain I saw it but no one else reacted.' You should sound a little shaken, but like you almost can't believe your own eyes."

I should point out that when people are shrunk, their voice tends to scale accordingly. They don't sound like cartoon mice or anything (more's the pity), just really quiet. So, if I want to absolve myself of responsibility for what I'm assuming is about to be a pretty morally questionable act by letting Tess make the call, that will mean unshrinking her, which will mean unshrinking everyone, and suddenly sharing a small phone box with Tess, Jackson, Tony and the preserved remains of Jesus Christ.

"Just a moment please, I'm a little shaken," I say.

"I quite understand, take your time." The phone woman really is friendly.

I look at Jackson for guidance. He pauses for a moment, like he's weighing it up, and then nods encouragingly.

"I hope you can help. I've just seen someone, I think it might be one of those... I don't know what the right term is, magic people? They... they weren't normal."

"I see."

"You need to say they had a job, say they're a cop." Says tiny Tess.

"But the thing is this person was a police officer. That's not right, is it? I thought it wasn't allowed?"

That gets her attention.

"A police officer? And they used their trick while they were working?"

"Yes, I'm certain of it. But I don't know that anyone else saw it. That's why I called."

"And what was the trick? What do you think you saw?"

Tess sticks her tongue out at me.

"They had a really long tongue."

"I see. I mean, some normal people have pretty long tongues."

"No, it was really long. They licked their eye with it." I feel like I'm losing her. "And it was forked, like a snake's."

I think we have them. Tess gives me the name and description of one of the cops checking tickets, and the lady on the phone sounds pretty keen. They want to know how long we think he'll be there, so hopefully they are coming right away.

"Christ be with you," says the cheery sounding lady on the phone.

"He surely is."

It's nearly thirty minutes before the X-Force arrives, which I guess is pretty impressive given that we are kind of out in the sticks, especially considering how well prepared they are when they do arrive. Still, it is a long time to stand around trying not to be recognised, given that I am apparently now the second most-wanted fugitive in the country. I sit on a tree stump in the shade with my hood up and try to conceal that I am talking to my tiny friends.

An SUV with blacked-out windows pulls up in front of the ticket office and two heavily armed men get out. I was already thinking "wow, this is a huge reaction for a man with a long tongue" when a second SUV pulls up behind and another two troops get out. One of the guys in the second car has a red-and-orange-painted weapon. I wonder if that means it is the same as the one that incinerated the deer. Is there maybe a universal system for these things, or are they just free-styling it? I suppose we are about to find out. Barbecuing a cop in the middle of a train station would certainly be a reckless play, even for the X-Force.

As the troops enter the ticket office, I try to get as close as I can to the entrance to the platform, ready to take any opportunity to sneak past. I can't see much, but I can certainly hear the commotion. Fortunately, Tess is able to get a front row seat in the form of a curious pigeon. What happens is this:

All five guys walk quickly over to the two police officers. As it happens, both officers are busy assisting a slightly confused lady. I think she asks them for some information about where her train is leaving from. These guys are standing by the barriers and seem to be checking tickets, so she probably just assumes they are railway staff. Anyway, credit to them, the officers are trying to help her.

"Sir!" says one of the X-Force unnecessarily loudly.

"Just a second please," says one of the officers with admirable restraint.

"Now please."

And at that point an X-Force guy towards the back raises and cocks his weapon, I assume to show he means business. And it definitely does that. As he cocks it, it lets go what looks like a large dart into the loud man in front of him.

"Oh, sorry John, I think it went off."

John looks down at the huge dart sticking out of his body armour.

"Jesus, be careful with that, would you? Ah man, I..."

I think he is going to say, "I think it went through." Because it definitely has. I guess it is a weapon designed to deal with people with particularly thick skin. The long dart has punched its way through the body armour and there is a slight delay before it injects its payload. Anyway, John basically melts.

"Now," says Tess.

And now the police are definitely taking these guys seriously. As if the message is "This is what we do to each other, imagine what we'll do to you!"

One of the police officers draws his weapon. I should point

out at this point that the majority of the British police force still use largely traditional weaponry. There are special teams that have some trickster-specific devices, but due to both budgetary constraints and general common sense, these are rare. The police officer's weapon is a taser, I think, one of the ones that fires out a pair of wires that latch onto the victim.

The officer immediately spots an issue though. All three remaining X-Force troops are wearing pretty robust-looking body armour. It is unlikely the taser is going to do much through that.

The one that had melted John seems a little shell-shocked, like maybe he's had enough firearms time for today. His weapon stays by his side. The other two are a different story though. Both shoulder their weapons and point them at a police officer each.

This seems like the ideal time to pass through the barriers and onto the platform. No one will pay any attention to us with all this going on.

We enter just in time to see the police officer tase an X-Force in the face. This is effective, and the guy spasms and crumples to the ground. Unfortunately, as he goes down, his gun fires out some sort of plastic goo that hits the confused woman square in the face.

"Freeze," shouts the other X-Force guy, before shooting both cops with what appears to be a conventional shotgun.

I hop over the ticket barrier and half-jog down the platform. I'm pretty sure that, given the situation, this behaviour would have been normal even if I wasn't a wanted criminal.

In a rare stroke of luck, a London train is pulling up to the platform just as all this is going on, and I'm not the only passenger trying to get off of the platform and onto the train as fast as humanly possible.

"Freeze, everyone freeze," I can hear him shouting as the doors close.

Tom Barnett filed a claim for libel against the newspaper and, somewhat necessarily, a criminal complaint against Felix Trent. He claimed that he had no recollection of the evening when the photograph was taken, after the point at which he was introduced to Felix by a mutual friend. He claimed that Felix had presumably used his mind-powers to trick him into making out with him, before going back to his place.

This would normally have been passed off by the police as a fairly ridiculous assertion, contrived presumably to add weight to his also frivolous libel claim. You have to remember, though, that these were the very early days of people coming to terms with tricks even existing. New, hitherto unseen powers seemed to be cropping up on a weekly basis, and there was a huge amount of pressure, both from the general public and the existing establishment, to set up a legal framework to protect people from any potentially super-powered criminals. Couple that with the fact that a "mind-bending predatory gay," as Felix was once memorably described, is amongst the British tabloid press' greatest fears, and you know that this case isn't going away anytime soon.

However, the prosecution knew that their case was weak. It was essentially just one person's word against another's, which should never be relied upon to convince a jury of a person's guilt "beyond all reasonable doubt". And so, they went about interviewing as many of Felix's former lovers as they could find and... there were a lot. As I have mentioned, Felix is a charming chap, and he was also a prominent and then not-so-prominent celebrity for quite some time. It's not hugely surprising that a number of people found him attractive.

The problematic thing for Felix was his particular taste in romantic partners. As the prosecution continued to dig, a pattern emerged — Felix seemed to favour successful men in their early twenties... straight men. Not a single person interviewed by the prosecution had been openly gay until their encounter with Felix, and very few had been single. Many continued to identify as straight afterwards, often remaining in their current relationships; others made some fairly dramatic lifestyle changes. It's important to note (I watched a pretty exhaustive documentary series on this very subject) that in early interviews, not a single person suggested that there was any kind of mental coercion, memory loss, or even any regret surrounding their encounter with Felix. Those all came later.

At the same time as the CPS was building its case, the British press had discovered a veritable news goldmine. They were avidly seeking out Felix's former conquests at a rate the prosecution could only dream of. It seemed like every day there was another story of an ostensibly straight person in the public eye who had "allegedly" or "was rumoured to" have had a relationship with Felix. Felix had mixed in some pretty well-to-do circles, especially in the early days, so it was hardly surprising that he was socialising with other celebrities. Among those being "probed in [the] ongoing enquiry" were two Premiership football players, a technology CEO and a TV chef whose photogenic family featured heavily on his show. What would normally have been considered fairly trashy journalism now had a genuine news value and was the key talking point in just about every current-affairs discussion show for weeks on end. Was it possible that he was turning straight young men gay? If he was, would that be a crime? He was on TV a lot, could he make me gay just by watching? Would that be a crime? If I think he turned me gay by watching his show, to whom should I apply for compensation? That kind of thing.

9

FATHER KNOWS BEST

I decide to hide in the train's tiny toilet for the whole trip. It seems like here we'll have the least chance of being recognised. I shan't bore you with the details, as I feel I've spent a lot of time describing my ongoing struggle of trying to remember to keep everything shrunk whilst not nodding off or losing my train of thought. It is somewhat like the plane trip but with slightly lower stakes, I suppose, as if something went wrong this time, I'd be less likely to cause the death of everyone on board.

The toughest moment is probably when the ticket inspector knocks on the door to ask if I'm OK. I don't think he really wants to know if I'm OK. Clearly he spotted that the door has been locked for some time and suspects (accurately, as it happens) that I don't have a ticket.

Fortunately, we are just approaching a station, and he is suddenly quite distracted by three pigeons trying furiously to cuddle his face.

I am really starting to appreciate just how useful Tess' trick can be. There is almost nowhere in the country where you aren't within a few hundred feet of a potentially useful animal.

What's more, they are generally pretty inconspicuous. Your average person, even in the country's current heightened state of awareness, won't stop to question if a rat or a pigeon is looking at them for maybe a bit too long. Tess is so practiced at it that she will usually keep a perimeter of small animals around herself at all times. As such, she is constantly aware of what is around every corner.

It is largely due to this that we are able to get from the train to the entrance to the old Post Office tunnels unseen. Everyone is back to full-size, except for the package, which I shrank again as we figured it would be easiest to keep in a pocketable size. Basically, it's all going really well, until it's not.

"Stop, stop," says Tess, raising a hand to Jackson.

He walks into her hand and looks confused.

"It's Spider-man," says Tess.

I sign this to Jackson, who seems intrigued. "Does he have...?" He mimes what I am guessing is a kind of web shooter.

I shake my head. "Maybe don't mention that to him. He might make you an omelette."

An omelette is actually one of the few foods that Jackson can eat. Because he can't chew anything, he's limited to foods he can shove down his oesophagus unchewed. Generally he sticks to protein shakes and the like, but I've known him to enjoy a soft scramble.

"What's wrong with Spider-man?"

"He's not there."

There aren't many tunnels in the old Post Office Railway. It used to be used to get post from one side of London to the other, until logistically it became both simpler and cheaper to just drive letters across town. The old tunnels have been abandoned ever since. The section that Jimmy et al. had made into their London base was only accessible from one of two entrances to the same tunnel. The theory being that it would be easy to keep these guarded with minimal resources. Phoebe would guard the tunnel from the other side, and if anyone was approaching, she would radio back to Chris who could make an ungodly racket. When I had previously visited, they had only been able to all come and have lunch together because Tess was there, and she could achieve the exact same result by intermittently possessing a couple of mice.

But Tess hadn't been there, and Spider-man wasn't on guard, so where was he?

It turns out that he'd been killed. In fact, they had all been killed. Before I tell you how, in case you aren't familiar with them already, I should probably tell you a bit about creepers.

Creepers can walk through walls, well, kind of. It takes them ages. A really thick wall will take maybe an hour or two to get through. So what they tend to do is stay in the wall itself and just watch and wait until they have an opportunity to come out. Their clothes cannot go through walls though, so they have to do this naked. The same goes for weapons, nothing that isn't living tissue can go through. So if a creeper wants to get to you through a wall, they'll arrive naked and unarmed, and it'll take them at least an hour to get out, so they're not as scary as some potential adversaries. As the name would suggest though, they are pretty creepy.

In the early '90s, creepers would often be found in bank vaults first thing in the morning. Sometimes they were caught, sometimes they'd get away. It was easy enough for them to get into the vault of course, even with thick walls. Given a whole night, they can get pretty much anywhere. However, once they were inside, they would realise that they could no more get the money back through the walls than you or I could. (Or just you maybe. I would actually have a shot if there was even a small hole and, come to think of it, I don't know what you've got going on. But anyway, creepers can't pull hard objects back through walls.) But sometimes they would decide that they were already too committed to just leave empty-handed, I guess, and they'd wait until morning to make a run for it with the cash. The first few times, before banks had procedures to check for them, they tended to get away with it. I imagine it was fairly startling to find a naked person in your bank vault first thing in the morning. Accordingly, they'd usually be able to just run past whichever hapless employee opened the vault with as much cash as they could carry.

As banks became wary of them, though, creepers sought out other illicit income streams. Given how proficiently they can bypass most security, assassin seemed a promising career choice. Fortunately though, they aren't any more naturally suited to murder for hire as they are to bank robbery, as illustrated by the fact that Jimmy, an overweight and naturally friendly man with no special abilities other than being able to eat huge objects, had seemingly taken out two of them.

I don't think all creepers are related, by the way. Some people do, but I think that's likely just one of those prejudices against people with tricks. When a parent first finds out that their child is a creeper, usually as they wake up somewhat terrifyingly having half dissolved into their bed for the first time, every parent must wonder for just a moment if there could be some truth to the king-creeper theory. "Theory" is perhaps too generous a term for this, but it's something people say, and when I say people, I don't just mean kids in the playground. I've heard political and religious leaders espouse this. The theory is that every creeper shares the same father (admittedly somewhat plausible given the Bobbett situation). This king-creeper is said to be the most prolific rapist of all time. For every creeper that is born, the mother would have been visited by the king-creeper around nine months previously, often without her noticing. Apart from the obvious implausibility of the theory (without noticing, seriously?), assorted creepers have now been genetically tested and shown to be essentially unrelated.

This gives you some idea of the regard in which society holds creepers though, and if you also have a low opinion of them, it's not about to improve when I tell you how they often make a living these days. While the inability to bring weapons in through walls makes them at best mediocre assassins, and the inability to bring money back out with them limits their abilities as thieves, it turns out that they are incredibly well suited to taking young children from their beds at night. Because the child is human or biological or whatever, unlike money or guns, if a creeper grips a person tightly, they can pull them slowly back through a wall. Provided, of course, that the person is small enough or incapacitated enough, and the creeper can keep ahold of them for the few hours it will take to get through the wall. And, of course, the victims have to be naked too. Correspondingly, even by the standards of tricksters, creepers do not tend to be popular.

───

We piece together a pretty reasonable approximation of what had happened, I think. The creepers had come in through the wall from the Bakerloo Line. Jimmy was presumably asleep at the time. Creepers are pretty vulnerable if you're not asleep, basically just an unarmed naked person leaking very slowly into your room. But they had been able to catch Jimmy off guard, and what's more, they had been able to get ahold of a weapon. When we find him, he has a knife stuck firmly in his right eye. It's a knife for cheese, so not a particularly brutal weapon, but it doesn't really have to be if you're asleep and someone shoves it in your eye. I figure he must have been asleep because, well firstly, they had managed to get him right in the eye, which wouldn't have been easy with a moving target, and secondly, because the knife has gone right through his eyelid, so I figure his eyes must have been shut at the time.

Amazingly, this hadn't killed him right away. Jimmy must have woken up and started fighting for his life with everything he had. The room is in total disarray like these two had been going at it hard. Blood covers almost every surface, it could be Jimmy's, could be the creeper's, likely a bit of both. Jimmy had evidently thrust a broken bottle into the top of the creeper's leg, and I think he must have cut an artery.

Tess is understandably reluctant to take a close look, but I suppose my day job has inured me to the intrinsic horror of these things. I just want to figure out what had happened.

I study the creeper for a bit. He is pasty white. Not like a pale person, or even an albino, more like if you shaved a hairy creature like a monkey or a cat, like his skin has literally never seen sunlight. Maybe it is from the blood loss, maybe he just didn't get out much. Creepers probably don't get invited to many parties.

His leg wound is maybe fatal on its own, or at least it would have been given time, but he also has a phone cord wrapped tightly around his neck and his hands are reaching up desperately. It's like Jimmy had throttled the guy from behind and then just let him drop. And I think I know why. What with being stabbed in the head and everything, he was probably conscious that he might not have long left to live. To be honest, it's a phenomenal performance to have got anything done at all considering his injuries. He'd grabbed a pen and paper from his desk and began to write a note to Tess. Annoyingly, he'd only managed to write "Tess" and nothing else when the second one had got him.

I think it must have been while he was writing, hunched over his desk with a cheese knife sticking out one eye, that the creeper had bludgeoned him over the back of the head with a heavy object of some kind, probably the chair leg. We found the leg outside the room with a lot of blood on it, so that makes the most sense. He had presumably used it to kill Chris as well. It looks like he'd been clobbered hard with something, also in the back of the head.

It's not surprising that Jimmy hadn't thought to check for another creeper. I'm pretty sure this is the first time I have ever heard of them working together. As contenders for being the very least liked type of tricksters, or human in general, they tend to be solitary. The McMillan brothers are possibly even more hated but they are thankfully, as yet, a one-off. Creepers, on the other hand, are relatively common. That said, as it is a fairly easy ability to hide, as unless someone catches you halfway through a wall there's really no way to tell, I'm sure the vast majority simply keep it to themselves. There must be a lot of creepers that, provided they somehow managed to keep their name off the register, are living happily as members of the general public.

I figure that after being struck on the head, Chris must have been able to raise the alarm, because both Spider-man and Phoebe had been heading in his direction when they had been shot. This is the real conundrum that creepers pose. As much as you might want to arm yourself at home, to protect yourself against a surprise visitor, you could very well be playing into their creepy hands. Undoubtedly, there are more people who "keep a loaded gun by my bedside just in case" that have been shot by creepers with it than have successfully used it to defend themselves.

Chris did have a small handgun though. It was the one that the fox who had been following me had. The gang had shared it, for emergencies. Unfortunately, the emergency had snuck up behind Chris and caved his head in with a chair leg before he had a chance to use it. Once the creeper had been armed with the only gun, the others didn't really stand a chance.

"I'm just wondering if I should leave it in."

Tess pushes Jimmy's corpse back and grabs the knife firmly. "I don't want to do any more damage, but no one wants to wake up and have to pull a knife out their skull, right?"

She yanks hard on the knife, and it must be lodged in there pretty good because she stumbles backwards as it comes out. This turns out to be incredibly lucky. If she hadn't lurched back at exactly that moment, then the bullet would have hit her right in the face.

The naked creeper standing in the doorway fires again, and this time he hits his target. Fortunately, his target was Jackson. The bullet to the head knocks him to the ground, and the creeper turns the gun to me. My instinct is to shrink him, but the problem is that I still have the package shrunk and in my pocket and I'd have to return it to full size before I could do anything. As it happens, I don't need to do anything else as the robust coffin, now full size, makes a solid barrier between myself and the creeper as he fires. Jesus, not for the first time, takes one for the team.

This had to have been an unusual event, even for a creeper, generally no strangers to unusual events. Anyway, it is enough to give him pause before firing again, and the pause is long enough for Jackson to bounce back to his feet and charge the guy. He wrestles the gun from him and, perhaps anxious to save ammunition, beats the creeper to death with it. As it turns out, there is only one round left anyway, but I suppose it's still a saving of sorts.

We arrange the shrunken corpses inside the cheddar cheese Tupperware, not the creepers obviously, just the good ones. I hope that if we leave the cheese in between them it will form a kind of buffer to stop them getting too smashed up if we have to run or something. Jackson, perhaps the world's foremost expert on being a temporarily tiny person, takes this one step further and presses the bodies into their own individual cheese blocks to prevent any movement at all. It looks like a cheesy action figure presentation gift box.

I also shrank Jackson, as his permanently exuberant facial expression tends to stand out in a crowd. He opts not to travel in the cheese box though, which is understandable, I suppose. From the perspective of a shrunken person, it is basically a large shipping container full of giant cheese and dead bodies. He chooses instead to ride a pigeon. Pigeons are also a big help in us getting onto another train unseen, as Tess makes sure that there are birds covering all of the main security cameras in the station. We buy tickets this time and everything, so all we need is a small distraction as we get past the barriers. There are four uniformed police officers in the station, I don't think this is any more than usual, which seems like a good sign.

I'm hoping that this distraction will be slightly less fatal than the last one, and Jackson doesn't disappoint. Simply flying in on his pigeon to set off a fire alarm in one of the station's coffee stands seems to be enough to get the attention of the police. Tess and I then just jog as casually as we can to our train. By the standards of the last couple of days at least, I could almost call the journey "uneventful."

"Seven, I think," says Tess. "Maybe even eight if there is one inside the guard box."

"Are they all Bobbetts though?"

"It's difficult to tell."

"How old do they look?"

"Old."

We are maybe two-hundred metres away from the main gate, halfway down the grandiose driveway at T-BAIT.

"Do they have guns?"

"Shotguns, yeah, I see at least three shotguns."

I'd read somewhere that Terrence favours shotguns for his Bobbetts, as they are weapons he can obtain legally. Since he had lost his government contract, he was no longer allowed to purchase military weaponry, but there is nothing illegal about a "farmer" with the correct license purchasing shotguns. The Bobbett skillset is probably more suited to close-range combat anyway.

"And I think one has a machete."

This is going to be tricky. Even if Terrence Bobbett is going to help us, and I'm still not totally convinced that he is, we'll still have to explain ourselves to six heavily armed Bobbetts. Previous encounters I've had with Bobbetts have not led me to believe that they are the most rational of creatures. Once, one had grabbed a Cornish pasty straight out of my hand. I'd gone to grab it back off her, and she'd jumped head first off of Black-friars Bridge. She must have righted herself in the air because it looked like she'd broken her leg on impact. This didn't seem to faze her that much though. She had hopped off eating the pasty.

"I could take them," signs tiny Jackson. And I have no doubt he is right. Especially at full size. That doesn't seem like the best course of action though. Firstly, it would mean bringing all the bodies back to full size, something no one was looking forward to. And secondly, this would probably involve Jackson killing all the Bobbetts with a machete or a shotgun, not exactly the kind of interaction that is going to endear us to someone we are about to ask for a big favour.

"What if we distracted them? They look like they'd be easily distracted."

"With what?"

"Horse?" says Tess. "There's one not far away, couple of sheep too."

"I don't know, I don't want one of them to shoot a horse. We're going to have to introduce ourselves at some point anyway, if we're going to talk to Terrence."

"What, so, just wander up and say 'hello'?"

"Yeah, they're probably more scared of us than we are of them."

"That's foxes," says Tess. "And they're not, you know," she says, with some authority.

"Well, it's the best plan I have."

"It's not really a plan, is it?"

Tiny Jackson shrugs and jumps back on his pigeon.

"I'm doing it."

I think that the key is not to spook them. As we get closer to the large gates, I can see that Tess was right, they are old. I don't know the exact maths on it, but I'd guess that, if they were normal people, they looked about eighty to ninety years old, which I think in Bobbett terms would make them around ten. This made some sense, as it was reportedly only the very oldest Bobbetts that were trusted with firearms.

It's just like having a conversation with a ten year old, I tell myself, you can do that. A ten year old with a shotgun.

I hold my hands high above my head as we walk towards them and gesture to Tess to do the same. I don't want them to think we are trying to sneak up on them.

"What does that say?" says Tess, under her breath.

The words "PATER SCIT OPTIMUM" are inscribed above the iron gate.

"I think it means 'father knows best'." I'd read that some-where. I don't speak Latin, and I'm assuming, neither do the Bobbetts.

And then one fires.

I'm so startled by the shotgun blast that we are nearly immediately joined by the cheese corpses. I hadn't been watching the Bobbett that fired, so I can t tell if maybe it had been a warning shot into the air or if he had been aiming to kill us. It is impossible to tell now as the force of the shotgun blast had knocked him off his feet.

We definitely have their attention now though, and two shotguns are pointed straight at us.

"Wait!" I say, hoping I can think of something better to say.

"We're friends!" says Tess, holding her hands high above her head.

"Friends of your father."

There is another shotgun blast, and for a moment I think we are dead. Luckily, the blast hadn't come from either of the guns pointed in our direction. It isn't all good news though. The Bobbett who had fallen to the floor had evidently been using his loaded shotgun as a crutch to help himself up. The butt of the gun had been pushed into the floor, so the barrel of the gun was pointing skyward. He had either knocked the trigger with his foot or just jolted the weapon hard enough to dislodge the firing pin. Either way, the blast had caught him in the bottom of the chin, and he'd fallen back to the floor.

"You know Dad?" says the Bobbett with the machete. She has an innocent, almost excited tone to her voice.

"Yes, yes. We are friends. We need to speak to him," says Tess.

"Is he OK?"

I'm not sure why I say this. The Bobbett on the ground is clearly not OK, the bottom half of his face had come off. This would have been a catastrophic injury for anyone, but for someone of his age, I really don't fancy his chances of survival. None of the other Bobbetts seem to be paying any attention to him though.

"To Dad?" says machete.

"Yes, if we could, is he here?" says Tess.

The Bobbetts all look around as if he might be standing right next to them.

"I mean, is he home, could you call him for us?"

"Dad!" shouts a Bobbett in a deep baritone. The mixture of childlike mannerisms and mature features doesn't stop being surreal.

"He won't hear that," says machete.

"And I'm the best at shouting," says the deep-voiced one, casually scratching the side of his head with the barrel of his shotgun.

I don't doubt that they are both right.

"Do you have maybe a phone or a radio you could call him with?"

"Not allowed," says machete. "Only Eric can use the radio."

You can approximately age Bobbetts using their first names. Terrence apparently works his way through a baby naming book, only skipping names he thinks either he or the young Bobbett will have a hard time remembering. Every January though, he moves to the next letter of the alphabet. When I'd read this, I think the very last C-reg Bobbett had just died of old age, and this was a while back, so Eric, an E-reg, has to be getting on a bit.

"Who's Eric?"

Somewhat predictably, she points to the presumably dead Bobbett with the shotgun wound to his face.

"Do you think that maybe *we* could use the radio?" says Tess. "I don't think Eric is up to it right now."

Shaking of heads all round. The Bobbett pokes Eric's face

with the end of the machete, just to confirm that he isn't up for a quick radio chat.

"What if you let us in and..." A lot more shaking of heads to this. "If we all walked down together to find your dad?"

"Got to stay at the gate," says the good shouter, loudly.

"Can't let anyone past," confirms the other, with a swing of her machete.

Tess taps me on the arm. It feels like we're at an impasse with the Bobbett negotiations, so I'm not sure what she wants.

"Uh-oh," says Tess.

And then Jackson lands his pigeon on the machete wielding Bobbett's shoulder. This was an incredibly bold move on Jackson's part. Bobbetts are famously prone to startle and often attack with little provocation. Terrence reportedly keeps them on a pretty hefty steroid regiment to keep them physically strong as they age, and this, combined with them being essentially bizarrely raised children, can lead to some unorthodox behaviour. For a moment I think she might take a swing at the pigeon with the machete and do it, or herself, some serious damage, but she is surprisingly unperturbed by this tiny man gesticulating wildly from atop a small bird on her shoulder.

"They're coming," signs Jackson. "Lots of them, and fast."

"How fast?"

"There are two out front on quad bikes," says Tess. "They are quick... Oh wait, one of those hit a tree."

And then I spot the camera. I don't know why I hadn't seen it, mounted high up on the gate. I suppose I had been distracted by the Latin. I presume there is a video feed connected to the main house.

"Shall we run?"

It has been hard enough trying to negotiate with just a few of them, I don't fancy our chances with a mob.

"No," says Tess. "Just try and look friendly."

I put my hands higher above my head and take a step away from the dead one.

A Bobbett on a quad bike is charging towards us, until he suddenly veers off the road into a ditch. He flies a good few feet over the handlebars and then makes a crunchy thud as he lands. Tess and I just keep our hands raised above our heads. Tess has a really innocent expression on her face. I try to do the same, but I'm sure it isn't as good.

The first Bobbetts to arrive are pretty young looking, maybe mid-twenties in conventional ageing. Every one of them is incredibly muscular, and their faces have the furious intensity of a puppy trying to get to a ball that's just out of reach. Fortunately, there is a gate between us, or they probably would have trampled us to death. They are just too excited for their own good.

As more and more Bobbetts arrive, the average age increases markedly. Even the more mature ones have a real intensity to them though.

And then there is the sound of a loud air horn, and the whole energy changes. The youngest ones stop looking at us and instead their eyes dart back, eagerly searching for the source of the sound.

"Everybody..." comes the loud, nasal voice of Terrence Bobbett, and the crowd waits with bated breath. "Down."

Every Bobbett hits the ground instantly and lies face down. I say instantly, it takes some of the older ones a little while longer, and a number of them seem to use their presumably loaded weapons as a kind of walking cane. Thankfully none of them go off.

Finally, we see Terrence, the only Bobbett left standing, walking slowly towards us.

I don't think he cycled here. I only say this because he is wearing cycling shorts. The really fitted kind that maybe an Olympic cyclist or a Tour de France competitor would wear. He isn't wearing another pair of shorts over the top of them or anything. It's really just those shorts.

"Everybody..." The younger Bobbetts are already twitching in anticipation. "Stand on the grass."

The first move almost has some military precision to it, albeit maybe a kind of Dad's Army military. The second is just mayhem, like a game of musical chairs at an eight year old's birthday party where everyone has had way too much sugar. Some Bobbetts make a fairly rational route towards the grass verge at the side of the road, but they are in the minority. The youngest ones either don't know what grass is or are just too excited to care. They frantically dart back and forth, copying each other's actions in the hope that one of them is right.

Credit to them though, eventually they all manage to get over to the grass and stand in a loose kind of formation.

"Everybody... sit." And they do. There is one accidental shotgun discharge, but I don't think it hit anyone.

"Careful now, gently with those," says Terrence, approaching the gate.

10

AN OBVIOUS MANIAC

May 14th 2001
7 days before the General Election

Bobbetts had been laying waste to the UK for nearly a year before Terrence proposed a solution. I'm not sure why he had left it so long, perhaps to let both the government and the people of England see how futile their situation was without his help.

And it definitely was. I think the real key to understanding just how bad it had become was not so much how people reacted to the Bobbetts, but how they now didn't. I once saw a fairly respectable-looking person push a presumably dead Bobbett into a heap on the floor, just to take her seat on a train. I'm pretty sure she was a Bobbett. There's a somewhat distinctive look that they get past a certain age where they are certainly physically decrepit but their skin is incongruously youthful. If it turned out to have just been a regular old person with a particularly good skincare regiment though, the point stands, the Bobbett invasion had made the country into a colder, meaner place.

The hardest hit by this were people who were struggling to begin with. Disdain for the homeless had risen to the point of open hatred in areas with dense Bobbett populations, where to ask any stranger for money was to take your life in your hands. An older Bobbett will often look to steal any easily visible valuables from a passing stranger, so people had become fairly defensive of their personal space. It wasn't uncommon to see commuters carry a basic defensive weapon to keep all strangers at a distance. The baseball bat is a classic choice as it is (a) legal and (b) capable of knocking a Bobbett to the floor without a huge chance of killing them. Bobbetts, even fully grown, are fairly robust. The same unfortunately cannot be said of the genuinely elderly people that are often mistaken for Bobbetts. Many a retiree has been shoved to a premature death by rushing commuters, in a hurry to catch a train or whatever. Golf clubs were also a popular weapon. Apparently indoor-putting championships became popular in a number of larger offices. I suppose if people are bringing the clubs in anyway, it makes sense to use them.

Anyway, this is a long way of saying that things got pretty bad. And so, when Terrence Bobbett not only proposed a solution but demonstrated it's effectiveness, he absolutely had the government's attention. He chose the town of Royal Tunbridge Wells to demonstrate. It's not a huge town, but it had been particularly hard hit by the Bobbetts. The Pantiles in the south of the town had become somewhat of an open Bobbett breeding ground, whereas the shopping mall towards the North was more of a retirement community/cemetery. You could essentially witness the entire Bobbett lifespan in a half a mile wander up the high street. And that's pretty much what Terrence did. At the bottom of the town, he blew a whistle three times and started barking out orders through a megaphone. I think the words were just his own invention, as no one could identify the language, but whatever it was, the Bobbetts understood it. Or at least the Bobbetts that were old enough to have been raised and trained by him at T-BAIT did, and the younger ones were happy to follow. In a matter of minutes, there were hundreds of them following him in a slow, orderly march past Fenwick.

Fenwick is a small department store that had been abandoned to Bobbetts entirely, only weeks after they arrived, but it had only taken a matter of minutes for every single one of them to be out on the street and marching in an orderly fashion behind their father/grandfather/undisputed leader. At the top of the town, he had arranged for a convoy of military-style troop transport trucks to collect them, and the Bobbetts hopped willingly onboard. The whole thing didn't even take a day, and just like that, the people of Tunbridge Wells had their town back, and upwards of five thousand Bobbetts (a huge increase on the few hundred that had originally been dropped off) were on their way to T-BAIT.

And so, when Terrence explained to the Prime Minister in a private meeting, that he would be willing and able to do this in every Bobbett populated area in the country, the PM was keen to hear him out. But first, Terrence explained that he would require a few concessions (he never called them "demands" although that's what they definitely were) from the government.

———

Fortunately, Terrence had seen me on the news and so decided to let us in. Unfortunately, he insisted on giving us a pretty thorough tour of the facilities.

"Do you know what a super-food is?" asks Terrence. This is a trick, and not a good one. He'd already asked several questions like this, and other than "please God don't tell me", I don't think there was any answer I could give that wouldn't result in him explaining anyway.

"Yes, I think so," says Tess.

"They're essentially magic, but natural, so much more affordable. Pomegranates are super-foods." He is holding a kiwi. "These too." He bites into it like an apple.

"I eat eight to ten super-foods a day. Sometimes even fifteen. Sometimes I have very few calories left for regular foods. I saw a cancerous person on TV the other day, they looked a right state. I could cure you in a minute, I thought. Didn't even have hardly any hair at all, and this was an Italian woman, I think, they usually have loads of hair."

"Really?"

"Famous for it. Do you know why she didn't have any hair?"

"Chemotherapy?" I hazard.

"Maybe she wasn't fully Italian, she might have just been born there or something," tries Tess, an answer that Terrence definitely appreciates more than mine.

It gets a point of the finger and a "Good thinking, she didn't even have any eyebrows though. Where would that be from?"

"Portugal?" says Tess.

"I don't think so," says Terrence. He is contemplating it though, a nation without eyebrows.

"Super-foods, that's what she needs. Couple of cases of pomegranates, and it would clear right up, you mark my words. I would have sent her some, but they didn't give her address or anything."

"On TV?"

"Probably for the best. She might have needed quite a lot actually, state she was in, and I need mine for the troops." He gestures to the large crates of fruit, stacked ceiling high in this industrial-sized kitchen.

"Do you know how many of my troops have got cancer?"

"Yes." I am just saying anything at this point, but it doesn't seem to make a difference.

"None, ever, not a single one. You know why?"

"They only live for about ten years."

"They eat even more super-foods than I do. One year, the G's, we tried on an entirely super-food diet. Fruits and seeds. Probably the healthiest year yet, fastest beep-test average. We only discontinued it because they were stealing beef from the H's. I think all the fruit made them crave the meat. Questions?"

Tess has a hand up.

"Why is there only one kind of banana?"

"I'm not sure I know what you mean."

"Like in a shop," continues Tess. "There's all kinds of apples, Cox, Russet, whatever, but a banana is just a banana. You seem like an expert, so…"

"Brilliant question. Kirsty, could you look into that?"

I'm not sure why I hadn't noticed Kirsty before, as I suppose she's been with us the whole time. She nods at Terrence, and smiles broadly, but writes nothing down in her pad.

"You're a smart one," says Terrence, and throws Tess a kiwi. Which annoys me for some reason.

"You know he means *for a Bobbett*, right?"

Irrespective of Terrence's non-mainstream scientific ideas, the facility he had built was undeniably impressive. The facilities for the youngest Bobbetts were the most intensely staffed. There were lines upon lines of these large Perspex cribs.

"In the early days," Terrence explains, "we lost a few because they sometimes get strong enough to climb out of a standard-size crib. They're fast as well, on all fours, and essentially fearless. A couple of them had got to the swimming pool before we even knew they'd escaped."

"You have a swimming pool?"

"Olympic length, one of the best forms of cardio, swimming is."

"And they can swim?" says Tess.

"Some of them, sure. Not those ones, sadly."

"Oh."

"So now we've got the Perspex cribs. These were custom made. We can see them better, and they are coated with a non-slip, non-toxic gel that prevents them from climbing it."

"Non-toxic?"

"It is now, yes, the whole thing is a learning process. We're constantly perfecting it."

"Are these the mothers?" Tess points to a woman feeding a particularly big Bobbett with a bottle.

"I wish!" says Terrence. "The vast majority of the Ps are second or even third generation. The mothers would be too busy with their training and other obligations to raise a child, even if they had any interest in it, which they largely don't."

"So these are all professional nurses?" I'm guessing from the uniforms.

"I suppose, in a sense, we don't require any formal qualifications at this stage, it's basically just babysitting. Did you know we are the third biggest employer in Coventry?"

"Impressive." I'm not sure if I'm even being sarcastic.

"The real training starts when they are old enough to start running."

And boy are they running. There are maybe forty of them jostling for position as they run around the four-hundred metre track.

An elderly Bobbett, who is inexplicably wearing a pin-stripe suit, waves excitedly at us as we head over.

"Any outliers?" Terrence asks the pin-stripe Bobbett.

"Almost all of them are fast, well above the average human, but some can be exceptional," he confides in us.

"Fast times? New records?"

The Bobbett looks at the stopwatch around his neck, as if it might hold some answers.

"Who is the best?" says Terrence, in a clear, slow tone.

"I am," says the Bobbett, smiling shyly.

"What's your name?" says Terrence, with a hint of disappointment.

"Edward," says Edward.

"Yes, I remember now. That gun loaded is it, Edward?"

It's only at that point that I notice Edward appears to have a handgun tucked into the waistband of his suit trousers. As I try to make sure that Terrence is in between me and the happy looking old chap, I notice Tess is doing the same.

"Best hand it here." Terrence holds out his hand.

There is a thunderous roar as a herd of Bobbetts run past at a staggering pace. A few of them are waving and shouting at Terrence.

There is a loud sound of a gunshot, and all the Bobbetts stop running. Terrence had fired the handgun, which turns out to be a starter's pistol, into the air. I didn't know either of these things though. I, or at least my subconscious, assumed that someone had just shot me. A startling enough thought, it turns out, for me to lose concentration on my trick.

There is a loud cracking sound, and suddenly we are surrounded by corpses.

"Crikey," says Terrence, "where did they come from?"

My backpack is in tatters and there is nothing to be seen of the Tupperware container, presumably the sheer force of the bodies returning to full size had shattered it.

"Has that guy got four arms?"

The Bobbetts have already started to crowd around the bodies, tentatively poking at them.

Then I spot a flailing man-sized object falling fast towards the earth in the distance. This is why people without Jackson's unusual resilience shouldn't ride small birds. The poor pigeon, presumably already having a slightly rough day, must suddenly have found itself to be carrying 80 odd kilos of excess weight. There is a loud thump sound as Jackson bounces off the ground. Terrence looks to see what has caused it, and I try my best to keep his attention on us.

"They're with us, that's what we need your help with."

"Are they alright?"

An eager Bobbett is tugging at Spider-man's rigor-mortised arms.

"They're dead," says Tess.

"Leave that alone dear." Terrence pulls the Bobbett back.

"I'm not sure I can help much with that."

Terrence Bobbett's *request* to the Prime Minister was fairly simple. He wanted a new law passed that would "more accurately and fairly take into account the accelerated development of his offspring." Essentially, he wanted it recognised, in law, that his children aged faster than the rest of the population, and accordingly, they should acquire legal rights at an earlier age. Rights that "reflected their physical and mental development, rather than their biological age."

He had made quite the scientific study of the Bobbett ageing process at his institute (This is according to him. A political commentator who apparently got the chance to evaluate his "research" described the report as "the semi-demented scribblings of an obvious maniac") and he had devised an "age equivalence chart". I won't tire you with the details, it had apparently involved any number of physical tests on "an extensive sampling of his offspring", but the long and the short of it was that by 3.5 years old, a Bobbett was around 18 years old in regular human years. Terrence wanted this new law to reflect that. When a Bobbett turned 3.5, he wanted them to have all the legal rights of any other adult citizen in the UK.

If we set aside the presumably unscientific techniques Terrence had used to reach these conclusions, and accept that maybe a three-and-a-bit-year-old Bobbett is at least physically the equivalent of a human adult. I guess this doesn't seem like too unreasonable a request. There were a couple of stumbling blocks though. Firstly, the thought of a Bobbett behind the wheel of a car was a pretty terrifying prospect. Given the damage they can do unassisted, it seemed like a spectacularly dangerous idea.

Various legal scholars pondered this for some time. Giving these child Bobbetts all of the rights of an adult would seemingly confer the right to drive a car, and that was surely something no one wanted. However, to specifically revoke a person's rights based solely on their parentage seemed ethically unpalatable. It certainly wasn't a precedent they wanted enshrined in law. The solution was simple though. Being an adult does not, in fact, automatically confer the right to drive a car, merely the right to apply for a license. To legally drive you, of course, need to be able to pass both a driving theory and a practical driving test. Terrence assured everyone involved that despite his best efforts (the mind boggles), he had been unable to get even a very old Bobbett up to the standards required to pass either of the required tests. "They quite like it on the whole, the speed especially, but they simply don't have the patience for the exams." So, that was kind of solved.

There was another thing, and trust me, I'm no more comfortable discussing this than any of the mumbling British barristers involved in crafting the new laws. In fact, the only person who seemed to enjoy this topic was Terrence Bobbett himself, who apparently had "extensive and graphic notes". We need to talk briefly about sex with Bobbetts.

One of the other legal rights that would inevitably come about as a result of their newly acquired adulthood is that Bobbetts would now legally be able to have sex. Don't get me wrong, it's not like the law had been preventing this in the past. Bobbetts have sex with each other like other people high-five. It was something that most of the population had gradually learned to ignore. This wasn't the issue at hand though. More contentious was the legal status of the large, and rapidly growing, number of the non-Bobbett population who had begun intimate relationships with Bobbetts.

These people were currently considered legally (and by the majority of other people, actually) to be paedophiles. Even the ones that had hooked up with Bobbetts that were a long way past middle age were technically sleeping with children. The law, quite understandably, treats this as a very serious offence and mandates significant jail time. And this is exactly what people found to be in relationships with Bobbetts got in the early days. There were so many of them, however, that this rapidly became untenable. It was estimated by one researcher, that if every case of Bobbett on non-Bobbett intercourse (their phrasing) were to be prosecuted, the resulting convictions would be enough to exceed Britain's existing prison capacity fifteen times over.

One solution would of course be to relax the country's paedophilia laws, something I don't think any serious politician has ever suggested in the entirety of history. To put it mildly, it would not have been a vote winner, apart from I assume, within the paedophile community, a community that is not often actively courted by politicians. And so, it seemed that this new Bobbett law might actually help the legal system out of a rather tricky situation, distasteful as it may be.

After a lot of excruciating debate, the Terrence Bobbett

Accelerated Maturity Act (T-BAMA) became law. Terrence toured the country collecting up hundreds and thousands of his multi-generational offspring in giant convoys of vehicles and returned them to his rapidly expanding institution.

City centres returned to normal. Or almost normal, for months on end, shops and parks and pubs saw unprecedented booms. The population rejoiced, and the Prime Minister achieved his highest approval rating since taking office. There was a lot of chatter that he may call a snap general election to capitalise on his newfound popularity. Frustratingly, he opted not to. A number of strange people married Bobbetts, but even that didn't seem to dull the public mood.

And then Barnaby Bartholomew, the right honourable MP for Coventry South, fell down a staircase.

Terrence had decided that it was best to cut short the outdoor portion of the tour, as both he and the Bobbetts seemed to now be more interested in how I'd been able to fit an assortment of human bodies into a small backpack. This means that we missed out on visiting the firing range, an ominous-looking shed where the older Bobbetts are supposedly trained to handle weapons. This felt like dodging a bullet, probably literally.

Instead, a well drilled collection of middle-aged Bobbetts carried our fallen comrades and the Jesus package up to a huge hanger-like structure referred to simply as Big School.

I could have shrunk the bodies again of course, and simply carried them myself, but I didn't feel comfortable doing my trick in front of Terrence. There is something about him that I don't trust, maybe it is because he's an MP, or a sex offender, or because of the cycling shorts.

Oh, while we're on the topic of him being an MP, that is the first thing we saw in Big School.

The huge hanger provides Terrence with the scope to build up any number of real world simulations. He has a team of set designers that he has apparently hired "from Hollywood". This seems unlikely, as one of them sounds more like he is from Bradford, but I assume he just means that they have worked in movies.

"You see, detail is key, especially to a young mind. Whilst you or I will understand the purpose of each action and can therefore react reasonably to unanticipated obstacles, the younger ones don't have that luxury." Terrence gestures to the set.

"This is a reconstruction of St Christopher's Primary School reception room. It was used as a polling station in the by-election, and they are going to use it again in the general. The actual one is only a few miles from here, and it's where around 15 percent of the students are going to be voting on election day. Look at this..." He points to the patterned and worn hardwood floor. "Even the floor is identical. We reconstructed it from photographs. Taking those wasn't easy either. It's a primary school every other day of the year."

I decide not to press him on this.

"So, while you or I would be thinking 'I just need to go into any booth and vote for the candidate I want', the young mind isn't going to understand that. They could be thinking 'I go as far as the big blue floor stain, and then turn a bit to the left and walk forward three big steps until I see a window', something like that. We used to sit them down in classrooms and try and explain everything from first principals, but our biggest break-through in training was probably when we decided not to care about those. As long as the result was the same, what did it matter? If you obsess over making them understand stuff, they'll be physically well past their prime before they can do anything useful. But the new results-based training," a Bobbett who has presumably voted correctly is being given a small slice of chocolate cake and a medal, "coupled with incentives for good work, has led to excellent results with even very young students."

"Impressive," says Tess, I think genuinely. I mean, it kind of is.

"This is just the first step though. Come with me. Many of the older and smarter students are able to take on board much more general concepts. One of our earliest projects was to teach them to pay money in at the bank." I have a brief flash-back of some disturbing security footage. "Almost all banks have a different layout, so there would be little sense training them like that. It would limit us to one branch of a bank, and they'd probably just shut it. We had to think about it in a different way. All banks are different, but all paying-in machines are similar and often identical. Look at this…"

The next room is much larger than the school reception. There is a functional grey carpet and office-type partitions dividing up the space. There are maybe twenty or so different machines arranged around the room including a pinball machine, a payphone, a photocopier and what looks like a fully functional ATM with paying-in facility.

The door to the room opens, and an eager young (about twenty to my eyes, in regular person years) Bobbett excitedly gallops in. She has an envelope in one hand and what I'm guessing is a bank card in the other. She eyes up a dustbin, and then a lamp, before trotting confidently towards the payphone. I think what has drawn her to it is that it has a card slot, prob-ably for phone cards. Anyway she sticks the bank card in it and then suddenly spasms and falls to the floor.

"Close!" says Terrence, and then "again!" to whoever is running the show.

Three relatively mature Bobbetts drag the first one back towards the entrance.

"Is she dead?" says Tess.

"I shouldn't have thought so, depends how long she's been going. It's a simple electric shock system with a voltage that increases each time they make a similar mistake, that way we can find their optimum learning voltage. We've experimented with both positive reinforcement, like the cake, and negative, like you see here, a combination of both is most effective."

"And the orgies? In the banks?" Because when else am I going to have a chance to ask?

"It is a strong motivator... Oh see, she's fine."

The same Bobbett runs back into the room with her card and envelope, her enthusiasm seemingly unaffected. She seems much more wary of the payphone this time, giving it a wide birth. It looks like she is going to head straight past it to the ATM, but she has a last minute change of heart and turns back. The Bobbett sticks the card back into the payphone and immediately receives a larger electric shock.

"Some of them are slower learners than others. This one may be better suited to something else. I'd be surprised if she makes it as far as firearms training."

As her convulsing body is pulled back to the entrance, I feel confident that this is for the best.

A lot of people have since suggested that Mr Bartholomew's death was not accidental. And when I say *suggested*, I mean *loudly shouted*. Terrence Bobbett gets "murderer" shouted at him a lot. It doesn't seem to faze him, mind. This is a person that has appeared twice in court, accused of having sex with children. I'm not sure he did have the MP for Coventry killed anyway. He was apparently found at the bottom of a long slippery staircase in a park near his home.

The cause of death was found to be "a combination of myocardial infarction and sudden head trauma". Either he had fallen and had a heart attack, or he'd had a heart attack and fallen. I suppose a Bobbett could have pushed him. A lot of people seem to think so. Certainly the park's explanation of the lack of security camera footage is less than ideal. "Someone wet changed a tape and it got wet."

Anyway, the death isn't important. I'm sure it was to him and some friends and relatives, sorry Barnaby, but for our purposes, what is important is what happened next.

If you aren't familiar with the process, when a member of parliament dies while in office, there is a by-election. This is a little local election to fill the vacant House of Commons seat. These only usually garner a lot of press attention if there is something unusual about them. For example, if the result is a huge surprise or someone notable is running. The by-election for Coventry South garnered a huge amount of press attention.

Terrence Bobbett announced that he was going to be running for election on the day of Barnaby Bartholomew's funeral. It was exactly this kind of tone-deaf approach to public relations which caused a number of pundits to pour scorn on Terrence's "laughable" entry into politics. Unsurprisingly, he would not be representing one of the major political parties. He did not have the kind of image that they (or anyone really) was keen to associate themselves with. He had formed his own party (apparently it's not that hard) which was, somewhat bizarrely, called "Freedom Healthy."

This was all treated as a generally lighthearted bit of fun by the press. And understandably so. An accused sex-offender was running for the office of a man he was suspected of having killed, under the banner "Freedom Healthy". It was a strange situation. What people initially failed to take into account, though, was that Coventry South is not a particularly large constituency. Barnaby Bartholomew, it turned out, had been elected with 24,000 votes, beating out his nearest competition by about 6,000. Also, the Terrence Bobbett Institute for Accelerated Development is located in Coventry South, and houses a staggering number of Bobbetts. Bobbetts, as people gradually realised, that now had all of the legal rights of a regular adult citizen of the UK, including of course the right to vote.

And Bobbetts really love voting. That, or they really hate queueing, and voting means that they don't have to queue anymore. Anyway, when election day came, there were vast numbers of Bobbett celebrations outside the few polling stations in Coventry South. I'm not going to go into any more detail on Bobbett celebrations, I think you get the picture by now. But suffice to say, they were jubilant to be not queueing anymore. And there had been a lot of queueing, as apparently Terrence wasn't taking any chances. His opposition candidate, the unfortunate widow of Barnaby Bartholomew, managed a very respectable 33,521 votes, but was just pipped at the post by Terrence's 481,735.

Terrence Bobbett was duly elected as MP for Coventry South, and Freedom Healthy had it's first parliamentary seat. It was immediately clear that British politics would never be the same again.

The third room (seriously, this tour was suspiciously extensive) is another voting-booth-type situation. This time, he explains, it is "to condition them more on the general principals of the thing."

"Every time the room is reset, we move everything about a bit so they can't just learn what to do in the abstract, based on the position of things."

An elderly Bobbett walks into the room and immediately strides confidently to a desk with a similarly aged person sat behind it. There is something different about the one at the desk though. She doesn't have the same keenness behind the eyes and jerking staccato motion that he does. It occurs to me that she is perhaps not a Bobbett at all, but a conventionally aged woman. Despite them looking a similar vintage, she likely has seventy odd years on the Bobbett.

"I am here to vote," says the Bobbett in a booming voice, as he presents his polling card to the suitably startled woman.

"Masterful," commentates Terrence.

She hands him the ballot paper, and he takes it straight over to the booth without missing a beat.

Terrence is enthralled with this Bobbett's command of voting. Before long he'll probably assign this one a massively unsuitable weapon.

I look for Tess but she seems to have wandered away from the tour. This seems like as good a time as any to bring up the purpose of our trip.

"While we are on the subject of the election, there is something you could perhaps help us with."

"The corpses you brought with you? I was wondering when we'd get to that."

"They can help with the election."

"I don't see how, there's not very many of them. Even if you could get them all to vote, it's not exactly going to move the needle numbers-wise." And then, still distracted by the Bobbett, "Textbook."

The Bobbett has clearly voted successfully as he is awarded a piece of cake. I see that's where Tess has gone. The Bobbetts are eyeing her suspiciously, guarding their cake from her as she wanders past them.

"It's not that, it's that they have some information. At least one of them does. And if we could get it to Felix, he thinks the information could be enough to sway the election."

"Felix Trent? Good luck getting to that guy. Got to be about the most guarded place in the country. You'd sooner break into FIDA."

"Yes, that's why we came to you."

At least I have his attention now. It seems like a good idea to feed his ego. "Because you're maybe the only person in the country that could get to Felix."

"Agreed," he says.

I assumed that he would ask how, but he doesn't. Maybe he's already figured it out, but this seems unlikely.

"Because you are a Member of Parliament," I explain, "they'll let you in to see Felix."

He doesn't respond. For once, he is keeping his cards close to his chest, or maybe he is thinking about something else entirely, but I push on.

"It might look suspicious if I show up with a wagon full of corpses. What's that, my entourage?"

"It won't though, look."

I glance around for a demonstration subject. The elderly lady manning the polling desk seems like the most suitable candidate.

I shrink her, along with the chair she's sat on, to about the size of a tennis ball and carefully pick her up and put her on the desk.

"I can shrink them, you could carry them in maybe a pocket or a briefcase. See, she's fine."

The little old lady does not look fine, she looks intensely alarmed.

Terrence isn't so interested in the old lady though.

"What's in it for me?"

"Sorry?"

"If I do all this, deliver your corpses. What do I get?"

"Well, for one, we'd win the election. That's what Felix says, anyway."

Terrence doesn't look impressed. I look over to Tess, hoping she might have a better angle on this. What I see is worrying. She has a pile of the Bobbett's *successful* ballots in her hand.

She shakes her head slowly left to right, with a grim look on her face.

I remember noticing that the little old lady had snapped back to full size. This must have happened at exactly the same time as someone, probably an elderly Bobbett, jabbed me in the head with an electric cattle prod.

I'm not sure how long I was unconscious for, but when I come back around, Terrence is staring down at me and I can't move my arms. On the upside, I've suddenly figured something out.

"The votes, they were all for Barnett. You're teaching them to vote for Barnett."

He nods.

"You've done a deal with the Church, haven't you?"

"A really good deal," says Terrence, with a smile that is smug even for him.

I see that they got Tess with a cattle prod as well. Two Bobbetts are wrapping her in a straitjacket. This is somewhat reassuring for two reasons, it means that she probably isn't dead and also potentially explains why I can't move my arms either. But Terrence is wandering away, and I still have questions.

"I'm guessing the only way for you to get a better deal than you currently have would be... for Bobbetts to be not considered tricksters at all but to be..."

He can't help himself. "Miracles."

"Oh hell, of course they are."

"It's in the Bible and everything. 'Go forth and multiply.'

And no one's denying that's what I do, probably better than anyone ever!"

There is a twisted logic to it. In fact, there seems to be a kind of twisted logic to everything Terrence does. If the Church and the new government guarantee that his trick will be regarded as a miracle, why should he care what happens to any of the other tricksters? He and his family will be safe from persecution.

"I have a question though."

"Go on."

"Why are you campaigning so hard for the Prime Minister if you want him to lose?"

There's a pause. He doesn't seem as eager to answer this.

"All part of the plan."

"For you to campaign for the opposition?"

"Politics is complicated, you wouldn't understand."

"Try me."

"They have metrics," says a definitely less interested Terrence. "Polls, stats, that kind of thing. Apparently, the more I campaign *for* the Prime Minister, the less likely a large majority of the general population are to vote for him."

"That... makes a lot of sense."

11

THE SECOND TRIAL OF FELIX TRENT

By the time the trial began, things were not looking good for Felix. The narrative had shifted, and there were now a lot of people who believed they had been in some way tricked or mentally manipulated by Felix into sleeping with him. Furthermore, a lot of people now seemed to have almost no memory of the encounter. I think this was more likely due to the overwhelming tabloid pressure than anything nefarious Felix had done. Essentially, a large number of well known people were given the choice between having a rather challenging conversation with their family and friends about their fluid sexuality, or alternatively, blaming the whole thing on an evil magic man. Unsurprisingly I suppose, a great number took the latter option.

Felix's defence at his first trial had been spectacular, and he thought that if he was to have any chance of getting out of this one without a significant criminal conviction, then he was going to need something equally sensational. The difficult thing was that his honest defence was that he had barely used his trick at all.

In poker, Felix had liked for there to be a lot of money on

the table. The more financially invested the player was, the more emotionally invested they would be, and the better his trick would work. In life, few things incite stronger emotions than sexual attraction. With that much emotion in play, it is very easy for Felix to read people. In short, Felix knows if you want to sleep with him. This is partly because of his trick but largely because of the huge insight into the human condition his trick has given him. Felix can walk into a room of fifty people, and within ten minutes or so, he can tell exactly who in the room is attracted to him. He could also likely tell you, with absolute accuracy, who else everyone in the room is attracted to, but this is generally of little interest to Felix.

That example isn't hypothetical. This sort of thing essentially happened all the time. Especially in the early days of his celebrity, Felix would often be invited to movie premiers, gallery openings, exclusive parties where beautiful, successful people would gather en mass. They were target-rich environments, and Felix is a precision marksman.

This is how he explained the situation to his legal team, who seemed to generally agree that, while he didn't exactly come across brilliantly, and was perhaps unlikely to win back the advertising contracts he had lost once he presented this defence, it should be enough to keep him out of jail. Felix had, among other things, been a spokesperson for a chocolate brand, tagline: "you read my mind" — they had dropped him recently, citing a morality clause in his contract.

The prosecution was still facing an uphill battle. Although they now had numerous alleged victims to testify that Felix had used some sort of power to trick them into sleeping with him, there wasn't exactly a law against that, at least not yet.

And so, the prosecution attempted a risky tactic. They put forward a case so vague that it couldn't be disproved, presumably in the hope that a general fear of the unknown would move the jury to find Felix guilty. Witness upon witness testified that they had somehow spent the night with Felix even though this was something that was totally out of character for them, ergo there must have been some sort of wizardry involved. As, at the time, using an actual trick wouldn't have been illegal, the prosecution chose to ignore that Felix had any special abilities whatsoever and insinuated that he must have in some way drugged or rendered his victims unconscious in some other way. There was, of course, no physical or any other kind of evidence for this. Even the prosecution didn't believe it.

Somewhat reluctantly, after eight days of apparently heated deliberation, the jury was agreed. Unfortunately, the only thing they could agree on was that they were never going to reach a unanimous verdict. The judge even agreed to accept a majority verdict but to no avail. Half the jurors felt Felix had probably used his trick, and half felt that he hadn't; half felt he should go to jail, and half felt that he shouldn't. Those weren't even the same halves. By the end of the deliberation, they could no longer even agree on a lunch order. The most talked about case of the decade ended in a hung jury.

It would now be up to the prosecution to decide if it would be worth the time and money to attempt yet another Felix Trent trial. At least it would have been, if someone named Infinite Wisdom wasn't about to save them the trouble.

I never would have believed it at the time, but things might have been better for everyone in the long run if it had gone the other way. With a guilty verdict, maybe a little jail time for Felix, the press and the establishment could have had their pound of flesh. That was what a lot of the furore was about, I think. Felix was obviously having a lot of fun, and he didn't seem to have paid a price for it, that always gets people het up.

As Felix hadn't been found guilty of anything, papers would

tend to talk about a "mind-rapist" as a hypothetical person, rather than Felix specifically. As this person was a figment of the tabloid press' collective imagination, there was seemingly no limit to his powers. He could have you and/or your loved ones commit any number of indecent acts with legal impunity unless we "Ban Mind-Rape Now."

But it wasn't just the "mind-rapists" that the tabloids were worried about. New tricks were appearing all the time. There was a child in Bangladesh whose voice was supposedly hypnotic. What if someone with a similar power marched the streets like a modern day Pied Piper, abducting children. Would that be legal? Was it legal for someone who could see through walls to watch people on the toilet? As far as I'm aware, there wasn't even anyone with a trick to see through anything at all at that point, but all the discussion of tricks was always weirdly sexual. Every discovery of a new trick always had four or five articles accompanying it, generally about how someone could use it to covertly grope you, and it would be totally legal unless we changed the law immediately.

On top of this, there were growing national security concerns about how other countries would be using people with tricks. The US government was particularly worried about the potential for tricks to be used for assassination. A girl in New Jersey could dehydrate pretty much anything from a distance of up to about eight hundred metres. Before Billy Winn came to power, the CIA were apparently having her deflate animals in different situations and planning how to get her close enough to various target individuals. Then the Secret Service pointed out that they should probably be radically changing their own President's security protocols, in case there was someone out there with similar powers that wished the US harm. For what it's worth, the dehydrating kid was never heard from again. I saw someone do something similar on *Darwin*, but I don't think it was her. They didn't survive *Darwin*. These niche tricks don't tend to do well.

The rumour was that Israel already had a well developed program. They had called upon all Jewish people with tricks living anywhere in the world to repatriate to Israel "so that their gift from God could be best put to use." There were powerful incentives, outside of the fact that tricksters were being persecuted fairly universally worldwide, and so a lot did. They later added the stipulation that the trick must be "of use to the military". I can only imagine that this was as a response to a number of people with pretty mediocre tricks clogging up the system. A leg-flopper is not a particularly useful military asset, regardless of their religion.

And everyone was concerned about China, mostly because there had so far not been a single story about a person with a trick coming from China. Either there was something on a genetic level that precluded Chinese people from developing tricks, and even with the genetic research in its infancy this seemed highly improbable, or the Chinese state was concealing information... which seemed fairly probable.

The public fear of domestic trickster sex-offenders started to be balanced in the press against the fear of armies of Chinese superhumans razing cities to the ground with hitherto unseen superpowers. In short, whether you had a trick or not, it was a scary time.

And thus came about the World Congress on New Human Potential. It was held in Zurich, although pretty much in name only, as almost no one wanted to actually go. They were presumably too worried that if they said something the US didn't like, a small girl from New Jersey would suck all the water out of their body.

The general consensus was that it would be best for everyone if we just totally outlawed tricks. If no country was allowed to use them at all, ever, then maybe within a generation or two, they would just go away and everything would be back to normal. There was no scientific reasoning, logic, or even sense to this theory, but that didn't stop it from being a popular opinion. What did hinder it was that no government trusted the other nations not to maintain a secret army of superpowered assassins.

And so, some sort of controlled solution had to be found, something where governments could monitor any special abilities closely and prohibit anything dangerous to national security or society as a whole. The answer, of course, was schools.

In most countries, it would be compulsory for anyone exhibiting any kind of skill or ability that was "strange or unique" in any way to be appraised by a special-school admissions board. If they were judged to have a potentially powerful trick, they would be added to a semi-public register, and it would then be compulsory for them to attend one of the newly constructed special schools. There were five to begin with in the UK, with plans to build more as required.

Upon graduating from school, each person would be assessed and restrictions to the use of their abilities could be applied on a case-by-case basis. The general impression I got was that people were almost never allowed to use their trick without restriction. The assessment boards were career bureaucrats, none of whom wanted to take any responsibility for someone with a trick doing something crazy on their watch.

Felix wasn't incredibly surprised to be shot. I mean, I suppose he was at the time. It was about a month after his second trial, and he had been eating breakfast in a restaurant near his home, the now notorious Griddle Me This cafe, when he was shot in the head. The gunman also accidentally fatally wounded the cafe's owner, The Griddler, as I like to think of him. Anyway, for that brief moment, Felix was probably very surprised, and then he was dead. In retrospect though, he wasn't that surprised that it had happened.

The gunman was an aspiring rapper called Infinite Wisdom. Felix had allegedly slept with him a few years previously, and his name appeared on the prosecutions list of victims (I'm pretty sure that the "allegedly" is unnecessary, as Felix didn't deny sleeping with any of his supposed "victims", and the shooting would seem to imply that something had probably gone on, but that's how it was reported at the time). They had met at a party and went on to have a fairly lovely evening according to Felix. The prosecution had submitted such a long list of "victims" that Felix had barely even noticed Infinite Wisdom's name on the list. This was doubly easy to do as his legal name was sadly not Infinite Wisdom. Unfortunately, another rapper that this guy was apparently having a public feud with at the time had spotted his rival's name on the documents and made a pretty decent song about it. Infinite Wisdom had been humiliated by the whole thing and decided the best thing to do to salvage his reputation was to shoot Felix in the head.

Felix had almost anticipated that at some point someone might shoot him. He had given plenty of people plenty of reason. Also he has a pretty good idea of what most people want at most times. He was, however, surprised to wake up a few days later at a secret government facility on a disused oil rig in the North Sea.

As luck would have it, the selection process for special schools had just begun. Anyone that had shown any kind of unusual ability in childhood was being evaluated by a panel of experts to see if they required ongoing supervision. It was going to be both a method for the country to make sure that any exceptional individuals were given the "opportunity to thrive" and a way to curb the development of any potential turbo-powered-ultra-criminals.

Each panel of judges contained at least one representative from the clandestine services. They hoped to cherry-pick anyone with abilities that might be beneficial to national security. It didn't take them long to strike gold, and when I say gold, I mean a skinny little Luxembourger called Max, who could literally bring people back from the dead.

Max had recently escaped the civil war in Luxembourg, with his grandmother, sadly his only relative that had survived the massacres there. Even more tragically for Max, his grandmother died only days after they arrived illegally in the UK. The gang that had smuggled them across the border had apparently required her to pay for their trip by cultivating huge quantities of cannabis. The gang had used rented suburban houses as growing locations, and they found that elderly women raised the least suspicion from neighbours. Also, they tended to make for pretty conscientious gardeners. The fact that she had a young child with her was the icing on the cake, an even more innocent appearance and good leverage if she tried to back out.

Unfortunately, in order to circumvent the electric metres (a tactic that growers often used to avoid suspiciously high electric bills), they'd had someone plug the power for the house directly into the electric grid, and this person had done a lousy job. One evening, as Max's grandmother was adjusting the giant UV grow lights, she had been electrocuted.

Max knew she was dead, but the poor guy had no one else in the world to care for him and no idea what to do. He sat there in the dark, holding her hand, for several days. He was so lost, he just intensely wished, again and again, for her to be alive, for none of this horror ever to have happened... and then it happened. She was alive again... kind of.

People that Max brings back from the dead aren't quite "good as new". His grandmother had been very badly burned by the electric shock, and that didn't get any better. Her heart had started beating again occasionally, but it didn't seem to be a totally necessary part of her continued existence, like a toddler occasionally half-pedalling a bike that their parent is pushing along. But compared to the alternative, they both took it as a big win.

His grandmother took this second chance at life as a blessing from God. She tried her best to cover the burns with makeup, and they carried on as best they could. When the schools for children with special abilities were announced, this seemed to her like a further positive sign from the almighty. Surely Max's ability was so special that the schools could overlook his questionable immigration status?

I imagine that the selection interviews for special kids in the early days must have been a fairly excruciating experience for the members of the various judgement boards. The public impression was that the children selected were going to be given "the best possible advantages in life". Britain was going to be at the forefront of whatever this new thing was, and the key to that was going to be nurturing the talents of these gifted children. But, of course, every parent thinks that their child is special. I'm sure that for every child like Max with a genuine new human ability, there would have been at least a hundred "look, she can read at a fifteen year old's level and she's barely even eleven" and "he's the fastest hundred metre runner in his age group in the county apart from two other boys but I'm sure they're actually older 'cos they've got beards." Those were two actual examples I'd heard from one of the more chatty teachers at school.

Max's ability isn't easy to demonstrate. Firstly, it requires something dead. Did it need to be a person? Secondly, it had potentially taken days the first time. And thirdly, he didn't even know if he could do it again. And so the board decided that the best thing was for his grandmother to come along as evidence, a kind of "here's one I made earlier". Even this was easier said than done, as she was basically a prisoner in her own home.

She told the whole story to the board (well, not the stuff about an illegal off-grid electric connection and compulsory cannabis cultivation) about how she had been electrocuted and had been dead for days until Max had brought her back. She removed her makeup and showed them the horrific burn marks up her arms, which indeed looked like the shock should have been fatal. They let a doctor take her irregular pulse, which he agreed was "utterly bizarre", however, he confessed he had no way of knowing if it was her or Max that was the medical curiosity.

Someone on the board proposed that what they really needed was "to see him bring something back from the dead, live", as it were. Max was happy to give it a go, but he wasn't sure how long it would take or if it only worked with people. Much to the misplaced joy of his proud grandmother, the man from MI6 assured them that he would be able to find something appropriate and escorted her to the train station before bundling Max away in an unmarked car.

Tricks don't come with an instruction manual. I'm sure there are hundreds or thousands of people with incredible powers that they don't even know they have, because they haven't thought the right thing, or pushed their body the right way. But it works the other way as well. Sometimes you only find out the limitation of your ability by pushing it too far. You see, it turns out that people Max has brought back only remain alive while they are near him. Max's grandmother was once again dead by the time her train arrived home. The burned body on the train was an unusual find, not least because it appeared to have been dead for several months, and news of it swiftly found its way to Dr Shears, the person in charge of

Max's assessment. She decided that it was best they not pass this information on to Max though, as he was making strong progress, and she thought that an emotional strain like the second death of his last living relative might be a distraction. This proximity limitation was interesting though, and something she intended to evaluate.

Initially they had tested Max out on the newly dead. In order to recreate the conditions as closely as possible to the situation where he had first performed his trick, the scientists had fatally electrocuted a goat. They didn't tell Max this, they just brought him the animal's body and told him to try his best. After a couple of days, he said the best thing he could do was maybe make a curry out of it. This wasn't the strong progress I mentioned, although the curry was apparently delicious.

Jennifer Stratton had fallen to her death from a fourth-story window while attempting to take a photo of herself cleaning it. That wasn't even the strangest thing that happened to her that day. Max held her hand and concentrated as hard as he could and literally willed her back to life in a few moments. This was the strong progress.

Jennifer and Max had a chat, while military doctors ran some tests, but the results seemingly raised more questions than they answered. The X-rays showed that Jennifer's spine was still broken, and yet she was able to walk around perfectly normally, albeit with her head at a slightly jaunty angle. She had some skin lacerations from a windowsill that she had clipped on the way down, but she wasn't really bleeding, she just looked like she was about to. The EEG results were equally bizarre. She did have something close to normal brain function occasionally, usually as she spoke to Max, and then it would fade away to something between a coma and death.

The most important test, from a military perspective, was

what distance Max had to be, relative to Jennifer, to keep her going. However, there didn't seem to be a way to let Max know what they were testing without also letting him know the unfortunate news about his grandmother so they just told him that Jennifer was better now and was being sent home. To simplify things further, this is also what they told Jennifer.

A helicopter ambulance took off from the oil rig and hovered, as Jennifer's vital signs were monitored. It would then fly a hundred metres and hover again as the process was repeated. At four hundred metres from Max, she became incoherent although not unconscious, and by six hundred metres she was once again dead.

And then Felix Trent was shot in the head.

The powers that be (i.e., military advisors. The Prime Minister isn't the type to think up plans of this nature.) decided that it might be worth taking a shot at bringing him back.

This wasn't an act of altruism; no one, for example, had suggested they bring back The Griddler. Rather, that with all of the startling new discoveries of human potential that had been arising, it had long been noted that the one that foreign leaders seemed to fear the most (certainly until The Angel of Death started to do her thing) was still the original trickster, Felix Trent. I suppose the fear that someone could divulge their deepest desires to the public instilled more fear in political figures than pretty much anything else. Felix was an asset worth hanging onto, dead or alive, hopefully kind of both.

His body was airlifted to the disused oil rig where Max was under observation, just as the corpse of Jennifer Stratton was being returned to the morgue where they had found her.

Max had recently started to ask if he could return home to his grandmother. He had shown them his trick as best he could and quite understandably wanted to go home. They asked for just one more demonstration, just so they could be sure that he was suitable for a place in a special school. Max agreed.

Max was then shown the body of the recently deceased Felix Trent. This was quite a shock even for Max, who had admittedly seen a lot of horrific things for such a young person. He had apparently been a long-time fan of Felix, and this was a pretty disturbing way to find out he was dead. Also, Felix had been shot in the head and was not looking his best. He'd been shot just behind the right ear, and he had an exit-wound, around the size of a satsuma, where his left eye should be. This didn't get any prettier once Max brought him back to life. His wound never bleeds but, as with Jennifer's, it always looks like it's about to. It's an appearance that takes some getting used to.

And so Felix was back, and for all intents and purposes, he was now the property of the British Secret Service. This whole scheme had been put together admirably quickly, but they soon realised that perhaps they didn't have the diplomatic-super-weapon they had hoped for. Cynics would argue that rather than the mind-reading ultra-negotiator they had envisioned, they instead had resuscitated a degenerate gambler with only half a face who was now mortally dependent on a twelve-year-old boy.

YOU GOTTA STOP GOING TO THESE PLACES

The Reverend Billy Winn's gatherings had been getting progressively larger even before the TV coverage, but afterwards, the growth became exponential. What didn't make any sense to me about the popularity of these events is that now there seemed to be almost no chance of actually being cured of anything. He would hold these rallies in mega churches or sometimes football stadiums, as they were the only places big enough for the numbers he was drawing. As before, towards the end of the event, he would pick a few people out from the adoring invalids in the front few rows and he would cure a few. But the ratio of spectators to people actually getting any benefit from him was now so skewed as to make them virtually pointless for the chronically sick to bother with. Also, he was now going for more flashy stuff. The problem with curing cancer, from the perspective of creating spectacle, is that you can't really tell it's happened. The person still basically looks the same, and they won't even know themselves until they have had a fairly thorough medical examination. So he didn't really do that anymore, instead he would go for things with more visual clout.

These people would obviously have been picked in advance, as he would have some prerecorded footage ready to play on the big screens, maybe a shot of them in a wheelchair, or sitting down at a wedding when everyone else is standing, that sort of thing. There would almost always be at least one person he'd help to walk again at any event. Those had that immediate visual payoff that everyone was after. I guess if you were going to bother going to one of those things, and there was clearly no chance he was going to cure your gonorrhoea, at least you would hope to *see* a verifiable miracle.

My personal favourite was Jim Fenton, an actor who had previously appeared in a number of fairly popular action movies. He took pride in (and wouldn't shut up about) doing all his own stunts. It wasn't a stunt that did the damage though, rather a drive home from a bar where he had been reportedly drinking for some time, although he was apparently not breathalysed at the scene of the accident. He'd wrapped his sports car around a tree stump and broken his spine.

The nature of the incident didn't play exactly to Billy's clean-living, holier-than-thou image, but Jim was fairly famous and largely popular. In fact, his popularity had soared since the accident, I think mostly because he seemed to be taking it with such good humour. "I told my mother, 'I've broken my spine in two places.' She says, 'You gotta stop going to these places!'"

For Billy, the fact that this was a well known celebrity, who now famously couldn't walk, was too big of an opportunity to pass up. For context, his sermons had recently turned a bit more towards the fire and brimstone sections of the Bible. He had been vociferously condemning homosexuality, adultery, homosexual adultery, drink, drugs, you know the kind of thing. Nevertheless, in front of a crowd of one hundred and ten thousand people (seriously, it's like people have nothing better to do on the weekends), Billy put his hand on Jim's head and restored his spine to it's former glory. But first, for balance I suppose, he'd had him read about eight Bible passages about how he was sorry for all the drinking and once he was blind but now he could see and the scales have fallen from his legs or whatever. It was exactly as tedious as it sounds, but it made what happened next even more amazing. Apparently Jim had decided to give his new spine a thorough testing out in a motel just around the corner from the stadium, immediately after the show. He was arrested as a result of an altercation with hotel security following a noise disturbance. In the room with him at the time were nine prostitutes, three unregistered handguns, and a quantity of drugs with a street value of twenty-six thousand dollars.

I would have hoped that this would have taken the wind out of Billy's sails a little, especially with the telling everyone what they should be doing with their lives schtick, but no, if anything he doubled down. He didn't mention much about drinking anymore though. In fact, he didn't mention much of anything other than his new "public enemy number one — abominations". By which he meant, of course, anyone that could do a trick... like him.

So far, the US had been not greatly dissimilar to the UK and the majority of Europe in that people with tricks were largely being educated in special schools. Initially, this had been fairly universally welcomed, possibly only as a means of preventing a running back at Notre Dame, who could run sixty yards in a matter of seconds whilst dragging twelve fully grown men behind him, from totally destroying college football. A huge programme was being set up to find the best and the brightest and give them all possible advantages in life. Billy had a different idea for people with tricks though. The Bible was pretty clear on this (2 Kings, 24), these people were "abominations unto the Lord" and should be treated as such. He started saying this a lot.

The Bible calls for death for a lot of things, and quoting it will usually get a pretty big cheer from the kind of crowd that Billy was drawing in, so no one paid too much attention to this specific pronouncement when he first made it. He might as well have called for death for people who ignore the sabbath, or curse their parents. You're going to get an "Amen" or two, but no one's going to expect you to be lining disrespectful kids up against a wall anytime soon. But this is where people underestimated Billy Winn. After all, he can cure cancer, and in the right light he looks a little bit like Jesus, provided you don't really care what Jesus actually looked like.

It also seemed to go against the prevailing mood with regard to tricks, which was generally one of excitement and hope. A young lad with superhuman grip strength had recently scaled the Empire State Building like a tiny King Kong, and an eleven-year-old girl had just beaten a kung-fu grand master to death with his own nunchucks. Both of these achievements had been largely celebrated. In fact, before Billy Winn's rise to power, new tricks were usually greeted with more excitement in the US than almost anywhere else. If anything, there had been *less* of the trepidation there that had been so commonplace in the rest of the world.

The first victim, as far as anyone could tell, was Stacey Bradshaw. And victims of The Headsman (as she was then known) are fairly distinctive, so it's unlikely that any were overlooked. Stacey had missed a morning class, which was unusual for her. So unusual in fact, that her roommate Becky returned to her dorm room to make sure everything was OK. She found Stacey still in bed, presumably asleep, with nothing obviously out of place in the room. When, after several attempts to wake her failed, she shook her, she discovered to her horror that Stacey's head had been severed from her body completely. The cut was so fine that barely any blood even escaped the body until it was moved.

The college dorm was fairly well covered with security cameras, and the tapes from the night before showed Stacey entering her room at just after 11 pm. No one else entered or left the room, with the exception of the roommate, until the following morning. The only plausible explanation was that Becky, for some reason, had decided to decapitate her roommate during the night, and had done a phenomenally good job at it, with a weapon that she had presumably subsequently disposed of. Fortunately, the detective in charge of the case had a great deal of experience, and his gut reaction was that this simply was not something that Becky could have done. He called in some favours and dug a little deeper. The first accounts of creeper kidnappings had started coming out of the UK by this point, and it occurred to him that this could be something similar.

The UK department responsible for crimes involving tricks was fairly overwhelmed at the time, but they assured him that this didn't sound like a creeper because of the use of a weapon. It was probably either the roommate or something new. Fortunately for Becky, it didn't take long for someone else to "wake up dead".

Jeb Spencer III was the current CEO of the Spencer's Coffee chain and was a wealthy man. The chain had over sixty outlets in five states and was a popular destination for a reasonable cup of coffee at an unreasonable price. According to Jeb's wife, she had gone to bed early as she had a Pilates class in the morning. Jeb had presumably joined her at some point in the night. She liked to read a little when she woke up, and she would usually borrow one of Jeb's pillows to sit up on. He apparently liked to sleep on a big pile of them, but he didn't mind her grabbing one. This time when she grabbed the pillow though, Jeb's head had rolled off onto the floor. She said that,

"Before that moment, there was no sign he was anything other than totally fine."

The detective running the Bradshaw case would likely never have been alerted to the link, as it wasn't in his jurisdiction, but luckily the bizarre decapitation of a prominent business figure was a big enough story to make the national news. This was particularly fortunate for Mrs Spencer, as she had already been arrested and would almost certainly otherwise have been prosecuted for first-degree murder. Much like the dorm room, Jeb's home was pretty well covered with security cameras. There were none covering the bed itself, but enough to be sure that the only people in that room that night had been Mr and Mrs Spencer.

There are now two divergent opinions about why the killer had chosen these particular victims, so let's get the ridiculous one out of the way first. The story goes that God appeared to The Angel of Death in a dream, and he told her that he had a job for her, a very special job that only she could do. He then bestowed upon her the power of invisibility and "a special holy weapon" that He Himself had made. He then told her the names of people that had displeased Him. It's not clear exactly what young Stacey Bradshaw had done to displease God so much. Maybe she wore mixed fabrics or something. I could give you more reasons that God might have been mad at Jeb, but instead, let's get to the more plausible explanation for the whole thing. Stacey Bradshaw had recently begun dating college football player, and all around great catch, Buddy Thompson. Jeb Spencer III had recently initiated a new policy in his coffee shops wherein all tips were to be shared between staff and counted towards the minimum wage requirement. This drastically reduced the staff wages at Spencer's Coffee, particularly for attractive female staff, who tend to get tipped pretty well.

Kitty Campbell has a trick. She can't exactly turn herself

invisible, but she can very rapidly change the colour of her skin to mimic her surrounding — a technique you will be familiar with if you have ever seen, or failed to see, a chameleon. Basically, if she stays close to a wall and moves slowly, you'd be very unlikely to see her. She also just happened to have been dating Buddy Thompson before he'd broken up with her to pursue a new relationship with Stacey Bradshaw, a few days before she was decapitated. Oh, and Kitty worked in a Spencer's Coffee shop and had been particularly vocal about how the new wage policy was "unfair and someone was going to pay." So those could have been the motives for the killings, or God came to her in a dream — it's definitely one of those two reasons.

In fairness, the rest of the victims may as well have been named for her in a dream. She had killed twenty-four people before she was caught, and they can't all have wronged her. Most of them were seemingly unknown to her.

I don't know Kitty personally; for most people, meeting Kitty is very much the end of the road, but I think I know the type. There was a kid at school with prehensile toes on his feet. Monkeys have these, I think. It helps them to grip on to branches. His weren't quite like monkeys' feet though, more like long hands on the end of his legs. The point I'm trying to get to is that they didn't seem particularly useful, not outside of the world of climbing trees. But then this kid played a bit of football, and he got really good, really fast. It turns out that his grabby feet were a real asset there, like the control you would get from catching a ball with your hand, but with the power of the leg muscles for kicking. For what it's worth, if monkeys were into it, I bet they'd be really good at football. But I digress, so within a few weeks of discovering that he was good at football, it became this kid's whole personality. He was wearing football shirts all the time, reading football magazines, and he quickly became an inexhaustible fount of tedious football trivia. This is what I reckon happened with Kitty. This kid wasn't good at football because it was his passion, it was his passion because he discovered he was good at it.

Invisibility, or the close-enough-if-she-stays-next-to-a-wall approximation of invisibility that Kitty has, isn't actually useful for all that much. In killing though, she had found something she could do better than maybe anyone else. When she was finally arrested, she was found to be carrying a garrotte made from graphene tied between two Perspex tubes. If it wasn't moving, I would guess it was about as invisible as she was. Graphene is incredibly strong, and so a relatively thin cord is all she needed. So thin, in fact, that it was as sharp as a scalpel. She would get behind the person as they slept and saw through their neck in only a few minutes, usually making barely enough sound to wake anyone else in the house.

Billy Winn would no doubt tell you that all those early victims had sinned, and God had chosen to punish them. I'm sure he could find a reason for each of them if he could be bothered. If you ask around about even the most pious person, you're going to find some deadly sins somewhere. Especially if you read the Bible with the willful misinterpretations that Billy is prone to. But I think Kitty picked those people virtually at random, maybe because they were easy, maybe because they were a challenge, but she killed them for no better reason than that she was exceptionally good at it. She's probably a sociopath or something like that as well, but you can bet dollars to donuts that those people would all be alive now if Kitty couldn't go invisible, the same way that the kid from my school only knew every FA cup winner because he got the monkey feet.

An Academy for the Exceptionally Gifted (an AEG, this is what they called the Special Schools in the US for the brief period that they existed) was under construction in Cambridge, Massachusetts. It was apparently going to share a number of teaching staff with Harvard. It was thought that this new generation of exceptional Americans could be studied by the finest minds at Harvard, whilst also being educated by them. Before the foundations were even completed, a man disguised as a construction worker drove a truck filled with a crudely explosive mixture of fertiliser and industrial hydrogen peroxide into the centre of the site and detonated it. The explosion was not precisely targeted, but it was so huge that it didn't really need to be, it did substantial damage to almost every structure in a four-block radius. The immediate death toll was over two hundred people, but a far greater number were injured. It was the injured that Billy Winn saw as a huge opportunity.

He flew immediately by private jet from his home in Tennessee and was at the scene in a matter of hours. This was the first time anyone had witnessed what Billy was capable of in a disaster situation. Rather than immediately going to nearby hospitals, Billy and his entourage went directly to the scene of the explosion itself. The bomb blast had hewn a giant crater out of the ground, and emergency services were still pulling victims from the rubble when he arrived. When a body was discovered, Billy would be let through before even the paramedics, such was his reputation. There was nothing he could do for the dead, so he would just say a prayer and move on, but anything short of death and he was admittedly able to work miracles. Battered and broken bodies would be pulled from the ground only to be walking and talking moments later, after Billy had laid his healing hands on them.

One of the most visually powerful moments was when a young woman was pulled from the rubble. She was unconscious and missing her left arm entirely. Billy placed a hand on her forehead and said a silent prayer. He then spoke to the emergency services, and a frantic search began. Within a few minutes a firefighter came running over brandishing the severed limb (I assume it was hers. It's not impossible that it had belonged to someone else). He placed the arm next to her bleeding torso and whispered as he pressed them together. In a moment, the woman hugged Billy with fully functional arms.

And then Billy Winn announced he would be running for President of the United States in the upcoming election. You can't fault his timing. At that point even I would have voted for him.

As he then toured Cambridge Hospital, where a large number of the wounded from the explosion had been brought, he outlined what would be his election platform, in between restoring peoples' sight, limbs and otherwise incurable ailments.

His first key stance would be the "eradication of all abominations", by which he meant any and all people who could do a trick of any kind. This was a fairly strange stance for several reasons, not least that he surely was one of the people he was planning to eradicate. Secondly, he was currently curing the victims of an explosion caused by a group with exactly that aim. A pro-human activist group (that's how they described themselves) had claimed responsibility for the destruction of the Cambridge AEG.

And here is the genius of Billy Winn. As a political tactician, he can be pretty masterful. As he placed his hand on the forehead of a construction worker that had been in a coma since the explosion, he declared that "this kind of indiscriminate violence is not the way to confront the issue of the rising number of abominations in America. Such attacks are ineffective, unhelpful and, above all, un-Christian."

As the young man's eyes opened and he saw Billy and realised what must have happened, he began to thank him profusely.

"Instead, my administration will perform a much more

targeted, humane and thorough destruction of the abomina-tions, without unnecessary innocent victims."

He shook the hand of the unnecessary innocent victim that he had just brought back to life.

So yeah, he's an outside-the-box thinker. He just suggested genocide as a presidential platform and made it sound like the moderate option. Want another example? Let's not get too bogged down in US politics. Billy was about to render the whole process pretty irrelevant, but here goes.

I don't want to make sweeping generalisations, but I think it's fair to say that you might normally expect a person of Billy's religious background to be a member of the Republican Party. At least, you would have done. In fact, his second key platform besides the "eradication of abominations" was "a return to biblical Christian values." This is Republican bread and butter. At the time, the current president was finishing up an eight-year term and could not run again, so both parties were gearing up for hotly contested primaries. Billy's candidacy announce-ment sent shock waves through various Republican hopeful's campaign teams.

Political parties tend to lean towards their base in primary season, so for Republicans, that was going to mean a lot of talking about "Christian values". Billy Winn, a preacher who quoted some of the most fire and brimstone sections of the Bible nonstop, and could literally perform miracles, was going to be tough to out-flank from the religious right. I imagine therefore, that Republican presidential hopefuls greeted the news with relief when Billy announced, to the surprise of essentially everyone, that he would be running for the nomina-tion of the Democratic Party.

This was "insanity", said the pundits. Surely he couldn't win the nomination from the Democratic base, where his hard-line religious views and anti-gay, anti-abortion, anti-trick stance would be seen as a huge negative. And then, even if he did win, he would be running against a Republican, who surely a lot of his supporters would vote for, no matter which name was on the ticket. As the Democrats geared up for the early debates, Billy was assumed by most to have squandered his opportunity to be a Republican front-runner, to surely be eliminated early in the Democratic primaries. His celebrity alone was enough to get him an invitation to the first televised debate though, and pundits were, not for the first time, about to be proved very wrong.

The first question was a softball for all the candidates, just a two-minute opener where they could explain their platform. Billy began with a line that no one on that stage was going to disagree with, "The Republican Party is broken."

Big cheers.

"They are disgraced by perversions of nature, they allow and tolerate abominations to walk among us and they celebrate their unholy acts. There is no place in Christianity for this corrupted party."

A gentle smattering of, at best confused, applause.

A softly spoken senator from California named Todd Brooks stepped up to his mic and interjected. "I don't mean to speak out of turn, but I really must register my offence here. I believe that not only are people who can perform these incredible physical or mental feats, 'tricks' as I would call them. Not only are these people likely a key part of the future success of our nation, but they are undoubtedly *gifts* from God, and should be celebrated as such."

The crowd was on Todd's side. There was a great cheer, in fact a deafening cheer, as a member of the audience clearly had a trick that allowed him to make a noise at about the volume of a Concorde crashing into another Concorde.

When the noise finally died down, he continued, "And may I say that I find it particularly hypocritical that a person such as yourself, who can perform such a wonderful and useful trick, would be so reluctant for others to use their abilities in the same way."

The loud trickster cheered again, and the whole stage shook. This guy really wasn't doing us any favours.

Billy waited a moment for calm. "The miracles I perform are no 'tricks'. It says so very clearly in the scriptures. The Lord God is merciful, but He is also vengeful. Which will He be with you, Senator Brooks?" And with his point made, Billy walked off the stage.

If you were wondering about his last question, the answer was "vengeful." The next morning, when Senator Brooks' wife went to wake him, his head rolled cleanly off his body and into the bathroom.

The police investigating Senator Brooks' death immediately drew parallels with the Kitty Campbell case. It is, after all, a fairly unusual cause of death to be decapitated while sleeping. It still took far longer than it should have for the combined forces of a number of US agencies to realise that, rather than being either a copycat killer or perhaps someone with the same trick as Kitty using the same technique, this murder might have been carried out by the actual Kitty Campbell.

She was being detained at a maximum security facility in Texas, in a regular federal prison as there were, as yet, no facilities designed specifically for people with tricks in the state. At least, she was supposed to be. It turns out that the last time Kitty had actually been seen by the guards was four days ago. The head warden at the prison had been "concerned that it may cause panic" if he had made public the fact that Kitty had gone missing, and that he was "almost certain that she was still within the walls of the prison." He was right about the first part. An invisible killer on the loose probably would have caused a significant panic. I think we can safely assume now that he was wrong about the second part.

Kitty had not yet been convicted of anything and had therefore been allowed some leeway with regards to visitation. As well as her regular defence attorney, she had been visited twice previously by a lawyer named Christopher Goldwater, whose other notable clients included the Reverend Billy Winn and the Church of Divine Justice, a tax-exempt religious entity under the control of Reverend Winn.

If you are the sort of person that enjoys watching people that are obviously terrified for their lives discussing tax reform bills, then I'd hugely recommend you check out 1998's New Hampshire Democratic Primary. Three candidates had chosen not to attend the debate at all. They didn't pull out of the race officially though, as I guess they were waiting to see how things progressed.

The moderator asked the opening question, which was about how each of the candidates proposed to reduce the national deficit. I can't remember what the first couple of people said. They certainly didn't address the elephant in the room. That elephant was, of course, the recent murder of Todd Brooks. His decapitated corpse might as well have been propped up in the middle of the stage, that's how heavily it loomed over the proceedings. Billy, predictably, said that he would greatly reduce government spending by cutting "all funding for special schools and facilities for abominations against humanity."

It wasn't until the third question that finally someone brought up the murder. Justine Wilkins from Arkansas, a relative unknown in politics until that year and a firm outsider for the nomination, showed herself to be the bravest person on that stage. She segued in from another topic. "I had the pleasure of working with Senator Todd Brooks on a bill that would do exactly that..." conspicuous pause, "a senator who will be greatly missed, not just by myself, but by all free-thinking people of this great nation. And I, for one, will not stand idly by while his murderer continues to run for office with impunity, and furthermore, has the audacity to preach the gospels. Reverend Winn, last week you stood on a stage, not unlike this one, and threatened the senator with 'God's Vengeance'. And this week, the senator is no longer with us. I would like to ask you what you believe happened to him?"

Billy Winn seemed entirely unfazed; he didn't rush to answer, but stood and soaked up the expectant silence.

"I made no threats. I simply stated my beliefs, as is the right of every American. It was my belief that God would pass judgement on Senator Brooks. The Lord has many angels and archangels, as you would know if you read your scriptures more closely." He turned to the audience. "Bringing daily Bible reading into public schools is a key part of my election platform. I would hazard a guess that Senator Brooks was visited by Azrael, the Archangel of Death."

Justine stood dumbstruck by the audacity of it for a moment. "Oh, really? You think it was an angel that cut my colleague's head off? You don't think it was perhaps the escaped serial killer Kitty Campbell? A serial killer with *a trick*, by the way, which I believe in your eyes, would make her an abomination? You don't mind these 'abominations' when they are doing your dirty work!"

There was significant applause from the studio audience, which Billy quieted down with a hand gesture, as if it had been for him.

"Allow me to clear up this misunderstanding you seem to have. I don't know how it is possible to confuse some monster with an extra leg with the Lord's work, but you seem to have, so let me help you. The Lord created man 'in his image', and we have continued to live with his blessing for thousands of years. These new creatures are not 'in his image'. I read today of a girl who could breathe underwater like a fish. That is not 'in his image'. She is an abomination and should be destroyed."

There were a lot of boos but also a couple of cheers from the crowd. This was apparently not an entirely unpopular view, even among Democrats.

"These are not *my* opinions, but the words of the Lord God right here."

He pulled a well-worn Bible from his back pocket.

"There is a person in this book who can do what I do, who can heal like I do, perform miracles as I do, and He is the Son of God."

That was about as clearly as he ever laid it out. If it is in the Bible, it is a miracle, if it isn't in the Bible, then it's just *a trick*, and the person who can perform it is an abomination. Later on, there would be all kinds of reasoning from his followers, with convoluted explanations and obscure passages from bizarre translations of the Old Testament. What it really boiled down to was, if Billy found a need for you, or if you had donated a large sum to his election campaign, then it turned out that you could perform a 'miracle', if he didn't or you didn't, then you had a 'trick'.

There was even a boy who could straight-up walk on water. I'm no Bible fan, but I'm pretty sure that's in there. Still, he was denounced as an abomination, maybe because it was a little too Christ-like and Billy wanted the monopoly on Jesus tricks. Anyway, they drowned him somehow.

"Do you believe in God?"

Justine Wilkins stood her ground. She had started down this road and there was no sense turning back now. "I do believe in God, and I do not believe that this is his message or that you are his messenger."

"Well, let's just see what the Lord has to say about that."

Justine's head fell off the following Thursday, just when people were beginning to think that she might have got away with it.

And so, the Reverend Billy Winn became the Democratic nominee for President of the United States. After Wilkins, The Angel of Death didn't even have to visit any of the other hopefuls. They all found reasons for dropping out of the race that came short of saying "I don't want to have my head cut off while I sleep." But no other politician came right out and called Billy a murderer. It just wasn't worth the risk. Why put a bullseye on your neck for The Angel?

When a prominent paper published a front page piece entitled "*The Angel of Death" is the End of American Democracy*, they were entirely right, but not for the reasons in the article. The paper had two editors at the time, and The Angel visited them both that night, as well as the journalist that foolishly took the by-line on the article — and *that* was the end of American democracy.

But there was still an election to come, and it was going to be a strange one. The Republican nominee was spaghetti-hoop mogul, Cranston Jarvis. I'm assuming his company made something other than spaghetti hoops as well, as he's ostentatiously loaded, but that's what they're mostly known for. He was left in a tricky position for several reasons — the first, and I'm sure foremost in his mind, was that there was a good chance that God would kill him at any moment. He had apparently taken to sleeping inside a concrete reinforced panic room on his estate. The door could only be opened from the inside, and he had taken the very wise precaution of installing thermal imaging cameras. Before he entered the room each evening, it would be flushed entirely with nitrogen for twenty minutes, before being refilled with air. He was assured that no living mammal could survive this.

But this was, in many ways, the easiest of his problems to address, at least if he still hoped to be president, and given the trouble he was going to, we can assume he did. On every issue that he was already right wing on, Billy was more so. Cranston was a long time hunter and a huge favourite of the pro-gun lobby, at least until they saw Billy Winn's platform. Billy thought that not only should Americans be free to own a gun, he believed it should be compulsory. It was every American's sacred duty to defend himself as best he could "against the abominations in our midst." And given that some of these abominations had some pretty significant abilities, they were going to require the "most vigorous firepower available."

The prospect of entirely unregulated ultra-weapons sent firearms manufacturers' stock prices soaring. But there was no need to contribute any of this new wealth to the Republican campaign though. For once, a Democratic win would be even more profitable. On almost every other issue, Cranston was also out-flanked on the right. Billy was so pro-life that he didn't even believe in pregnancy tests. Women should be in a "constant state of readiness" for new gifts from the Lord.

I suppose Cranston could have tried to move to the left to pick up some votes. After all, actual liberals didn't really have a nominee, as a vote for the Democratic Party was a vote for Billy Winn. But to be seen to flip-flop at this stage would surely have been political suicide. Besides, there was the possibility of an independent challenger from the left. Grover Pleasance was a human rights lawyer from Denver. He had previously been a noted commentator on a number of public safety issues but had been particularly vocal recently. He foresaw what would surely be human rights abuses down the line for anyone with a trick. He noted that Billy Winn was singling out these "abominations" in the same way that racial and religious minorities had been scapegoated in the past, with horrific consequences.

The intriguing thing about Grover is that he had no particular affiliation to either party. Currently in his seventies, he had previously supported both Republicans and Democrats on various issues, but always from an apolitical human-rights promoting stance. He was clean-living, married only once, with a wonderful family, and had several decades of experience debating hot-button issues on TV. This was a once in a lifetime opportunity for a sea-change in American politics.

When he announced that he would be running as an Independent candidate, both parties' nominees had to take note. Democrats, who rightly felt that their party had been hijacked, would now have a candidate to vote for that didn't have radically different views to them, and moderate Republicans would now have someone to vote for. Grover Pleasance was the right man, in the right place, at the right time, and he almost certainly would have been America's next president if he hadn't been decapitated in an elevator shortly after announcing his candidacy.

Billy Winn won the presidency by a landslide.

13

SQUIRREL CHARADES

The brilliant thing about pigeons is that they barely have a mind of their own. This is according to Jackson and confirmed by Tess. I don't really have any strong opinions on pigeons one way or the other.

Once you get on them and they're flying, they will essentially just go in whichever direction you point their head. Grip them firmly just behind the eyes and it's about as responsive as a car's steering wheel or the yolk of an aeroplane. The challenging thing is getting on one in the first place, or at least it was before Tess was involved.

Jackson flew his first pigeon because I dared him to do it. This wasn't uncommon; I used to dare him to do a lot of things. It's the single most reliable way to get him to do anything. I think I may have pushed my luck once by daring him to make me a sandwich, but providing there is some actual challenge in the thing, dare Jackson to do it, and it's as good as done.

We had been trying to break into the house of the manager of a first division football team. His team had just been knocked out of the FA cup at the quarter final stage, and he had given a rather unsportsmanlike interview after the match, in which he blamed their defeat on the "unholy abomination of a centre-forward those cheats fielded."

This was post Winters Act, so it would have indeed been considered cheating for a team to field a player with a trick, as being a professional sportsman is a form of job, albeit a pretty cushy one. He hadn't directly called him a trickster, but the word "abomination" was so loaded that we all knew what he meant. I don't even know if the player had a trick. As far as I could see, he just had long legs and an admittedly huge head. I'm not sure that was enough to qualify as a trick though, and obviously he had managed to keep himself off the register, otherwise he wouldn't have been allowed to play. I guessed that the manager was just rude and fairly bitter about the spectacular header that had cost his team a place in the semi's. As I often did in those days, I had decided that this guy needed to be taken down a peg or two and, as equally often occurred, I roped Jackson into helping by way of a series of escalating dares. He needed the money anyway. This guy probably had all sorts of expensive goodies, and Jackson always needs money.

Usually being a tiny invulnerable person is enough to get you into pretty much any property. I'd shrink Jackson and he'd jump up through a cat flap or a small ground-floor window. No such luck with this guy's house though. In fact, the only likely point of entry looked to be a chimney on the roof. It was a three-story house, so getting up there would be no easy feat. I can throw Jackson pretty far, but this was probably out of reach.

As we were pondering this, a couple of pigeons landed on the chimney we were staring at. I barely needed to say it at all.

"Dare you."

And before long I was throwing the shrunken Jackson at every bird we could see. It took about an hour before we got one. I had pretty much lost interest in the whole thing, but

Jackson is relentless. Once the dare has been made, there's just no way he's going to stop.

Anyway, that was the day he learned to fly a pigeon, and he wreaked no small amount of havoc with it inside the house. He got so good at steering though, that he even managed to fly it back up and out of the chimney. Ever since then it's pretty much been his preferred way to travel.

And so it was that he was scoping out the facilities at T-BAIT from a few hundred feet up in the air when suddenly he found himself plummeting towards the earth, holding a now relatively tiny pigeon between his legs.

He let go of the bird and tried to get into a decent landing position. I would have thought he should just land on his legs, but he prefers to hit the ground almost head first and roll. Whatever works for him, I suppose.

He lands in what would have been, for a regular person at least, maybe the worst place in the entire complex. It is an open piece of land, and he sticks the landing pretty well, only to be immediately shot in the shoulder and the leg by an elderly Bobbett in some sort of chair weapon. He dives to the ground and tries to figure out what is going on. There are paper targets towards the end of the range, the kind that have a cutout of a human figure, and they are being absolutely obliterated. The Bobbett is still firing away, having apparently not noticed that an actual human figure had briefly appeared and absorbed a few of his rounds.

A challenge that Terrence had routinely faced with armed Bobbetts was that by the time they reached a level of mental maturity where they could be trusted with a weapon, they would often be so physically deteriorated that they couldn't carry them effectively. This contraption is likely an attempt at a solution to that problem. The device the Bobbett is sitting in looks like a fairly conventional wheelchair, but with robust-looking, chunky, off-road tires. Attached to the side of the chair is a fully-automatic rifle, presumably acquired back when he had a military contract. It is being belt-fed rounds across the Bobbett's lap from a weighty-looking ammunition canister on the other side of the chair.

Provided they don't hit any organs, bullets will go through Jackson without doing any real damage at all. His rubbery bones just kind of congeal back together. Still, getting shot is incredibly painful, and he isn't eager to take another hit, so he thought it best to crawl face down out of the line of fire. I should probably also point out that, even if Jackson is hit in major organs, it's unlikely to do him any serious damage. He's really not easy to kill. He particularly doesn't like getting hit in the heart or the lungs though. That sort of thing can cause him to have a bit of an extended sit down.

Did you know that the first congratulatory phone call that a newly elected US president receives is always from the UK prime minister? This quaint old custom, I suppose, was usually something of an honour, but this year that wasn't really the case.

International reaction to Billy Winns rise to power had been somewhat tempered. Usually if a prospective world leader was to run on a platform promising the extermination of any proportion of their own population, you would expect at least some pretty vocal condemnations from other world leaders. The fact that the country in question was the United States meant that it was unlikely that most nations would throw any overt military threats into the mix, but at least there could be some blustery high-horse grandstanding about how morally reprehensible the whole thing is. Maybe even a resolution everyone could sign. It wouldn't change anything, but it would at least be something. With Billy Winn, there hadn't even been that.

When he was asked by a back-bencher at Prime Minister's Questions to make his position clear on Billy Winn, the PM had looked like he'd just been called up to the front of school assembly and been asked to tell everyone which girls he fancied and why. Because, always lurking behind Billy (metaphorically, I suppose, although often, in fact, she could be there physically; she is good at hiding) is The Angel of Death. It hadn't gone unnoticed, I'm sure, that people who disagreed with Billy often woke up without heads. So, for a prominent leader to publicly denounce Billy would be a very dangerous act. You know how in action movies when a villain is explaining some horrific weapon or trap, and some character who's said nothing yet decides this would be a great time to shout something brave or stupid, seemingly just so the bad guy can show us what the weapon does? That's what it would have been like for the first-world leader to speak out against Billy Winn.

And so I image the "congratulatory phone call" was an exercise in talking without saying anything at all. As luck would have it, this is something that the Prime Minister is particularly good at. It was going well, until Billy insisted they meet in person with a visit to Camp David, an honour the Prime Minister attempted repeatedly to turn down.

I wake up in what appears to be a padded cell, the kind that I imagine you would find in a Victorian-era insane asylum. So the straitjackets we are wearing kind of make sense, I suppose. There is a theme. I don't suppose the property had already had a padded cell when Terrence bought it. Everything else appears to be newly constructed. Which means, presumably, that this is also something that Terrence had had built, perhaps for insane Bobbetts, but how he can tell if one of the "students" is more insane than the others is anyone's guess.

Tess is slumped over in the corner of the room. She looks unconscious. It's difficult to tell with Tess. Sometimes she's just concentrating really hard on getting some creature to do something it doesn't want to do and she blanks out for a bit.

"Tess," I whisper.

"Wave something in front of that window," she says.

I hadn't even noticed that there was a window, but there is indeed a recessed hole about seven feet off the ground with prison-style bars in it.

"Wave what? I'm wearing a straitjacket."

"Can you at least jump up or something? I'm trying to figure out which room we are in."

I jump up and down on the spot. I can only see out of the window at all at the very top of my jump.

"See anything?"

"Bars. Thick bars."

"Now?"

"Still there."

"Urgh, how many other cells has this place got? Oh, there you are."

"Monkey!"

"Ah man, these are thick."

"Monkey with a hacksaw."

Tony has already started sawing away at the bars. He is no stranger to breaking and entering.

"This is going to take all day," says Tess, pushing herself against the wall as she gets to her feet. "There are bars on the windows all the way along this side of the building, I dread to think who else this guy has locked up. I had him pegged as a fairly harmless eccentric."

"We need to get out of here. The ballots, they were all for Barnett, right?"

Tess nods.

"He's done a deal with the Church of Divine Justice. They're going to declare him "a miracle", rather than an abomination or whatever, and leave Bobbetts out of any new regulations."

"*If* they win."

"Which they definitely will. I mean, they were looking likely to win even without the Bobbett vote. If anything, I think people have been underestimating how many of these he can mobilise. They're absolutely going to win, and not by a small amount."

"Maybe not. Not if we can get to Felix. He reckons we can really make a difference."

"Jesus? Really? I don't buy it."

"Christians love Jesus. What are they going to do, ignore him?"

I was about to say that "yeah, that's almost certainly what they would do", but Tess suddenly seems deeply preoccupied.

"What's up?"

"This is bad."

As the Prime Minister prepared to meet Billy Winn, he had a number of quite understandable concerns. What if Billy Winn proposed something he couldn't go along with or if he did something else to upset him? If he criticised his death-camps, for example, was he going to have to spend the rest of his life sleeping in a concrete bunker with doors bolted from the inside like Cranston Jarvis? He convened a council of security advisors.

As Billy Winn had a trick, Dr Kim Sheers, who had been heading up MI6's Special Abilities Research Department, was brought in to consult. Kim had just recently returned from the helicopter ride where she had watched Jennifer Stratton die for the second time. It was that kind of research.

The Prime Minister's biggest concern was that he wouldn't even know if he had displeased the President. What if he *seemed* happy but he intended to kill him at a later date? Regardless of how well the meeting went, he would never know what Billy was thinking... and this is where Dr Sheers finally had something helpful to bring to one of these meetings.

She explained that the recently assassinated mind-reader, Felix Trent, was not, in fact, dead (kind of, this didn't seem to be the right moment to explain the idiosyncrasies of young Max's resurrection trick). If, somehow, they were able to bring Felix along to the meeting with the new President, then they could hopefully both figure out whether or not he was likely to have The Angel of Death pay the Prime Minister a visit anytime soon and also get some sort of insight into his intentions for his nation going forward.

The Prime Minister tried not to let on that he was almost exclusively interested in the first piece of information. He was genuinely excited by the plan though, having been a keen viewer of Felix's TV shows — he thought they provided a valuable insight into human nature that was useful in politics. Also, it was fun to see how much everyone else lied all the time, confirming his long held suspicion that it wasn't just him.

"That's fantastic! I suppose we could disguise him somehow, make out he is some sort of advisor," said the PM.

Dr Sheers hesitated for a moment, and the minister continued, "I mean, he was quite a public figure for a bit, maybe not as much in the States, but we wouldn't want someone to recognise him."

"I don't think that will be a problem," explained Kim. "As you might recall, he was recently shot in the face."

Jackson did such a good job at blending in with a group of Bobbetts that it takes the squirrel a few passes to find him. In fact, it is Jackson that spots the squirrel doing a kind of confused double-take. I've seen this as well with animals that Tess controls. There is sometimes something unusual about their movements. It's not quite human, but it's not entirely squirrel either.

I should also point out that this is probably a unique experience in Jackson's recent life, blending in. With his permanently excited expression, he tends to stand out in any crowd, but seemingly not here. He had found a group of suitably aged Bobbetts and was queueing up with the rest of them to have a go at axe throwing.

At this point, he doesn't know that we've just been kidnapped and imprisoned by an MP with a very dubious criminal history, so this had seemed like a reasonable way to pass the time. For all he knows, I'd either just forgotten about him for a moment or I needed to shrink something else so I had to return him to full size, both of these are things that have happened in the past. As I often say, "If you don't want to suddenly fall out of the sky, don't ride a pigeon with your tiny self." Or words to that effect.

Jackson is so unconcerned that he doesn't give up his spot in the queue to see what the squirrel wants right away. His axe throw is impressive. I think he must have done it before. It's not a huge challenge to outdo some middle-aged Bobbetts, they essentially have the minds of toddlers after all, but Jackson scores two bullseyes with sequential axes. His fellow Bobbetts are excited, potentially too excited, and a couple of them start to tear off clothing in celebration.

The instructor, a man dressed as a Second World War colonel and sporting a tremendous moustache, makes some approving sounds and looks to see which Bobbett had managed it. It's only at this point that Jackson thinks it a good idea to make himself scarce. This is easy enough to achieve as the celebrating Bobbetts are getting rambunctious.

"Steady, Irene, steady. Save it for recreation time," warns the colonel.

"Tess?" signs Jackson.

He has hidden himself in a corner, and the squirrel has come to join him.

"Yes," says the squirrel. This is being very generous to the Tess squirrel. Squirrels don't have a voice box that is in any way similar to a human's. The sound that comes out is more akin to a frustrated drunk, mumbling obscenities. There is a noise, but it's not really an identifiable word or anything. But, combined with exaggerated gestures, it's sometimes possible to interpret.

I should also point out that Tess' sign language is shaky at best. She had picked up a little from Chris, her very loud former hideout mate, but beyond her name and a few basics, this was essentially charades. Squirrel charades. It would have been adorable if our lives didn't literally depend on it.

Max's excitement about his upcoming trip to America was tempered by his gradual realisation that his grandmother was probably dead. He's a smart kid and he just couldn't think of any other reason that he would have to travel to America for the meeting with Felix, other than that Felix was somehow dependant on him. There had been other things, he had started to realise that he could feel things that Felix felt. Only lightly, but there was some sort of link between them. He realised now that he had shared the same link with his grandmother but hadn't noticed it until now. When he had felt nervous about the school interview, when he had felt excited that he had done well, those emotions had been amplified as he had been feeling his grandmother's fear and elation on top of his own. And now he realised that she had gone, because everything felt watered down.

Dr Sheers had reluctantly told Max the truth when he confronted her. They hadn't "wanted to upset him" she'd said.

Kim had bigger concerns at the time. She was trying to figure out a way to get a celebrity sexual predator with half his face missing into the same room as the President of the United States. This was the early days in the program and her human resources were limited, she had a kid with sticky arms, a girl who could excrete an intensely toxic oil from her sweat glands and a guy who could eat huge things was on the way over from New York, but nothing that seemed like it would help with the Felix situation. The best anyone could suggest was a Film and TV make-up and prosthetics artist they had worked with in the past.

For reasons of security, the make-up artist was not fully briefed on the project, which is why Felix had arrived for his meeting with the President looking like a flamboyant pirate with both an eye patch and an earring. Fortunately, this seemed to work as an elaborate double bluff on the Secret Service operatives, who reasonably assumed that no developed nation would attempt any kind of covert operation this ridiculous.

The Prime Minister, the newly inaugurated President Billy Winn, and National Security Adviser Ron Johnson (AKA Felix Trent, now dressed as a pirate who'd just got a job in insurance) met at Camp David to discuss the future relationship of the two nations. Max accompanied Dr Shears in a nearby lobby, where they both hoped desperately that no one suggested moving the meeting to somewhere more than a couple of hundred metres away.

"I believe your nation is angry, Mr Prime Minister, the abomination situation is out of control over there."

The Prime Minister had very much gone into this meeting with the hope of making a good impression. It had even crossed his mind that they might become friends or allies. The least he was hoping for was coming away confident that Billy Winn wouldn't have him murdered in his sleep. This bold opener from the President was making even the third option seem like wishful thinking.

"I'm not sure that angry is entirely accurate. There have been some challenges, I'd certainly accept that."

"Man I saw was furious, jumped out a window." Billy Winn had a point.

"Oh, him. Yes, I don't think he was representative of the population at large though, a vocal minority perhaps."

"I don't buy that at all," said the President, taking a seat in front of Felix. "Not with the infestation I saw."

"Infestation?" said the PM.

"The old retards, I've seen the pictures, what do you call them again?"

"People have been calling them Bobbetts, their father is named Bobbett. They aren't retarded, quite the opposite. It's just that physically they grow at an accelerated rate, so in comparison..."

"Stop," Billy interrupted. "I don't care."

It seemed like it really wasn't worth the effort of bringing Felix along. Billy certainly wasn't holding anything back or even attempting to be diplomatic. If he was going to have the Prime Minister killed, he'd probably just come right out and tell him.

"That's been resolved though. We found a solution that everyone is happy with. Their father is actually a Member of

Parliament now. Strange man, but some of the very best MPs are a touch eccentric."

"What happened to your eye?" Billy had barely been listening to the PM, his attention was on Felix.

"I was attacked by a bird, someone with a trick, I think."

"Sounds about right. You know, I could fix that for you. Do you still have the eye?"

"No."

What if he wanted to see it? This guy was clearly pretty fixated on people with tricks. Surely he would recognise Felix, the original trickster. "The bird ate it."

"Shame, would be a good one. I'm sure we could find you an eye." Billy looked to his advisors behind him, but none of them responded. And then the Prime Minister realised that the look hadn't been directed to his advisors, but to the wall behind them. The Angel of Death was in the room with them. Of course she could find an eye, she could be out the door and back with a whole human head before they finished their biscuits.

"Thank you, but it's OK, I like it."

Billy narrowed his eyes suspiciously.

"It's a reminder... Of what we're up against."

"Good answer... What we are up against. Let me tell you what I have in mind."

And Billy Winn continued to lay out a proposition for the Prime Minister and Felix.

For a statesman that was usually so broad-strokes in his public pronouncements, and someone who wasn't shy about essentially publicly executing people, his proposal was surprisingly nuanced. Someone on his team had clearly taken great care to make sure that this was something the Prime Minister would be able to sell parliament and the British people on. He also used a negotiating tactic that had worked for him in the past, by which he starts from such an outrageous position that anything else seems reasonable. Billy's opening position was a total genocide. He wanted the UK to implement a similar programme to the one he had instigated in the US. It was clear to see why Billy would want this. In his blanket destruction of tricksters, he was likely concerned that he had left his nation at a disadvantage from a military perspective. Any number of tricks had potential military uses, and in the US this was going largely untapped. Of course, he did have the get-out that if someone was born with an exceptionally useful ability, he could certainly classify it as a miracle, but it would be even better if no other nations had tricksters at all. He had decided that the UK would be an excellent place to start.

Admirably, this was something that the Prime Minister was unwilling to do. Somewhat less admirably, he compensated by giving Billy essentially everything else he asked for. He agreed to legal immunity for the Church of Divine Justice's members to "defend themselves against people with inhuman abilities", and thus the X-Force was created. He sanctioned the building of four new mega-churches in which CDJ followers could congregate, with the first one to be located at the site of the old Battersea Power Station. And he made promises to consult the Church on future policies.

Such is the Prime Minister's nature, that after the meeting he was less concerned that he had just essentially given away his nation and more concerned that he perhaps hadn't done enough to please the President.

The PM had not come away from the meeting happy at all, and he had taken his anger out largely on Dr Sheers. He complained that Felix had offered "nothing but criticism of every decision I made" and had given him "absolutely no help at all on the President's intentions."

Felix had come away from the meeting looking shell-shocked and was uncharacteristically silent.

"What is more, when he did shake the President's hand, he..." the Prime Minister paused, looking for the right phrasing, "aggressively soiled himself." He found it.

"He's the devil," muttered Felix.

"You're fired."

"Me or him?" said Dr Sheers.

"Both of you," said the Prime Minister.

14

GREAT WEATHER FOR DUCKS

I t was shortly after the Prime Minister met with Billy Winn that the Winters Act came into effect. I remember it clearly because I was just starting my second year at the special school and it radically changing the focus of the lessons. In the first year, there had been much more of a sense of a promising future for all of us. Because of the nature of tricks, it isn't really possible to have a one-size-fits-all approach to teaching. The thinking was that if each child was to be given the best possible opportunity to excel (and this was initially the idea of these schools) then we would need one-on-one tutoring, tailored to our specific ability.

As far as I can recall, this had worked pretty well. We would all learn normal subjects like maths, English, science, or whatever, in one big class, but for two hours most days, we would be taken off for private tutoring where we would each be given the opportunity to nurture our own ability.

One of the challenges, of course, was that some of the abilities were so unique that no one could be considered an expert in them. Instead, the teachers were recruited from an assortment of willing tutors with science, sports coaching, and military backgrounds. My teacher was a strict but fair retired Navy officer named Lieutenant McKinley. She had spent her whole career on submarines and naturally thought that would be a fantastic vocation for me. I can't argue with the fact that being able to shrink things down small would be useful in such a cramped environment. The fact that I can't do it for very long did seem to be a limiting factor. Also, even at the time I remember thinking that being the sailor responsible for shoving giant quantities of rations into people's footlockers might not be the most imaginative use of my particular skill. That's usually what a our lessons involved, building up really huge and well ordered piles of things (we used gym mats), shrinking them down, and putting them inside small things (we used a biscuit tin).

The point I'm making is that the lessons had a purpose, and a feeling that after school I would be in demand from employers because of my trick. It was similar for the other kids. Ziggy, whose trick would mean he would now unfortunately be referred to as a "creeper", used to spend an hour or two most days half-being a tree. He was a really big fan of animals, and he thought that perhaps he could be a wildlife photographer. He had practiced so that he could push almost all of his body into the tree, and then have just a hand and the bit of his face poking out. He used to take incredible pictures of nesting birds really close-up, without them being aware at all of his presence. And this was all encouraged and nurtured by his teacher. As his teacher was another ex-military person, I assume they were thinking it would be easy enough just to swap out the camera for a sniper rifle, and the wildlife for assorted enemy combatants, but maybe that's just me being cynical.

Anyway, this is how it was until the Winters Law came in. Johnny Winters, who the law is named for, was a passably entertaining meteorologist. He did the weather reports for a major UK broadcaster for twenty odd years. The television studio he reported from was at the top of one of the tallest buildings in London, and the huge glass windows behind him overlooked the city. It was a nice enough way to get a quick idea of what the weather was like. The issue for Johnny was that, unfortunately, he was neither as entertaining or, it turns out, as good at predicting the weather as a sixteen-year-old-girl with a trick and a duck. Kelly Goodwin's weather reports had been gradually growing in popularity for some time, but recently there had been a surge on account of an article in a national newspaper.

Kelly's setup was far less grand than Johnny's. She would simply stroll down to her local park, put a camera on a tripod and deliver a weather forecast for her local area for the next week or so. These were a kind of "and finally" segment on a minor regional broadcaster, for people who found the actual weather forecast too formal or something. The hook was that she was supposedly getting these weather reports from a duck named Bill. She would stand by the pond and call out his name and Bill would come paddling over. She would then pick him up and whisper a few things in his ear, and Bill would usually quack a bit. Then she'd pop him back in the pond and send him on his way.

Like most people, I'd assumed that the trickiest thing going on here was training a duck to respond to his name. If you were planning a day out with a friend, you might jokingly check The Duck Forecast, and sporting events would sometimes light-heartedly allude to The Duck Forecast if rain stopped play. It's not like anyone was using it to plan critical events or anything.

The thing is, though, they should have been.

A statistics PhD student had been looking for some data to analyse for his thesis, and they had decided to use weather reports. The object was to compare a lot of reports and see if there were statistically meaningful differences. They had chosen the forecasts of a handful of national newspapers, the

TV reports from the major broadcasters (including Johnny Winters') and, almost as an afterthought, they had thrown in The Duck Forecast. According to the student, this was as close as they could get to a control group, as in their mind, it was someone taking a random guess at what the weather would be like with no meteorological equipment. Their idea was to apply a number of cutting-edge statistical analysis tools to the data, something about "small sample size minor variation analysis of..." you don't need to know all that. The point is, that there was no analysis really required. The Duck Forecast had so far broadcast 232 weather reports and not been wrong once, about anything. If Kelly said it would be raining at 4 pm, it was, every time. For comparison, the other reports were right about 70-90% of the time on general predictions and 50-80% on specific predictions. It didn't need a statistics PhD to tell you that Kelly had some sort of trick. Either ducks can predict weather with 100% accuracy and Kelly's trick was being able to chat with them or, as I think is more likely, Kelly's trick is being able to perfectly predict the weather, and she just happens to have a duck friend.

The student's report got picked up by the papers, and before long a major broadcaster offered her a job as a full-time meteorologist. This was Johnny Winters' job.

Johnny had apparently already been quite staunchly anti-trick. Felix had met him at a party years before this and described him as "possibly the most instantly-dislikable person" he had ever met. Anyway, after Johnny had been handed his notice, he still had a few shows left to do. He didn't forgo the opportunity to tell the world about the menace of these tricksters. It wasn't "just me", he ranted. "Eventually these abominations (I'm guessing he was a Billy Winn fan) would soon be taking all our jobs, our livelihoods, and our way of life. All over the country," he said, "people were being put out of work by tricksters. There were factory workers out on the streets, replaced by freaks, postal workers would be a thing of the past, with whole towns serviced by just one abomination, and this was just the beginning."

In fairness, there was actually some truth to Johnny's rant. A small shoe factory in Kent had replaced its workforce with just one employee with a trick. The employee happened to be the son of the owner of the factory. He did also have a trick though. I don't know exactly what it was but apparently it made him very good at making shoes. And three postmen had been reassigned and replaced with a postal worker with a trick. He was just a pretty fast walker. It wasn't a particularly exceptional trick or I think he would have got a better job. That wasn't what had made Johnny's rant memorable though. These stories were already pretty well known. What made Johnny's rant really memorable was that he concluded it by running at full speed into the glass window at the back of the studio. The first time, the glass cracked but Johnny bounced off. He turned back and, with a bloody, broken nose, stared straight into the camera and shouted, "You're next, you're all next!" Then he had another go, and this time the glass gave way.

The network was too slow to interrupt the broadcast, and the whole thing went out live. Trying to avoid just showing a broken, bloody window, the producers had cut to the under-standably startled newsreader, who panicked and just started reading the Autocue.

"Thank you for that, Johnny, and for your many years of wonderful reporting. On behalf of myself and everyone else at the network, we wish you all the best with everything in the future." She paused for a moment, seemingly aware that John-ny's future of a pavement at speed was not something you could wish someone "the best with", and then just continued to read.

"It's great weather for ducks! Well let's hope so, as next

week we look forward to greeting our new weather correspondent, the lovely Kelly Goodwin and her adorable helper Bill."

It was an incredibly memorable piece of television, especially for a weather report, and it certainly got the nation talking. And then someone stabbed the fast-walking postman to death.

In response both to a "public outcry" and the incessant campaigning both in parliament and in print of Virgil Barnett, politicians got to work drafting new legislation. The stabbing of the postman enabled the government to frame the upcoming bill as something "intended to protect people with non-standard attributes from hostility." As well as being a measure to "even the playing field for the conventionally-abled in the employment arena."

The act is technically called something like the Special Abilities Protection Statute, but in recognition of Johnny Winters' spectacular swan dive into the history books, it is usually referred to as the Winters Act. The Winters Act forbids any person gaining an "employment advantage by reason of use of a non-normal ability" and mandates giant financial penalties for any company that flouts it. There have been cases of large corporations brought close to bankruptcy for employing even one person with a trick. The Church of Divine Justice will pay a bounty to any person who reports a trickster at their job. The general public were encouraged to get involved as well, with a tabloid newspaper running a wildly popular "Sneak on a Freak" feature, where they would investigate any person reported by their readers. It was out of character for the press to come right out and call people with tricks "freaks", but I guess the search for a rhyming headline had taken priority over subtlety.

It's almost impossible to prove you aren't using your trick to gain some sort of advantage if you happen to have one, so essentially, if you have a trick and you have a job, at some point there is going to be trouble. And so we all became basically unemployable. At school, there was an immediate shift as soon as the Winters Act had been voted into law. I didn't have any more lessons with Lieutenant McKinley, as apparently there was no longer a promising future for me in packing crates of beans onto submarines. Ziggy wasn't going to be a wildlife photographer/sniper.

When I went back for the second year, the majority of the teachers had not returned. Year groups had been merged together, and there were no longer any specific classes on how to use our tricks. In fact, the exhibiting of any form of special ability was now forbidden. There was now a mandatory school uniform, a highly visible jumpsuit type thing. This was apparently to make us easy to spot if we got lost in the grounds. Being as we were never allowed out into the grounds, what they meant by this is if we escaped. This was probably smart on their part, as there was almost no one who wasn't considering running away. The challenge was that all of the budget they were saving from not having any form of decent teaching staff seemed to have been invested into a giant squad of armed guards. Supposedly for our protection, these burly military types with thermal imaging goggles and tasers would now patrol the facility at all times.

Jackson was faced with a fairly unusual tactical conundrum, one likely never faced before in military history. The squirrel had tasked him with putting on a rescue mission wherein he would infiltrate a compound guarded by potentially tens of thousands of armed combatants, on his own.

There was no doubt that this was going to be an intensely challenging task, but there were a couple of factors that convinced him that it might be achievable. Firstly, his bouncy bones make him almost indestructible. Secondly, most of the people he had to get past were Bobbetts, who while often incredibly physically strong, do not usually have a great capacity for tactical thought.

He had miraculously managed to have a fairly long, if somewhat ambiguous, conversation with the Tess squirrel without alerting his fellow Bobbetts to his non-Bobbettness. He'd stayed on the fringe of a large group around his age, and slipped away near the armoury building at the rear of the firing range. The key giveaways were his frozen-joy-face and the squirrel poking out of his front pocket, but so far no one seemed to have noticed either.

As he peered into the armoury, he'd realised that perhaps the biggest consideration was going to be more moral than tactical. It turned out that Terrence Bobbett had managed to get hold of an obscene amount of weaponry. At the rear of the shooting range, a guy in military fatigues that didn't look much like a Bobbett, in that he appeared relatively young but didn't seem to be utterly thrilled at absolutely everything, was handing out big guns to old Bobbetts.

From a purely tactical consideration, the easiest thing for Jackson to do would have been to just storm into the armoury and grab the most sinister weapon he could find and turn it on literally everyone. Sure, he'd probably get shot a fair bit, but nothing too serious. Maybe not even that. All the heavily armed ones had their guns pointed down the shooting range, so he could probably kill most of them before they even had a chance to turn around. Old ones are almost slow, and the guns are heavy. But before you go thinking that Jackson is a murderous monster, remember that this is if he were to consider his options from a purely tactical perspective. He isn't, and he didn't. He decided that he was going to have to try and accomplish his mission while killing the fewest number of Bobbetts possible, that number ideally being zero. Bobbetts are, after all, essentially innocent. It's not even like they have much choice in any of this. They've been raised without knowledge of any other way of life, and most of them will never even survive to be teenagers. The other people dotted about, Terrence Bobbett's hired help, Jackson figured were fair game. If you accept a job militarising ultra-toddlers, you've got to be willing to face some consequences. So, having established the ground rules, he then has to figure out the best way to proceed. Would it even be worth his trouble to get a machine gun? Probably not. It's easy to think of Bobbetts as slow-minded, but they really aren't. In many ways, they are hyper-vigilant. Walking back through the armoury with a weapon would be akin to sneaking past a six year old's birthday party with a cake. One of them is going to see you, and a fuss is going to be made. And, much like at the children's birthday party, that fuss would likely be catastrophic.

He figures the safest approach will be to arm himself as best he can with whatever is nearest, and try to make his way to Big School without raising the alarm. He finds a claw hammer; in fact, he finds a lot of them. He decides to scurry and crawl through a patch of woods that lead a large part of the way to the main house, and it turns out that the woods are positively littered with hammers. Terrence had recently become convinced that they were ideal weapons for a young Bobbett. They had several advantages over a machete, which he had also experimented with. They were similarly effective in combat, in that you really wouldn't want to be struck hard by a muscular six foot Bobbett with either one of them, but hammers had other advantages. Firstly, the Bobbetts were much less likely to hurt themselves with them. Hammer accidents did happen fairly frequently to be sure, but they were significantly less destructive than the constant machete limb-severing incidents that had plagued generations F through H. Secondly, they were easily attainable. Sure, anyone can buy *a* machete, but put in an order for twenty thousand of the things and questions are going to be asked, more than likely, in parliament. Twenty thousand hammers, on the other hand, could be passed off as the kind of grand incompetent construction project that Terrence Bobbett was becoming famous for. Bobbetts are forgetful and easily distracted though, and so they would often drop their assigned hammer as they wandered off to do something more interesting. Jackson probably could have picked up fifty as he went if he wanted, but he figures that two will probably be plenty. The squirrel in his pocket nods in agreement.

———

"It's your daughter, Prime Minister. Emily... she's been killed by guerrillas."

"What?" said the understandably shocked Prime Minister.

"I'm so sorry," said his private secretary, who had already made a number of career-ending mistakes.

Firstly, he had decided that this news was so earth-shatteringly urgent that he should burst in and tell the Prime Minister right away, even though the PM happened to be in the middle of a soon to be televised meet-and-greet with a fireman that had rescued six puppies from a burning building. Accordingly, this whole tragi-baffling conversation was recorded for posterity. Secondly, he had not taken the time to ascertain the exact facts of the situation before barging in, so when the fireman broke the uncomfortable silence to ask "guerrillas or gorillas?" The PM's secretary actually wasn't sure.

"What?" said the secretary, buying some time.

"What?" echoed the shell-shocked PM. I'm quoting this verbatim.

"Sorry, was it 'guerrillas'?" said the fireman. He mimed someone shooting someone, presumably Emily, in the head.

"Or gorillas." He mimed a primate tearing something, presumably Emily, apart with its hands.

The PM looked understandably devastated. I can't imagine this encounter did a huge amount for the fireman's career either. On that note, I should also point out that, in rescuing the puppies, he had neglected to rescue the human occupants of the building, two of whom had died in the blaze. The British public's love for pets was such that this was merely a footnote to his heroic rescue though.

"There were three of them, apparently," said the secretary, checking his notes.

"Guerrillas?" choked out the devastated PM.

"Or gorillas," said the fireman, doing the mauling mime again.

I'm not sure if the fireman knew this but the PM's daughter was currently on a school expedition to Rwanda, one of the few places on Earth where it was entirely plausible that she had been killed by either the armed militia-type *guerrillas* or the hairy forest-dwelling *gorillas*. For this reason, the personal secretary made the belatedly sensible decision to double-check his facts before continuing.

If you don't know already, I shan't spoil it for you, but the important piece of information for our purposes is that she was confirmed to be very much dead. Ironically, the PM had been very encouraging of the trip. The meeting with Billy Winn had gone badly, so badly that he had been fretting over not just his own but his family's personal security ever since. It had seemed like an excellent idea to have her as far away from him as possible. And so she had gone, and now she was dead, and he wouldn't even be able to tell her how sorry he was... And then, of course, he realised that he could.

15

THE HELICOPTER TO NOTHINGNESS

G iven how many X-Force members seemed to arrive based on just an anonymous tip about a made-up superpower, I suppose it is no surprise that they arrive in force when they are notified by Terrence that he has detained a genuine wanted trickster. He actually has two, of course. To his future regret, I'm sure, he hadn't thought to ask if Tess had any kind of trick.

And it is thanks to Tess' trick that, from inside our padded cell, we know that so far, a total of six SUVs and a troop carrier have arrived at the entrance of the main T-BAIT building. The troops happen to arrive just ahead of Jackson. His first instinct had been to approach this issue in the same way I had once seen him put up a shelf, from behind with a hammer. Fortunately he doesn't, as I'm assuming it would have led to similarly disastrous results. Upon seeing the ridiculous quantity of experimental weaponry they are pulling from the vehicles, he decides to stay hidden until he can better assess the situation.

It's difficult to ascertain the exact hierarchy within the X-Force. I think because they are essentially a volunteer organisation, they are pretty free and easy when assigning ranks. Not many people want to give up their free time to be a private, and as such, I don't think I've ever seen an X-Force with that rank. In fact, I've never seen anyone that wasn't some kind of officer. Even in the UK, they seem to be using the US military ranks as a starting point, but this has been merged somewhat with positions from within the Church. These bizarre concoctions are printed proudly on the front of the officers' uniforms, so at the moment we know that three Reverend Captains are consulting with a Bishop Major about the best way to approach and, presumably, kill me.

We know this because they are having this conversation within listening distance of two Alsatian dogs that they have brought with them. X-Force often travel with dogs, as they aren't nearly as susceptible to tricksters with camouflage or transparency type abilities as people are. Dogs tend to use smell as their primary sense, rather than sight. What this gives Tess, though, is a useful window into their ongoing debate.

"Judging by the carnage at the transport van, I think one of them might have some sort of fire power," says the Reverend Captain, with an air of experience.

"So, you think we need *more* firepower?" says the Bishop Major.

"No, well, yes. Maybe. But I mean it may literally have the power to set things on fire. Apparently, the guys in the prison transport were melted to the bone."

"Body armour, then?" says another Reverend Captain. "I think there is a fireproof one, like racing drivers wear, maybe with a gas mask."

The Bishop likes the sound of this. "Sure, see if you can find one of those." He shoves him in the direction of the troop carrier. "Let's see what he comes up with. Maybe we can send him in first, see what they make of him. You got thermal imaging?"

The Reverend nods.

"See how hot he gets, if it sets fire to him or anything."

Just as he is checking his thermal imaging camera, the Reverend suddenly spots something and raises a rifle to his shoulder.

"Freeze."

"Wait, wait, wait! I'm not one of them, I called you!" said Terrence, seemingly unaware how close he had just come to being shot. This is the first time I've seen them leave even the smallest of gaps between shouting "freeze" and firing.

"I'm Terrence Bobbett, this is my institute, I'm on your side."

"It's him," confirms the Major. "I recognise him from TV. He was campaigning for the Prime Minister."

As Terrence approaches the group, the Alsatians start barking ferociously. Maybe this is Tess' doing, or perhaps dogs just find him to be about as creepy as most people do.

"I'm Bishop Major Stock." He shakes Terrence's hand. "I understand you have secured the suspect."

"Two of them, in my cool-down room."

"What's a cool-down room?"

"Oh, it's a secure room. If one of the students is acting up, or overly aggressive, we can shut them up to cool off for a bit. I've locked them in."

"It's cool?" says the Bishop, possibly hoping it will help with the fire threat.

"No."

At this point, one of the Captains, apparently his name is Dawson, returns wearing what looks like a firefighting outfit with armoured plates somewhat randomly applied.

"I think this is it. It said 'retardant'."

"Well you sure look retardant," says the other Captain, and then to Terrence, "Where is this room?"

"It's on the second floor. Go up the main staircase and it's the furthest room straight ahead on the left. The door is double bolted from the outside."

"Careful, he's a rapist!"

Terrence had stepped quite close to the Bishop to confide this information to him, and one of the soldiers milling about, an Admiral of the Fleet Archdeacon or something, thought it helpful to shout a warning.

"And what tricks can they do? Have you seen?"

"It was statutory, and those charges were dropped." He turns back to the Bishop. "I'm on your side, for Christ's sake."

It perhaps doesn't help that several Bobbetts, of varying ages and abilities, have followed Terrence out of the house and are currently investigating their new visitors. Possibly as a result of some previous training, this often involves reaching their hands into any pockets on clothing that they can get to, to see what is in there. The soldiers don't seem to like this at all.

At this point I don't know what happens, as Tess is currently giving her full attention to the squirrel, or rather to Jackson via the squirrel, in order to convey, via the medium of mime, our current location.

Jimmy's first few days on the oil rig had involved a lot of eating, none of it good. It seemed that the scientists were keen to find out what kind of size and weight of object he was able to keep down. At first, these were progressively larger and larger plastic bricks. The scientists would time each one and note the results. This was far from the worst thing that had happened to Jimmy since he'd been sentenced. In fact, he was somewhat enjoying finding out what he was capable of in such a regimented fashion.

The tests became more disconcerting though, as the focus turned to how long things could survive inside him. This involved him eating a cat with custom SCUBA gear, wrapped in an oversized sandwich bag. It was a deeply unpleasant meal and, judging by the internal wriggling, the cat hadn't enjoyed it much either. Jimmy wondered what exactly the scientist was writing in the extensive notes he seemed to be making. "Feline test subject dislikes both breathing apparatus and being consumed by large man."

What was the purpose of this? Was there some sort of secret mission that would require a well-known cat to be smuggled somewhere inside his stomach?

And then the cat kicked him in the kidney and he threw up. He threw up a cat. It doesn't say a huge amount for the US prison system that he was still regarding this as a slight improvement in his situation.

The return of Felix and Max improved his mood further. The scientists would initially only rarely conceive of experiments that required one of them. Sometimes Felix would be asked to consult on various things. He'd watch tapes and look for signs of deception. He really needed to be there in person to use his trick fully, but he had enough of a sense of human character that he was fairly accurate with the tapes.

Once they had got the general idea that if something was smaller than Jimmy, that he could probably eat it, there didn't seem to be much else to be learned from further experimentation. So, the prisoners would be pretty much left to their own devices. There was no heightened security or anything. There didn't need to be as they were on an oil rig in the middle of the North Sea. They would play pool or poker and just chat. They got on well. Also, Felix is a ridiculously good source of celebrity gossip, and Jimmy eats that stuff up like a comatose cellmate.

Later, Max had a much tougher time of it, as eventually the researchers found something genuinely useful for him to do. One of the MI6 officers on the rig had previously worked with Scotland Yard, and he was chatting with an old colleague about a real head-scratcher of a case. It was an apparent suicide by hanging with the door locked from the inside, but something about the scene didn't look right to the detective assigned it.

He couldn't figure what it was, but something was off, perhaps because the victim had apparently purchased a new rowing machine on the morning he had supposedly killed himself, which just didn't seem right to the veteran detective. The impulse to take up rowing, and the impulse to end your life, just seemed to come from different states of mind. The detective had suspected foul play, but given that the victim had been found hanging inside a room locked from the inside, he thought that perhaps some sort of trick had been involved. As the MI6 guy was running through a list of the tricks he knew of that could enable someone to hang someone inside a locked room (Creepers were the go-to trickster for this kind of thing. They're capable of it and it's in keeping with their general reputation), he'd had a brilliant idea. Why don't we just ask the victim?

They had kept the cadaver in storage while the investigation was ongoing, and the special unit had the sort of reach that could get these things done. The corpse was flown out to the oil rig that very afternoon, and Max had him up and chatting in no time. Somewhat disappointingly, it turned out it was a suicide after all. The rowing machine had apparently been ordered on a whim months earlier and had taken a long time to arrive. Like many suicide survivors, the reanimated corpse seemed to be experiencing a new appreciation of life. He mentioned that he was now especially eager to try out the new rowing machine. Obviously, this wasn't going to happen, but there didn't seem to be any particular need to tell him that, as they loaded him happily onto the chopper back to the mainland.

This was just the beginning though. Everyone was happy to have something more tangibly beneficial to the public good come from the unit than Casandra-esque political advice and cat eating. A memo was quietly circulated around ongoing murder investigations — they were looking for cases where the victim would potentially be able to identify the killer. Priority was given first to cases where the body of the deceased was still in the morgue, but later on, once the program had shown itself to be remarkably effective, the police began to exhume the victims of some classic whodunnits.

In a landmark case, the video testimony from two victims of a serial killer was shown in court and led inevitably to his conviction. The amount of press this generated led to an absolute deluge of requests for Max's assistance. There were requests from police departments all around the world, begging Max to let them interrogate the often long-dead. The vast majority, however, were from people already convicted of murder. Somewhat surprisingly, it seemed that almost every convicted murderer in the world was convinced that the victim would completely exonerate them if only they were given the chance. There was a guy in Ohio who, and I swear I'm not making this up, was willing to finally reveal to the police the location of his wife's body, on the condition that they bring her back for one last interview.

But still, the biggest victim in all this was probably Max. A young boy who was already painfully alone in the world, having lost his whole family, now spent most days returning people from the dead, only to let them die again moments later. He'd never really had a friend his own age. He didn't even get much of a chance to hang out with Felix and Jimmy anymore, as he was in constant demand for crime solving. For red-ball cases, where it was feared the killer might strike again soon, recently murdered bodies would arrive at all times of day and night, to be magicked back into existence for a few terrifying moments to attempt to identify their killer.

This troubled Felix. It wasn't just the physical toll that

performing his trick so frequently was taking on Max, but the emotional damage it was doing. This non-stop parade of death, anger and revenge was going to break him eventually, if it hadn't already.

Jackson is still crouched in the grass, waiting for the right moment to get involved, but the dogs are going crazy, barking and tugging at their leashes. He worries that they might have seen him, or smelled him, or something. And then, he remembers that he essentially has Tess in his pocket, and if anyone can sort the dogs out, she can. So he pops the squirrel out in front of him and starts signing. The squirrel looks confused, so he points at the dog and starts playing out making a distraction, but as a dog, miming biting and the like. Anyway, she seems to understand. Then one of the dogs bites Terrence on the leg, and he starts shouting furiously.

Pretty much everyone is looking at Terrence, the X-Force guys because he is shouting, the Bobbetts because they always seem to look at Terrence if he's about. Anyway, it's the perfect opportunity to sneak up behind these guys without being seen. Jackson dashes across the driveway and scooches in behind the big SUV that is furthest out.

He thinks he got away with it, but unfortunately an X-Force officer walks around almost immediately. She stands still for a moment, in silence, looking right at him. In fairness to Jackson, he doesn't have long to make a decision, and he is very aware that he really needs to prevent her from raising any kind of alarm. Anyway, he swings both hammers at her face as hard as he can. He uses the side for pulling out nails, so they perform more like axes than hammers. They clank together right in the middle of her head. I'm sure someone would have heard it if the dogs hadn't been making such a racket.

He thinks about taking her gun, but it has an ominous yellow barrel and he doesn't know what it does, so he figures he'll stick with the hammers. They've been effective so far.

A couple of the Bobbetts, young ones by the looks of it, have been grabbing at the pockets of a pair of X-Force officers, and they are pushing them back. The X-Force guy is shouting in the tall Bobbett's face, but this just seems to make it more keen, like they are playing a game. He pushes it hard and then pulls up his rifle, aiming it right at his head, but the Bobbett doesn't seem to mind at all. He is kind of trying to look right down the barrel, and this guy is really starting to lose his temper. The soldier is so focused on the Bobbett in front of him that he doesn't spot the little one behind him swiping the sidearm from his holster.

He's shouting like a drill instructor for this Bobbett to back off, and the little one shoots him in the back of the head with his own pistol. Now they have everyone's attention. The X-Force guys are all brandishing their rifles, spinning in circles, not sure who to go for first.

Terrence shouts, "Wait, no!" but it's too late, as one of the Bishops with some kind of flame thrower has just incinerated the young Bobbett with the pistol. He doesn't die right away. He spins around shooting rounds in every direction, which of course gets the other X-Force troops firing away.

"Stop, stop," shouts Terrence, and then he blows his whistle and says, "Down." And in a second, every one of the Bobbetts, including the one that has just been shot about nine times and is on fire, sits down on the floor where they are.

"Which one of you morons gave Mickey a gun? Huh?"

No response. I don't think anyone else saw him take it.

"He's not old enough, he's not been trained. He was one of the good ones as well."

He seems genuinely upset.

"Right, get in there and get what you came for. I want you all off my property in five minutes."

It had been impossible to keep the fact that the Prime Minister's daughter had been killed a secret for long. There was a tape of the PM receiving the news, after all, that the documentary crew were very reluctant to relinquish no matter how hard various Downing Street staff had insisted.

The current stance from the Downing Street press team was that "she had been badly injured" but was being shipped back to the UK where "a world-leading NHS facility" was going to attempt to revive her.

The world leading NHS facility was a young boy called Max, and it seemed unlikely that reviving her was going to pose any significant challenge. He could probably revive most of a full-English breakfast if you asked him nicely.

It didn't help matters that the Prime Minister had remained almost entirely in seclusion from the general public since it had happened. He had apparently been reluctant to leave his daughter's side even for a moment, ever since the tragedy. In the first few days, the press had been somewhat respectful, giving the first family "as much space as they needed in this challenging time." Which, as it turns out, was quite a lot of space, as they were on a secret oil rig in the middle of the North Sea. Before long, though, questions were being asked, questions like "Where exactly is this NHS facility, and what exactly does it do?", "Would it be so hard to pop out for a quick press conference or something?" and "Wait, was it *gorillas* or *guerrillas*?"

It took an industrial-size international incident to finally get the Prime Minister to return to the mainland. An incident that would have consequences he could barely have begun to anticipate.

Felix Trent is a realist, probably above all else. A lifetime of perceiving people's inner desires will surely do that to you. The moment young Max had revived the Prime Minister's daughter, he was very conscious that his days were numbered. Now, it was surely only a matter of time before they sorted out new accommodations for Max. There was perhaps a faint possibility that Emily would be left on the rig, and the PM would just visit occasionally, but her father's presence was surely already drawing way too much attention to this supposedly secret facility. No, that wouldn't be it. There was also the faint possibility that the PM could just let his daughter die. That's what they had done with everyone else, after all, a few key questions and then back on the helicopter to nothingness. Everyone except for Felix that is.

And then one night, Max confirmed it. The poor kid had been crying all day. Apparently the PM's people had been discussing the new arrangements. He was going to have a whole new flat built just for him, and they were going to arrange for private tutors to give him "the very best education available". They'd wanted to know what his favourite games and hobbies were so they could get everything prepared for him.

Felix had consoled him, "It's for the best, Max. This could literally be the best thing for you. You'll have a pretty normal life, and you won't have to worry for anything at all. Anything you want, just ask, they can't say 'no' to you!"

"They did," said the sobbing Max. "They wouldn't give me anything I actually wanted."

"Why?"

"I wanted for you and Jimmy to come with us."

"Oh," said Felix.

It can't have been a hugely challenging choice for the Prime Minister, between his daughter, and a mangled trickster he had met once and disliked.

"Well, Jimmy will be OK. Hey, he survived federal prison."

"Only just... and you'll die."

"I'm already dead, kind of."

"Not to me," said Max.

16

A KIND OF MEAT ONESIE

A lot of people refer to the McMillan's murderous rampage as "the straw that broke the camel's back" of the whole trickster situation. Admittedly, this hypothetical camel had already sustained some pretty significant spinal injuries in the form of robberies, kidnappings, Steve the Ripper, and the whole Bobbett fiasco. Before the McMillans, though, it was perhaps still just about able to move its metaphorical hooves. The brothers from Ipswich put an end to that.

I would like to think that Joe and Chris McMillan's homicidal instincts are nothing to do with their trick, that they would maybe have been murderers anyway, that perhaps their trick just made them more effective murderers. However, I'm not sure that could be true. Murder is such an intrinsic part of their trick that it only seems reasonable to assume it came as a package deal.

The McMillan's trick, like a number of other tricksters, is that they can do a really good impression of pretty much anyone. Sadly, the person being impersonated won't be around to witness it though because, thankfully, unlike any other tricksters yet discovered, the way they can make the impression so uncanny is by removing their victim's skeleton and organs and wearing their skin as a kind of meat onesie. It doesn't just look like a skin-costume though, that wouldn't really be a trick, more a horrific outfit.

Once they have put on the person's skin, within a few minutes it has become one with them. To all intents and purposes, they would be indistinguishable from the living person. Their height and weight change to the approximate physiology of their victim, and they can do a pretty good vocal imitation using the victim's own voice box. It's already easy to understand the devastating consequences such a trick might have, but the way in which Joe and Chris use it seems to be designed to deliberately inflict the most emotional damage possible. I'll skip over some of the worst examples, but here's enough to give you a flavour.

In the last known pictures of the brothers, they appear to be between twelve and fourteen years old. No one knows what they would have looked like beyond that point, as they were permanently inside someone else's skin. It seems unlikely that they even have their own skin anymore, just a perpetual succession of new victims, like constantly re-wallpapering a room without ever stripping back the old layers.

Chris was the first to discover his trick. He killed a school friend (Stacey Lawton) and buried her skeleton in the woods. Subsequently, he lived with her family for around ten days, before the skeleton was discovered by a dog walker. He had correctly ascertained that it was only a matter of time before they'd identify the body and wonder what the creature was that had been living in Stacey's house all this time. This would be the most startling answer imaginable to the mystery of her declining maths grades. Also, Chris McMillan had of course been reported missing. In a video in police archives that is particularly chilling, Stacey Lawton herself is interviewed about Chris' disappearance.

Chris then decided to return home. His father recognised this Stacey girl as one of the last people to see his missing son, and let her in. Chris had apparently either become bored of being Stacey, or he just wanted to test out his new trick some more. He killed his father, Gregory, at some point during the day. He put on his skin, collected the remaining bones and organs in bin liners and put the bin liners under his bed. The less we imagine about the next bit, the better, but it was eight days before anyone discovered that anything untoward had even happened to Gregory McMillan. He even went to work a few times (Gregory had been a gas safety inspector, and Chris apparently just told everyone that their gas was fine. This won't be the only example of Chris McMillan having a rather casual attitude towards the safety of others).

Eventually, the smell emanating from the boys' room became so strong that their mother went to investigate. As she was staring in disbelief at her husband's remains, Chris smashed her over the back of the head with a toaster oven and then waited for his brother to get back from school.

Joe had a lot of new information to take in. Firstly, his father was dead. This was a particularly challenging piece of information to take on board, as it was, from Joe's perspective, told to him *by his father*. Chris informed him with glee that it had in fact been him rather than his father living with them for the last week or so. This explained his father's inability to help Joe with his maths homework, but posed many more questions.

I should point out at this point that seemingly none of those questions was "why?" It apparently seemed innately obvious to both of the McMillan brothers that as soon as you had the opportunity to kill your parents, this was definitely something that you would do.

Joe was excited to see if he could do the trick too, and Chris was happy to show him the ropes. Before long, their mother was up and strolling to the local pub, and there was another set of bones in a bin liner under the boys' bed. The boys spent the next few days drinking in a few different establishments, a drinking binge that many of the locals understood to be a reaction to their son's tragic disappearance.

Over several drunken days, the boys developed the seed of a plan, a plan that would eventually become perhaps the most polished and sinister modus operandi in British criminal history.

If you were to encounter Chris or Joe McMillan, and I hope for your sake that you never do, you'd probably like them. You may, in fact, love them, but let's start at the beginning of a new chain.

Chris would usually do his scouting for victims as a young child. Joe favoured the body of an attractive woman when it was his turn. You can hear them weigh up the pros and cons of each in interviews they later gave from captivity. Apparently, people are less suspicious of the child and more likely to be honest, but younger victims will often be reported missing more quickly.

So, you meet this chatty lost child on the street. He'll tell you something along the lines of "my parents didn't pick me up from school because they were in an accident" or maybe "I got separated from them when they were shopping, and I don't know how to get home." A number of people survived these encounters, so there are several accounts. Few ever suspected there was anything disingenuous going on. It was usually random chance (they were in a hurry or not local) that saved them, rather than any suspicion of Chris. This little kid is going to try and find out a few things from you: where you live, who you live with, what you do for a living, what your partner or parents or children do for a living. He doesn't need all of this information, and this inquisitive little child is going to make it sound very friendly and natural. If he gets some answers he likes, he is going to try to get you to a quiet place where he can stab you in the lower back and remove your skin. More often than not, this will be your own bathtub. I know this won't come as much of a consolation, but you probably haven't even had the worst available experience for a McMillan victim. At least your part is over; for your family and friends, this is just the beginning.

Generally, Chris or Joe would try and get a sense of the person's life from their house. Once you have access to a person's home, you have access to a lot of their personal information. Combine that with looking and sounding exactly like them, and it is easy enough to, say, make a bank transfer or simply withdraw some cash. They did this with their first few victims, collecting up sports bags full of banknotes, until they realised that there wasn't really any point. With every layer of skin, they had perhaps moved further and further from any sense of self. Who they were right now was who they were full stop. In short, they stopped looking to take things away from people and started looking to become people whose lives they would enjoy.

Starting with relatively simple aspirations, Joe spent nearly a month living in the home of the boy from his school who had the best selection of computer games. Chris wasn't so big on computer games and had mostly spent his days fishing. This would almost sound wholesome if it didn't inevitably imply that there would be some bin bags full of bones in a cellar somewhere. As time passed, though, and they expanded their horizons, they would seek out people with access to fast cars, glamorous lifestyles and luxury apartments in exotic locations. What they had discovered was that, in a *Six Degrees of Separation* way, almost any person was only a few friends or relatives away from someone living the high life. If they started with someone with a half-decent job that was living in a nice area, then they were probably only one or two steps away. You see, when the curious little kid on the street with the sob story about being lost on a school trip asks you all those seemingly innocuous questions, it's probably not because he's after your stuff. More than likely, he just wants to borrow your skin for a bit so he can get to your sister's ex-husband's beach house.

A typical discovery of a McMillan victim would be something along the lines of someone not returning from a three-week tropical vacation, a vacation they had departed on suddenly, with little or no notice. Perhaps they had been acting strangely for the day or two prior to departure. They may have had slight memory loss or asked unusual questions. It would not be uncommon for other family members or a close friend to go missing at a similar time, which would add to the impression that maybe they weren't dead, maybe they had run away with an old childhood sweetheart. It would usually be months before the bones were found, if they were ever found at all. The boys had got better at that as well. Later on, they would burn the remains or dump them out at sea. Even now, some families will never know what happened to their loved ones. Maybe they had decided to fly to the Bahamas on a whim? Maybe they are still out travelling the world? Anything had to be better to believe than the possibility that their bodies had been burned on the beach while a fourteen-year-old psychopath took their skin for a two-week joyride.

It's possible that they never would have been caught if it wasn't for the crisis of conscious of an Italian hotel proprietor. After all, it would require a huge leap of imagination for a detective confronted with a bag of bones and an out of character Caribbean vacation to start looking for... whatever the

McMillan brothers are. It turned out that for many years, the hotelier, a mild-mannered pervert in his early sixties named Joseppe Russo, had placed secret cameras in a number of the bedrooms and bathrooms of his hotel. This luckily included the honeymoon suite, where Chris McMillan had been staying. Chris was checked in as Donatella Brigante, the 24-year-old heiress to a freight shipping company. She had been sharing the suite with her fiancé, Maxwell Thomas, a 32-year-old lever-aged-buyout specialist, for nearly a week, when Joseppe witnessed something horrific.

He was reviewing the tapes of the suite's opulent shower when he saw Ms Brigante drag in the unconscious body of Mr Thomas. Ms Brigante then proceeded to cut a long strip along the line of her fiancé's spine using the foil cutter of the waiter's friend corkscrew from the hotel minibar. Joseppe watched, in shocked amazement, as Ms Brigante expertly removed the man's entire skeleton and placed it in an oversized drinks cooler. This was made all the more bizarre by the fact that Joseppe had just spoken to Maxwell Thomas that morning. Mr Thomas had arranged a car service to drop him at a local marina. He checked the time stamp on the video and confirmed that it had definitely been recorded the night before, and then watched in bemused horror as Donatella Brigante climbed into the skin of her former fiancé and then reached behind herself to zip him up like a cocktail dress.

Joseppe was confronted by a moral dilemma. What he had caught on tape was obviously something that demanded immediate police attention. This wasn't just a murder but a dangerous trick that had never been witnessed before. There was nothing illegal about having a trick in Italy. In fact, trick-sters in most of Europe were legally protected from discrimina-tion. There was, however, a particularly virulent anti-trick movement that Joseppe imagined would be gaining a lot more members if this tape ever saw the light of day.

The dilemma for Joseppe was that he was very aware that anyone he took the tape to was hardly going to be able to ignore the fact that he had obviously been video recording the shower area of the honeymoon suite in his hotel. If he took it to the police, questions would surely be asked, rooms would be searched, hidden networks of cameras would be discovered. The alternative, he supposed, was just to pretend that he never saw anything and hope that they checked out soon. It was the second of these two options that Joseppe initially considered to be the more prudent course of action.

Chris McMillan returned to the hotel that evening, and Joseppe noticed that he still had the large drinks cooler with him. He correctly deduced that he had disposed of the skeleton at sea but had hung on to the cooler (apparently coolers large enough to fit a complete human skeleton are pretty hard to come by). That wasn't what had grabbed Joseppe's attention though. He was more focused on the young local girl who was chatting and laughing with Chris. They had gone to the hotel bar for a drink while a porter took the cooler to the room. Joseppe made up his mind. If they went to the room together, there was a good chance she was going to be leaving in that cooler, and that just wasn't something that he could allow to happen. He had a daughter at a similar age, and he knew that he could never live with himself if he let this young girl be murdered. When Chris McMillan ordered a bottle of champagne to be sent to the room, Joseppe called the police.

The police did not exactly excel themselves on this occasion. Joseppe had spent some time explaining that he had good reason to believe that "the person currently staying in the honeymoon suite is a murderer, that he had murdered one of the guests a few nights before, and he was surely about to kill again."

"Who did he murder?"

"Maxwell Thomas, an American, I think. He took his body out in a cooler, and now he has brought a young girl back."

"And who is in the room now?" asked the officer.

"The young girl."

"And..."

"Maxwell Thomas."

"I thought he was dead."

"So did I."

"So, who is in the room now?"

"Maxwell Thomas."

"This Maxwell Thomas is the killer or the victim?"

"Yes."

Except in Italian I imagine it was even more confusing. Anyway, the police were entirely unconvinced and reticent to interrupt this obviously wealthy and potentially influential businessman's romantic evening. At that point, Joseppe threw caution to the wind and showed them the live video feed from the room. A video feed that showed Maxwell Thomas, the supposed murder victim, and his date, enjoying a romantic moment.

The police called for backup. There were live video feeds to a great number of rooms in the hotel and secret recording equipment that had no doubt captured countless romantic moments. They would need all kinds of officers to catalogue the number of crimes that this hotelier had committed. Joseppe was placed under arrest as he desperately pleaded for the police officers to save the young girl. Fortunately, he was able to convince the officers to watch the tape of the murder before they entirely lost track of the matter at hand. They called for more backup.

Chris McMillan was placed under arrest on suspicion of murder. Or rather, somewhat complicating the matter, Maxwell Thomas was placed under arrest, on suspicion of the murder of Maxwell Thomas. There is no mechanism in the Italian legal system (or any other that I am aware of) to accurately book a suspect inhabiting the still walking corpse of the victim, so this was the best they could do. This was all about to be moot, as the Italian authorities were about to discover that keeping someone with the McMillans' particular trick locked up is not an easy task.

They didn't even make any obvious mistakes. There were protocols for dealing with people with unusual abilities in place. Chris was immediately taken to a maximum security facility where he was kept in total isolation from all other prisoners. For extra security, he was supervised at all times by a sniper team and monitored using a thermal imaging camera. This, or something similar, is fairly standard practice for any prisoner in the developed world suspected of having a trick. Thermal imaging will mitigate most camouflage-type tricks, and there aren't a lot of tricksters that will do well after being shot by snipers.

Things were about to get even more legally groundbreaking, though, as Chris used the substantial wealth that he had access to (Maxwell Thomas had been doing rather well for himself financially) to hire a prestigious legal team. A legal team that currently had their work cut out for them as, as well as the criminal matters, their client was also being sued by Maxwell Thomas' actual parents. They were understandably attempting to prevent their son's obvious killer from using his savings to pay for his criminal defence. This resulted in court case after court case where huge amounts of novel legal work was accomplished and almost nothing was decided. This was pretty much the point of the thing for Chris. He was legally entitled to attend every one of these hearings, and eventually someone would slip up.

It was during a recess for an extradition hearing. Mr and Mrs Thomas had been lobbying to have the case moved to the United States, as they were presumably hoping that their son's murderer would be executed. I suppose extradition would have made sense as both the victim and the murderer were American citizens. They were both Maxwell Thomas.

Evidently on this occasion, the court security officer had not been briefed as thoroughly as he should have been on the very specific precautions that should be taken with this prisoner. Chris had been left in a holding cell with two other prisoners, also waiting for court appearances, and he must have taken his chance immediately. By the time a bailiff came to fetch Maxwell, the other two prisoners had already returned to court. All that was left in the cell was the McMillan's trademark pile of bones, internal organs, and clothes. Neither of the prisoners, upon being collected from the cell, had mentioned anything about what they had seen. This was presumably because one of them had just witnessed something absolutely horrific and was rightly terrified of the man next to him, and the other one was Chris McMillan in a new skin suit.

And so began the largest and most ill-defined manhunt in criminal history. The suspect could be of any race, sex, height, weight or nationality. They could reasonably be in any country in the world. They could be someone you have just met or someone you have known for years.

An international task force specialising in people with tricks took over the search. They were impressively able to work backwards from the murder of Maxwell Thomas through four previous victims. Before Maxwell, he had been Donatella Brigante, and before that he had been Christine Montford, who had attended an international school with Miss Brigante some five years previously. Apparently, Christine had contacted Donatella out of the blue suggesting they go for drinks and a catch-up. Donatella had suggested a bar, Christine had preferred a walk on a beach. It was around a hundred yards from that beach that Misss Montford's bones and discarded clothes were found, double-bagged in bin liners and buried under a few feet of sand.

The police were eventually able to establish Jason Trudeau as a likely previous victim, and the link to Christine Montford. Although his remains were never found, he had gone missing at around the time that he had met up with Christine, an ex-girlfriend. His banking records also showed a sharp increase in spending at around that time.

Based on these victims and witness testimony, the task force was able to put together an advisory on things to look out for. Key warning signals were: 1. A friend or relative you haven't seen for some time getting in touch. 2. Friends or family making out-of-character large purchases, luxury vacations especially. 3. Friends or relatives asking you any questions at all about your income and/or assets.

The reports to the international hotline were too numerous to individually investigate and, apart from decimating the multilevel marketing industry overnight, little good came of it. It did, however, instil a deep suspicion in all people of all people, that remains to this day.

Chris McMillan was caught, by pure good fortune, when an off-duty police officer in Miami walked into a public bathroom to find a young boy climbing into the skin of a local club promoter and instinctively shot it four times with his service weapon. Incredibly, Chris survived, and was taken to a local hospital. This was surely just a temporary reprieve though. Billy Winn had been President for some time at that point, and there were mechanisms firmly in place for dealing with trick-

sters. Once a court had imposed a "differently-abled" designa-
tion, he would almost certainly be transported to a processing
centre and exterminated. The fact that he was the most wanted
murderer in the world wouldn't help his case, but was inci-
dental at this point. The previous week, Judge Susan Vance (the
person in charge of these things in Florida at that time) had
designated an entire a cappella group, The Tone Rangers, as
tricksters, and marked them for destruction, purely because
they had an abnormally large vocal range. A boy who had literally been found climbing into another person didn't seem to
have a chance. A small side note on that, one of the a cappella
group professed to have no trick at all. He was staying within a
totally reasonable human vocal range with the rest of the group
carrying the tune on the high notes. This was subsequently
shown to be true but far too late to have made any difference
to him.

Billy Winn had evidently decided that this was a perfect
opportunity for a bit of grandstanding. Even the most ardently
trickster-sympathising liberal was going to find it hard to
defend the actions of Chris McMillan, currently known (much
to the chagrin of the Watkins family) as Timmy Watkins, the
nine-year-old boy he happened to be occupying at the time of
his arrest. A stadium was booked, and Billy Winn was no doubt
preparing a truly sanctimonious speech.

These things take a little bit of time to organise though, and
accordingly, Timmy Watkins' Special Abilities tribunal, where
he would presumably be found to be a "non-person" (the
language had been softened from "abomination" on its way
into law) and sentenced to death. There is no appeals process,
so the execution could be carried out the same day. It seemed
that, if things had gone according to plan, Billy Winn would
have had a live feed of the execution played at his rally, as he
had done on previous occasions. I'd assume that Timmy

Watkins was due to be sentenced to, what was colloquially known as, The Quad.

I should explain how The Quad came about a little, as otherwise it's going to seem like a horrific and bizarre form of punishment. Don't get me wrong, it is definitely both of those things, but there is at least some logic behind it.

Billy Winn had wanted to start executing the differently-abled as soon as possible after he was elected to office. However, there were concerns that some tricks may allow people to survive current methods of execution. These concerns weren't hypothetical. They had become clear during the execution of Dani Kino, a convicted murderer, in Wisconsin the previous month. The execution was unrelated to the fact that Mr Kino had a trick. In fact, it seems unlikely that he even knew he had a trick, being that his trick seemed to be limited to having an incredible tolerance to toxic substances. This isn't the sort of trick you'd usually become aware of in the course of a normal life. One of the only ways I imagine a person could learn that they had this specific trick was if, as happened in this case, a person measured out and administered them a fatal dose of toxins.

Due to objections from the American Medical Association, doctors are not permitted to be actively involved in executions. The person administering the usually fatal drugs in this case was "a taxidermist and amateur vivisectionist" named Gordy Plank. There was a doctor in attendance, but his sole duty was to confirm that the prisoner was indeed dead, something that it took him quite some time to do. After the first injection, the doctor had quietly informed Gordy that the prisoner still had a heartbeat. Gordy, a little puzzled, had then injected three further vials of the lethal solution into a cannula in Dani Kino's arm. This time, the doctor wasn't required to confirm the death, as Dani had begun to ask questions. Understandable questions like "Is this your first time?" and "Do you know what you are doing?"

It turns out that Gordy was particularly sensitive about people impugning his professional abilities. An unfortunate sensitivity for Gordy, as it was something that was about to happen a lot. Offended, angry, and out of poison, Gordy opted to stab the prisoner repeatedly in the throat with his pocket camping knife. This impulsive action received a mixed response from both the witnesses present and the public at large. I guess the best that could be said for it was that it was eventually, inarguably, a successful execution. It didn't seem like the sort of display the world's most powerful nation should be putting on too often though.

A White House council, somewhat defensively, pointed out to the infuriated new President that inventing and testing a more robust execution method, one that would be effective against a variety of differently-abled victims, and then passing it into law, could take many years. They could, however, get it done faster if they chose from the methods currently allowable under federal law; these were electrocution, cyanide gas, firing squad, hanging and lethal injection. Billy Winn apparently liked the sound of all of those, apart from the last one. Lethal injection had, after all, been developed to reduce the suffering of the victim, something he didn't think was entirely appropriate.

And so, The Quad was developed. The prisoner would be strapped to a stiff board and a noose would be placed around their neck. Electrodes would then be attached to their shaved head, hands and feet. When the signal was given, they would drop through a trap door into a chamber pre-filled with cyanide gas, as twenty thousand volts of electricity surged through their body. A computer-controlled mini-gun would then fire two thousand rounds in thirty seconds into their generally already dead body. Not everyone was accorded the grandeur of The Quad of course. It was expensive, time-consuming, and messy. The Tone Rangers would, under normal circumstances, just have been finished off with a couple of gunshots to the back of the head in an old office building once someone could be bothered to get around to it. But The Quad is what the crowd, booked-in for the evening's entertainments at The Miami Dolphin's stadium, would have been anticipating seeing little Timmy Watkins going through on the big screens.

Incidentally, human rights lawyers had petitioned the supreme court, arguing that The Quad was a *cruel and unusual* punishment, but the court ruled that in order to be unconstitutional, it would need to be simultaneously cruel *and* unusual. The justices accepted that The Quad contained elements of cruelty, and was undeniably unusual, but at no point was it simultaneously cruel *and* unusual.

Timmy had not been charged with any crime other than those under the new regulations against abnormal human abilities. This would generally have been a smart decision by the District Attorney. In previous cases, prosecutors had found that having other charges could slow matters considerably. Bobby Dugan, a transparent trickster convicted of sodomising the Mormon Tabernacle Choir during the recording of a Christmas album, had been charged and convicted of multiple counts of assault. It subsequently turned out that he was legally required to serve his complete two-hundred-and-twenty-five year sentence for those crimes before he could be executed under the new legislation. If they had ignored the other charges and just gone straight to the abomination statute, he could have been dead before dinner time. Incidentally, that album went on to be the Tabernacle Choir's biggest ever seller by quite some margin, largely because of the publicity, I suppose, but at least some sales have to be attributable to people just wanting to know what it sounded like.

And so, for the reason of expediency, in cases involving non-persons, the DA had decided it was best just to leave the rest of the charge sheet blank. The sentence was going to be death after all, it always was.

Until it wasn't. The prosecution's case consisted of the eyewitness testimony of the off-duty police officer that had shot the boy, coupled with horrific photographs from the scene. An Emergency Room doctor, who had treated Timmy for his bullet wounds, also testified to this creature's bizarre anatomy. I won't recount the testimony because it turned out to be entirely irrelevant, but unsurprisingly I suppose, the McMillan brothers have got some pretty mad stuff going on internally. Certainly enough abnormality to get you a death sentence in the United States without any further questions being asked. Coupled with that, the prosecution also showed the video from the Italian hotel room. This wasn't really necessary as continuous news coverage had made it one of the most viewed bits of video footage of all time, but it neatly reinforced their point. This creature was not only an abomination, but potentially the most dangerous non-person yet captured.

So it came as a huge shock to almost everyone in the courtroom when, without any deliberation, Judge Vance declared Timmy to be "free of any abnormalities" and, as such, ordered that he be released from custody immediately. The DA looked thunderstruck and immediately shouted "objection" to no one in particular, and when that didn't seem to accomplish anything, he shouted it again, repeatedly, into the small child's face.

The only person that didn't seem shocked was Timmy Watkins. He politely confirmed, "I'm free to go?"

"This is insane, the President is coming, we need to kill this child!" sputtered the DA.

"You are free to go, and I suggest you do so quickly," said Judge Vance.

"Objection, objection, abomination."

As Timmy strolled, unimpeded, out of the front doors of the courthouse, the judge insisted that the DA meet privately with her in her chambers. When the DA reappeared some time later, he seemed much happier with the decision. He wouldn't be pursuing "any further prosecutions of tricksters" he said, and he was right about that at least. His bones were found in Judge Vance's chambers later that afternoon. Her bones were found, along with those of her husband, in the cellar of her townhouse later that evening.

Joe McMillan, in probably the most ingenious act of his short life, had found his way to the Judge's husband, a dentist with a relatively small private practice. It had been simple enough to book an appointment for the day before Chris' hearing. On reflection, his secretary had found it a little strange that he had arrived carrying a large drinks cooler.

Joe had been sure to book the last appointment available that day, so when the dentist had headed straight home, it wasn't considered out of the ordinary. The fact that *he* was now carrying the drinks cooler (no doubt containing his skeleton and internal organs) was definitely odd, but not the sort of thing you contact the police about. And the rest is legal history.

So, the public was dealt the double-blow that not only was this super-powered killer on the loose again, but worse, there were two of them. Billy Winn was incandescent with rage. I know this because he chose not to cancel his rally that evening and instead spent the whole two hours visibly shaking with anger at these "unholy abominations". To be fair to Billy, in this fairly unique case, that doesn't seem like an unreasonable description of the McMillan brothers, but the impact was tempered somewhat as he had previously used the exact same phrase to describe a child with exceptional night vision.

He chose not to miraculously cure anyone that evening, a usual staple of his live performances, instead opting to stick with just the rant and the video feed finale. I think this may have been a last-minute decision as there were a number of people in wheelchairs next to the stage who looked more than a little disappointed.

Evidently, Billy was out for blood though, and the crowd was treated to four executions using The Quad. Presumably because there was no one more obviously threatening to public safety available at short notice, all four members of The Tone Rangers were hanged, gassed, electrocuted and then shot. It wasn't what either the crowd or The Rangers had been expecting, but it was certainly a dramatic end to the evening.

Billy Winn is not the kind of person to forget a grievance, and he held the McMillan brothers in particular disregard among all abominations. When eight months later they were captured, he was chomping at the bit to get them in front of a mini-gun. There were, however, a few obstacles in his way. Firstly, they had been captured in the UK.

The fact that the brothers had been caught at all is testament to the voracious appetite with which they were moving through victims. Their trick should make them all but impossible to catch. All they would have to do would be to climb inside the skin of a couple of people with few friends or family, and they could live out the rest of their days in relative safety. But they had apparently developed an appetite for the high life that proved to be their downfall. The bones of Chester Hampton, who had apparently made a lot of money in natural gas (I'm not sure what he did with it. Sold it, I suppose. I can't imagine he generated that much of it.) were found by a cleaner, in the closet of his Bermuda holiday home. Evidently, this was earlier than the boys had hoped they would be discovered, and the local police were quick to inform Interpol. Interpol then discovered that Chester was currently supposedly on board his private jet and due to land at London Heathrow shortly. The jet was met on the runway by seemingly the entire British Armed Forces. This was not an opportunity they were going to miss.

Everyone on board the plane was arrested and placed under the highest security available. Medical experts were quickly able to ascertain that they had got very lucky indeed. The creature inside Chester Hampton turned out to be Chris McMillan, but another passenger on board the plane shared the same bizarre physiology, as well as a large portion of his DNA. Joe McMillan had apparently recently decided to get into bodybuilding but had evidently decided to take a shortcut and instead get into a bodybuilder, the already huge MMA fighter Dion Mitchell.

Billy Winn was insistent that the pair of them be extradited immediately to the US "to answer for the crime of the murder of a federal judge..." etcetera etcetera. What he really meant was the crime of spoiling his rally, but the result would be the same; warm up The Quad. Billy Winn was notoriously sensitive to any form of perceived humiliation. Jim Fenton, the actor who's post-miraculous-healing hotel antics had displeased the President, had been visited by The Angel of Death only recently.

The Prime Minister explained that while he would "absolutely love to extend the President such a courtesy, the European Statute on Human Rights prohibits us from extraditing a person to any country where they might expect to face the death penalty." He might have added "I tried my very best, please don't have me killed", but I guess they didn't write that bit down. However, rest assured that for the numerous crimes they had committed, they would surely be handed full-life terms of incarceration in our new ultra-high security prison, the newly completed Facility for the Incarceration of the Differently-Abled.

And it is certainly an impressive institution. In fact, it took almost four months before Chris McMillan escaped. I won't go into all the details, but you get the picture by now. It involved a lot of piles of bones (his lawyer, a guard, and then an investigative journalist on this occasion) as he body swapped his way to freedom. Good news though, they got him back. After the authorities intercepted a letter that Chris had sent to his brother in FIDA in an apparently "childishly transparent code", they had calculated an approximate idea of his current location. Actually capturing him, though, was far from simple. It had involved essentially quarantining a major city until every single person could be DNA tested. A process that was reportedly about as fiscally burdensome to the British government as about half a Bobbett invasion. The important thing was he was back in custody. The fact that he looked very much like an eight-year-old schoolgirl at the time of his arrest had only dampened the celebrations slightly.

17

A PRESSING OF A PERSON

"Can't he saw any faster? At this rate I think it'll take him the rest of the day."

I feel bad, Tony is already occasionally shaking his hands and licking them as he continues to try to get through the bars of our cell.

"I don't think so, they're really strong. Can't you just shrink them or something?"

"No."

"Why not?"

"Because they're attached to the wall either side. I can't shrink things if they are attached to something else."

Tess looks at me very dismissively, like she is a teacher and I haven't done my homework or something.

"What if..." she says, before I shrink her to the size of a field mouse.

A few moments later, the tiny Tess emerges angrily from the arm of the straitjacket. To an onlooker, it might seem like I'd just shrunk her to stop her giving me tips on how to use my own trick, and granted, they might not be one hundred percent wrong, but there was another more legitimate reason. It had just occurred to me that there was something I could shrink that might help in the current situation: Tess. I had thought that maybe this was what she was about to say when I shrunk her. But judging by the grumpy look on her tiny face, it wasn't.

"You should really give people a heads-up if you're going to do that."

I let her back to full size, and she starts to undo the buckles on the back of my jacket.

"I'm sorry, I got excited when I thought of it. This is good though, progress!"

<hr />

It had been easy to convince Jimmy to go along with the escape plan. In a recent experiment, one of the scientists had accidentally let slip that they were testing how different explosive compounds would fare in his stomach. Someone had clearly had the idea that he might be an excellent vessel for a large amount of explosives, and it seemed entirely possible that they would choose to detonate him with them.

The unlikely trio didn't foresee any major problems in getting out of the facility. There were, after all, long periods of time when both Jimmy and Felix were unsupervised. The issue was going to be getting off of the oil rig and back to the mainland. The only way they had ever seen anyone arrive or leave was via a helicopter, presumably both for reasons of security and legal deniability. That is how someone in charge had wanted it. The rig was far enough out to sea to be in international waters and was technically unaffiliated with the United Kingdom.

Construction was well underway on the new prison facility for people with special abilities at this point. Jimmy realised that he was almost certain to be sent there when it was ready. It wasn't like there were a huge number of criminals with tricks, and they were going to need some inmates to fill the thing; otherwise, it would be pointless. Or, even worse, he might be deported back to the United States, an almost certain death sentence for a trickster since the election of Billy Winn.

But without a way off of the oil rig, any escape attempt would be futile. Just when they thought it was hopeless, some good news arrived. It arrived, somewhat surprisingly, in the shape of a Chinook filled with militant Islamic fundamentalists.

I don't know enough about it to go into too much detail I'm afraid, but to put it offensively mildly, Billy Winn's "I am God's messenger" shtick had rubbed a lot of people the wrong way. There was far from a consensus of opinion anywhere on what the status of people with tricks should be, but I think it would be fair to say that the majority of Muslims thought that Billy Winn was not the right person to tell us God's opinion on the matter. This particular group had thought this so profoundly that they had stormed into the new UK headquarters of the Church of Divine Justice armed with large knives and golf clubs. This was the first of several new churches planned for the UK. The idea was to have a mega-church-sized building big enough to make it worth Billy's time if he wanted to come over and address his British followers in person. It was a grandiose and intimidating structure. They had basically stuck giant gaudy steeples on top of the chimneys of the Battersea Power Station. It looked like four already oversized churches having a cuddle.

The terrorist group's plan had been to destroy the building during Billy Winn's first service, so as to wipe out as many of his followers as possible, as well as hopefully killing the man himself. But they had arrived to find the building disappointingly empty. There had been some confusion regarding the date. It was listed on the promotional material as 7/6, which the British terrorists had read as the 7th of June, whereas Billy was actually due to address the new church on the 6th of July. Once the operation had begun, and the police were surely incoming, they had decided that they may as well martyr themselves anyway and destroy the ridiculous building in the process. Explosives were placed in each corner of the building and detonated, causing the giant steeples to collapse inwards and bury the terrorists in a pile of rubble.

Reportedly Billy Winn was furious, partly because he considered it to be an attack on him personally (which it undoubtedly was), but mostly because of the lack of support from the British population in general. With the exception of his admittedly growing fan base in the UK, most people (64% according to one poll) seemed to think that the attack was a good thing. It's somewhat unusual for the majority of the UK to side with terrorists, but this group had a number of things going for them. Firstly, no one, apart from the terrorists themselves, was killed in the attack. The mix up regarding the dates was never made public, so people had assumed this had been a rare humanitarian gesture from a terrorist group. Commentators reminisced about the good old days when you could always expect at least a courtesy phone call if a bomb was going to go off somewhere. Secondly, it was a powerfully unattractive building, and thirdly, a lot of people seem to think that Billy Winn is, to quote a lady on a vox pop, "too full of himself by half."

I'm sure that all kinds of pressure was being applied to the British government by the President though. This was the first event to pull the Prime Minister away from his daughter's side since her death. I'm sure he'd assured Billy that he was going to do his absolute best to investigate the attack and prosecute the perpetrators. And when it came to investigating crimes, there were no better tools available to the British government than the team of little Max the necromancer and his mind-reading sidekick, Felix Trent.

The emergency services were assigned the unenviable task of collecting together the remains of the terrorists and boxing them up as neatly as possible. The building had collapsed in on itself, and none of the terrorists had survived, but some were in considerably better states than others. Suffice it to say, this was potentially going to be Max's toughest challenge yet.

The X-Force are coming. They seem to be arranging themselves into some sort of quasi-military formation outside of the entrance to the building.

Someone shouts out a bunch of commands, and about fourteen heavily armed troops hunch down behind the guy wearing the fire suit. He looks like he has been very reluctantly selected to fight a bear or something.

"Captain Dawson, you have the lead." says a Bishop, very much from the back of the formation. "Everyone else, you are to wait for my orders. We will proceed behind Captain Dawson and provide covering fire if required. Questions?"

Captain Dawson has a lot of questions, but the answer to all of them seem to be that "if you didn't want to go in first, you shouldn't have put on the fire-proof suit."

And then the whole lot of them move forward to the building and start to go up the central staircase.

They are going really slowly. I figure that Dawson is hoping that something else will happen that will somehow mean he isn't going to have to face whatever fire breathing thing he's imagining. Still, Jackson doesn't have much time if he's going to make a move.

Luckily, Bobbetts are a curious bunch on the whole, and a few have already started following closely behind to see what is going on. They'd all been really good at sitting down when they were told, but it doesn't last long. It won't even be a minute after they've been told to do something that they'll start doing something else. Either they forget, or they just see something more interesting to do. Terrence doesn't seem bothered by it anymore, anyway. He's just stood at the bottom of the stairs, waiting for it all to be done.

This works out well for Jackson, as it gives him some cover to stay close to the X-Force without being spotted. The Bobbetts aren't bothered by him, and as long as none of the troops look straight at him, he blends in fine. Besides, they are all eyes-front. He just keeps his head down and, much like Captain Dawson, hopes that he can think of something to get him out of this mess.

Before long, the troops are at the door to our cell, forming a semi-circle around Dawson. Someone hands him one of the net-firing weapons.

"Ah come on, I need something better than this. Can't I use yours?"

"I'll use mine," says the Bishop to the now rather frantic Dawson. "If they need shooting, I'll shoot them, but the orders are to bring them in alive if at all possible."

The crowd of Bobbetts had got pretty close by now, close enough to be poking and grabbing at the soldiers' weapons. Jackson sneaks nearer with them, keeping his face looking away from the door in case any of the soldiers turn around.

"On three," says the Bishop, unbolting the door.

"Three."

Jackson still doesn't even have a fraction of a plan, but he figures it is now or never if he is going to do something.

"Two."

He thinks that maybe he can scramble over the top of the troops. If he can swing Dawson around just as the door opens, maybe he can get him to fire the net the wrong way.

"One."

The soldier turns just as Jackson is reaching for his shoulder. From the look on the guy's face, Jackson can see right away that he's realised that he isn't a Bobbett. He levels his gun to Jackson's face and fires.

The Bishop shouts "Now!" and flings the door open.

Jackson ducked, but the first round still caught him right on the top of the head, and the force from the thing was immense. It threw him backwards, and he rolled back down the stairs head-over-heels. Still, the guy keeps firing at him. Normally, people lay off once they've scored a headshot, but apparently not this time.

Jackson gets shot in the face again, and then things get worse. A stray bullet, that had presumably been aimed at Jackson, hits Terrence Bobbett. He is absolutely furious, understandably I suppose, as from the way he is doubled over, it looks like it has caught him in the groin area.

"Cease fire! Cease fire!" the Bishop is shouting, pushing the trooper's gun towards the floor. I think he realises that this has gone very wrong indeed.

Terrence Bobbett blows his whistle, and every Bobbett in the place is suddenly silently watching him, just waiting for his next command.

"Mr Bobbett?" says the Bishop. "Are you hit?"

The Bishop looks pretty worried. He doesn't even seem to be paying any attention to Jackson, which is good because Jackson is pretty disorientated from having been shot in the head and falling down the stairs.

"Mr Bobbett, the cool-down room, it's empty."

Felix had spotted the opportunity the moment he'd been briefed on the operation. There were twelve terrorists in total, and Max had been instructed to bring as many of them back as possible simultaneously. Individual cells were hastily being constructed on board the oil rig to detain the terrorists. They would then all be interrogated individually in order to ascertain both who had financed and planned their operation and if there were any further attacks planned. The interrogations would be carried out by British Secret Service and a CIA specialist named Agent Connor, a ghoulish man who managed to look pasty and unwell, even when standing next to Felix, a re-animated corpse. Felix was to be on hand throughout to consult and to alert the interrogators if he believed the subject was being untruthful at any point.

The Chinook helicopter had arrived with the boxes of remains, and Max had had the first three terrorists up and thoroughly confused in no time. They had presumably been anticipating arriving in some form of paradise, so to be woken up in the middle of the North Sea by a little Luxemburger has got to have been at least a little startling.

Max had decided to resuscitate them in order of difficultly, starting with the easiest first, so his earliest subjects had sustained only minor injuries. "Minor injuries" should be taken in context. They weren't minor in the more conventional sense, given that they were very much fatal.

Agent Connor's first priority was to find out who the leader of the organisation was, and if he had been killed in the attack or was still at large. This was information that Felix was also keenly interested in, having spotted the potential for an escape attempt. If he could somehow team up with the terrorists, they would almost outnumber the military personnel onboard.

He also knew that there was no way he was going to individually convince each of these people to go along with his plan. However, if they had an accepted leader that they would follow, then he might have a chance.

Progress was slow to begin with. Agent Connor would hammer rapid-fire questions at the terrorists almost immediately as Max brought them around. The terrorists, in turn, usually had some pressing questions of their own. A typical exchange would be:

"Who is your leader?"

"Who are you?"

"Was he part of the attack? Who planned the attack?"

"Where are we? Who is the child?"

"Are there further attacks planned?"

"Where is my arm? Is that a golf club sticking out of me?"

Furthermore, it turned out that people brought back by Max aren't vulnerable to physical coercion in the same way as the genuinely living generally are. Agent Connor, conscious that time was a factor and eager for quick results, had waterboarded the first subject within an hour of beginning the interrogation. He'd initially thought that he might have killed him before realising that breathing seemed to be an entirely optional pastime for these half-dead creatures, and the terrorist, upon being strapped down on his back, had taken the opportunity to have a nap.

With seemingly the majority of the CIA's enhanced interrogation playbook irrelevant at this point, the onus began to fall on Felix to get the information they required. He did this in what he considered to be the most humane way possible, by offering them a cup of tea and explaining the situation as clearly as he could. It only took a couple of hours for Felix to have three of the terrorists independently name Tariq Malik as their leader.

The CIA operatives were confident they had their man, and what's more, he was in box number seven and would be with them shortly. Aside from getting this information, Felix had been keen to impress upon the group the nature of their situation. They were here right now solely through the powers of the little boy next door, and without Max, they would soon be dead. Felix had never believed anyone when they claimed that they didn't fear death, and he wasn't about to change now.

A large steel girder had impaled Tariq through the shoulder as the building had collapsed. The firefighters at the scene had cut through the metal just above his head, which meant that whenever he turned his head to the right, he thought that he was just about to walk into a giant steel girder. However, right now this was the least of his problems. Identified as the leader of the terrorist organisation, he had become the absolute focus of both the Secret Service and the CIA's investigation.

Agent Connor was having a very ominous conversation on a special phone about what constituted a "living person", and the legal consensus seemed to be that they could do some pretty monstrous things to Tariq if he didn't give them the information they required. Legally, at worse they might be guilty of *desecrating a corpse*, an offence with no international bearing. Becoming aware of this was presumably key in Tariq being predisposed to consider Felix's plan favourably. He was in a horrific situation, and he didn't really have any of the information these people were after. He didn't have any superiors he could name or financiers he could point a finger at. This whole operation had been his plan, but that apparently wasn't the answer that they were looking for. It was clear that things were going to get worse before they got better, and better was going to mean, at best, death.

While the MI6 and CIA were discussing the next steps, Felix had a few moments alone with Tariq. He'd laid his cards on the table as swiftly as possible. He wasn't a government employee, he was a prisoner just like Tariq. If they helped each other, they might all escape.

"There's something critically important," said Felix. "Can any of your men fly a helicopter?"

Tariq's answer was both good, bad, and worrying. The worrying thing was that a number of the group had been learning to fly for quite some time, using flight simulator soft-

ware. The good news was that this simulator had included heli-
copters, and Tariq was confident that, given enough hours with
the simulator, they would be able to fly the real thing. Only one
of them had done any flying with the helicopter though. For
most of them, the simulator had just been part of their training,
and it hadn't seemed particularly likely that they would ever
need to pilot a helicopter. It was only Kamal that had actually
really enjoyed flying and had tried out all the different aircraft
on offer. Tariq reckoned that, given the opportunity, Kamal
would have a good chance at being able to pilot a genuine
Chinook. The bad news was that Kamal was in box number
twelve.

Max had numbered the boxes in the order of how difficult
they would be to reanimate, and Kamal had been assigned the
very last slot, with good reason. When the building collapsed,
Kamal had been crushed by a giant flat piece of masonry. He
had been lying face down at the time, having been knocked
down by the shock wave of the initial blast. The emergency
services had packed him up as best they could and shipped
him over, but he didn't so much resemble a person as a
pressing of a person. In short, regardless of the quality of the
flight simulator and how many hours he had put in, it didn't
seem likely he was going to be flying a helicopter anytime soon.

But Max is a miracle worker (not in the Billy Winn sense;
for Billy, he's obviously an "abomination"), and he managed to
get the contents of all twelve boxes into some form of
consciousness by the end of the day. It turned out that Kamal
was at least able to talk, "What am I?" being his quite understandable first question.

That night, Jimmy and Felix were hurriedly planning when
suddenly all the lights went out. A power cut? Had Max or
maybe Tariq made a break for it already? Either way, it seemed
like too big an opportunity to pass up. As time passed, it
seemed likely that security would only get tighter, so acting

now, when there was only a skeleton staff on duty, would give them the best chance. The oil rig had not been designed as a prison, so there was nothing preventing Max and Jimmy from getting up onto the platform, providing of course that they weren't seen. The blackout provided by the power cut helped a lot on that front. The challenging thing would be getting Max and his new entourage of undead Islamic fundamentalists out, without raising the alarm.

This was made considerably easier when they arrived at the new interrogation cell to find that Agent Connor had electrocuted both himself and the two military officers accompanying him. He had attached electrodes to Tariq, in a tried and tested interrogation technique, but he hadn't taken into account a few things that were different in this situation, from standard electrocutions he was presumably used to.

Firstly, Tariq was basically dead. While Agent Connor was definitely getting a reaction out of him, it was requiring much larger voltages than normal to get an adequate pain response. By the time Felix and Jimmy had arrived, the machine was set to the maximum value. Secondly, unlike the concrete prison cells they normally operated in, the floor of the new interrogation cell on board the oil rig was made of metal. And thirdly, unlike any person Agent Connor had interrogated previously, Tariq had a steel girder protruding from his body. It looked to Felix like the first time the girder had touched the floor while the juice was flowing, a circuit had been created that electrocuted everyone in the room. This had presumably also been what had knocked the power out for the whole rig.

Tariq took it as a sign that God was on their side; Felix took it as a sign that maybe the CIA shouldn't electrocute people. Either way, it was agreed that now was their chance to escape.

In the darkness, Felix and Jimmy called out for Max, and Tariq called to his men. Eventually there was a reply. Unfortunately, the reply came in the form of a volley of gunfire that hit

Felix in the head and Tariq in the girder. Given the almost complete darkness, these guys were good shots. Tariq was about to fire back using Agent Connor's handgun, when Jimmy stopped him. "Don't, you might hit Max."

Fortunately, the bullet that hit Felix had been so close to his existing bullet wound that it had essentially passed straight through his head without doing further damage.

One of Tariq's men shouted out, communicating both that they were all alive and that God is great.

"Is the small boy with you?"

More gunshots.

Tariq shouted for his guys to get between him and Max, and they did, forming a human shield, so he could fire blindly into the dark. He loaded another clip and fired until no fire was returned.

"You OK, Max?" shouted Felix.

The somewhat muffled reply came back. "I'm OK, what's going on?"

"We're getting out of here!"

There were a lot more cheers about how great God was at that point.

I don't know how many people they shot getting out of there. Felix insists that he's not a violent person, so I think the fact that he basically instigated a standing gun battle between a terrorist organisation and the secret service doesn't sit well with him. It was definitely a battle that he wanted the terrorists to win though, and they had. It turns out that in a gunfight in the dark, you really want to put your money on the walking dead. It did, however, take them some time to get to the helipad, given that a number of them were missing limbs and a couple had large pieces of Battersea Power Station embedded in them.

Felix had also wisely opted to bring the Prime Minister's daughter along for the ride. This seemed like a much better option than leaving her on the oil rig to die, as Max was obviously coming with them. She didn't have much choice, but she seemed admirably game for the adventure.

Kamal was disappointed that he wasn't physically able to fly the chopper because he was now essentially a paper-person, but he was able to coach another of the group through the process, to the extent that they were able to take off and eventually fly back to the British Isles. Landing was significantly more challenging, but again, the fact that most of the passengers were basically already dead played to their advantage. Pilots apparently say that "any landing you can walk away from is a good one", and by that criteria, theirs can be considered a partial success. At least some of the passengers could somewhat walk.

18

FOR WANT OF A KINDER NAME

I hadn't even heard of Virgil Barnett until Felix's trial, and I assume I am not alone in this. Any newspaper articles from that period refer to him as something like "Father of Tom Barnett, alleged assault victim of Felix Trent." If you are a politician and the most notable thing about you is that your son slept with a game show host, it's probably fair to say that you are not a prominent politician. Before the trial, he was apparently the Shadow Secretary of State for Transport, and after the trial, he wasn't even that anymore. He resigned from that role, apparently in protest at the "absence of justice in the British legal system". It was a somewhat bizarre protest, given that shortly after the trial Felix had been shot dead. I'd assume maybe Virgil could have found some justice in that, but apparently not.

Most people guessed it was just a way for him to save face, an excuse to step back into a more private role, as obviously he had found the whole episode rather embarrassing. But also, apparently not.

He was notably the first MP to use the word "abomination" in parliament, in reference to people with tricks. Although admittedly, this was in reference to Terrence Bobbett. That was just the start though. It quickly became clear that he had decided to set himself up as a single-issue MP, and that issue had nothing to do with transport.

Not a single topic could be discussed in parliament from that point on without Virgil Barnett somehow making it about people with tricks. How to curtail the rise in childhood obesity? "First we should deal with the abominations in classrooms. There's one child who weighs eighty-five stone. If we dealt with him, then surely that would bring down the average."

Should Gatwick Airport be allowed a new runway? "It shouldn't even be allowed to operate as an airport, as long as it allows abominations to fly freely into the UK."

Should there be a raise to the national minimum wage? "We could afford to, if so much money wasn't being spent on facilities for abominations, but also, no."

This did nothing for his popularity amongst other MPs, I'm sure. He was routinely booed whenever he rose to speak. Several MPs would surreptitiously hum the theme-tune to Felix's TV show, which was funny by virtue of how much it clearly annoyed him.

That's not to say his opinion wasn't popular with the public though. It didn't take long for the tabloid press to spot his single-minded determination and begin championing him as a "restless defender of the normal man". He had two separate newspaper columns, one daily in a tabloid, and one in a weekend broadsheet, in which he could more exhaustively express his views. This seemed to be a more effective vehicle than boring parliament with them, and before long, he seemed to stop bothering with his day job at all. Instead, he campaigned, both in print and on television, to "stem the tide of the descent of humanity, and to stop treating monsters like humans."

Eventually someone on Billy Winn's campaign team

spotted an opportunity, and Virgil began to be invited to speak on US television in defence of the candidate. This helped both men's careers. It made Billy seem like less of a loan crackpot, as another politician that not only sounded intellectual but British, seemed to agree wholeheartedly with everything he said.

Not long after that, Virgil travelled to the States to appear alongside Billy at a few of his church revival speeches.

When Virgil returned, not only was his political movement conspicuously well funded, but he seemed physically revitalised. His acne scars were gone, and he no longer walked with a limp. Every newspaper column he wrote and TV appearance he made would invariably be accompanied by a photo of him vigorously shaking the hand of Mr Winn, presumptive presidential nominee of the Democratic Party, and almost certain serial assassin. It's not that he won the presidential election for Billy, but it perhaps gave his win an international legitimacy that it might not otherwise have had.

After the leader of the opposition died in an unfortunate step-aerobics accident and his party was left looking for a new leader, Virgil Barnett seemed like a pragmatic choice. He was popular with a large section of the general public, had name recognition, was tacitly endorsed by the newly elected leader of the free world, was filled with an alarmingly youthful energy these days, and most importantly of all, he absolutely refused to shut up about "the threat that abominations posed to the nation". This was an issue that the Prime Minister was clearly weak on. He had often been criticised for being "soft on tricksters", even before his daughter was being held hostage by one. Keeping the trickster issue front and centre was clearly going to be key if they were to oust the PM in the upcoming election.

Virgil Barnett undeniably gave his party the clearest shot at winning back parliament, so, despite no one really liking him much and some people still humming TV themes at him whenever he stood to speak in parliament, he was elected as leader of the opposition.

———

Terrence is visibly furious, what with being shot in the crotch and all. Every single Bobbett in the room is staring intently at him. I think mostly because he blew his whistle, but also they are fixated on the injury.

Jackson just about gets his bearings and tries to figure out the best way to handle the situation. He gets to his feet and stumbles a bit. What he hasn't really counted on is that all of the Bobbetts are miraculously standing absolutely stock still, so the fact that he is moving at all means he draws everyone's attention. Certainly he has the attention of the Bishop Major, or whatever his title is. There isn't a lot that Jackson can do now. He can't exactly hide. Also, the fact that he is still stumbling around after being shot twice in the head is probably freaking them out a touch. It is probably this consideration going through the Bishop's head when he utters the poorly considered command "Shoot him again."

The next thing to go through his head is an axe.

Because, of course, Jackson isn't the only person who has been shot, and a fair few of the Bobbetts have clearly interpreted his utterance as an order to shoot Terrence again. One, at least, isn't a fan of this order at all and rewards it with a very solid axe throw.

The Bishop tumbles down the staircase with a kind of hollow crunching sound. Everything else is deathly silent. Jackson looks at Terrence to see what he will do, but he seems to be struck as dumb as everyone else. Essentially, everyone except Terrence has a wide-eyed, mouth open, shocked expression on their face not dissimilar to Jackson's.

And then one of the X-Force decides to take the initiative

and shoots one of the Bobbetts. It could have been the one that threw the axe, but it seems just as likely it wasn't. Then he shoots another and another until a few of them charge at him with machetes. The Bobbetts are screaming a high-pitched war cry as they hack away at him. The moment that starts, the rest seems somehow inevitable.

Every other Bobbett in the room starts up with the cry as well, as they charge down the remaining X-Force troops. Terrence looks for a moment like he might blow his whistle, but then he seems to think better of it and limps towards the exit. Not even he can get out quickly though because of the sheer quantity of Bobbetts pouring in. They are all screaming at the top of their lungs. Each scream is about the volume and tone of a fully grown large adult shouting as loudly as they can but with the intensity of a young child that is absolutely losing control. They arrive by the hundred — every Bobbett on the compound must have been able to hear the war cries, and it seems they all want a piece of the action. The X-Force doesn't stand a chance.

The soldier that puts up probably the best fight has a very serious machine gun. With the number of rounds he is laying down, the Bobbetts can't get near him from the front, and he is building up a monstrous pile of corpses. Reloading his weapon takes a few seconds too long though, and eventually a few of the younger ones get through and smash him with hammers.

It's around that point that Jackson realises there is not a lot he can do either way to help out. He figures he should probably sneak away before they finish off the Christians and start looking for something else to focus their blood lust on.

Felix knew right away that it was going to be almost impossible to blend back into society. Their unorthodox troupe consisted of, in no particular order: The Prime Minister's daughter, a spectacularly large man, twelve terrorists that were currently collectively at number two on the FBI's most wanted list and were physically all kinds of exploded, Felix himself, not exactly an unknown to the general public, also conspicuous for having been shot in the head twice, oh and Max, probably the only one on this list that wouldn't attract an immediate armed response on any street in the civilised world.

The group couldn't really split up either, as they mostly needed to stay within a few hundred yards of Max or they would drop dead.

There was, however, a pretty strong trump card in their hand. Any attempt by the authorities to send in an armed unit to kill them all would clearly carry the huge risk of also killing Max, and by extension, Emily. In Felix's experience, while politicians are relatively gung-ho about sacrificing the lives of other people's children, they are considerably more reticent when it comes to their own.

Felix, the de facto leader of the group by virtue of master-minding the escape, and Tariq, the leader of the terror cell, had discussed the situation thoroughly and decided on a strategy. They wouldn't so much hide in plain sight as revel in it.

Previous to devoting himself entirely to large-scale terror-ism, Tariq and his brother had run a restaurant located not too far from the site of their crash landing, called *Tonight We Dine in Hull*. It seemed like as good a place as any to set up shop. So, literally, they opened the shop back up.

It was, of course, key to demonstrate as quickly as possible that Emily was alive and well (or whatever approximation it is that Max rustles up), so that the Prime Minister could factor this into his decision-making. They staged what was officially a press conference outside a kebab shop; unofficially, it was more akin to a *proof of life* hostage video.

Emily read a hastily written speech to the collected press

about the "groundbreaking medical attention she had received at a pioneering facility of which all of Britain should be very proud." She said there was still "a long way to go with her recovery" and, as such, she would be convalescing, for the foreseeable future, in the wonderful city of Hull.

"In the kebab shop?" asked a local reporter. It was a fair question, and the shop's glowing sign had been prominent throughout the press conference so far. Apparently Tariq had wanted it that way, confident that it would be great publicity. In fairness, it was.

And then Emily answered with one of the more memorable quotes in the history of British journalism. "To answer that, and any more questions you may have, I'd like to hand you over to Felix Trent."

There was a stunned silence, then some murmurs, laughs even. As far as the public was so far aware, Felix Trent had been shot dead more than six months ago. Either this was some sort of joke or a miracle... and then Felix appeared, looking somewhere in between the two.

Felix's head wounds look so obviously fatal that it's borderline impossible to think of anything else as he is talking to you. I'm sure very few viewers paid any attention at all to his opening remarks, thanking Emily for her kind introduction and wishing her well with her ongoing recovery. They did, however, probably pay some considerable attention to the second part of his speech, that addressed the Prime Minister directly. He encouraged the PM to allow not just Emily, himself, and their "fledgling community, but people with tricks everywhere, the space and freedom that they need to thrive."

And so the PM and Felix had arrived at a sort of a stalemate. The government clearly had no option but to leave Felix to his own devices.

I'm kidding, of course; the government immediately sent in the SAS to kill everyone.

Top military commanders, once apprised of the unusual situation, had apparently advised the Prime Minister that it would be "a relatively straightforward operation" for a crack team of operatives to get in and extract Emily and Max simultaneously. While it wouldn't be altogether simple, this was "just the sort of thing that these guys are trained for."

What they had neglected to take into account, as seems to be quite common, was that the combatants they were facing were, for the most part, already dead.

Under cover of darkness, they had approached the restaurant and shot the men on guard outside repeatedly with silenced weapons. Under usual circumstances, this would likely have enabled them to remain covert, but in this situation, the victims had shouted very loudly that "there are soldiers coming and they have shot us in the head a bunch."

Felix and Max had prepared for almost exactly this eventuality, and Max immediately donned the feline SCUBA equipment that Jimmy had presciently decided to hang on to. Apparently, before deciding on explosives for the Battersea Power Station attack, Tariq had considered a poisoned gas attack. It is worryingly simple to create a rapidly deadly chlorine-based gas using cleaning products, easily available to any high-street restaurant, and that is exactly what he had done. As soon as Max had his mask on, Tariq released a valve on a storage container, and the gas rapidly started to fill the basement.

It's not unusual for SAS teams to wear gas masks on this type of mission, generally if they are planning on using gas themselves, but apparently they had opted to go without on this occasion as it would give them better visibility. I'm sure if you asked them now (and somewhat surreally, you could), they would agree that this was a tactical error on their part. All but two of the eight-man team succumbed to chlorine poisoning, and the last two were hacked to death with those big knives kebab shops use for slicing doner meat. Given the option, they probably would have gone with the gas.

This mission was already deemed by the government to be an abject failure, given that an entire elite team had been wiped out and none of their objectives had been accomplished. An unexpected development the next day, though, put it into a whole new category in the pantheon of Special Forces catastrophes.

Max had brought the gassed team back to life one at a time, and Felix had sat them individually down for a chat. It had taken some time to get over the shock of the thing and to overcome their resistance to what was initially perceived as *joining the enemy*, but eventually Felix had all but one of them convinced that the best way that they could serve themselves and their country would be to remain at the restaurant and protect young Max from any further attempts on his life. Felix is, as I know I have mentioned, very persuasive, and he'd had the added advantage that it was in the soldiers' best interest to keep in close proximity to Max. This fact was aptly demonstrated by the one soldier he failed to convince. He had dropped dead while jogging back to base, presumably about six hundred metres from Max.

And so, not only had they failed to kill Max, but now Max had his own protection unit of highly trained soldiers that were not only heavily armed but effectively immortal.

The Prime Minister wisely decided not to authorise any further attempts to extract either Max or Emily from their location. He didn't stop there though. From this point onward, Felix and the PM shared a common objective — to keep Max out of harm's way. Which made it all the more frustrating, from the PM's perspective, that Felix seemed to be trying his very best to get himself killed.

Before Felix had been shot in the face, he had of course been somewhat of a TV personality. Given that several people who presumably wanted him dead already knew where he was, and that didn't seem likely to change anytime soon, he figured that he might as well see if he could do some good.

At the time, there were a number of public figures expounding on the dangers of tricksters, the most prominent in the UK currently being Virgil Barnett, but there were also others who had risen to prominence towing a variation of the Billy Winn "tricksters are abominations that don't deserve to live" line. This was all despite the fact that, if a member of the general public were to have been asked to name the first person they could think of that had a trick, more often than not it would probably have been Billy Winn himself. In short, people with tricks were rarely, if ever, represented positively in the media anymore. Felix decided that was something he was going to have to try to remedy, if tricksters where going to stand any chance at a better future. He happened to be in a unique position to make this happen.

He proposed putting together a television broadcast, an "informal chat", where he could discuss "the issues surrounding living with a trick in the UK, and hopefully, put a more human face on the struggle." There were a couple of stumbling blocks to accomplishing this, not least of which was that he didn't really have much of a human face anymore. Another issue was that the British Armed Forces had formed an impenetrable perimeter around their current location. Having, since the wildly unsuccessful SAS mission, more thoroughly researched Max's abilities, they calculated that around a 1 km radius from his location should guarantee that they won't be bothered by any undead terrorists and/or special forces. More on the perimeter situation in a moment, as it's something that is about to be pretty relevant to our current situation, but for the time being, the issue was that they didn't yet have any way to communicate with the outside world. Felix had reached out to some old TV contacts and they were largely keen to be involved in what would likely be headline-making television. The issue was they had no way of getting to him.

Emily, the Prime Minister's daughter, provided the solution. She convinced her father that it would be in his best interest to allow a TV crew into the compound. And she was right, given how vociferously the leader of the opposition, Virgil Bennett, hated tricksters. The PM had, almost by default and certainly against his will, become the leader of the *pro-trickster* party in the upcoming general election. If Felix could indeed succeed in shining a more favourable light on the trickster situation, it would be a great help to the PM politically.

Felix re-introduced himself to the world. He began the first broadcast with a bandage wrapped around his head, presumably not to alarm any first-time viewers that had somehow managed not to see the previous press conference. He then discussed what had happened after his trial. Surprisingly to most, he didn't seem particularly bitter about the shooting, and even more surprisingly, he took this opportunity to apologise to his "victims".

"You weren't victims of my trick, I can assure you. In fact, few people have been since I quit playing cards for money a long time ago. You were, however, I have come to realise, victims of my indifference to other people's feelings. It is for this indifference that I'd like to take the opportunity to apologise today. I paid a price for my actions, a heavy price, but it is something I deserved, and I pay it gladly." And then he removed the bandage to show the giant exit wound that had demolished his left eye.

"The only reason I can be here to talk to you right now, in any number of ways, is because of the incredible skill of a phenomenally brave young boy named Max. I'd like to introduce you to him now."

Then Felix and Max chatted for a good long while about how Max had first discovered his own trick, the tragic death of his grandmother, and his subsequent treatment at the secret government facility. I won't go on, I'm sure you've at least seen clips from it. For a time it was all that anyone was talking about. Odds are, though, it probably didn't change your opinion on people with tricks. In my experience, people who watched it and found Max to be an inspirational miracle worker probably already didn't have any particular issue with tricksters. If, going in, you already thought that anyone with a trick was an abomination, it seems unlikely that this was going to change your mind. In fact, this parade of walking dead monsters was likely only going to solidify your beliefs.

And that is largely what happened. The country was no less divided on the issue, but now there was this unlikely focal point of a kebab shop in Hull for anyone who felt particularly strongly about it. And people did feel strongly.

In the next few weeks alone, over a hundred people had headed to *Tonight We Dine in Hull* with the express intention of killing either Felix, or Emily, or Tariq, or even Max. The perimeter security in those days was nowhere near as comprehensive as it is now, and more than a few managed to get pretty close. Close enough, at least, to be killed by the undead SAS troops that now made up Max's permanent guard.

But Felix had some fans as well, of course, some of them equally enthusiastic. A great number of tricksters, or people with family members with tricks, or people who just like inserting themselves into the middle of topical events, made the journey. They were usually met with similarly lethal outcomes. The military guard around the perimeter had developed a pretty robust "shoot first, probably nothing else will be required later" policy for any member of the general public breaching the perimeter. After all, people attempting to break into the compound were either going to join Felix and Max, something the government frowned upon, or to kill them, also something they were trying to avoid.

The result of all this was that a section of the city of Hull, a couple of kilometres in diameter, was pretty soon littered with corpses. Max was keen to bring them back from the dead, if only for the aesthetics of the place. The worrying thing was, of course, that a great number of them had probably come there to kill him. They devised a convenient solution.

The majority of the city centre had been essentially deserted, most shops had shut and almost all of the former residents had abandoned their homes. There was apparently some sort of scheme to compensate these people. I won't go into the details here, but it was sub-adequate. That's not to say that everyone left, some people are stubborn. Also, especially for older residents, those inside the military cordon now had a rather unique advantage in that, if and when they died, there was a good chance that Max would bring them back. So, more on that:

The police station was one of the buildings that had been abandoned. It's not like there wasn't already enough of a police presence. With the police and military combined, it was probably the most heavily guarded area in the world. However, the station contained four holding cells that became very useful.

I should point out that once Max has brought someone back to life, he can't just turn them off at will, at least he hasn't chosen to thus far, and they had no intention of making him do it even if he could. The kid's life had been traumatic enough.

And so, the process went like this. Jimmy, who was essentially the only genuinely living member of the gang, would collect up four prospective recruits, i.e. corpses of people that had been shot dead trying to enter the compound. He would place one each in a holding cell in the police station. He would search them thoroughly for weapons and often handcuff them just to be on the safe side. Then, Max would pop by and do his thing, before going to sit with Jimmy in the cafe next door, a cafe that was still run by one of the more stubborn/optimistic genuine living locals.

The next step was for Felix to have a conversation with each of the possible recruits. He would chat to them about anything that would get their emotions up. For a lot of them, it would be politics, tricks, religion, that kind of thing — anything to provoke an intense reaction would do. It doesn't take Felix long to figure people out. Also, if someone has travelled across the country with the express purpose of killing someone because of something they saw on TV, they probably weren't the most emotionally guarded character to start with. And if that's the case, if they came with murder on their mind, Felix just leaves them in the cell. If, on the other hand, after a thorough chat Felix ascertains that they mean them no harm, he unshackles them and releases them from their cell. They are then welcome to return with him and join his, for want of a kinder name, ever-increasing army of the undead.

The old police station is a good nine hundred metres from *Tonight We Dine*, so there's no further step necessary. Max just heads back home when they are done, and anyone left in their cell will soon be a corpse again. Jimmy will take them to the *unsuccessful applicants* area, which to the untrained eye might resemble a pile of rotting corpses in the stock room of an abandoned TK Maxx.

Very rapidly, Felix Trent had once again become a staple of mid-afternoon British television. Except this time around, rather than demonstrating his own trick, he would typically be chatting to someone else about their experience of having a trick and why they had travelled to Hull to join him. I think he called this section of his show *Tales From the Underground*, but everyone else called it *Freak of the Week*. Despite the pejorative title though, I think he actually did quite a lot of good for the way the public saw people with tricks.

Due to the nature of the tabloid press, generally before, when you heard about a trickster, it would be within a context of fear. What danger is this new ability going to pose to you and yours? You know the kind of thing. Felix's show didn't have any of that type of sensationalism. It was the kind of thing you could put on while you did the ironing. Just a brief, sometimes entertaining, sometimes moving, glimpse into someone else's life. He spoke at considerable length with a lady whose trick was that she would exactly mimic the voice of whoever she was talking to. This is one of those tricks that almost sounds like a gift, and I'm sure it would have been if she could turn it off like some tricksters can. The thing is, for her it was involuntary, and it turns out that people really don't like being mimicked, especially with uncanny accuracy. Even Felix was clearly finding it distracting as she replied back to him in his own commanding baritone. As people got annoyed with her she said, they would begin to shout. Involuntarily, she would then start shouting back. Even though she was apologising and trying to explain her unusual situation, the fact that she was screaming at them meant that arguments often escalated quickly.

After the Winters Act, she had lost her job. She had worked in data entry and surely hers was one of the few cases where the trick was obviously not of any benefit to her work at all. Still, they had let her go. Her former boss, a man with a particularly shrill voice, had apparently been looking for any opportunity to fire her, and the Winters Act had been a convenient excuse. After that, she had eventually lost her flat and, for a time, had been begging on the street. She would try to keep conversation to a minimum, but eventually some generally well-meaning soul would start chatting to her, she would mimic them back and they would invariably think she was mocking them, just as they were trying to help. They'd shout, she'd shout. She was physically assaulted on a fairly regular basis. When she had seen that a community of tricksters seemed to be developing around Felix, she'd thought that maybe it was a more accepting environment, somewhere she could finally fit in. I'm not sure she had been entirely right about that. Felix was looking progressively more annoyed with her as the interview went on. Anyway, she had managed to get over the fence and make a run for it. She'd been shot several times by the perimeter guards, but nothing that Max couldn't sort out.

As well as offering a window into the potential struggles of living with a trick, the show had done a great deal to solidify Felix's position as the de facto *leader of tricksters*. Whenever any issue hit the news that even tangentially involved people with tricks, someone would be on the phone for his take on it. It helped, I suppose, that journalists always knew where he was, and it's not like he had a lot else to do with his time.

Eventually, presumably because the authorities were concerned that Felix had amassed too large of an entourage, or perhaps because they were just plain tired of shooting people, or maybe just because the basement of TK Maxx was full, a more robust perimeter fence was constructed. It was just before this that Jimmy and Felix had parted ways. I don't think there was any animosity between them. Jimmy had just preferred not to be permanently barricaded inside the city of Hull. The new fence was apparently designed by the same team responsible for the construction of the Facility for the Incarceration of the Differently-Abled (more on that later, it's quite the institution) and showcased a number of features to keep out even the most motivated trickster. It was apparently un-climbable, impenetrable, and under constant thermal and biological surveillance from both sides. In short, almost no one was going to be getting in or out.

Which was about to be a rather immediate problem. See, since the new wall had been constructed, the only people who had been allowed to enter the compound had been politicians, an unusual and unintentional situation brought about entirely by some inept politicking from the Prime Minister. He had understandably wanted to visit his daughter within the walls of the compound. This had seemed like a reasonable request to pretty much everyone involved, and arrangements had been made for a very guarded trip. So far, so good, at least in the PM's recently lowered expectation of "good".

As he was there, Felix thought it might be a fun idea to have him on his afternoon show. It would be an opportunity to have a public discussion about political decisions affecting people with tricks every day. Much mirth was had in the press that the PM was to be *Freak of the Week*.

The PM and Felix did not agree on a lot, but the discussion was at least cordial. In fact, it was so civil that many argued it qualified as an endorsement of the PM by Felix. Keep in mind that as Virgil Barnett, the leader of the opposition, was currently all but calling for the mandatory execution of tricksters, and very specifically Felix Trent, this endorsement had been largely assumed anyway.

Mr Barnett disagreed though. At Prime Minister's Questions the week following the interview, Mr Barnett accused the PM of using his position to derive an unfair advantage in the upcoming election. As the interview had been broadcast on the BBC, a publicly owned broadcaster, he argued that they also had an obligation to allow him a rebuttal. And for once, Virgil Barnett, the honourable MP for Orpington and leader of the opposition, was actually right. The national broadcaster was obliged, by government mandate, to hear his opinion.

The PM, potentially joking, as there did seem to be a reasonable chance that Felix would kill Mr Barnett given the opportunity, said he would be happy to arrange a visit. Virgil called his bluff though, and said he would head to Hull at the next available opportunity. Then, for the rest of the question time, it seemed that every back-bench MP and their secretary wanted to pay Felix a visit, presumably just for the chance to get on TV. Eventually a motion was tabled, that any elected MP would be allowed access to the secure compound should they so desire, and it was swiftly voted into law.

Virgil Barnett's subsequent appearance on Felix's show had been almost civil. Barnett had called Felix an "ungodly pederast that will surely burn in Hell" and had essentially promised to kill him as soon as it was convenient and/or legal, but these were statements that he had made so frequently in print already that few people paid much attention.

19

FREAK OF THE WEEK

<u>May 15th 2001</u>
6 days before the General Election

And so, that is why it is important that we have a Member of Parliament with us. It is surely the only way to get the package to Felix unharmed. Our MP doesn't seem very happy about the situation though, and for good reason.

Firstly, he had been shot in the groin. This is the sort of thing that would put a dampener on pretty much anyone's day.

Secondly, as he had been receiving medical attention for his gunshot wound, his surgery had been interrupted in possibly one of the most startling ways possible.

Jackson, wielding two hammers, had burst in to the operating room with a message for Terrance crudely scrawled on his T-shirt in blood. The message had read, "tell the squirrel where the bodies are".

I don't know why Terrence seems to think this whole situation is our fault though. It was the X-Force that had shot him, not us. Also, it looks like the doctor had done a pretty good job with the injury. I'm going to assume it was actually a doctor rather than a Bobbett, based on the quality of the job they had done. Terrence seems to have lost a bit of the spring in his step as we walk towards Checkpoint Foxtrot, as the entrance to Hull city centre was known, but that is understandable given his injury.

The second thing that may have taken the spring out of Terrence's step is the bus. We had made the journey to Hull in a Terrence Bobbett campaign bus. While the checkpoint guards are legally obligated to allow Terrence access to the city, it seemed unlikely that they'd allow him in with an entourage of wanted tricksters and corpses. We'd decided the best thing to do was to put everything into the bus, except for Terrence and myself, and for me to shrink the whole thing.

Terrence had looked reasonably happy with this part of the plan, presumably because it didn't involve him being shrunk, something almost no one likes. Talking of things no one likes, the final part of the plan was to put the bus into Terrence. Something that Tess had initially thought to be an excellent idea, until she remembered that she would be on board the bus.

"Hear me out," I said to a distinctly scowling Tess. "If they search him at the gate and he has what, a mini campaign bus on him? How is he going to explain that?"

"It could be anything, a toy, a novelty souvenir from his campaign," she said.

"What if they shake it? Or just bin it?"

Tess seemed to be contemplating if either of these things would be preferable to a short journey inside Terrence Bobbett. "What if he swallows it instead?"

"No." I feel like I'm quite the authority on this. "God knows how long it will take to come out the other end."

"We don't need to wait that long, just until we're inside

then..." She mimed a bus exploding out of Terrence Bobbett and then checked to make sure he wasn't paying attention. He wasn't.

"If there's a delay, though, you could be digested. Trust me, this is the best way."

"Easy for you to say."

"Yeah, yeah, I've had such a discomfort-free experience so far."

In fairness to him, Terrence has been quite a good sport about the whole thing. Perhaps because he has concerns that his deal with the Church of Divine Justice may be void, given that his Bobbett army had killed so many of them. Maybe he's decided that getting Felix on his side is the best way to go. Or maybe it's because, if at any moment I lose concentration, the double-decker bus will suddenly burst back to full size. Who knows? Either way, he is being relatively civil to me as we approach the checkpoint.

"What's the biggest thing you've ever shrunk?"

"Height or total volume?" I'm trying to think of something, because the honest answer is "the bus, by quite a long way."

"Either, I guess... height?"

"A giraffe."

"Where did you shrink a giraffe?"

"Zoo."

"Why?"

"Fun."

See, we're getting on great.

"Aren't they going to wonder how we got here?"

"Say your assistant dropped you off. They don't allow vehicles to approach the checkpoint anyway."

"Aren't you supposed to be my assistant?"

Tess had coached us on the plan. Terrence had paid close attention, probably because it involved putting a bus in him.

"I was thinking about that. I don't think you should say I'm your assistant. I think you should say I'm your physician."

"Why?"

"For your trick."

"Miracle."

"Fine, for your miracle, say that you require constant medical attention."

"Or what?"

"Or they might not let me in."

Terrence stops walking. We are almost at the checkpoint and a bright light has been trained on us.

"No, I mean, what happens if I don't have constant medical attention?"

"Just make something up, they won't know how your trick works. Make it something they wouldn't want to happen so they have no choice but to let me in." This much is true, as far as I'm aware. Terrence's trick is thankfully unique.

"I'm Terrence Bobbett." He has his hands up.

"I know who you are," says the guard, conspicuously not lowering his weapon.

"Terrence Bobbett is approaching Checkpoint Foxtrot," says the other guard into their radio.

Terrence keeps his hands up, which seems wise. I hadn't thought to raise mine, and at this point it seems ill-advised to make any kind of movement.

"The pedophile?" squawks back the radio.

"That's the one," confirms the guard, with his gun pointing at Terrence.

"Correct," confirms the other guard into his radio.

At least they know who he is, I suppose.

"I'm a Member of Parliament, MP for Coventry South."

"What does he want?" says the radio.

"You have to let me in, it's the law," says Terrence.

"I think he wants to be on *Freak of the Week*," says the guard into his radio.

And then they both turn to me.

"I'm a doctor," I say, "a specialist, his abilities require constant medical supervision."

"What abilities?" scoffs the guard.

"I'll impregnate people," says Terrence, "without medical supervision."

And no one doubts him.

Felix Trent strolls surprisingly confidently towards us. I say "surprisingly" because it looks like the top half of his head might fall off at any moment. Also, there's any number of people who would love to assassinate him, so I don't expect him to be the first person we see, but here he is, hand outstretched to Terrence.

"Great to see you, thanks so much for travelling all this way."

"I didn't have much choice."

Felix stares into Terrence's eyes for a moment. I imagine this would be quite a daunting experience even before his injuries, if you know his trick, but given that looking Felix in the eye now means staring through his head, it's even more disconcerting. Still, Terrence doesn't flinch.

"Then you have my thanks even more... Bus, a whole bus. That is impressive. Your doing, I presume?"

And I shake his hand.

"It's a pleasure to meet you." It really is, even though his hand feels strangely cold. And then for a moment I'm so distracted wondering what Felix is getting out of my mind that I nearly forget about the bus.

"Follow me, let's get you two settled in."

There seems a sense of urgency to his stride as he leads us forward.

This part of the city isn't entirely deserted, but it is definitely quiet. The few people we do pass stare directly at us. I try to figure out if they are dead people that had been brought back by Max, or just regular residents of Hull that had refused to leave despite the madness that currently surrounds them. It's kind of tricky. None of them look exactly healthy. And then there is an easy one. I'm guessing he is one of the terrorists that had escaped with Felix from the oil rig because Felix greets him enthusiastically, and he looks crushed. I mean, he seems happy enough to see Felix, he just actually looks crushed, like you could probably get his left arm through a pasta roller on a medium setting.

Terrence comes out from the bathroom holding the tiny bus in his hand. I'm not sure if it's pride on his face or relief. A little of both, I imagine.

"Where do you want it?"

"Middle of the road, I guess?" It seems as good a place as any.

"Everyone should probably stand well back."

We have attracted quite the crowd, it seems all of the terrorists have come out to watch, as well as a number of assorted, presumably dead, tricksters.

And boom, bus.

Jackson is first out and he doesn't look happy at all. That's surely just me projecting though, based on what they had just been through. Tess is next out, and her expression does little to dissuade me of my assumption that it must have been pretty awful. Even Tony looks traumatised.

"Great job, young man, thanks for your help." Felix gives Jackson a hearty pat on the back.

"I swear to Christ, that's the last time I let you shrink me," says Tess, not for the first time.

"Talking of…" says Felix.

"He's on the bus?"

"Amazing, you must be Tess." He shakes her hand and jumps aboard the bus. "I can't thank you enough for all your hard work."

And in another few seconds he is back at the door.

"What happened to Jimmy?"

I don't know how to answer this, I don't want him to think it was our fault or anything. Fortunately, Tess does.

"Creepers got him. Thought we should bring him with us and maybe you could bring him back."

"You did the right thing," says Felix, glancing back inside. "Max will be thrilled. And the others?"

"Creepers too."

"The more the merrier. Still, creepers, rough way to go. Can I get a hand?"

He looks at me with his one remaining eye, and for a moment I think he wants me to help him drag Jimmy's huge corpse somewhere. Of course he actually wants me to shrink them.

A short while later, Jimmy confirms that being killed by creepers had indeed been a rough way to go.

"My eye! Why does it have to be in the eye?"

It has got to be a pretty startling way to return to consciousness, made worse by the fact that he can still see through the eye that is no longer in his head. He can hold on to the cheese knife and turn it to have a look around the room. Even the SAS soldiers are looking a bit grossed out by this, and I think we can safely assume that they aren't delicate types.

So I'll gloss over the process of little Max bringing everyone else back to life. Suffice it to say, it's a fairly unsettling event for the person being brought back. First, there is the realisation that they are dead, not *you might die*, not even *you will die*, but *you are dead*, it happened, creepers got you. That's got to be rough, but then there is the upside, *you're back*... kind of. I'm sure it's a lot to take in, and no one takes it exactly well. Chris lets out a super loud yell of frustration like only he can, and Spider-man is kind of crying.

Everyone is back, apart from Jesus. We haven't even opened the casket yet. Given what a baffling experience it has been for the others, people who had died only recently and already knew about Max's trick, I have to admit that I'm pretty intrigued to see how Jesus will take it. Especially if his last memories are what... crucifixion? Wait, "What language does Jesus speak?"

"Don't worry about that just yet," says Felix.

"Aramaic," says Tariq.

"Let me show you guys around!" continues Felix, with an excitement that no one else seems to share.

"Does anyone speak Aramaic?" I'm not sure why I hadn't contemplated this before, maybe because I didn't think that we would ever get this far.

"Not here, but yeah," says Felix. "That's why we're going to do it live."

"That sounds risky. Are you sure?" says Jimmy, who is currently attempting to tape the cheese knife with his eye on it to the side of his face. "What if he doesn't say what you expect?"

"Oh ye of little faith. Besides, if it goes out live, at least we'll have something. The worst case would be that he refuses to do the show at all and this whole thing will have been a waste of time."

"Like Churchill, you mean, and that was more of a waste of my time than yours," says Jimmy.

"I'm not convinced it was him," says Felix. "He was surprisingly racist."

"I think it was him," says Tariq.

"Well, it was in his grave," says Jimmy. Tony perches on his shoulder and pokes at the side of his head. I'm not sure if it is Tess trying to get Jimmy's attention or it is Tony acting on his own accord, maybe trying to figure out what is different with him.

Emily doesn't seem to have any visible injuries. In fact, compared to the rest of the walking dead, she is positively vibrant. It seems like a different world. While the kebab shop had a definite *armed resistance* vibe, Emily's flat directly above the shop is more akin to a quaint holiday cottage, or at least it would have been if it wasn't full to bursting with reanimated corpses. This atmosphere is only enhanced by the fact that Emily herself seems to be blissfully unaware that there is anything unusual about her situation at all.

"I've made biscuits that are ready now, or if you wait fifteen minutes, there will be a pie."

"If I have a biscuit now," says Jimmy, taking a seat in an armchair, "will I forfeit my chance at a slice of pie later?"

"Not at all," says Emily, with a cheeky smile, seemingly entirely disregarding the fact that this huge visitor has one eye shoddily taped to the side of his face and a monkey on his shoulder.

Tess opts for biscuits as well. I decide to wait for pie.

Jackson is unfortunately unable to consume either pie or biscuits in a socially acceptable manner.

"So, you really think Jesus will vote for Dad?" asks Emily, with a smile that gradually disappears as we stand silently, presumably all pondering how phenomenally ill-conceived this plan is.

"He's hardly going to be a Virgil Barnett fan, is he?" Felix breaks the silence. "Or Billy Winn for that matter. Let's not get too political right out of the gate though. The key thing is that we establish who he is and try not to freak him out too much."

Jackson signs to me.

"What he say?" says Spider-man, holding three biscuits.

"He said 'it's a solid plan'," I lie.

"Look, I think the key is that we don't ask him any significant questions right away. If he says something that Christians don't like, they'll just refuse to accept that it's actually him. I think to start with, we just keep it civil, let him say whatever he wants to say, thank everyone for watching. Then, people are going to have nearly a week to come to terms with it. There are going to be some naysayers, but there are almost certainly going to be believers as well, I think probably even the majority. It's not like people don't know what Max can do. Look at me, look at all of us!"

Jimmy nods in agreement.

"The key thing is that we'll then have some time. I think that was maybe the mistake with Churchill, not enough time. It's a lot to take in."

"Is he still in TK Maxx?" Doesn't seem right. I'm not volunteering, but it seems like someone should probably put him back.

Tariq nods solemnly.

"Then we'll have a few days to explain the situation to him."

"In Aramaic?" Tariq points out.

"I have a guy we can phone, a scholar."

He looks unconvinced

"More importantly, the voters have time. The way I see it, Christians are going to have a few different ways they can react..."

I start to feel like if we'd maybe had this discussion in London a few weeks ago, I could have saved myself a pretty awkward trip.

"Firstly, they can just refuse to accept that Jesus is back. Let's call this group the *doubting Thomas'*."

"I think there might be a lot of *Thomas'*." Tess looks daggers at me. "What? I'm just saying, I'm not sure I'd believe it."

"But," says Felix reassuringly, "there will be a lot fewer than if we'd gone in straight with the politics questions. If he hasn't said anything controversial, there's a lot less reason to argue that it's not him."

This is probably true.

"And then, there is the second group.' I get the feeling Felix has maybe given this speech a few times before, or at least he's thought about it a lot. "They think that there is a pretty good chance that we have, in fact, brought back Jesus, but they could go either way on it. In all likelihood, it'll depend on what he says and whether or not it conforms with their existing beliefs. Let's call them *suspicious*..."

"*Steves?*" I suggest. I don't know why I am being flippant. I think I get nervous around people I respect, and tend to over-compensate.

Felix doesn't seem bothered though. "The *Steves*, there's not a lot we can do about. I think it will mostly come down to how persuasive Jesus is."

"He's gotta be quite persuasive though, right?" says Tess, for some reason consistently optimistic on this plan. "Isn't that kind of his thing?"

"He does have that reputation. That said, he'll be a skeleton speaking a dead language, so it might be an uphill struggle with everyone except the third group, the *true believers*. These are people that are immediately going to accept that this is the Son of God brought back to life, and are going to basically do whatever he says. So the hope is that firstly, there are a lot of these, and that secondly, Jesus doesn't turn out to think that we are all actually abominations."

"But this is where I think we have the advantage," says Jimmy. "The people whose minds we are trying to change, the people who would otherwise be voting for Barnett, are probably Jesus fans anyway, so they're going to be more likely than most to believe he's back."

"And what about the second bit," I say. Everyone's eyes turn to me and, not for the first time, I wish I could shrink myself. "What if he hates tricksters too?" This doesn't seem unlikely now I think about it. In general, older people have been much less accepting of people with new abilities, and this guy is going to be about two thousand years old, on paper at least.

"I don't think so," says Felix, with somewhat reassuring confidence. "Not if the Bible is anything to go by. He loved a trick, water into wine and all that."

"Oh oh, of course!" says Tess. "Let's have him do that!"

"What?"

"Water into wine. That ought to bring round some of the *Steves*, maybe even a *Thomas* or two!"

"I don't think it would work that well on television," says Jimmy, and he has a point. If an Aramaic-speaking skeleton hadn't convinced them, it seemed unlikely that some water changing colour would win them over. And that's assuming it was red wine, white wine would be even more visually underwhelming.

"What else can he do?"

"Walk on water maybe? Do we have a lake or anything?"

"Perfect," says Tess excitedly. "Maybe he could turn a whole pond into wine, and then walk on that?"

"He's not a performing monkey," I interject, as it seems that we've perhaps gone off track at this point.

"I just want it to be the best it can be " says Tess, as her own performing monkey glares at me.

"Why don't we see if it works first, gauge the public reaction, see what he's up for? When is the show?"

"We're live at five," says Felix.

I should have known that, firstly because it rhymes, and secondly because Felix had kept his old game show time slot, even though he now hosts probably the most talked about show on television.

"Talking of which, we should head over to the studio and have a quick run-through."

He looks right at me.

"What?" My heart skips a beat in anticipation.

"I like to keep it informal and chatty, but we usually block the show out roughly for lights and camera. Have you done any TV before?"

"No." I don't think the clip of me swallowing Jesus that has dominated the news recently counts as *doing TV.* "I'd rather not, if that's OK."

"Nonsense, you have to do the show, this will clear your name. People will know how important what you were doing was, why you crashed that plane."

This doesn't sound like it will help at all. "I think I should probably just go home."

⸻

I don't go home though, of course. Partly because I can only leave when Terrence leaves, and he has apparently decided that he wants to stay around for the show. Presumably because he thinks he's going to be on it. I had assumed he wasn't, mostly because audience research has shown him to be literally the least popular person in Britain, but also because the other guest is Jesus.

So instead, we all find ourselves in screen two of the local cinema, which has been semi-converted into an ad-hoc TV studio. I say "semi-converted" because it is still apparently used as a cinema on most days. It is within safe range of Max's usual hangout in the kebab shop, so the undead can often be found catching a matinée screening of something or other without fear of dropping dead again.

"Should we open it up?"

Max is eyeing up the Jesus crate that has been placed upright in the middle of the set. If you haven't seen Felix's show, then "set" is probably too grand a term to describe the decor. Usually it's just Felix sat on a folding chair, chatting to one or two guests on their own folding chairs. The crew consists of five spectacularly-wounded former terrorists, three with cameras, one that I assume is recording sound, and one with giant cue cards that I think Felix is going to be reading from. I'm not very familiar with how normal TV is made, but I'm pretty sure it's not like this. Anyway, back to Max's very good question.

"I think we need to do the whole thing live, so they can see that we've not planted anything or coached him on what to say."

"What if I can't bring him back?"

"Of course you can. There's no one you can't bring back, Max. Just look at Kamal." Felix gestures towards the paper-thin man leaning against a camera.

"Five, four, three."

The audience starts to cheer impressively loudly, as the terrorist with the cue cards signs "two, one."

"Goooooood evening!" intones Felix, in a style that is perhaps more suited to someone hosting a game show than someone about to resurrect Christ, but the audience seems to be into it. The old cinema is absolutely at capacity. It has happened so fast I haven't had a chance to take it in. I'd still had loads of questions in the run-through. It doesn't seem like we are ready at all. Beyond that even, it seems unreal.

But at a quarter to five Felix had happily given the word to open the doors, and in the blink of an eye, every chair in the place was full. I can't make out the audience in detail, but I'm guessing it is largely Max's handiwork, tricksters that had been killed trying to enter the compound and are now bound to him indefinitely. I just can't imagine that the previous residents of Hull would be as invested in what Felix is saying as this crowd clearly is.

I can't see their faces though, the light is too intense. Apparently they have rigged a projector to act as a spotlight, and it is blindingly bright.

"And boy, oh boy, do we have a show for you! Obviously the general election is coming up in a matter of days now. An election that I don't think it would be an overstatement to say 'will be the most pivotal in the history of this nation.'"

Another big cheer from the optimistic crowd that I can't see. Oh, and I haven't even got to the worst part. I have the bright light pointed right at me because Felix had insisted that I be on stage with him from the start. There is Felix, sat at his desk, a plinth with the Jesus coffin on it, and then to the side are Max and me. I tried several times to give up my seat, and Terrence was eager to take it, but Felix had insisted. It is "important that people know where the body has come from," Felix says, and I am key to that story. There really hadn't been time to argue.

"Are you OK?" whispers Max.

"Why?"

"You were mumbling something, 'kebaby'?"

I hadn't even known I was doing it. "I'm just hungry, I guess."

Why am I lying to this kid?

"I think it's because I'm nervous."

Now the crowd is booing, I figure that Felix has been talking about Barnett or something.

Max places his hand reassuringly on mine. His fingers tap rhythmically, like a heartbeat.

"On this stage in the past I have had many discussions, debates, arguments might be a more accurate term, 'fights', some might say."

A knowing laugh from the crowd. I'm assuming in reference to his interview with Barnett, where they had famously nearly come to blows.

"I feel I have been fair in giving anyone who wanted one, a forum to lay out their views and, of course, I've had a lot of opportunities to lay out mine. But, there are some people, a lot of people, where no matter how compelling any argument, any critique, any appeal to reason is, they simply cannot be won over. This is because, rightly or wrongly, their beliefs do not come from a place of reason but from a place of faith. A faith in a higher power. In those cases, nothing I can say, nothing anyone can say, is going to change their mind. It's not like we can just ask God his opinion on the matter... Which brings me to today's guests..."

And then all the cameras are on me, and my heart is pounding in my head. I don't even hear what Felix says, but the crowd cheers, so that's nice, I suppose. I'm just trying not to hyperventilate. I do a little wave. It seems like the right thing to do when people cheer, but on the recording it looks ridiculous, like I'm there to collect an honorary degree rather than to explain why I brought down a 737. The "interview" is no better. I just about manage to apologise for the plane crash. I had wanted to explain that it was an accident, but it really doesn't come across that way. The workings of my trick are challenging to describe at the best of times, and I was having a terrible time.

Fortunately almost no one remembers my bit because of what happens next.

I'm trying to explain that I would never have taken such a risk if it wasn't important.

"And why was this package so important?"

"Because... Jesus?" I sound like a child at Sunday School.

There is a growing murmur from the audience as a couple of them guess at what I might have meant.

"Because... Jesus," says Felix, turning to the casket in the middle of the stage. Finally the cameras are off of me. Max squeezes my hand reassuringly again.

"You did great," he lies.

I really hope Max is better under pressure than I am.

"All the way from Jerusalem, Israel... " says Felix, like he is introducing an Elvis Comeback Special, something that Max could probably also have arranged. "This vault, containing the earthly remains of Jesus Christ, was sealed when his still intact tomb was discovered, near the site of his crucifixion. It has not been opened since. We only do so now with the utmost respect and reverence so that he may hopefully bring further wisdom to humanity. Gentlemen..."

And then, onto the stage come two undead militant Islamic fundamentalists, brandishing some respectful crowbars.

The first thing that I notice is that the room has gone silent, totally silent.

And then I see that the guy with the cue cards is slumped down on the floor. The guys with the crowbars never make it to the casket, everyone has stopped at the same time. Even Felix is motionless, only held in place by his desk.

I realise that Max isn't squeezing my hand anymore.

I must have known what had happened, the only thing that could have happened, before I shake Max by the arm and his head slides cleanly away from his neck.

20

THE FACILITY FOR THE INCARCERATION OF THE DIFFERENTLY ABLED

W hen the Facility for the Incarceration of the Differently-Abled was first proposed, it was almost universally regarded as a good idea, by both parliament and the general public. However, when it came to actually building the thing, no one had wanted it anywhere near them. It didn't help that, at the time, most papers had been dominated by a story of a botched creeper kidnapping. A mother had opened her son's bedroom door one night to find the poor kid halfway through the wall. They were a wealthy family and presumably would have paid the ransom had the child been returned, so this was really the worst possible result for the unfortunate six year old.

I've explained creepers before so it's best not to dwell on it, but otherwise you're just going to be wondering, so I'd better, I suppose. The creeper had successfully squelched through the wall unnoticed by around two o'clock in the morning, at which point he had held a chloroform soaked rag to the face of the young boy and successfully knocked him unconscious. Everything was going well, from a creeper perspective, and to be honest, better than some even from the boy's perspective.

Apparently it's harder to knock someone unconscious for an extended period of time than most people think, either that or creepers are just really bad at it, perhaps because they are generally unarmed and naked. Whatever the reason, a number of children where beaten to death with very little being accomplished at all before most creepers seemed to learn this lesson. In this case, the creeper had poured the chloroform in through an air vent onto a T-shirt on the floor of the boy's room. This would suggest that he was a resourceful and conscientious kidnapper.

Anyway, the creeper had successfully managed to knock the boy out without killing him and was pulling him back through an exterior wall when the mother had interrupted them. Apparently she would always kiss her children good-night, regardless of what time she got back in the evening. That night she'd stayed late at some work function and got back at about 3.30 am. She wasn't going to wake him, just kiss him goodnight, I'm sure more to satisfy the habit than anything else. She'd enjoyed a succession of cold drinks at the work do though, and had clattered in fairly loudly. The creeper was nearly all the way back through the wall, and he had chosen just to make a run for it. By the time the slightly worse for wear mother had realised that her son wasn't in his bed and had flipped on a light, the creeper was already well on his way. The sight that confronted the mother has to have been sobering to say the least.

The creeper had been dragging the naked kid through the wall waist first and had got about as far as his ribcage, so his head and the top of his chest were still in the room. His mother had tried to wake him without success. She had called for the emergency services, and they'd arrived rapidly. They all assumed that the boy was surely dead, he was, after all, more than half wall. Unfortunately though, he wasn't. The boy regained consciousness as the chloroform wore off and was therefore able to explain to the paramedics how excruciatingly painful it was to wake up with a wall in you. Whatever it is that allows creepers to pass through physical objects was wearing off slowly. Bit by bit, over half a day, the wall became more solid, until mercifully the poor child died. This is the horrific tale that had been dominating the press, reinforcing in the public consciousness that tricksters can be both incredibly dangerous and incredibly hard to imprison. So while everyone seemingly wanted this new prison to exist they simultaneously wanted it to exist as far away from their loved ones as humanly possible.

Normally in this situation, the government would have chosen an area with as small a population as possible. This would have the dual benefit of making the land very cheap and permanently enraging the fewest number of voters. However, the proposed facility had a number of logistical requirements that just couldn't be met out in some abandoned Scottish moor. The power requirements, for one, were going to be astronomical. A lot of the technologies proposed to incarcerate these tricksters involved huge amounts of electricity. To even hold ten or so creepers simultaneously, it was going to require the power draw of a mid-sized town. It wasn't unreasonable to expect that the finished facility might use as much power as even a major city. Couple that with demands for huge quantities of water (high-pressure hoses were another big feature) and it made more sense from a cost perspective to build in or around an existing city. Obviously no area wanted it, so they ended up looking for the city in the UK with the least political clout, or that was deemed by the general population to be the most expendable. Either way, the answer was Newport.

FIDA had been completed only six months after Felix's escape from the oil rig which, according to the the prevailing public mood, was about six months too late. "Gay Mind-Bender On The Loose" was my second favourite headline of the time, surpassed only slightly by "Mentalist Escapes With Fundamentalists."

On the downside, the Prime Minister had angered Billy Winn by allowing the terrorists that destroyed his sassy new mega-church to escape. The Angel of Death was ever present in the Prime Minister's mind. She understandably hung like a sword of Damocles over the head of anyone that perceived themselves to be on Billy Winns' enemies list.

The PM had correspondingly upped his personal security significantly. While having four armed guards wearing thermal imaging goggles in the bedroom with them every night was causing tension with his wife, it was at least allowing him to get some much needed sleep. On the upside, his decision to build a giant specialist prison for tricksters now seemed to have been both prescient and judicious, two things he had never been called before.

And now that the facility was finally completed, there was considerable public pressure to fill it up with monsters and throw away the key.

The Winters Act had made it almost impossible for anyone with a trick to get a job of any kind. Even if you kept your trick a secret and had no intention of using it at work, or even at all ever, it was standard practice to cross-reference all prospective employees with a publicly available government database of people with tricks. Even if the company had no specific political agenda themselves, it just wasn't worth the risk of hiring someone on the database. All it took was for one person to make a call to the Church of Divine Justice (picking up a generous bounty for their trouble) and all kind of devastatingly expensive proceeding would begin.

Some tricksters would rely on family or friends for support, but this was usually a temporary solution at best. It was incredibly frustrating to be a healthy adult, both willing and able to work, but with no possible means of employment now or seemingly ever again. Unsurprisingly, a lot of tricksters turned to crime.

The first trickster to be sent to FIDA had been given a four-year sentence for credit card fraud. They had stolen the credit card details of a number of customers at a restaurant they used to work at and had ordered several expensive items over the phone. They'd had them shipped to their home address. Like most of the early cases, these weren't master criminals, just regular people that were out of options. They hadn't even used their trick to commit the crime. Their trick had involved a resilience to high temperatures. They had worked the grill at the restaurant and been fired as soon as the Winters Act had come into effect. It's not like they needed a special facility to incarcerate them either. Unless they had otherwise been planning to keep them in a cage of fire or something, a regular prison would have done the job fine.

And so it went. It seemed like the only news we ever heard about people with tricks for a while was the sentence they had received for some sort of stupid crime. Shoplifting, mugging and burglary were common. Sometimes people were assisted in this by their trick, but more often it was of no help at all. There was a girl who could shrink herself down to about the size of a cocker spaniel. She would grab money from the tills of high-end jewellers and then shrink and run away. It was ill-conceived. It wasn't like she was invisible or anything, and shrinking herself had just made her that much slower at running. Eventually a passer-by just grabbed her by the jumper as she tried to scuttle past with a handful of cash. They'd held onto her until the police arrived. I say police, but it would almost certainly have been the X-Force. The police had outsourced pretty much any situation involving tricksters to them. Tricks are so varied that it's difficult to be prepared for every eventuality, and the police were on an increasingly tight budget.

The X-Force have the kind of weaponry that the police could only dream of, also a whole load of video equipment for dealing with the invisible. A thermal imaging camera will see through most transparency tricks, although they won't do you much good against creepers. Creepers apparently take on the temperature of whatever substance they are slowly splurging themselves through. While we are on the subject of creepers, I should briefly cover how they imprison them. A pair of captured creepers were the first cases, to my mind at least, where the new special prison was genuinely justifiable. They had been arrested for unrelated robberies, one of a bank, one of some sort of money processing centre.

To start with, the guards didn't even bother putting them in a cell, they just drew a two metre by two metre square for each of them in the middle of the prison yard and told them that if they attempted to leave it, they would be shot without warning. This was an effective but resource-intensive solution, as it required a team of snipers working full time. Eventually, a more finessed solution was completed. Cells were constructed with a tightly woven copper mesh beneath the surface. Every five to ten minutes, a giant electric current would blast through the circuit, enough to make an ominous humming sound. Any creeper that happened to be halfway through the wall when that happened would be incinerated. These cells were expensive to construct though, and creepers are particularly crime-prone, as tricksters go. At one point there were apparently about twelve creepers to every specialised cell. I don't think anyone was particularly worried about their living conditions though.

It was a self-perpetuating cycle, the more the general public was bombarded by story upon story of tricksters committing crimes, the more we became shunned by society as a whole. They hated us, and we resented them. I can hide my trick, unless I choose not to, but not everyone is so lucky, and people were starting to be attacked seemingly for no other reason than the fact they had a trick. A stripey person was pushed in front of a bus by a mob in Barnsley. As far as I can tell, that was the full extent of their trick, being stripey. It certainly didn't do anything to protect them from being squashed by the bus. What's more, no one was even convicted of a crime for basically murdering a person in plain sight. Apparently, it was not possible to see clearly on the CCTV footage exactly who the fatal shove had come from. To me, the message of the whole thing was pretty clear; murdering tricksters was fair game.

At school, everyone began practising how best to hide their trick. It wasn't just anyone that had been sent to the special schools, these were the children with the most exceptional abilities. The problem was that this made a lot of us pretty easy to spot. One kid had three sets of knees on each leg and two elbows on his arms. He was about nine foot tall and could jog at sixty miles per hour. They wouldn't exactly have to check his identity papers to find out that he had a trick. Lucky he was so fast, I imagine he's had to run a lot.

So, contrary to my expectations, not only was FIDA almost instantly at full capacity, overcrowding was already an issue. Terrence Bobbett's political aspirations had won him few friends, and there had subsequently been a crackdown on any stray Bobbetts for minor crimes like shoplifting, loitering and prostitution. Bobbetts aren't that challenging to imprison. A strong fence could comfortably restrain a few thousand of them provided they aren't startled or aroused. However, rigorous implementation of the Winters Act meant that any number of more powerful tricksters were being sentenced on a regular basis. Winters Act violations carry up to a ten-year sentence, and the Church of Divine Justice had been awarding cash prizes for reports leading to convictions.

People with a vast range of unusual skills now needed to be imprisoned, and the government was understandably reticent to build specialised accommodations for every single type of trickster.

Say, for example, a woman is convicted of murdering her husbands. I say "husbands" plural because this isn't actually a hypothetical example. Her name is Carol Chambers, and she wasn't caught until the seventh one. Apparently, if she caresses a man in a certain way, it will cause an immediate myocardial infarction.

She claims that the first two were accidental, and it seems plausible enough. I'm not sure how you could even figure out that it was a trick you could do without at least nearly killing someone. The progressively increasing life insurance policies of her subsequent husbands, though, suggested a different story. At some point this had almost certainly become an intentional act. Carol was sentenced to life in prison, a rare "full-life" term, reserved only for the country's most notorious offenders. She was now the permanent responsibility of the Facility for the Incarceration of the Differently-Abled.

So now, FIDA administrators have got to figure out what kind of investment permanently securing Carol from the general public is going to be worth. There are a number of factors to consider here. Firstly, is there already a cell in FIDA that could safely enclose her? If so, is it available? Slim chance, more likely was that they would either have to rehouse the present occupant of a suitable cell or, even better, find an available cell with an occupant with which Carol could safely share.

Because, if none of these criteria could be met, the next

question would be, how much money is it worth investing in new units that can safely house Carol and/or her ilk? Talking of ilk, is Carol a one-off, or perhaps the first of a new common phenomena? A worrying thought, given how many premature deaths Carol had caused before being caught.

I imagine that, to begin with, solving these kind of issues might have been an intriguing and somewhat rewarding exercise. FIDA was very much in the public eye and was, as such, fairly well funded in the early days. Each new inmate had been assessed by some of the best minds in the fields of both incarceration and the relatively new field of enhanced human ability. For Carol, they would have surely recommended solitary confinement with maybe some strictly supervised exercise time.

Budgets were far more constrained by the time she had been convicted though. By this point, the warden was unlikely to authorise the construction of new units for any reason at all. Instead, she ordered that Carol should share a cell. On assessing her criminal history, she realised that this was a risky proposition, so the governor took the precaution of making sure Carol was sharing with a particularly annoying inmate that everyone disliked. As it turned out, Carol didn't get along with this inmate any better than the governor did, and within a couple of days he was dead.

Perhaps it was subconsciously that the governor began to place other "problem" inmates in with Carol. She claims that it was never intentional. And then, arguably, the warden put the wrong person in with her. Carol had developed quite the deadly reputation at this point, and her fifth new cellmate in as many weeks, a person with no discernible trick, that must have had truly appalling legal representation to have been sent to FIDA at all, pre-emptively clubbed her to death with three tuna fish cans stuffed into a gym sock.

This was the start of a pattern though, of housing inmates

together in potentially lethal combinations. Before long, the death rate a FIDA was almost high enough to keep up with the accelerating rate of new convictions. In many ways, what later became *Darwin* was just a formalisation of this process. Some might say it evolved.

21

JUST OUT OF REACH

6 weeks after the General Election

Remember Ziggy? The creeper I went to school with that wanted to be a wildlife photographer. Well, I suppose unsurprisingly, that didn't exactly work out. He didn't even get to be a sniper or whatever it was they had been training him for at school before the Winters Act had come into effect and rendered him permanently unemployable.

Instead, he had turned to crime like basically every other creeper. Credit to him though, he had decided that ransoming kidnapped children back to their parents was just too sleazy a way to make a living. In case you have understandably chosen not to remember or care about the problems of creepers, the issue that they often face is that while they can easily enter pretty much any locked premises by slowly osmosing themselves through the wall, they can't really bring anything back with them, nothing that isn't organic anyway. And even organic things need to be something they can hold still for the few hours it takes for them to get through a wall. Which, as I'm sure you don't want me to remind you, is why some creepers choose to drag naked incapacitated children back with them. Ziggy had decided this was no way to make a living. Which almost passes for noble, until I tell you what he decided to do instead.

Essentially, he had traded in secrets. He would break into the residences of essentially anyone rich or influential and snoop around, looking for any secrets that he could profit from. For example, he had been able to sell some information regarding a large company's hidden financial losses to a hedge fund that apparently made a fortune selling the stock short. Or more commonly, there was evidence of infidelities that he could blackmail a cheating spouse with. So yeah, maybe not a noble way to make a living but probably preferable to kidnapping.

Often, the best secrets would be contained within a very robust safe, and this is what had led to his downfall. He had developed a pretty ingenious technique for reading documents inside of a safe. He could stick his head and hands into most safes in about thirty minutes or so. Of course, this wouldn't be of much use if he couldn't see anything once he was inside, and unless they happened to have stuck a torch in there, it would be pitch black. Obviously he couldn't use his own torch, it's not organic and so couldn't pass through the safe's exterior. Instead, he would totally coat his face in a bioluminescent gel he'd made from mushrooms that glow in the dark. This organic material was susceptible to his creeper trick and could pass through objects with him. It apparently provided enough of a glow for him to read for at least a couple of hours.

This was part of his undoing in the end. He was taking his time, really trying to digest the implications of some legal documents in a safe in the penthouse apartment of a top property investor, when the guy had arrived home unexpectedly.

Ziggy didn't even hear him come in because his head was in the safe, and even then it's not like there was a lot he could have done about it because his hands were also inside the safe to turn the pages of documents. The man could probably just have phoned the police and waited for them to deal with it. Even if Ziggy had heard him, it would have taken him at least thirty minutes to extricate himself from this ridiculous situation. Instead, the homeowner had grabbed the nearest thing to hand and administered a savage beating. The nearest thing to hand had been a sturdy fire poker, and the beating had inflicted some serious damage. No one is entirely sure exactly how creepers work, but we can now assume that it somehow involves the spleen. After laying down any number of "suppressing whacks", the property mogul had opted to use the poker in more of a "controlled stabbing manner". The long and the short of it was that Ziggy couldn't creep anymore. He'd lost his trick, and this really couldn't have happened at a worse time. Those quotes, by the way, are from the property investor's interview under caution. He wasn't charged with a crime.

In fairness, victims of creepers suffer an even more horrific response if the creeper is incapacitated or killed while they are mid-object, but still, this was pretty unfortunate for Ziggy, as not only his head but both his hands were now stuck inside the fifty-kilo safe.

To add insult to grievous bodily injury, the property investor refused to tell anyone the combination to the safe. Ziggy was permanently stuck in total darkness, without the use of his hands, which is presumably why he had been assigned as my cellmate in the Facility for the Incarceration of the Differently-Abled.

Overcrowding being the issue it was at FIDA, there was no way that even a "high risk" inmate like myself was going to get a cell to themselves. There is a fairly thorough triage process though, and they had decided that it would be unwise to put me in with anyone that they wouldn't want shrunk. I don't think Ziggy would even notice if I shrunk him, with the safe on his face the way it was. He could hear me surprisingly easily if I was close enough, and I could hear his reply provided I cupped my ear to him like a safecracker from an old movie. It was an annoying way to have a conversation though, even if it hadn't been for our other cellmate constantly interjecting that he wanted to hear too.

Hugo had apparently been reaching to get his wife's hatbox down from the luggage rack of a train, when suddenly his arms had extended to two-and-a-half times their previous length and then flopped to the floor. He was fairly old for this affliction to kick in, so it must have come as quite the shock. I'm not sure how he had presumably manage to go the first thirty-six years of his life without trying particularly hard to reach anything. He has to be regretting the hatbox incident though, as his wife left him shortly afterwards. She says it was for "other reasons", that they had "grown apart". It's hard to imagine that him turning out to be an arm-flopper wasn't a contributing factor though. He certainly seems to think so, he won't shut up about it.

The time in the cell, though, had mostly afforded me a lot of thinking time. Time to reflect on how our admittedly ill-conceived plan had gone more wrong than even I could have anticipated. I figured that there was a small possibility that The Angel of Death had joined us at T-BAIT, but it made more sense that she had been tracking us for much longer. Disturbingly, I realise she had most likely joined us in the prison transport, all that time with the doors wide open and the big empty space the X-Force had left in the back of the van, that and the weirdly high scream I'd heard.

The only consolation is that I don't think it went quite as she had planned. I've never heard of The Angel of Death killing anyone in public. With only a few exceptions, her victims have usually been asleep, with a maximum of one other person in the room. I can only imagine that she must have been told that under no circumstances was she to let the resurrection go ahead, otherwise I'm sure she would just have waited until Max went to bed to do her thing.

I don't want to dwell on the aftermath of Max's death. It was largely captured on the live broadcast, and you can watch every horrific moment if you are that way inclined. I wouldn't recommend it.

I hadn't been totally sure what percentage of the studio audience was genuinely alive as we were recording the show, but my suspicion had been that the majority were dependent on Max. His untimely death unfortunately confirmed this. Essentially, the entire crowd was suddenly dead, a fate in which I was about to join them.

It's easy to see why no one wakes or struggles when The Angel of Death comes for them in their sleep, the sensation was almost imperceptible. It felt perhaps like someone tickling the front of my neck with an ice cube. To even call it painful would be overstating it, and yet now when I touch the wound it left, it's got to be half a centimetre deep. It wasn't even the sensation of the cut that had caused me to duck back and likely saved my life, it was the sight of Jackson coming at me fast, as crazy mad as I have ever seen him, about to punch me in the face.

She's not entirely invisible, Kitty, especially if she's not pressed up against a wall or an object, and thankfully Jackson had appraised the situation faster than I had. He'd known that she'd have to be close, and he had caught a shimmer of movement behind Max, moving towards me.

He hadn't been trying to punch me in the face but rather to rapidly push my head out of harm's way. Anyway, it had caused me to duck so I'm not complaining, with the added benefit that he'd followed through and punched The Angel of Death in the face.

Then he punched her again.

The first blow to the face had caused a spray of blood to come out of her nose, and this had been the clearest way for Jackson to see where she was. He kept on punching just to make sure there was a continuous stream of blood and he could keep track of her, at least until she had sustained enough injuries that she'd lost control of her trick.

I'm sure I don't need to remind you at this point that, because of Jackson's facial paralysis, to the inexperienced observer, he can look like he's happy, unreasonably happy, ecstatically happy even. Which is an unusual expression to have on your face as you are beating a naked teenage girl to death with your bare hands on live television. If you've not seen it, it's an undeniably compelling bit of footage.

"But why didn't she kill you before?" said Ziggy, at least I assume he did. I pressed my ear up against the safe.

"Say again?"

"But why didn't she kill you before? There must have been loads of opportunities when you were travelling. You must have slept or had a rest. Why wait until the last minute?"

"I don't think that was the point."

Ziggy shrugged.

"I mean, even if she'd killed all of us, Felix would still be there. He had a lot of power, a lot of influence, and he really had the Prime Minister over a barrel with the whole mutually assured destruction Max thing. Security was so tight there, I don't think even The Angel of Death could have got to Max without us."

I pressed my ear to the safe as Ziggy started talking again.

"So you're saying the whole situation would have been better if you'd just done nothing?"

He was annoyingly right.

"Say that again," said Hugo, trying to press his face against the safe.

"I mean, it's not like Jesus swayed any voters, and without you, Max would still be alive, they'd all still be alive."

"Who'd all still be alive without who?" said Hugo. I trod on one of his floppy arms, maybe not entirely by accident.

I decided to stop talking to Ziggy for a bit. There was a TV in our cell. This wasn't a treat for us, it was deliberately locked onto a news channel.

———

Virgil Barnett won the election by the way. It hadn't even been close. The general consensus from the public seemed to be that the concept of bringing Jesus back to life with a little magic boy was pretty sacrilegious in the first place. Felix was definitely seen to have finally gotten what was coming to him, with Max as admittedly unfortunate collateral damage.

It can't have helped that the Prime Minister had refused to make any further public appearances in the week preceding the election, instead choosing to mourn his daughter in private. I don't think it would have made a difference though, too many people wanted him out. Oh, and judging by the numbers from Coventry, it looks like the Bobbetts voted for Barnett en mass. I'm not sure if Terrence had managed to re-negotiate his deal or he was just attempting to win favour with the new government. I don't think he's been arrested yet though, so maybe it worked.

Talking of which, I should probably fill you in on what happened next.

As the video feed had been going out live, the news that Max had been killed was public almost instantaneously. Given the speed of the response, I'd have to assume that this was an eventuality that the perimeter guards had trained for.

Tess said "they're coming, they're all coming", but it was in such a defeated tone that I don't think she was planning on putting up much resistance. It's not like there's a lot she could do anyway. I doubt there are enough badgers and foxes in the county to take out the heavily armed force that was heading for us. The only one of us that stood a chance was Jackson.

"Get out of here," I insisted.

He looked devastated.

I shrank him before he could object, and then seemingly within moments there were shouts through bullhorns outside, telling us to "raise your hands above your heads and walk slowly towards the exit."

We were lucky to be arrested by the conventional police. If the X-Force had been allowed through, I'm sure we would have been killed right then. I say "lucky", but it's starting to look like that may have been a preferable fate.

Virgil Barnett's government has enacted a number of new policies since taking office... Oh, a couple of notes on Virgil that I recently found out, they should give you a good idea what to expect from the man. He killed his own son. Wait, it was more cowardly than that, he'd had his own son killed. I figure that's why The Angel of Death had even been in the country to begin with. Barnett must have borrowed her from Billy Winn for this particularly sensitive job. That's why there had been bloody sheets in the dryer already when I was cleaning the sofa. She must have killed him in his sleep, as per her usual MO, and then concocted the hanging afterwards as a way to disguise her handiwork. For once, this was a murder she couldn't take credit for. I can't be sure why Virgil had thought it so necessary, but I'm going to assume it was some nonsense about "the shame he had brought on the family". That had certainly been the general attitude he had taken whenever the subject came up, that he was "perhaps, in death, hoping to atone for the errors he made in life."

We eventually surmise that The Angel had probably been

tracking us since the very beginning, and she had probably still been at the crime scene when I arrived to clean it. Maybe that was something she often did. She could observe the police response that way. And then, when a pair of tricksters turned up and started shrinking things and controlling animals, it makes sense that she would have kept an eye on us. It seemed to be well within her skillset to follow even someone as tricky as Tess. In fact, following people is something she's probably even more qualified at than killing people.

It's more than likely that, as Tess was tracking me with a selection of compliant animals, she was herself being tracked by one of the world's foremost serial killers. Something that may have amused either or both of them if it hadn't led to their deaths.

I assume that it was only Jimmy's elaborate thermal imaging setup that saved him from decapitation. Not that it did him a lot of good of course. They'd just used creepers instead.

As you'd imagine, Ziggy was full of fascinating facts. Apparently it was pretty common knowledge that Barnett had previously hired a creeper, that everyone called The Ghost, to do his dirty work. Interestingly, apparently The Ghost got the nickname because of his incredibly pale complexion, the fact that he mostly came out at night and killed people was just a happy coincidence. Instantly that made me think of the pasty creeper that Jimmy had seen off and, for once, I was able to tell Ziggy something he didn't already know. The Ghost, I told him, was probably dead.

"The Ghost is on our side though, right?"

"No, Hugo, pay attention." I'm beginning to realise that his wife, in fact, had a number of good reasons to leave Hugo before he even got the floppy arms.

I'm also beginning to wonder if the former leader of the opposition's step-aerobics fatality was entirely accidental. According to Ziggy, The Ghost had worked exclusively for

Barnett for the last year at least. I suppose he had seen how effective The Angel of Death had been for Billy Winn and had cobbled together his own off-brand equivalent. So, there was another reason to dislike our new Prime Minister, but there are oh so many more.

The first bit of new legislation on the books was that *Darwin* was now going to be far more frequent. Instead of one a month, there would be two shows a week. This would have previously been unsustainably regular. See, there really aren't as many tricksters as most people like to make out (excluding Bobbetts, I'll admit there are a surprisingly large number of Bobbetts). And even then, it's only a small sub-section of tricksters that would voluntarily take a chance on *Darwin*. Even with the overcrowding as bad as it is, I think most of us would just stick it out in FIDA if it came to it. That was certainly my plan.

There had apparently been a number of attempts to find a way to make *Darwin* compulsory for all tricksters. Most of the pundits on the news these days seemed to think it was the obvious way to go, certainly on the news channel that was left playing incessantly in our cell anyway. Legal experts would contradict them though. The games were already playing in a legal grey area, a grey area that often required, as a point of law, that the contestants' participation be voluntary. The whole category of "Death by Misadventure" for example, which contained a number of audience favourites, would fundamentally not be legal in a compulsory game.

It all very much seemed like pointless semantics to me. Surely if they wanted to kill us, eventually they would just kill us, but it was the only thing other than the news that we were allowed to watch, so we'd of course watch *Darwin* and all the post-game analysis twice a week.

Every Wednesday and Saturday at 9 pm it would be shown on every TV in the prison. It used to be on at 7 pm, but it had been decided that a post-watershed time slot was more appropriate. Not apparently because of the brutal violence visited upon the majority of the contestants, but because when the brutal violence happened to people, they would sometimes swear loudly enough to get picked up by the crowd mics. Somewhat unexpectedly, Ziggy was a huge fan of *Darwin*, apparently he always had been. Given that he was in a safe, he couldn't exactly watch it anymore, so I would have to cup my mouth to his door and describe every horrific moment of it to him.

A lot of *Darwin*'s obstacles come up repeatedly. This is presumably because some of them are fairly expensive to construct, but also, I think, because some are just popular. Most people have theories on how they would take on some of the classics, but for tricksters it is even more resonant as there is, more so now than ever before, a significant chance that they will sooner or later have to put their theories to the test. Hugo was less of a fan, given that he'd only discovered he was a trickster fairly recently and didn't seem particularly happy about it. I guess this wasn't that surprising. Also, as he had a spectacularly bad trick, I can't imagine he was considering giving *Darwin* a go.

But I'm assuming that this is one of the reasons that Ziggy had clearly put so much thought into it before his injuries. He must have considered being a contestant at some point. Now that he has a safe for a head, though, I think his best bet would be to just sit down quietly at the entrance. This is not even a terrible tactic in terms of survival chances for most contestants. I think people just don't do it often because the crowd tend to boo people who do. Some of Ziggy's suggestions were actually pretty insightful though.

There is an underwater maze game, for example. If you've not seen it, I'm not sure what you'd need to know. It's a maze, like researchers would perhaps send a science mouse through, but it's big enough for humans. You enter through an airlock, and the whole thing remains filled with water. If you go the right way, it would probably take less than a minute or so to get in and out the other side. The route changes every time the maze is used though, so odds are that you are going to hit a dead end or two along your way.

"It's not the maze that kills them though, it's the panic. You can make every single turn wrong, and as long as you don't repeat a mistake, you'd still be out in a couple of minutes. It's not a big maze," said Ziggy.

"He needs to go faster," said Hugo.

As we watched the next contestant, I realised he was right. Not Hugo. Hugo was seldom right. Ziggy had a point though. I'm not sure what the guy in the maze's trick was, but he was definitely strong and he'd set off at a decent pace, half swimming and half striding along the bottom. He was even lucky with his route, and I think most of the crowd thought he was going to make it through, as there was a hint of grudging respect in how quiet they were being. But then he reached a dead end. It shouldn't have posed a problem but he did exactly what Ziggy had predicted, he turned around and got stuck in a loop, repeating the same last corner again and again, refusing to accept that his route was wrong and backtracking further. His actions became more and more frantic, but sadly, no more logical, as he was clearly running low on air. And now the crowd was anything but quiet, stomping and clapping in an increasingly rapid tempo until the poor guy took a huge panic breath, his lungs filling with water only metres from the exit.

"If he'd just stayed calm... There's so much focus on the physical, you see, but most of *Darwin* is mental."

Ziggy was again right. Easy for him to say though, as creepers are essentially immune to claustrophobia, otherwise they wouldn't be able to do what they do. Also their whole respiratory system is different. They can take a lot more oxygen in through the skin than normal people, and they don't need much of it because their metabolism is so slow. Come to think of it, I don't think I've ever seen one not make it through the water maze. Much to the disappointment of the audience I'm sure, creepers perform disproportionately well on *Darwin*. No one likes creepers. The fear of one being pardoned and released could only be slightly mitigated by the hope that the prize money would hopefully mean that they might be less inclined to kidnap children in the future. The audience sure likes seeing them killed though, so swings and roundabouts, I suppose.

Ziggy would have been an exceptionally welcome contestant, a creeper at an almost insurmountable disadvantage would be a surefire crowd-pleaser. I hope he would have proved them all wrong.

———

Another result of being a high-security inmate is that I was only allowed to leave the cell for one hour a day. The authorities weren't doing us a favour with this either. Apparently they hadn't wanted to let us out at all, but one hour was the minimum allowable in accordance with EU human rights legislation. Evidently this was a fight that not even Barnett's government wanted to pick. The questionable legality of *Darwin* was contentious enough among the more liberal nations and was doing little good for the UK's reputation in Europe, as reflected by our increasingly poor performance in Eurovision. It can't have helped that our most recent entry had been performed by Reasonable Force, the *Darwin* house band. Nul points.

Anyway, once a day I would be escorted from our cell for an hour of exercise. This would comprise of walking up and down an enclosed area not much bigger than the cell, whilst being monitored by a team of snipers. While the walking wasn't particularly strenuous, the thought of the sniper's itchy trigger fingers was enough to get my heart rate up. The exercise wasn't compulsory, but the thing that made it worth the stress was that it was outdoors, or at least it was the minimum amount of outdoorsness that was legally permissible. I was surrounded by four thick walls, but I could see the sky through a wire mesh roof. More importantly, I could see the birds that would perch on the mesh.

Either the guards were not aware of the nature of Tess' trick, or they simply had no way to prevent her from using it. She could stay sat in her cell and communicate with any prisoner she wanted while they were out for their daily exercise. This had made her almost instantly the most informed inmate in all of FIDA, certainly in quantity, if not quality, of information.

Most inmates were happy to talk to her. A lot of them would have been happy to talk to anyone, usually because their trick precluded them from contact with other inmates. An inquisitive crow or squirrel or seagull or whatever made a good listener.

The problem was that Tess didn't really have any solid way of separating paranoid conspiracy theories from genuine conspiracy facts. On the whole, people with tricks tend to believe that the state is out to get them. This is because, generally, it is. An early rumour that I dismissed as paranoid hyperbole had turned out, in fact, to be true.

Tess had told me that *Darwin* was moving to a new venue. In order to fit more contestants into each show and to allow for more elaborate obstacles, the whole thing was being moved out of the Birmingham NEC and into the Millennium Dome. If you didn't happen to visit it, don't worry, you are in the majority, the Millennium Dome is essentially an oversized circus tent that was conceived to celebrate some things the UK was proud of.

Presumably, given that it had not been particularly popular, someone had suggested trying the opposite approach. It was now going to showcase something that we should rightly be pretty ashamed of, the bi-weekly blood sport that is *Darwin*.

This had sounded improbable to me for a couple of reasons. Firstly, it just didn't seem necessary. I was amazed that they were finding enough contestants to fill the two shows a week they have now. The promise of a decent monthly paycheque just isn't enough to get anyone but the chronically desperate to volunteer to participate in something as dangerous as *Darwin*. Secondly, it sounded incredibly expensive. "Circus tent" maybe doesn't do the venue justice. It's one of the biggest indoor spaces in the world. The government wasn't exactly flush with cash either. The Bobbett invasion alone had cost the country an estimated 23% of it's GDP for almost two years, a thought that briefly made me feel more fondly of Terrence Bobbett than is probably appropriate.

"Trust me," squawked the crow that was Tess, "it's nearly ready."

Apparently they had tricksters working on it in the early stages, a pair of super-strong brothers with prehensile tails had told her.

Anyway, it turned out the crow was right. A few weeks later, the *All New Darwin* had been announced on the news. In a collaboration with a large US television network, the Church of Divine Justice and, somewhat surprisingly, Honda, it was indeed going ahead. The building was to be renamed the Darwin Dome and was going to be the new permanent home of the games. The inaugural event was to be in only three weeks' time, and was going to feature an opening address by none other than President Billy Winn, in his first public appearance in the UK.

The day after it had been announced, Tess' squirrel was gesturing at me so fervently that a sniper shot it.

The sponsorship deals explained the funding, I suppose, and Tess now had a pretty decent idea of where they were getting so many contestants from. She'd spoken to some inmates who had been in FIDA pretty much since it opened, and apparently the current situation was far from normal. In the early days, there would maybe be one or two inmate arrivals a week. There was time for them to individually assess each new prisoner and find the most suitable accommodation.

Post-election was a whole different thing though. Tricksters were arriving most days by the bus-full. They were being stuffed twelve at a time into the creeper cells, probably the most universally secure cages in the building. Ironically though, probably the worst possible place for a creeper in the short term, unless you wanted them dead, I suppose. A creeper won't usually do well in a large group. As I'm sure I've mentioned, they're not popular.

This had apparently been brought on by the drastic increase in the rate of arrests of the differently-abled. Under the former government, most trickster arrests had been for one of two reasons, either the trickster had been reported for using their trick for some sort of gainful employment, a Winters Act violation that could get you up to ten years in FIDA, or they had been caught trying to get money some other way, usually theft, which would usually get you an even longer sentence.

Now, though, Tess said she had spoken to people that had been arrested for crimes as minor as vagrancy and trespassing, crimes it is almost impossible to avoid if you are homeless and have no legal means to make a living. Tess had spoken to a whole family that had been arrested just for living in a tent. Both parents had tricks so they'd had almost no money, they had tried to make a go of basically living off the land, planting fruit and veg in some public woods. They'd all been sent to FIDA, including the nine year old who didn't even have a trick, not yet anyway. The family thought it best not to mention it though, lest the poor kid be sent somewhere else on her own.

She had even spoken to Kelly Goodwin, the weather forecaster with the duck, who had recently been arrested, admittedly for a genuine Winters Act violation. She had been selling her forecasts to a futures trader. Apparently you can make pretty decent money trading with infallible weather information. Eventually the trader had decided he could make more money faster, though, by selling the whole story of his nefarious deal to a tabloid. Kelly had looked pretty down apparently. The chatty seagull that Tess was using at the time had reminded Kelly of her duck. The X-Force had apparently shot it while making the arrest, either out of the mistaken apprehension that it was dangerous or out of pure spite.

"Can she still tell the weather without it?"

"I don't know," squawked the crow. "It didn't seem like the right time to ask."

"That's fair," I said, secretly annoyed.

But the worse news by far to come from Tess, the news I had really wished wasn't true, had been about Jackson.

Jackson hadn't been arrested when we were. I'd shrunk him to about mouse size, and there had been a lot going on. Coupled with his innate invincibility, it had been easy enough for him to get away. What he did after that though, it's difficult to say. He would have gone back to full size once I had been driven off, but I was pretty sure I had given him enough time to stash himself somewhere safe. And indeed, when he hadn't been brought to FIDA in the first few days, we had been pretty confident that he'd escaped. If there was ever a trickster that actually justified the elaborate excess of FIDA's security though, it was Jackson.

His problem is he can't really blend in anywhere. It's not just that the fact that his face is frozen in place that immediately marks him out as unusual, but that the expression on his face seems so startled and excited, people can't help but wonder what has just happened to him. Also, he had just beaten a naked girl to death live on television, so there was that.

I suppose I was hoping he would just find some uninhabited area to hide out. I think that's what I would have done. On reflection, though, it did seem overly optimistic to expect it of Jackson, and indeed, he had decided to take a rather more proactive approach to the situation.

The first we had heard of his antics was about two months into our incarceration. The rumour was that there had been an attempted escape. Then it turned out that it had, in fact, not been an escape attempt, but instead someone had been attempting to break in to FIDA.

The building is located around five miles outside of Newport itself, in a large desolate area that used to be a poorly managed dairy farm. Jackson presumably thought that he would be able to get fairly close to the building before he encountered any security, but unfortunately this was far from the case. While it was true that the sniper cover surrounding the property covered only around a five-hundred-metre perimeter, it turns out that was not the only external security in place.

I half remembered this story from a couple of years ago, but Tess had the full details. "His name is Teddy Swann and he is properly mad. He'd managed to keep it a secret his entire life that he even had this trick. Apparently not even his parents knew."

Teddy had been living a perfectly normal life with a

perfectly normal job, which is pretty much living the dream for someone with a trick, credit to him. Then, one weekend he had been watching a live chat show on TV, one of the guests said something that rubbed him the wrong way, apparently something about squash not being a "real man's game". It was a fairly innocuous comment and would almost certainly have gone by unnoticed by almost anyone else, but apparently this was something Teddy was hyper-sensitive about. His dad had reportedly been a passionate squash player and had passed away recently. Perhaps not entirely rational, but Teddy's an unusual chap. Anyway, the show was being broadcast live. He'd known where the studio was, and he'd just run there and grabbed the guy. It was one of those shows where someone is cooking something as they chat, and he had grabbed the guy that had made the squash comment and drowned him in leek and potato soup. As he killed the man, he delivered an impassioned speech straight-to-camera about, not only the physical benefits of playing squash regularly, but also its all-round manliness. The content of the speech was perhaps a little overshadowed by the fact that he was both crying and drowning a man in soup as he made it, but other than that, he made some reasonable points. Then he ran home.

Here's the thing though. He'd lived around thirty miles from the TV studio, and the time between the guy making the comment about squash and his face hitting the soup was only about seven minutes. Even if he'd not stopped once and kept an exactly constant pace, he had to be capable of running at about two hundred and fifty miles per hour. And he'd somehow kept this secret his entire life.

Anyway, Teddy had been sent to FIDA. Some people in the press had raised the concern that, no matter how good the snipers were and how high tech their gear was, if this guy got loose at three hundred odd miles per hour, he was going to be hard to hit. Given that a few of the journalists raising these issues themselves hosted live TV broadcasts, this may actually have been a personal concern on their part. God knows what other bizarre peccadilloes Teddy had that he might attack people with food to defend. So eventually, a representative of FIDA had publicly explained that the institution has a special dispensation from a number of international agreements regarding landmines. There are more landmines in the two-mile perimeter of the FIDA building than there are on the North/South Korean border. The spokesperson reassured the journalists that, regardless of his speed, if Teddy was to make a break for it, it would be both short-lived and explosive.

Jackson presumably had not got the memo on this, and what we can assume had been his first approach at FIDA had indeed been explosive, if not exactly short-lived. There were contrasting reports from different inmates, but we could be pretty sure that at least seven landmines had been detonated the previous night. This had led the general prison population to assume that there must have been a break out on a grand scale. Hey, if seven got caught by the mines, maybe a few got away.

What Tess had realised though, without passing it on to the other prisoners, was that no one was missing, at least there certainly weren't seven people missing. She'd spoken to enough people in enough areas of the prison to figure that out at least. Secondly, from what people had heard, the barrage of fire from the perimeter guns had come after, rather than before, the mines went off. Surely it wouldn't have been possible for seven people to get past the snipers unseen. Some optimistic inmates thought that maybe a whole team had charged towards the facility simultaneously. This hadn't seemed hugely likely to me, but I had to admit it did a better job of fitting the facts.

A news report the following day, though, had made sense of the whole thing. Jackson's face, a recent shot presumably captured on a FIDA night-vision camera, was shown on the news. The population of Newport and the surrounding area were being warned to be on the lookout for this "incredibly dangerous" person. They were told "not, under any circumstances, to approach him".

It was also made very clear during a press conference that, despite the location, the public were not to assume that he had escaped from FIDA, which we were assured "remains escape proof".

And then it all fitted together. Not a group of people approaching FIDA at once, but one very persistent person. A person who, despite being blown up by at least seven land-mines still kept on coming, presumably only turning around when the snipers started shooting at him as well.

Tess was optimistic that he would return for another go. She reckoned that she might have found a way through the minefield.

"When you say 'found a way'..."

"Best not to ask."

And that was the last time I spoke to her. The next day, when I went out to exercise, there was no creature waiting for me on top of my unit. The next day was the same, and then the next.

I was worried. The best case scenario I could think of was that maybe she had been moved somewhere so far away that her animals couldn't reach me. Or maybe that they had found some way to stop her doing her trick, drugged her or something, because the other alternative was too grim to contemplate.

"She's dead," said Ziggy, and I smacked him right in the safe.

"I'm sorry, but what else could it be?"

He wasn't helping, he was the only person I had to talk to though. I really didn't want Hugo's take on the situation.

"How though? She wasn't on *Darwin*, we would have seen."

"You think that's the only way they kill tricksters?"

But before I could answer, the loud lockdown buzzer went off in our cell. This meant that we were to stand against the far wall with our hands behind our backs, not Ziggy obviously, although this generally led to a shouting match followed by a poke with an electric cattle prod from every new guard that wasn't familiar with his situation. It was no easy feat for Hugo either, but I'd begun to enjoy it when they cattle-prodded him a bit.

Anyway, the buzzer had only previously gone off when one of us was about to be escorted out of the cell. I had already had my exercise time for the day, and the others didn't tend to take theirs. Hugo doesn't like getting his arms mucky, and as far as Ziggy is concerned, inside is very similar to outside. So this was presumably for something different.

We stood facing the walls until the buzzer stopped. I turned back around.

"What is it?" said Ziggy.

"I... it can't be good."

For the highest security prisoners, there is a special transportation procedure. A mini cell, almost the exact width and height of a human, is carried or wheeled between cells. It is never opened until it is affixed to the doors of whichever cell or vehicle they are about to deposit the monster into. And one of these was now attached to our cell door.

"You lucky people are getting a new cellmate," said the worryingly gleeful guard.

My only thought was that I should shrink it. How dangerous could they be if I made them tiny? A second buzzer sounded as the door of the cage opened, releasing the prisoner into our cell.

Ziggy turned and ran, clanking his safe into the wall behind us.

I froze, as suddenly in front of me was the familiar, excited, eager face of Jackson.

22

DEATH BY MISADVENTURE

The Prime Minister, I think somewhat reluctantly, had brought a bill before parliament proposing to reinstate the death penalty in the UK. It was a popular bill. Capital punishment has always been a divisive issue in British politics, but the McMillan brothers had given the pro-death camp (a lot of whom were actually also pro death-camp) a forceful argument that just hadn't existed before. It turned out that people existed for which life-long incarceration simply was not a reasonable option. Even if facilities existed in which we could be sure that they could never escape, it would surely be an unreasonable burden to place on the taxpayer.

Furthermore, this was currently only for one trick. Who knows what nature has in store for us in the future? It seemed clear that it would be best for everyone, including possibly the criminals themselves, if we could just put an end to them. It didn't do any harm to their case that the McMillan's had, between them, committed possibly the most reprehensible series of crimes in human history.

I had been at school at the time, so essentially all of my friends were tricksters of one kind or another. We knew this could potentially mean bad news for us down the line, but I can't think of anyone who didn't want to see the McMillans put to death as horrifically as possible.

Anyway, the death penalty bill had passed through the House of Commons about as decisively as any bill ever does, but that isn't the end of the story. It was immediately bounced back, almost unanimously, by the House of Lords. This isn't the right place for a complete overview of the British legal system so let's just stick to the key bits. While the House of Lords cannot prevent a bill from becoming law, they can throw it back to parliament for review. They can generally do this enough to significantly delay the bill coming into law or force a permanent change. And it turned out that the death penalty was something the House of Lords was immovable on. Regardless of the specific situation, their stance was that morally it would be a huge regression for the state to commit murder.

The PM had apparently had a call with Billy Winn where he had assured him that this was only a "minor setback". While there may be a delay, he already had a team researching the most practical ways to execute the McMillans and any future murderous abominations.

And that's how a television show provisionally titled *A Study of Evolving Human Abilities by Means of Natural Selection* had come about. It is now known simply as *Darwin*.

It seems bizarre to think of it now, as it has become such a broadcasting institution, but *Darwin* was not initially devised to be a TV show at all. The footage of what became the first episode was captured mainly as evidence to prove that the authorities were *not* guilty of murder. This was very important from a legal perspective, as in every other sense they were definitely intending to do some murder. The government had for some time been trying to figure out how they could legally kill the McMillan brothers, and some bright spark had suggested perhaps taking a leaf out of the Billy Winn playbook and rather than changing the law, simply working within the laws that already existed.

The President obviously had the advantage that the death penalty was already legal in the majority of his nation. The UK was going to be more constrained on that front, but maybe they could put the McMillans into a situation where they might fight each other? After all, that would presumably kill at least one of them without the government bearing any responsibility at all. Also, some sort of fight to the death would perhaps go some way to satisfying the public's understandable appetite to see the brothers pay a heavy price for their crimes.

There was a bit of an obstacle to this plan though. As this was to be a contest between brothers, you would probably then assume it would be a fairly even match up. As it turned out though, Chris was at a significant disadvantage. When he had been captured after escaping FIDA, Chris had been inhabiting the body of an eight-year-old schoolgirl named Jenny Mayhew. His brother Joe, on the other hand, had not changed his body since his initial arrest, when he happened to be inside the huge muscular frame of the MMA fighter Dion Mitchell. While it was important that the events that took place should be recorded as evidence, it would be tricky to justify to the public at large what would presumably look, to the neutral observer, like a bodybuilder beating a child to death.

The idea of some sort of contest was perceived to be a strong one though. After all, there were an ever-increasing number of differently-abled people being convicted all the time, and space at FIDA was limited.

Besides, it had become fairly clear to the government that changing the existing laws regarding capital punishment would be slow and challenging, two things that the Prime

Minister wasn't particularly keen on. Accordingly, a think tank was tasked with ascertaining if there was any way to execute the more troublesome of the criminal differently-abled, within the UK's existing legal framework. They would never use the word "execute" of course, but they weren't hugely subtle about what they were after. I saw this documentary recently, *Darwin, Origin of the Spectacle*, where they had interviewed a number of the original architects.

The group had been varied; it comprised of lawyers, I think a couple of corporate liability specialists, there was a retired judge, an economist and there were a few others, some from the world of PR, and a few people that had a history of killing people publicly without facing any legal consequences. A key protagonist was apparently a guy called Anderson Black who I can only assume was brought in because he had produced a TV show that had recently accidentally executed a contestant. The TV show was called *Hangman* and was based on the children's word guessing game, except I think the contestant had to answer trivia questions while models constructed an actual gallows around them. I didn't watch it, but they had apparently accidentally hanged a contestant because they couldn't name the drummer that Ringo took over from in The Beatles. I mean, he wasn't hanged by accident, they meant to hang him, I just don't think they meant to do it quite so effectively. The poor guy's family sued and did receive a moderate out of court settlement from Black Death Productions, the unfortunately titled production company behind the show. However, no criminal case was ever brought against the producers, and this turned out to be a surprisingly career enhancing moment for Anderson Black.

As recording a person being executed and not being prosecuted for it was exactly what the government intended to do, and Anderson Black was someone who had recently just done exactly that, I guess it made sense to have him on the team.

It's Anderson's TV background and "instinctive eye for the dramatic", to quote some idiot from the documentary, that really ended up shaping the project. What started as a way for the government to discreetly dispose of inconvenient prisoners while maintaining maximum legal deniability somehow became a prime-time spectacle. In a similar vein, a man who ran a popular Blackpool nightspot called *Dive Bar* had also been consulted. His was apparently the world's only venue to feature both a late-night liquor licence and an Olympic-height diving board. So far they had only killed two patrons, but they had injured numerous others and had as yet escaped any kind of criminal prosecution. I believe it's him we have to thank for a number of the popular water and diving based obstacles that make *Darwin* such a popular spectator sport these days.

One of the first concepts that the lawyers of the think tank thought was worth exploring was a term you'll be very familiar with if you've ever watched even a single event. I'm talking of course about "Reasonable Force". This quickly became a catchphrase of the show, and the *Darwin* house band, Reasonable Force, had a modest hit with "Feel The Force", a song that they continue to insist on playing more than surely anyone enjoys, but before that, it was a relatively seldom used piece of British jurisprudence.

In British law, it has long been established that any person may use "reasonable force" to defend themselves against anyone that is perceived to be attacking them, or with some exceptions, someone else. There are a few things about this law that appealed to the creators of *Darwin*. Firstly, it is deliberately vague. There is no specific definition of what might be deemed "reasonable". This happens a lot in legal definitions as it allows laws to remain relevant as customs change. Secondly, the term "reasonable" is fairly subjective. What may be a *reasonable* force to defend yourself from one person may be very different to what would be reasonable to defend yourself against a different person or in a different situation.

To go back to before the very first *Darwin* for a moment, the lawyers had suggested that, given their propensity for escaping, in the not unlikely situation that one or both of the McMillan brothers was to attempt to escape or was to brandish a weapon, it would likely be deemed to be a "reasonable" use of force to shoot them. They started with relatively simple ideas, nothing like the madness it has become these days. Say, if a gun were to be placed where one of the McMillans would be able to pick it up. Everyone was reticent to give these people weapons for obvious reasons, but it was pointed out that the gun didn't necessarily have to be loaded. This is a legal grey area, but being as they were trying to kill people, it seemed that they were going to have to play in some pretty grey areas. Essentially, all that matters in law with regards to what is "reasonable force" is what the person using the force perceives the situation to be. So, hypothetically, if Joe McMillan were to pick up an unloaded weapon and then point it in the direction of, for example, an SAS strike team that did not know for sure that the gun was not loaded, under British law, it would be perfectly legal for them to defend themselves with lethal force.

Other potential opportunities for legalised murder lay within the UK's traffic laws. As one "expert" put it, "Outside of military service, if you are looking to kill someone and not go to jail, then your best bet is to drive a big car fast." Of course, it's not always legal to mow people down in a car, that would be carnage, but the lawyers pointed out that, out of the thousands of road deaths every year, only a very small percentage led to the prosecution of a driver. Essentially, if you weren't drunk or going at a significant margin over the legal speed limit, it would be very difficult to prove that you were driving "without due care and attention", which would usually be required for a criminal prosecution.

An initial idea was to just find a way to coax the brothers into running across a busy motorway. Understandably, this idea had some significant drawbacks. If they were hit by a car going at eighty odd miles an hour, it might do some significant damage to both the car and the driver, that the organisers may be liable for. Or even worse, if they were to successfully cross the motorway without being fatally wounded, they'd have just released two serial killers. So, using public roads seemed to be out of the question, but in general it still seemed like a promising notion.

The final idea that the team had thought worth exploring was the legal concept of *death by misadventure*. From the lawyers' perspectives, the appealing thing here is that the brunt of the responsibility for the death is placed firmly on the victim. Unlike, for example, an *accidental death*, or ever worse a *death due to negligence*, with *death by misadventure* the victim is considered to have made a choice that led to their death. It's often the legal classification of deaths involving drug overdoses or dangerous sports. If the prisoners could be induced to make a choice that they knew to be risky and it resulted in their death, then it could more than likely be classified as a *death by misadventure*. Therefore, the event organisers would not bear any moral culpability or legal responsibility.

Early appraisals weren't positive though. Each of the legal concepts was individually assessed and found to have too many elements of risk to be effective. In order to kill someone with *reasonable force*, it would be necessary for them to brandish a weapon or at least threaten a vulnerable person. For someone to be hit by a car that was being driven *with due care and attention*, they would need to have made a choice to step into the road. A key factor in a death being classified as *death by misadventure* was that the victim had knowingly taken a risk. None of the ideas would work, for a combination of two reasons: Firstly, they all involved an element of personal choice, so the prisoner could simply choose not to comply, and secondly, even if they did partake willingly, there seemed to be a good chance that they might survive.

It seemed for a moment that they would have to devise something totally different or potentially scrap the whole idea, until an economist on the team salvaged the project. The answer to the first issue was that they needed some sort of motivating factor. In most economic models, the motivating factor was money, and it seemed that would likely work here as well, although it might be frowned on to offer large cash prizes to convicted murderers. There was another even bigger motivator they could offer though: freedom. If they were to set up a game where the convict could potentially win their own freedom, perhaps also combined with a more modest financial amount, something close to the national minimum wage, then perhaps they could be persuaded to take on even visibly dangerous risks. That is actually where the prize money for *Darwin* remains to this day. It is calculated as the national minimum wage at thirty-eight hours per week for the remainder of the winner's life. It's never been popular that the winner receives anything at all, but the public have been placated by two facts: Firstly, this is significantly cheaper than the cost of housing a differently-abled person in FIDA. Secondly, each *Darwin* show has a maximum of only one winner and usually features a significant number of deaths, resulting in a substantial overall net saving to the taxpayer.

This concept was understandably initially met with a huge amount of scepticism from the team. The point was to murder these monsters, not release them back into the wild. But the economist had continued undeterred. Providing there were multiple elements of risk at play, it would be possible to devise a system with an almost certain outcome. "Much like a collection of loans with a significant risk of defaulting can be packaged together to make a low risk security, a number of tasks with a seemingly small chance of injury could be packaged together to make an almost certain chance of death." He literally said this on the documentary, and yet, still every trickster I've met has reckoned they would have a pretty good shot at getting out if they ever ended up on the show. I guess we're just not good at calculating probabilities, or maybe it's that your own death always feels like something incredibly unlikely. It has, after all, usually never happened before.

It was using the combination of these ideas that the very first *Darwin* was devised. It took place in a disused steelworks on the outskirts of Sheffield. There was no audience, as such, this was not intended as entertainment and letting the McMillan brothers near any other humans seemed like an undue risk. It was necessary to have a relatively large area, though, as they needed space for the vehicles to maintain a decent speed.

The premise was fairly simple, at least compared to modern *Darwin* events. Contestants would enter at one end of the giant indoor space. In order to remove any liability that may have resulted from a death in police custody, they would be provisionally pardoned of all crimes and legally released from prison upon entering the building. The pardon was, however, contingent upon them leaving the building through the correct exit within the allotted time. From a legal standpoint, this is a sporting contest between free people. It was also important, from a legal standpoint, that survival would be a possibility. For the first *Darwin*, this possibility consisted of a white door at the very far end of the room. If they could be the first to reach that door by any means, they would be free to go. In order to get to that door, though, they would have to traverse a number of obstacles. Each of these obstacles posed a sometimes obvious, sometimes not so obvious, risk of death.

As well as the possibility of freedom at the far end of the room, there were other "motivating factors" to encourage the contestants to try their luck at the obstacles. I think the first event only had a couple of cars, I guess because it was a smaller venue. A circular roadway was constructed to run through the building. It was designated as the A999 and had a legal speed limit of 70 mph. Professional drivers were tasked with driving at or about the speed limit for the duration of the event. They were instructed to drive "with due care and attention to other road users".

I'm assuming it was made very clear to them that if, for example, a terrified differently-abled person was to suddenly jump out in front of their vehicle, that they would not be likely to face any charges if they were to inadvertently hit them at approximately 70 mph. They'd done a bit of research on the likely outcomes of an incident involving a pedestrian being hit by a car at high speed and picked a couple of tall SUVs for the task. They apparently offered statistically the greatest chance for a pedestrian fatality, with an almost negligible chance of the driver of the vehicle being harmed. I imagine they were largely the same instructions as the drivers are given to this day; basically, don't obviously aim for the pedestrians, but maybe don't go out of your way to avoid them either.

During the first *Darwin*, the cars proved their effectiveness almost immediately, by fatally injuring Joe McMillan after only a few minutes. Joe was the first contestant in, having apparently volunteered for that position. Now, of course, the running order is either decided randomly or, more often, everyone is just released simultaneously. Pundits have different views on whether it's beneficial to get in early and give yourself the maximum amount of time, or to start late so you can see what is ahead of you. It depends largely on who else is competing on the day as to what makes a good spot. For Joe, though, this was a bad spot. Being that this was the first ever *Darwin*, going first meant that he had absolutely no idea what to expect. He had entered the arena with the cocky self-assuredness of the MMA fighter whose body he currently inhabited. This confidence was misplaced, though, and was about to be proved so. The McMillan's trick, while incredibly versatile in the free world, conveyed very little assistance on *Darwin*. It had at least offered Joe the advantage of being in very good shape physically, and he was well suited to the first obstacle.

Contestants entered the steelworks via an elevator that they exited onto a raised platform. They would have then been able to survey the whole space — every obstacle that lay between them and the big white door to freedom at the far end of the structure. In order to get to the next obstacle, though, they would first have to get down from the platform, around 20 metres from the tarmac surface below. They were presented with the kind of simple "misadventure" task, that is very much the bread and butter of a modern *Darwin* event. In front of Joe were six strong-looking climbing ropes. These were hanging about a metre from the raised platform. They were close enough that it shouldn't be difficult for most people to be able to jump off and grab one, but they were just far enough out of reach that you couldn't give each one a tug. The reason for this became clear if you looked up to see what the ropes were attached to. While all six ropes went up into a dark box near the ceiling, only five ropes came out the top of the box, and then appeared to be securely tied off to a steel girder.

The message was clear, one of the ropes was not tied off at all, or at least not to anything that would take the twenty-odd stone that Joe must have weighed. Joe didn't even pause though, he just jumped straight off and grabbed the rope that was closest to him. As it happened, this was a lucky choice and the rope held. He climbed down to the bottom and started to do a bit of a dance. Some people reckon that his complete lack of hesitation was because he was so used to taking big risks that a one-in-six chance hadn't concerned him. I'm inclined to think that he just hadn't counted the ropes. He didn't even realise that one of them wasn't going to hold, he'd just thought it was a climbing challenge or something. Anyway, it was the little dance that got him, not the ropes. He had lowered himself straight onto the A999, and the small delay in having a little dance was enough time for one of the SUVs to get to him at an entirely legal 70 mph.

The next contestant was either smarter of more risk averse than Joe had been, or maybe it was that they could see Joe's bizarre remains spattered all over the road beneath them. The SUV had quite literally knocked Joe out of his skin. Anyway, the next contestant counted the ropes and had obviously figured that one of them was not going to produce the desired outcome. He'd stood on the platform contemplating his options for a while. Long enough that if there had been a live audience like there is with today's *Darwin* shows, people would have been booing and shouting abuse.

On *Darwin*, it's almost always an option to just stay put where you are. After all, having a contestant willingly, for example, jump off of a platform, has very different legal ramifications than pushing them off the platform. Contestants are accordingly entirely within their rights to wait out the whole event. There is, of course, a three-hour time-cap on any given show these days. The earlier shows had a far looser format but with a similar result. If the contestant manages to make it to the end of the time without winning, they will simply be returned to their cell at FIDA and can potentially appear on a future *Darwin* show.

As well as the progression towards freedom and modest prize money though, there are a number of other motivating factors that tend to keep people moving through the course. The first is that if you have already made it a pretty good distance, there is a very palpable feeling of sunk cost. You don't get to save your position or anything. If you don't finish and you come back another time, you will have to start from the beginning. Given that, often, to have got some way into the course would have involved a number of near-death experiences, this factor is not to be underestimated. Secondly, there is usually a contestant behind you. You don't usually know who the next contestant will be. Contrary to popular opinion, most tricksters are pretty reasonable people and aren't going to be looking to do you any harm, but it's often not as simple as that.

There is, of course, a possibility that the person behind you could be someone like Chris McMillan. That was certainly most people's fear in the first *Darwin*. Chris was in the body of an eight-year-old girl, so the common consensus was that he may look to upgrade early on. He had certainly proved himself very willing to kill people for a lot less. On the other hand, as he was only in the body of an eight-year-old girl, he was unlikely to be able to overpower all but the weakest of opponents without getting hold of a weapon of some kind.

These all would have been considerations rushing through the mind of the second ever *Darwin* contestant, a short wrinkly man with the ability to emit an alternating electrical current, as he eyed up the rope-Russian-roulette in front of him. He certainly considered the ropes for quite some time. His decision was hurried along considerably when Chris McMillan stepped onto the platform next to him. It looked for a moment like he was going to jump straight off the platform without grabbing a rope at all, but then he went in a different direction altogether and decided to curl into a foetal position and gently vibrate. It was an unorthodox strategy but effective. Chris ignored him entirely and took a running jump at the ropes. He jumped through the ropes diagonally which enabled him to take hold of two ropes simultaneously. One of the ropes fell straight to the floor, but Chris was able to swiftly descend on the other. The bloody remains of his brother on the road below alerted him to the danger of the A999, and he didn't linger in the roadway. Chris was off to an alarmingly impressive start. In fact, this became such a standard technique for overcoming this obstacle that for a while they didn't bother featuring it at all as it never caught anyone out. And then someone had the idea of bringing it back but with only four of the six ropes attached, with predictably fatal consequences.

If the chap left on the platform had been less busy vibrating, I assume he was electrifying himself or maybe it was just an unusual panic response, he would have realised that now was the perfect opportunity to shimmy down. Technicians would replace the dummy rope before the next contestant came in, but now he had a great chance to grab a rope which would almost certainly be safely tied off.

As Chris made his way to the next obstacle, he noticed a switch with the intriguing label "platform release". He looked suspicious, but as he definitely wasn't standing on a platform himself, I guess he figured it was worth a go. And he was right. Exactly as advertised, the switch released two bolts from the platform that the wrinkly man was vibrating on, and it dropped away like a trapdoor. The poor chap fell about twenty metres onto the road below. I think the fall killed him, but if it hadn't, then the SUV that went over him at 70 mph certainly would have.

And this is how the world learned of another motivating factor encouraging contestants to keep moving through the dangerous obstacles. While you are well within your rights to just stay put and wait out the event at any point of the course, if another person successfully completes the obstacle in front, there is a significant chance that this could have dire consequences for you. Sometimes this can be as simple as them voluntarily pulling a lever or pushing a button, as Chris had demonstrated. Sometimes it's a far more complex mechanism that is triggered automatically as an obstacle is completed. In short, staying put on *Darwin* can often be as dangerous as pushing on.

Chris actually did really well on *Darwin*, especially considering he had no significant advantage from his trick and was essentially an eight-year-old girl. It goes to show that it's not all about physical ability. A lot of it comes down to tactical thinking and luck. Of course, "doing really well on *Darwin*" is generally synonymous with "was killed on *Darwin*", and this was almost the case for Chris McMillan. In fairness to him, if he hadn't been on the very first show and had therefore been able to see a *Darwin* show before, he would have been unlikely to make the mistake he made.

He had been progressing through the course well and was getting close enough to the final exit door that I can imagine the organisers were beginning to contemplate a number of sinister contingency plans. I think they would have been perfectly happy for any of the contestants that didn't have the surname McMillan to get to the end. That would, after all, show how fair the process was. But the idea of having even one McMillan on the loose again was terrifying.

Chris had arrived at what looked like a relatively simple obstacle. There were three tubes in front of him. They may have posed an issue for some of the larger contestants, but as a small girl he was more than capable of crawling through. He wisely took some time to appraise the situation though. The tubes were long and they were not lit at all inside. It was possible to see light at the end of each, but it was impossible to see what was going on inside the tube. Also, there was a loud and disconcerting sound coming from them, reminiscent maybe of an old lawnmower. And so, Chris waited. He had maintained a lead throughout but it wasn't long before another contestant caught up with him. The contestant was a creeper, one of the earliest to be caught naked in a bank vault. She was understandably wary of Chris, and for a moment it looked like she was going to dive straight into one of the darkened tubes just to avoid him. She had a quick look in the first one, though, and thought better of it. Then she made a gracious "after you" gesture to Chris, which Chris repeated back to her even more graciously. Coming from a playful eight year old, this looked pretty adorable, until of course you consider the reality of the situation.

The creeper looked to be considering if she could simply throw this child into a tube to see what happened. She was certainly stepping towards Chris when he pulled the gun from behind his back. It was a small pistol; to this day we don't know if it was loaded. Sometimes they are, but more often they aren't. Usually there are blank rounds made up to look like the real thing. Closely examining replays will show that Chris had actually picked up the gun a few obstacles back. He had been crawling through a ball pit under some rotating blades and you can see him tuck it secretively into a fold of his dress as he leaves the pit. I guess he had assumed it was something that perhaps he wasn't meant to find, something that might convey an advantage later on. These are the errors he would be less likely to make if he had ever seen a *Darwin* show before.

He, once again, made the adorable "after you" gesture, encouraging the creeper into the darkened tubes. This time, though, with a gun in his hand, it was a lot more menacing. What he didn't see, or at least didn't catch the relevance of, was that two of the three *reasonable force* lights had come on. When the creeper didn't move, he brandished the gun more forcefully, pointing it straight at her head. The creeper perhaps would have obeyed at that point, it definitely seemed to be the less risky option, but then the third *reasonable force* light turned on, and Chris was immediately shot three times.

Apparently the organisers had not taken the trouble to explain the *reasonable force* system to the contestants. Following UK common law, any person is allowed to use reasonable force to defend themselves *or others*. As what is deemed to be *reason-able* is vague and subjective, the event organisers thought it best to have the unanimous consent of three legal scholars before taking any decisive action. These three legal experts, usually retired judges, watch the *Darwin* events unfold on a series of video feeds. They have access to a vast legal library, but they may not consult with each other. If they believe, at any point, that a contestant is posing enough of a threat to another contestant that they would "deem it reasonable to use lethal force to defend the other contestant(s)", they can make their opinion known. They are not aware of the other legal scholars' opinions, but if at any point all three experts concur that a lethal response would be deemed "a reasonable reaction to the current situation", hidden snipers are given the go ahead to take action. These days, this would of course be annoyingly accompanied by the song "Feel the Force" by the house band and sometimes a dance interlude and/or fireworks. Also, these days he definitely would have been hit by more rounds and likely in the head. They really don't take any chances with regard to the contestant surviving anymore, largely I imagine, because of this botched first use of the rule. Perhaps some snipers had been reticent to fire because Chris McMillan resembled a young girl at the time. Anyway, the three rounds had put him down but not out, and the event organisers had been legally obligated to administer life-saving medical attention.

In the end the creeper managed to win the first event and was granted a pardon and a modest income for life. This was an outcome that, I'm sure I don't need to tell you, literally no one was happy with. Combined with a lacklustre fifty percent success rate at terminating the McMillans, it's almost impossible to regard the first *Darwin* as a success.

We were given no warning that the schools were going to be shut down. This was surely by design. There was an official enquiry after the massacre to try to ascertain what had gone wrong, and it correctly pinpointed a "lack of adequate communication" as the biggest "roadblock to success". But of course, from the perspective of the Church of Divine Justice and their devotees, there were no roadblocks. The whole thing was an almost unqualified success.

The objective had apparently been to return all differently-abled children to the conventional educational system with "as little disruption as possible to their ongoing eduction". Which sounds fine, I suppose; these things usually do.

Billy Winn had apparently personally insisted on the X-Force assisting in the school closings to 'better guarantee the safety of surrounding communities". This is the point at which alarm bells should have been ringing for the PM. In fact, this should have been enough for the whole thing to have been called off, but I guess he was too far down the path of doing everything Billy Winn wanted to quibble over this seemingly minor detail.

The X-Force was already a robust institution by this point, and it was growing at an alarming rate. Their funding is supposedly from "private donations from concerned British citizens", but I'd be amazed if the President wasn't behind a lot of it. The Battersea Power Station church development alone looked to have cost hundreds of millions, and it was far from the only project they had going. Talking of which, much to the chagrin of Kamal et al., the bombing probably gave the Church more political leeway than they would otherwise have had. They argued that they were a "persecuted religious organisation" and as such "should have the right to defend themselves". As they argued that they were being persecuted largely by people with inhuman powers, they insisted that they should be allowed to use "any suitable weaponry at their disposal" in order to defend themselves. And it's a lot of weaponry. The existence of tricksters, or more specifically, the ongoing war against the differently-abled, has clearly proved to be quite a catalyst for innovation in the arms trade. It seems that every time you hear of a new and unique human ability, it will only be a matter of days before someone is advertising something specifically designed to kill those humans. There's a rare trick where some people's skin is intensely hard when hit by a fast moving object, and the harder the object hits it, the harder the skin surface becomes. As a result, these people are essentially impervious to bullets. At least they were for the few weeks it took for some sadistic innovator to come up with a slow moving sticky projectile that you could fire at these "abominations". The sticky bullet then injected a fluid, through tiny needles, beneath the skin which caused the person's internal organs to melt. Literally the only person I've ever seen with this condition is the poor chap I saw melting in the advert for this gun, but I bet they still sold thousands of the things. It's really rare, and it's even possible that they killed literally the only one when they were filming the advert. I guess weapon design had more or less plateaued with the invention of the machine gun. There's not a lot that one of those won't kill. The whole industry, it turned out, had just been waiting for a more challenging target.

The first time I ever saw the X-Force was when they showed up at our school. As far as I'm concerned, they are distinct pretty much in name only from the Church of Divine Justice itself. They had shiny new uniforms, though, and were armed to the teeth with cutting-edge assault weaponry. Nominally, they were only there to intervene if things got dangerous, like if one of the super-powered kids decided to go on a killing spree or something. It was utterly ridiculous, we were just school kids like any other school kids. If someone had told us what was going on and where we should go, I'm pretty confident the whole thing could have been accomplished without incident. People would only be likely to run if they were incredibly scared or incredibly confused, and unfortunately, they were about to be both of those things.

I wasn't in the first room they hit, but I heard how it went down. A government representative had interrupted a class for the oldest children in the school. These students would have been around seventeen, and the X-Force had assumed that they would be the most likely to cause trouble. While the government representative was addressing the class, one of the soldiers shouted "runner" and shot a student four times in the head. The kid had been closest to the door, but the person I spoke to, probably the only survivor from that class, says there's no way that he was running. His trick was something to do with prime numbers, like a crazy mental skill, he was a really quiet guy who just used to sit at the back and read.

"Another runner", and the same X-Force guy shot the girl closest to the window. She probably wasn't running either. At most, she maybe jumped up in reaction to the gunshot. *Now* people were running though.

And, of course, this is what the Church wanted. By the time it got to the classroom I was in, we didn't even get an explanation, just screaming children running for the exits, wailing that someone was shooting at them. There was a guy in my class called Seb that was pretty tough, and I mean that literally. It was like he was draped in a thick carpet made of old leather. Before the Winters Act, he had been training to be some sort of fireman, I think. Anyway, he stood in the doorway to take a look and shouted back at us that the Christians were coming for us. The class erupted.

This was about our biggest fear. We'd seen footage from the US of course, babies with extra limbs being dragged away from heartbroken parents. The bit of footage that haunted me was of a family that could all climb like apes. They had this extraordinary grip strength in their feet as well as their hands not unlike a kid I knew, and they could scuttle up just about any surface. It had been one of the early novelty stories of the whole phenomenon, watching three young kids dangling from the walls of their family's farmhouse. That's how I had remembered them, but now they were young adults and they weren't climbing, what good would it have done? When the local sheriff's department had come for them, they had just run into the corn field next to their family farm. A sheriff's deputy had picked them off one by one with a rifle without any trouble at all.

They were firing what looked like paint into Seb's face from some kind of giant water pistol. For a moment I thought it might be some sort of non-lethal crowd-suppression type device, or maybe the coloured paint was a way to mark him out as a troublemaker. It turned out to be far worse. The liquid was a quick-drying, intensely sticky, plasticky substance, and they'd got him right in the mouth with a huge chunk of it. He obviously couldn't breathe. He had fallen to his knees and was clawing at the gloop with both hands. His hands then became stuck to his face, so he was pretty defenceless when Verity Pool, a woman dressed in a purple cassock and a Kevlar vest, put a ridiculously large revolver to the top of his head and pulled the trigger.

She'd looked straight into my eyes right after she'd done it, as Seb crumpled into a sticky ball at her feet. It might not have been right at me. For all I know, she could have been surveying the room, trying to figure out who posed the biggest threat. She started to lift the gun and instinctively I shrank it. It just looked like such a stupidly big gun that I couldn't help it.

Verity looked a little startled by this and dropped the tiny gun to the floor. She stepped back from the doorway and was swiftly replaced by a big man with a lot of tactical gear on. I could hear her say to him, "the one in the corner is powerful", which was nice I suppose, but also troubling, as it was followed by "shoot to kill".

I got the impression that she was in charge, but I guess she wasn't the *follow me, lads* type, but more the *I'll wait at the back with this stupidly oversized gun and execute them once they are incapacitated* type.

Jenny threw a brick through a window and started running. This probably saved my life, because the military looking guy shifted his attention to her and fired a few rounds as I dived under a table. I don't know what kind of rounds he had, but Jenny had exploded. I guess they were prepared for people with some pretty serious defences. Jenny's trick had been that she could kind of sense the past of objects. It was bizarre. I don't even think there is even a word for it, but if you handed her a necklace or a book, anything people had touched, she could tell you where it had been for the last ten years or so. I don't think anyone had come up with anything particularly useful to do with this skill yet, but they might have done eventually if she hadn't just exploded.

I shrank the gunman and made a run for the window. I felt a series of sharp stabbing pains in by back. I realised afterwards that this must have been the same type of explosive rounds that he had shot Jenny with, but thankfully, shrunk down to a fraction of their original size, they were far less dangerous. Our classroom was on the fourth floor of the building, so diving through the window would usually have been a terrible idea. Fortunately, in this situation, it turned out to be one of the better things I could have done.

After Deitre had "fallen" to her death from a high window the previous year, someone had decided that it would be a good idea to put suicide nets around the whole building. This had been back when they were still fairly keen on keeping as many of us alive as possible, but no one had yet bothered to remove them. I hadn't remembered this, but maybe Jenny had when she threw the brick through the window. I was pleasantly surprised when I didn't just smash straight into the concrete driveway.

There were other kids running from the building, some more successfully than others. I saw a tall lad going at what had to be 50 mph in the direction of the woods. He was being chased by a guy on a quad bike, but over the uneven ground I think he had the edge.

We know now that similar scenes had played out at all the country's special schools. The Church had obviously decided this was an opportunity to wipe out a huge number of tricksters in one go. They had only been meant to intervene if there was an "immediate danger to the local population".

I suppose they had known that any panic would be self-perpetuating. Once they started one or two people running and opened fire, it would only be natural for everyone to start running, and then they would be able to shoot as many of us as they liked. It's not an unreasonable stretch of the imagination to assume that there were secret orders to a few key people at each school to shoot a few regardless of what happened, as many as it took to get people moving.

Anyway, I lay motionless in the net for a moment, amazed at my good fortune. I probably would have stayed there long enough for someone to come over to the window and shoot me if I hadn't been bounced into the air by someone landing in the nets next to me.

"The nets! I forgot about the nets."

This boisterous boy laughed, like this was the most fun we could possibly be having right now.

There were gunshots coming from the rooftop now, but they were aiming at the people furthest from the building.

"There are nets down here!" he shouted back at the windows. "Jump!"

Then he grabbed my hand and pulled us both off and onto the ground below.

"We should get out of here."

"Won't they shoot us?"

"I'd assume so," said Jackson. "I tell you what, you stay in front of me. Can you run OK?"

"Are you bulletproof?"

"Probably."

23

EQUILIBRIUM

The *Darwin* contestant cell is surprisingly pleasant. It seems that these have been newly constructed for the move to the Millennium/Darwin Dome, so presumably I am the first person to occupy this one. Also, everything about this new *Darwin* show seems to be quite lavish.

There is even a reasonably comfortable chair, which unfortunately I nearly manage to fall asleep in. I'm assuming I'm the first *Darwin* contestant to do this. People don't tend to sleep when they are facing imminent death, but I desperately needed it, I hadn't slept in days. On the upside, between the three of us and the nonstop 24-hour news channel, we had basically figured out what had happened.

Jackson had decided that attempting to hide was essentially a non-starter. It's not like he had ever really been one to blend in, but now was a whole new level. CCTV footage had been shown of him walking near the banks of the Humber, only a few miles from Felix's compound. Witnesses reported that he had looked "distressed" and had been signing frantically. The style of sign language that Jackson uses is not really something anyone else understands, so I'm imagining he had met with limited success. Also, it can't have helped that he was almost certainly trying to buy drugs.

The tabloid press was, somewhat predictably, not sympathetic towards Jackson's drug dependency.

"TV murderer at large, on crack."

With a picture of his face, which, if you put "on crack" underneath it, looks quite manic. Also, I noticed that whenever they were discussing Jackson, his victim would just be described as "a girl". Conveniently omitting that she was herself a convicted serial killer, who had, moments earlier, decapitated a twelve-year-old miracle worker. She was undeniably "a girl", but that doesn't really tell the whole story.

I'm also sceptical that he was "on crack". Don't get me wrong, if it was available, he'd probably have picked some up, but his drug of choice is heroin. And to say "of choice" is misleading, as I'm sure you are aware if you've encountered opiate addiction.

I should probably explain, Jackson's physiology is unique in that he is essentially immune to the dangers of drugs, in largely the same way that he is immune to the dangers of someone smashing him repeatedly in the face. He's not immune to pain though. Being smashed repeatedly in the face causes him a significant amount of pain, or at least it would if he wasn't generally on a heroic quantity of painkillers.

At school, this had been carefully supervised by his doctor. Over time, as his tolerance to opiates increased, so had the dose. From a military perspective, Jackson was one of the most promising pupils in the school. He was absolutely destined to be some sort of super-soldier that could be sent into situations likely to be fatal to literally anyone else. As the training he was undergoing pushed him closer to his limits, he needed greater quantities of painkillers to function. The dose kept going up and up.

The problems really started, though, when the schools had been shut down. Jackson was no longer entitled to a morphine prescription any more than any other addict would be. He was therefore almost immediately in an unbearable amount of pain. This wasn't pain from injuries, but from withdrawal. Much like pain from injuries though, this is a pain that can be mitigated with heroin.

Without medical supervision, Jackson had to acquire his drugs on the street, where, unlike in a medical setting, it is almost impossible to get an accurate idea of the strength of the drugs, as they will have been cut with assorted bulking agents. So, given that there is essentially no way for him to overdose, Jackson is pretty liberal with the quantities he takes. Anything for a break from the crippling sickness that would overtake him if he didn't take enough. So, post school, his drug use had inevitably snowballed. The more he took just to stay well, the more his tolerance increased, and the more he would need the next time.

Also, these huge quantities of heroin would make him sleepy. If he actually wants to get something done, he'll have to counteract the drowsiness with uppers such as crack or meth-amphetamine. So yes, the tabloids were possibly right. Given what Jackson evidently had planned, he was in all likelihood "on crack". I don't suppose they would have been any more sympathetic if he had been able to explain that it was only to balance out the gargantuan quantity of heroin he had just taken.

And I'm sure he had loaded up, because he was about to steal a bike. He usually does this by just waiting for one he likes to pull up at traffic lights. He walks up behind the driver and pulls their helmet off from behind and puts it on his own head. This usually leads to them punching him a lot, something that does him no harm at all. More often than not, they'll get off their bike to be able to take bigger swings, at which point he'll get on the bike and ride away. It's a pretty consistently successful technique.

In all subsequent CCTV footage, Jackson is wearing a motorbike helmet with a darkened visor. It's by no means a perfect disguise, but it enabled him to travel fairly inconspicuously across the country.

There was a robbery at a pharmacy on the border of Wales that was almost certainly him. He must have been desperate. He doesn't usually steal his drugs, he prefers to buy them with money he steals from people he doesn't like. When he's desperate, though, he'll do pretty much anything.

Right now is the worst I have ever seen him. Even with that frozen happy expression, I could tell he was in unbearable pain. The *Darwin* holding cell is enclosed on every side with solid metal panels, so it seemed like a good time to let him run around and see what he wanted to do.

But the Jackson in my pocket was not the Jackson I remembered, what he most wanted to do was frantically try to literally climb up the walls and then scream and claw at his face. When it had looked like he might actually claw his face off, I'd decided it was best to put him back in his pouch. I held his arms by his sides and wrapped him up tightly with a bit of bed sheet I had been using for this purpose. I put him back in my pocket just in time. There was a loud "clunk" sound that I'm pretty sure meant that my cell was no longer locked.

In *Darwin*, it often pays to be cautious, as most of the deadly events tend to require some sort of positive action on the part of the contestant. At the same time, though, you never want to rely on inactivity as a guarantee of safety. Once the game has started, there's no saying what kind of motivating factor competitors can activate in order to whittle away their competition. Also, as there can only be one winner of each game, there is a clear incentive for most contestants to get ahead early. It hadn't been some sort of deluded desire to win the thing that had got me to volunteer for *Darwin* though, I'd had no other choice.

Virgil Barnett, the newly elected Prime Minister, was giving a speech.

As I emerged from my cell, he was listing all the great accomplishments that his government had made in the short time they had been in power, how they heralded a return to the "Great Britain of old, with traditional family values, job security, and a return to conventional human abilities." It was pretty tedious stuff, but it gave me an opportunity to get my first look at this new *Darwin* arena.

Immediately, it was a terrifying construction to take in. Firstly, we were staggeringly high up. I had been transported to the venue in a high-security cage, which had almost zero visibility, but I'm still not sure how I didn't notice being lifted up so high. The cells for the contestants were suspended from the supports in the very centre of the building, almost touching the canopy. It is apparently around fifty metres high, which doesn't sound like a huge distance, but is absolutely eye-watering in person. The cell doors faced outwards and there was a steel walkway in a circle around them. I tentatively put one foot onto the walkway, and immediately, I was suspicious of it. It clearly wasn't connected to anything solid, but rather it was suspended from the ceiling by something with some movement to it. If you've watched nearly as much *Darwin* as I unfortunately have, you'll know that this is the kind of platform that is likely to fall away at any moment.

This precarious perch did at least afford me a view of the arena though. The audience surrounded us on three sides. It was presumably at full capacity as the sound coming off the crowd was quite something. Even in response to Virgil Barnett, one of history's least charismatic speakers talking about as un-invigorating a subject as long-term fiscal responsibility, the energy was electric.

Talking of which, Barnett was addressing the arena from the one side that had not been dedicated to crowd seating. He was standing in a kind of a royal box type enclosure. It was ornate and old-fashioned, like you would maybe expect to find in an old proscenium arch theatre. I guess this was in keeping with his *traditional values* message, but it looked jarring against the rest of the *industrial circus tent* aesthetic. Also, the fact that he was surrounded on three sides with presumably bulletproof glass didn't help. I suppose this was to be expected though, as the man sat next to him, the only other occupant of the box, was not one to take chances with security.

"It is with tremendous pleasure that I introduce an incredible friend, a longtime ally to both myself and our great nation, and a steadfast beacon of hope to the free world, in his first ever public address outside of the United States of America, ladies and gentlemen, President Billy Winn."

And the crowd, as I suppose had to be expected, went crazy. The noise from their shouting and stomping was shaking the walkway so much that I thought it would be safer to go back into my cell. I saw that the contestant to my left, an intimidatingly large chap with a profoundly hairy face, had clearly had the same idea. We were both out of luck though. The moment the cell doors had shut behind us, they had apparently locked. I should have seen that coming. *Darwin* constantly keeps the contestants moving forward. I'd been too absorbed by the spectacle though. I gave him a little wave, hoping that he wouldn't think I was much of a threat. He gave a surprisingly enthusiastic wave back, so that was nice. On the downside, as well as feeling like I might fall to my death at any moment, we now had to listen to Billy Winn giving it the big one about what "abominations" we were.

I'm sure you are familiar with his "we're all going to hell in a handcart" schtick by now, but I would like to highlight one detail because he singled me out personally! A live close-up of my surprised face popped up on the huge screens above his podium, as he described me as a particularly "insidious abomination that had remorselessly decapitated a child". This was met with widespread booing by the capacity crowd.

I'd like to think the booing was in response to how obviously untrue the statement was, what with the whole thing having been broadcast live on television and all. This seems unlikely though. I can only hope that it at least might have won me some sympathy from my fellow contestants, as the crowd definitely wasn't on my side. This could pose a problem. Technically, it shouldn't matter, but from what I've seen, the crowd will often have an influence on the *reasonable force* judges.

I'm sure I noticed the hairy face guy edging away from me. He'd seemed so friendly only a moment ago.

The contestant to my right didn't seem bothered though. He was too busy jumping up and down on his platform. Presumably, he had also noticed that it didn't feel particularly sturdy, and he had decided to test this by seeing if he could shake it loose, seemingly ambivalent to the fact that this would almost certainly cause him to drop to his death. I think he was at least half-Bobbett. Bobbetts pop up on *Darwin* disproportionately often as they are prone to volunteer for things.

I try and edge subtly away from him. As I do, I make the mistake of looking over the edge. Maybe it wasn't a mistake, I don't know, it's good to know what we're facing I guess, but it does not fill me with confidence. Below us, a long, long way below us, is what looks like a swimming pool.

I suppose this would be better than landing directly onto concrete or something else hard but, from this distance, probably not by much. Also, given that one of the original *Darwin* architects was famous for drowning his bar's patrons in a swimming pool, I'm not sure how much I would trust the depth of it.

More worrying still is that it basically confirms what I had been beginning to suspect. At some point, presumably once Billy Winn has finished his lecture on why we are awful, we are going to be compelled to jump off of this thing.

I'm looking for a staircase, but there is nothing behind me on this side apart from more cells. I'm assuming that there are contestants all the way around, as I can see maybe ten, and apparently there are fifty of us in total. I think I am free to walk around up here. I could try and see if there are stairs on the other side, but it's probably not a good idea. Stairs are actually fairly common on *Darwin*, albeit with some sort of catch like they are icy, or uneven, or there is something to compel you down them especially quickly. Before *Darwin* even began, apparently over a thousand people died every year in the UK from falls on stairs. I'm certain the games have added to that number quite considerably.

But yeah, sneaking around past fellow contestants is probably not wise. With Jackson shrunk and in my pocket, I can't shrink anything else, and I have no good way of defending myself if one of them turns out to be violent. Unless of course I un-shrink him, but the last thing I need with me on this platform is a full-size Jackson in his current state.

The crowd roars. I thought it had just been a response to one of the President's apocalyptic zingers, but it turns out that I hadn't even noticed his speech finishing. And then I saw the ropes. At least twenty or so thick, coloured ropes had just unfurled from above us. I suppose in celebration of it's new venue, this obstacle seemed to be a callback to the very first *Darwin*. A knowing nod for the event's super-fans.

The ropes were about a metre away from the platform. Predictably, they were just out of reach. Unless of course you just took a chance and leapt at them. A few contestants had already done just that, with mixed results. There was a sound of a splash, audible even over the sound of the crowd, which I assume means someone had just fallen to their death. They had either missed their rope, or their rope hadn't been attached to anything at all. This would probably be good information to have, and I look at the big screens. I didn't watch for long. They were showing a slow motion replay of the poor girl hitting the water. Whatever her trick was, it hadn't stopped her body essentially crumpling on impact. The crowd didn't seem to know what to make of this. It was cumulatively neither a cheer or a boo. There was the customary applause though. Any death on *Darwin* will always be followed with applause, albeit sometimes just a polite smattering, if it's not a particularly entertaining one.

The Bobbett to my right seemed to be having a much better time of it though. He must have immediately jumped at the rope in front of him the moment it had appeared, they are proactive by nature. He seemed to be shimmying down it quite effectively. Maybe he had been raised at T-BAIT. He would have climbed a whole bunch of ropes there.

Most of the contestants were wary, though, and remained on their platforms. Rightly so, it's a good rule of thumb on *Darwin* not to trust your weight on anything if you can't be sure what it's attached to. There were two ropes I could reach from my platform, one blue, one white. The way the lights were pointed down at us though, there was no way to see where the top of the rope went. It just disappeared off into blackness above. I didn't fancy jumping off at one of them. Even if I did manage to catch hold of it, who knows what would happen? The tactic I would have no doubt suggested from the comfort of my FIDA cell a few weeks ago would have been to jump through as many ropes as possible and to grab at least two. That was easier said than done though. I guess that's why game shows are so popular. Everything seems easier when you don't have to do it yourself.

The hairy guy suddenly leapt! He didn't seem to hesitate. Whatever mental contemplation he had obviously been doing, it hadn't manifested physically until he'd jumped. He'd got ahold of a yellow rope though, and it seemed to be secure enough... or was it? I think he was dropping very slowly, even though his hands weren't moving on the rope. I took a look over the side to see if the bottom of the rope was moving. It was hard to tell. Something else was happening though. It was the Bobbett, he was coming back up! This seemed to be confusing him as much as me, and he was climbing down furiously to compensate for it.

And then I saw something on the screens that I think just about made sense of it. A colossal woman, presumably from the cells on the other side, had grabbed onto a green rope, the exact same colour as the one the Bobbett was holding. She was descending at quite a rate, almost exactly the rate that he was coming up at.

I guessed that they had dampened the ropes considerably to slow them, but each side's ropes were clearly connected to the others. The direction your rope moved would depend entirely on the weight differential between you and the person on the other end of it. The speed it moved at would depend on the extent of the difference and, presumably, an element of luck. It would be typical *Darwin* game design to massively vary how much resistance they added.

I spotted an opportunity and I decided not to overthink it. I took a quick step to the platform where the Bobbett had been and jumped for the green rope. As I'm sure you'll be relieved to hear, I caught it. The audience on the other hand, not so much.

I tried to grip the rope with my feet, as my hands were already starting to slip. It might not have made a difference though, as I realised the rope was moving down quickly. Now that I was beneath the platform, I could see that the large woman on the other side, that I'd assumed was holding on to the other end of my rope, was moving up at quite a rate. She wasn't the only one. Contestants were shooting up and down on either side of me, some at almost free-fall speeds. And then it occurred to me. Whatever dampening was on the ropes that had been stopping the first contestants from just falling straight down wasn't random at all, it must have been on some sort of timer.

The game designers want to incentivise contestants to immediately jump. As a motivating factor, it was largely lost on us as it was our first time seeing it, but I dare say that the next time the game shows up, the contestants will be hopping right out like baby Bobbetts. Talking of which, I suddenly realised there was a critical issue with my current situation.

While the fact that the combined weight of myself and the Bobbett beneath me only slightly surpassed that of the woman on the other side was leading to a relatively controlled descent, I realised, to my horror, that this was surely about to end in one of two ways. Either the Bobbett would reach the water beneath and let go of the rope, which would result in me shooting skywards at a hell of a rate. Or, potentially even worse for everyone involved, the woman on the other side was going to reach the top and presumably get pulled into some monstrous pulley system. At which point I guess we would just stop, if she somehow managed to keep holding onto the rope. More likely though, she would let go and we would all fall to the water below, a worrying thought given that I was currently only maybe a quarter of the way down.

I'm sure that every variation of these outcomes will play out over the upcoming weeks on the *All New Darwin*, but my immediate realisation was that I needed to get down as quickly as I could. I started climbing faster, hand over hand, but there was no way I was going to be faster than the Bobbett. I looked down and could see that he was near the water already, certainly near enough to jump. I just had to hope *he* hadn't realised that.

There was only one thing for it. I took a fistful of my shirt into my hand and grabbed the rope with it, then I just let myself slide. I could feel the rope ripping into my skin even through the shirt, and then suddenly I was falling.

I had some time in the air to figure out exactly what had happened. The Bobbett had let go, either because he had reached the water or he had seen me sliding uncontrollably towards him. This had caused the weight differential on the rope to swing violently, which had jerked the rope out of my hand. Fortunately, I hadn't been holding onto it that firmly as I had been trying to slide as fast as I could. So anyway, now I was just falling to the water, and I had no idea if I had fallen from the kind of distance that one can survive an impact with water from. The fact that there was time for all these thoughts to go through my head before I landed can't have been a good sign.

It turns out that it was. I was probably helped by the Bobbett landing ahead of me and breaking the surface of the water. I have since learned that this can make all the difference. This was another reason that the first girl in had fared so poorly.

The pool was actually incredibly deep. So deep in fact, that it took me a while to even figure which way was up. Everything was just a dimly lit void. And then I found out in maybe the worst possible way. There was an obvious consequence to me letting go of the rope that I had so far been ignoring. Since the event, exactly how sadistically contrived this game was has become clearer.

The platforms are approximately fifty metres from the pool. The ropes are fifty metres long. Given that there is a pulley in the middle, if the contestant on one end has reached the end of their rope and is at the bottom, the other contestant is necessarily going to be at the absolute top. A good tactic, I suppose, would have been to buddy up with someone of a similar weight on the other side and both grab the rope of the same colour, climb as quickly as you can until you each reach the end of your rope and then simultaneously let go. You'll both have a fall of around twenty-five metres before hitting the water. This looks like a long way, but provided you land feet first and aren't unlucky enough to land on someone else, you should be OK. By the time people figure that out, though, I'm sure they'll have introduced ropes that are different colours on each end or attached to nothing at all or something. This is *Darwin*, after all.

A fall from fifty metres, on the other hand, is a different thing altogether. It is apparently survivable in theory, if you have both perfect form and excellent luck, but the woman on the other end of the green rope unfortunately had neither. Her horrifically broken body shot past me, still traveling at a seemingly impossible pace. It's an image that haunts me still. It was, however, how I knew which way was up.

The crowd was not happy at all to see me emerge from the water. I was relieved to be out though. It was starting to resemble a stock pot more than a swimming pool.

There seemed to be only one obvious exit to the pool area. This should make any *Darwin* aficionado immediately suspicious. What was even more worrying was that there was no way to see what was on the other side. Having gone from having an aerial view of the whole arena, we now had very limited visibility. I wish I had taken more in while I was up there, but I'd been too busy concentrating on not falling to my death.

The pool was surrounded by a clear plastic screen about five metres high. Presumably they'd made it transparent as they hadn't wanted to obscure the audience's view of the pool. As the wall tapered in towards the exit, though, it became gradually more opaque.

It didn't look like there was anything to stop us from walking straight out, but I had no intention of being the first person through. Not that I could have been even if I wanted. The most athletic of the contestants were already reaching the doorway. The first one out had skin between his arms, not unlike a flying-squirrel. Presumably he had just jumped straight off of the platform without worrying about the ropes at all. Terrible news for whoever happened to be on his opposite side, as there would be no one on the other end of their rope. Come to think of it, I guess I'd rather let down my opposite number as well, fingers crossed it was the squirrel guy. Talking of which, he, like many actual squirrels, was about to experience a fatal traffic collision.

The reasoning behind the obscured visibility was that a newly commissioned dual-carriageway, the A985, went right past the exit. The exit came out on a blind corner so the driver of the SUV, whilst going at or around the 70 mph speed limit and paying "due care and attention" to the road ahead, was unable to avoid the squirrel-man, who had been busy tucking his bonus arm skin into his sweatpants.

I reached out and grabbed the Bobbett in front of me, just in time to stop him jogging out onto the road. I think, maybe because we had shared a rope, I felt a comradeship with him. I can't think why else I did it. I'd definitely had a sneaking suspicion that this exit was a terrible idea, and I had done nothing to stop the squirrel. The Bobbett didn't thank me either, just shrugged free of my grasp and, seemingly oblivious to the bloody mess in front of him, proceeded to run across the road to the other side. I suppose, if he was raised in T-BAIT, he had probably seen his fair share of violent accidents.

Maybe he had the right idea though. Just one mad dash and maybe I'd be lucky. Then I felt a stabbing sensation in my stomach, and for a moment I thought I was finished. *Darwin* contestants generally don't fight each other unless they have to, but it can happen. It turned out it was Jackson though. In the swim, I guess his arms had come loose from his wrap, and he was lashing out furiously in my pocket.

Jackson clearly hadn't had much of a plan. This was not out of character for him. Being both impervious to harm and high on drugs will tend to make a person more of a doer than a procrastinator. And what Jackson had decided to do was to jog towards FIDA at night and see if he could find some sort of obvious way in or out. As previously discussed, and also like any number of Jackson's other plans, though well intentioned, this had not gone well. He'd hit some challenges along the way, and when I say "challenges", I of course mean anti-personnel mines.

The second night, Jackson had been about to give it another go when Tess, in bird form, had managed to stop him. Tess had persuaded him that it was best to abandon his efforts and adopt a new strategy the following night. This new plan was stupid, and morally questionable at best, but given that from Jackson's perspective it came from a distinguished-looking night owl, it had seemed very wise indeed.

The following day was the last time I saw Tess, when she had told me in hushed tones that "there may be a way through". I wish she had told me what they had in mind. Maybe I would have been able to talk them out of it. There's no sense judging at this point though. She'd been intensely sleep deprived and desperate, and Jackson had been strung out on pharmacy drugs. Between them, this is what they had come up with:

Cows.

There were several farms in close proximity to FIDA. In fact, almost all of the land that wasn't occupied by the prison itself was farmland. With the use of an assortment of birds in the early evening, Tess had opened up a series of gates, enough to allow a clear thoroughfare for a veritable Noah's ark of local animals to make their way to FIDA, or as was more likely, to make their way to an explosive ending some way short of FIDA.

This stampede of animals had, understandably, got the attention of the prison guards. It's not like they weren't on the lookout already. This time, however, rather than just Jackson, there were hundreds of moving objects all setting off explosions simultaneously. If you are familiar with cows, you'll know that even an unexpected shake of a feed bucket can be enough to set off a stampede. I can only imagine the kind of pandemonium that would ensue if one was to inadvertently step on ordinance designed to penetrate armoured vehicles.

All I know is that the whole prison was awake that evening. If for some reason you didn't hear the explosions, the nonstop gunfire was difficult to ignore. Presumably, having either failed to hit Jackson with sniper fire as he darted between the cows, or more likely, having hit him but failed to do any significant damage, the guards had adopted a more scattershot approach. Evidently there were a series of heavy-duty machine guns mounted to the walls of FIDA, the type one might use to repel an invading army as they stormed a beachhead.

Jackson made it through though. He was coming for us. He was coming for Tess, and he was coming for me.

24

THE TRICK

The second person to be killed on the A985 hadn't been nearly as foolhardy as the Bobbett or the squirrel-man. She was a middle-aged woman with the bearing of a primary school teacher. In fact, as she stopped at the exit and placed her hand on the ground, her expression seemed to say "wait here kids, I've got this."

Even the hand to the ground looked like a good idea. With the sound of the crowd combined with the house band blaring out of the speakers, it is all but impossible to hear any traffic coming, until it is far too late. I thought that I should probably just go when she did.

Fortunately, I didn't have time to. She jumped straight from her position crouched on the ground, directly into the wheel arch of an oncoming Honda. Either it wasn't possible to feel the vibrations of an oncoming vehicle, or this truck had made surprisingly few of them. Either way, the result was horrific.

The only upside was that her torso had got crunched into the wheel arch so thoroughly that it had caused the truck to swerve and then flip over. The driver of the SUV a short way behind, paying "due care and attention to other road users",

was able to stop in time. Still, the incident caused the temporary closure of the whole road while the wreck was cleared.

The crowd booed as the remaining contestants walked
cautiously across without incident.

I took this opportunity to let my guard down, an error at
any point in *Darwin*, and take in the spectacle for a moment.
What was really notable, compared to previous *Darwin* events,
was how much more intentional it seemed. The royal box, I'm
calling it that because I can't think of another term for it, even
though the Queen has kept a conspicuous distance from
Darwin, was positioned in such an elevated position that it was
almost impossible not to look at it. The only people presumably deemed worthy of such an esteemed position for this
inaugural event were Billy Winn and Virgil Barnett, and they
were playing along joyously. It had long been a *Darwin* tradition to buy an oversized, and presumably overpriced, foam
thumb that you could wave around in front of you. This would
often be used to give a thumbs-up of appreciation, for either a
particularly skilful use of a trick or, more often, a spectacular
death. Or, Roman-gladiator style, they could be used to give a
thumbs-down gesture to urge one contestant to kill another.
Billy Winn had evidently decided to join in with this tradition
and was only half-jokingly giving an enthusiastic thumbs-
down to the contestants safely crossing the halted dual-
carriageway. It's not like he needed the big foam thumb either.
The TV screens seemed to cut to his reaction constantly. And
this is what I mean by "intentional". The initial *Darwin* shows
had been almost apologetic about the violence on display. The
new government clearly not only revelled in it, but were keen
to take full credit for it.

Another change to the format was also becoming clear. The
scale of this new arena had allowed for a significantly longer
show. While it wasn't uncommon for early *Darwin* shows to be
essentially over in ten minutes or so, this was clearly set up to

take the best part of the evening for even the very fastest of contestants to complete. The only way to win on *Darwin* is to be the first person to get to the finish. In early shows, this had been a literal door, but we were briefed that the new format would feature a big red button. This button was fully enclosed behind some sort of half-tinted Plexiglas screen and was on an elevated platform just in front of the royal box. Apparently, the glass would only come down to allow access to the button in the event that the contestant approaching it had completed the course legally. This new restriction was presumably to prevent someone like the flying-squirrel chap from just going straight for the win from the top platform. I guess they didn't want to shortchange the crowd with a show that was over in moments, but still, it didn't seem to be exactly in the spirit of *Darwin*.

So yeah, this new show was long, not even including the artificial delays that had been implemented. At certain points of the course there would be a barrier. We were not to attempt to pass the barrier, it would come down eventually. This had been implemented to allow room for commercial breaks in the international editions of the live broadcast. During these breaks, the studio audience would be treated to a performance by the house band, and UK viewers at home, watching without commercials, would get a little highlights real. What it meant for contestants was that they would get a five-minute break every twenty minutes. But, more importantly, it essentially removed almost any advantage to going into an obstacle first, as the whole lot of us would just bunch up at the next barrier anyway.

A lot of contestants didn't seem to take this change on board, though, and enthusiastically jumped into the breach at any opportunity. I'm sure in the future they will implement a lot of motivating factors to keep boring contestants from doing what I did, but for this first show, I was lucky and my natural *wait and see* attitude seemed to be close to optimal. I won't go through every obstacle blow by blow. If you are a die-hard *Darwin* fan you can just watch the full tape of the show, it's probably heavily discounted by now.

If, however, you mainly picked up this book for tips on how to survive *Darwin*, then firstly, apologies for the rest of it. You probably didn't need to know all that stuff about Bobbett orgies and SCUBA cats, but secondly, here are the few things I learned:

On the merry-go-round obstacle, you've got to hug the horse. Don't just try to ride it normally or you'll probably be decapitated by blades in the ceiling. It's difficult to see them on TV but they're there. Do what I did and just hang from beneath, even though I looked like an idiot doing it. In all likelihood, eventually they'll add something new beneath the ponies to stop people doing this, so never be the first contestant to go.

Never be the first is actually solid advice for almost any obstacle, unless you are certain you know what the motivating factor is. The most obvious counter-example is the tube maze. Fortunately, when I saw the first contestant go in, I noticed a delay as they reset the airlock. If you see an airlock, then in all likelihood there is only going to be a limited amount of breathable air available. In this situation, it is imperative that you get in early. As you'll see on the tape, I got lucky and was able to push ahead of a claustrophobic contestant that was reticent to get into the tube.

Another possible exception here is zip lines. Often there will only be a limited number of handles at the top of a zip line. I would still be cautious in deciding to go first though, unless there is clearly no other way down. If they run out of handles, you can usually find something nearby that will work as a substitute, like the hose pipe I ended up using. Test it for strength first though, and don't trust anything too near the obstacle or too obvious.

This leads me on to my next point. *Be careful what you pick up*. It is within the rules to use anything in the arena, and there can be useful things dotted about, but a reasonable guide would be *don't pick up anything that doesn't have any other obvious purpose*. It has likely been put there to trick you into killing yourself *by misadventure*. Also, never pick up anything that could be confused for a lethal weapon. If you even accidentally brandish it at another person, this can often be enough to justify the use of *reasonable force*. Remember, depending on your criminal history, these days some snipers will feel safe taking you down with only two of the three *reasonable force* judge's lights showing green.

Talking of *reasonable force*, you'll notice that I basically don't use my trick at all during my *Darwin* appearance. This was largely due to a limitation specific to my trick — I can only shrink one thing at a time and I had tiny Jackson in my pocket, but in all honesty, I don't think I would have used it much anyway as the *reasonable force* judges are so leery of them. Let's say, for example, that I had shrunk another contestant, like the big bloke that looked like he was coming for me at the ring toss. Don't get me wrong, when I saw him coming, my instinct was to shrink him and run. This would have meant unshrinking Jackson, but even that seemed tempting. A dopesick Jackson probably would have torn the guy to pieces. But I'd had a fair amount of time to think about this, and I decided that it just wasn't going to be worth the risk of getting even a single r*easonable force* light. If a judge sees me shrink someone or, worse still, pull a tiny monster out my pocket that turns out to be a six-foot invincible man, they are likely to think that I am "an immediate danger to the safety of others around me" and bam, *reasonable force*, snipers, game over. As it happened, I got lucky and the guy grabbed a super-heated ring and then fell onto something pointy.

So that's my advice, unless your trick is both incredibly

useful and visually innocuous, only use it if it's the only way to escape imminent death. Despite the show's supposed purpose, most of the obstacles don't really favour having a trick anyway. There are only a couple that I've heard of that would give a significant advantage, and they are rare. A few tricksters can go for long periods of time without breathing. This is definitely useful and doesn't present an obvious danger to anyone else. Same goes for the girl I saw once that is resistant to electricity. There are a couple of games where she would do really well. In fact, as apparently she finds electricity irresistibly arousing, I'm amazed she hasn't been arrested and forced onto the show somehow. Sounds like it would be make for incredible television.

The key thing is that all obstacles are essentially legally required to be completable by a person of average abilities. Anything else would make the process a series of public executions, something it is trying to technically not be. This is evidenced by the fact that I got all the way to the end and, outside of my trick, my abilities are average at best.

What I hadn't anticipated, though, was how close I was to winning the thing. This was less due to me being particularly fast, and more due to the final obstacle being both new and unfathomably cruel.

When the door to our cell had opened to reveal Jackson, I'd been elated. I guess I should have been horrified that he had been caught, but I think I was just thrilled that he was alive.

But then somehow I knew that he wasn't.

Ziggy figured it out.

There had been rumours for months, apparently, that Chris McMillan had disappeared from his cell in FIDA. This initially had sounded like a lot of Ziggy's other conspiracy ramblings.

I'd nod along, which with Ziggy required saying "I'm nodding" quite loudly, but I wouldn't really believe them. But then I'd known for sure that Jackson wasn't Jackson. He'd taken a step towards me with his arms outstretched, and I'd shrunk him just in time.

"What they've done with Chris McMillan," said Ziggy, "is agree to release him on the condition that he work for them occasionally. He would be a political super-weapon. It's one thing to be able to assassinate your opponents, Billy Winn demonstrated that. But to be able to not only assassinate them, but then put whatever words you wanted into their mouth, would be on a whole new level."

Ziggy thought that after that first night when the landmines had alerted the guards to Jackson, the government had been concerned that he might actually be able to break into FIDA. Probably rightly so, Jackson is a formidable opponent. They had to have guessed that he'd be coming for me and Tess, and they had recruited Chris McMillan as a last resort, a fail-safe in case Jackson got through. Presumably by the time Jackson had got to Tess, she was already dead, her bones pulled out and dumped in a pile before McMillan had slithered in to this new person costume. It wouldn't have been difficult. I imagine all her attention had been focused on controlling cows outside. Maybe he had even been her cellmate for some time. Either way, it's not the sort of thing you'd expect.

And when Jackson did successfully make it inside FIDA, and all the way to Tess. He would have been equally unlikely to suspect that she was already dead, just a magic maniac in a skin suit.

———

The *Darwin* legal team had really outdone themselves this time. The final series of obstacles was surrounded by a gratuitous quantity of warning signs, some of them featuring fairly horrific cartoons demonstrating what could happen if you ignored the warnings.

The first one was simple enough, NO ENTRY, CONSTRUCTION SITE. But they rapidly became more concerning with SLIPPERY SURFACE, TOXIC MATERIAL, OVERHEAD LOADS, DANGER OF DEATH BY ELECTRIC-ITY... I could go on. Presumably having all of the warning signs so clearly visible was key in indemnifying the game's creators against the deaths that they were looking to cause.

By the time I had got there, the warning signs had seemed a little redundant. I could clearly see that it was a dangerous area because of the dead people it contained. Ahead of me was a long concrete roadway. It was seemingly the only thing between me and the end of the course, and it was only maybe forty metres of road. I imagine it had been just that feeling, that the end was tantalisingly close, that had led seemingly every contestant ahead of me to make a fatal mistake.

A Bobbett, I think it was my rope buddy from earlier, if not it looked a lot like him, had been hit by a falling wheelbarrow. With the pace he had been going at early on, he may even have been first in. Either he hadn't read the signs or had simply ignored them. Or possibly he had been too focused and trying to cross the wet concrete quickly and hadn't seen the numerous precariously balanced objects above him.

Concrete mixed to the right (or in terms of actual useful construction, absolutely the wrong) consistency, will become a non-Newtonian fluid. I had only seen something like this once before on *Darwin*, where there had been some sort of custard-filled swimming pool. I remembered the commentators explaining the unique properties of a fluid like this. It is basi-cally a thick liquid, but given enough force it will act as a solid. The contestants on that show, as far as I remember, had been far too tentative in their approach. Being cautious is generally a good policy, but on that occasion, the slower moving contestants had all drowned in custard.

Bobbetts aren't generally over-thinkers though, and I'd assume that he had been going at a decent enough pace to keep the gloopy concrete a solid, his error had been in not spotting the thin cables randomly spaced across the road. These cables were all tripwires of varying degrees of visibility. I'm sure the games designers have a more legally-defensible term for them, but to keep things clear, let's just call them tripwires. The Bobbett had presumably hit one of these at speed, and it had caused an assortment of heavy construction-themed objects to fall into his path. When I say "into his path", it looked like one had caught him squarely on the shoulders. If that hadn't killed him outright, then the slow sink into the concrete caused by his inevitably reduced pace would have.

That's what made it so cruel, if you even slowed for a moment to check for a tripwire or avoid a hazard, you would immediately start to sink irreversibly into the concrete. That is what seemed to have either already happened, or to currently be happening, to a number of the other contestants. I was just in time to see a screaming face slip beneath the surface at the very far end of the road. They had got so close! Cold comfort, I suppose. Maybe that was why they were screaming so hard.

There was a lady maybe halfway down who had only disappeared as far as her shins, but even this seemed to be unrecoverable. As she shifted her weight from one foot to the other, she just seemed to sink further and further down. In a bold move, that I really can't fault her for, she decided to give one of the tripwires a tug. I guess she figured that maybe whatever fell down might miss her as she wasn't moving. Unfortunately, it turned out that the cable she had grabbed wasn't a tripwire at all, but an exposed electrical cable.

For a moment, I thought that this might be the perfect place to release Jackson, but then I was rudely shoved from behind by a kind of lizard-looking person. If their lizard skin came with any additional benefits, politeness wasn't one of them. I fell face first onto the concrete as they barged past me. Maybe it had been seeing that the end was in sight, or maybe because they had just had a spectacular idea, they had decided to put on a turn of speed that they clearly hadn't used thus far.

And their idea was ingenious. Rather than running on the concrete and having to dodge tripwires, they had elected to run exclusively on the bodies of dead and dying contestants. There were enough of them dotted along the road that there was a clear route through using essentially only corpses as a path. The lizard's fatal mistake, though, was to stand on the woman that had just recently grabbed onto an electrical cable. The lights in the stadium dimmed as he was electrocuted. Big cheer from the crowd for lizard man, for that spectacular exit.

Fortunately, I had fallen face first onto the concrete with such force that it had remained solid. This was painful and I smashed my face in pretty good, but on the upside, I was able to push myself back to safety without sinking.

I'd like to think it is more down to the dehumanising nature of *Darwin* than anything intrinsically wrong with me, that my biggest take-away from the lizard man's horrific demise was that, the ending aside, it had been a pretty sound idea. The bodies of the dead and dying provide a much more solid footing than the soft concrete. Also, there is an added benefit that if you are basically following in the footsteps of previous contestants, you are far less likely to snag a tripwire.

I was halfway there, inelegantly hopping from corpse to corpse, before I even considered what to do for the last ten metres. I gave the electrified pair a wide berth and was able to survey the area from atop a very long but unsuccessful contestant. I had just about run out of options though, there was pretty much just virgin concrete ahead of me. But then, I crouched and saw the glint of a wire between myself and the spot where I'd seen the screaming face disappear beneath the surface. This was going to be my route. Better the trap I could see than something I hadn't. I hopped over the wire and landed my boot as close the human face as I could remember.

There was a piercing hiss from the crowd and some loud boos. This was to be expected, I suppose. I had been introduced to them as a child killer and Christ-abuser. In fairness, there were definitely also some cheers. After all, a *Darwin* with no winner at all is generally considered to be a poor showing, and there were by now very few contestants left. There was a very young-looking contestant eyeing up the start of the concrete death trap, presumably contemplating if it was worth a mad dash. It surely wasn't. Barring a few final formalities, I had won.

Whatever it is that Chris McMillan did, Jackson's incredible trick hadn't saved him. Unfortunately, I can only assume that given the nature of Jackson's trick, he was probably still alive as McMillan pulled his bones from his body. The one saving grace being that he was hopefully pretty high on a variety of drugs at the time.

He wasn't high now though. The Jackson they had brought to my cell had clearly already begun detoxing hard. That's not what had given him away though. I think it was the eyes. Jackson's face is of course frozen in an expression of something akin to ecstatic joy, but that is rarely mirrored in his eyes. Sometimes it is, that can be magic, but mostly his eyes are, his eyes were... Well, that's the key bit. When they opened the door to his cage and I saw him, it only took me a moment to realise that whatever was behind those eyes, it was no longer Jackson.

Instinctively, I had shrunk him. The murderous tiny little McMillan immediately gave up any pretence of being Jackson. He was feverishly trying to attack anything he could get his hands on. Obviously, he had got more than he had bargained for when he had crawled into Jackson's skin. Presumably, he would have taken on some of the healing ability that is key to Jackson's trick, but he was also enduring possibly history's greatest ever opiate withdrawal. Jackson was accustomed to a quantity of drugs that would have killed any other human long ago, and for the few days since Jackson's FIDA attack, presumably he'd had no drugs at all. This tiny little McMillan monster would clearly stop at nothing to get into someone else's skin. He was clawing at Ziggy's shin and screaming incoherently through Jackson's paralysed face when I'd grabbed him and wrapped him tightly in the bed sheet.

This was, at best, a temporary solution. We were stuck in a cell with this pocket monster. At some point, I was going to have to sleep, and the furious maniac was going to burst back to full size and pull our bones out. We had tried to kill it. Ziggy had stamped on it, and we had thrown it hard against the wall a bunch of times, but it was impossible. It was as indestructible as Jackson.

Ziggy and Hugo had, understandably, requested to be transferred to a different cell. This was not the sort of request that was granted in FIDA though. There was only ever one way out of here, and that was *Darwin*.

I had managed two full nights without sleep before I finally must have drifted off and my trick had stopped working. This was a new personal record, but I can't imagine this was of much comfort to Hugo, who had immediately been killed by the now full-size McMillan. Presumably, this was just because Hugo was the first person he saw, rather than Chris McMillan having a specific preference for long floppy arms. It speaks to how desperate he was, though, that he had already got most of Hugo's skeleton out before Ziggy had managed to wake me. I had immediately shrunk Jackson again and wrapped him back up, but it was surely just a matter of time before I drifted off again and he killed Ziggy and I.

Volunteering for *Darwin* had ostensibly been my idea, but Ziggy had definitely been hinting at it. If I got on *Darwin* and I took the tiny McMillan with me, I could just unleash it somewhere in the arena. Then all I had to do was survive the show. This is very much not a given on *Darwin*, but Ziggy had glossed over that bit.

But I had survived, better yet, I had only gone and won the thing! Or, at least, I was about to. All I had to do was press a button. And I was reaching out to do just that. This hadn't been the plan. There never was a plan. I hadn't even managed to get rid of Jackson.

And then there they were, seemingly right in from of me, with only the bulletproof barrier between us. In the royal box, Virgil Barnett with a condescending half-smile, and Billy Winn with his big ridiculous foam thumb pointed jeeringly down, a look of hatred on his face that reminded me why Felix had thought he was the devil.

And so I did what I did. There has been some discussion of the throw, like it was some sort of physical feat that I would have to have trained for, or it was part of my trick or something, but it really wasn't difficult. They weren't that far away, and I was admittedly used to throwing tiny Jackson, I'd done it hundreds of times. Also, in all honesty, if anything, I'd been aiming for Barnett. He'd seemed the more annoying of the two at that moment.

It was Billy Winn that Chris McMillan had gone for though, the moment he had appeared behind them, suddenly full size. He could have had the pick of either, stuck in there with him behind the glass as they were. I doubt he had thought about it much at all though. McMillan was visibly desperate, clawing wildly at the President's bones and organs, ripping them from his body.

Oh, I pressed the button, admittedly unsure what good it would do me at this point. The house band started to play, presumably almost involuntarily as the backing track had started up automatically. The jaunty music played and balloons fell from the ceiling, incongruously accompanying the sight of our new Prime Minister desperately clambering over the glass barrier, leaving his "staunch ally" to the monster climbing inside him. Several snipers took shots at McMillan, but the bulletproof-glass held firm. In seemingly no time at all, Billy Winn was standing again before us, Chris McMillan inside, limbering up in his new skin. This is certainly one for the history books.

I doubt that the United States constitution anticipated a psychopathic child in the skin of an evangelical preacher one day becoming President.

UPCOMING BOOKS IN THE SERIES